I0719713

THE COMPLETE QUARTET

ELEMENTS OF MIND

NISSA HARLOW

NIMBLE HOPE
PUBLISHING

Copyright © 2024 by Nissa Harlow

Brainstorm © 2022 by Nissa Harlow
Dreamflare © 2023 by Nissa Harlow
Mindquake © 2023 by Nissa Harlow
Headrush © 2023 by Nissa Harlow

All rights reserved.

No part of this book may be reproduced in any form or by any electronic or mechanical means, including information storage and retrieval systems, without written permission from the author, except for the use of brief quotations in a book review.

Names, characters, businesses, events, locales, and incidents are either the products of the author's imagination or are used in a fictitious manner.

ISBN: 978-1-7781397-1-0

Published in Canada by Nimble Hope Publishing

Cover and book design by Nissa Harlow

TABLE OF CONTENTS

For the storytellers.

BRAIN
STORM

IN WHICH
I ALMOST DESTROY A LIBRARY BOOK
AND MY DIGNITY IN ONE FELL SWOOP

Don't barf in the book. Don't barf in the book.

Saliva floods my mouth. My heart pounds. Clammy hands slip on the plastic slipcover of the book I hold in front of me as I try to focus my sparkling vision on the words. Something's wrong. But I need to find . . . I can't just—

Oh, shit. Something sour comes up the back of my throat. I slam the book shut and shove it back onto the shelf, leaving it sticking out a little so I can easily find it again. The noise alerts the cute boy who's perusing the DVD section. Damn it. Am I really going to puke in front of him?

Nope. No way. My legs shake as I turn away and rush for the bathroom. I'd rather go home, but it's a ten-minute walk, and besides, I'm not sure if I'd make it. It's dark out there, and if I pass out (which feels probable at this point), I might lie there for hours before someone finds me.

I absolutely *hate* public bathrooms, but I'm kind of beyond caring. I slam my hand on the door, push it open, and almost gag as the scent of stale lemon cleaner hits my sinuses. For some reason, all I can think about is that cute guy. I wonder if he watched me come in here. God, I hope he doesn't think I have diarrhea or something.

Not that what comes out of me is any less gross. I barely make it to the stall before my stomach shoots my last meal out of me with what feels like the force of a t-shirt cannon. Some of it actually hits the wall behind the toilet, and if I weren't feeling like I'm about to die, I might actually be impressed. Fumbling for the stall door, I manage to push it closed, just as another heave redecorates the wall.

Like I said, I hate public bathrooms, so I'm a little surprised when I come out of some sort of nausea-induced daze and find myself leaning against the stall, my head pressed against the cool metal. With a shudder, I straighten up and look down at the toilet. Damn, I have terrible aim. The stall is a mess. There's even splatter on my shoes. But at least I don't feel like I'm about to pass out, face first, in the bowl.

How long have I been in here? I wonder. I reach for my phone, only to realize my bag isn't on my shoulder. My heart screams into my throat, and I feel like I might be about to throw up again. But then I remember. I left my bag on the table near the shelf where I was standing to look through the books.

The stall door squeals as I pull it open and step out. I need to wash my hands, get my bag, and get out of here. But . . . I still need a book. Damn it. *Perfect timing, stomach. Of course this has to happen today.*

I step toward the sink, but startle and freeze as I register the figure out of the corner of my eye. It's the cute guy. Of course it is. I whip my head toward the mirror to check my appearance. Pale and sweaty. Great.

"You okay?" the guy asks.

I shake my head and force myself to walk to the sink to wash my hands. They feel filthy. It's probably all in my head, but—

"You don't look like you should be at a library."

"Excuse me?" I say, turning to him in disbelief. "What's that supposed to mean?"

He blanches a little. "Just . . . you look kind of sick."

"Oh."

"You *are* kind of sick," he mutters as he peers into the stall through the open door. Shit. I forgot to flush. Not that it would make any difference to the wall.

"I don't think you're supposed to be in here," I say, turning back to the sink and turning on the water full blast. I use three pumps of soap and try to lather it up, but that just makes my hands feel slippery rather than clean.

"Why not?" He has to raise his voice to be heard over the hiss of water.

"You're a guy."

"It's a unisex bathroom," he says. "The library switched them over last year." He falls silent for a few moments, and I finish washing the floral-scented slime from my fingers. When I turn off the water, the silence seems to wallop my ears. "You sure you're okay?"

"Yeah. I'm fine. I got it out of my system."

He grunts in amusement. "I see that."

Maybe he's not cute so much as annoying. I dry my hands with a paper towel, then give my front a quick once-over. There are a few flecks of puke on my shoes, but my jeans seem to have been spared. I toss the crumpled paper towel in the garbage and edge past the guy, who's still just standing there.

"What are you? Some kind of bathroom pervert? Move."

He skitters out of the way, and I yank open the door. My hand immediately feels gross again. Damn public bathrooms. But the thought is driven away almost instantly, replaced by a more pressing concern.

"What the hell?" I whisper, blinking into the darkness. "How long was I in there?"

The library is dark. Not dark like the power's out—the lights are still on in the bathroom, after all—but dark like the librarians have shut everything up and gone home. I can see a few tiny lights flickering in the darkness (computers or surge protectors, probably), and there's a faint glow coming in the windows from the streetlights outside.

"Closing time?" a voice says behind my right shoulder. I shake my head and edge sideways so the guy can get out of the bathroom. As soon as the door closes, leaving nothing but a thin line of light at the bottom, we're plunged into an eerie darkness.

"Wasn't there a warning?"

"Not that I heard." His shadowy form moves a little, and then a bright, bluish light illuminates the space in front of us. "Nice."

"Did they lock us in?"

"No idea. Locks usually undo from the inside, though, so we should be able to get out." He takes the light with him as he steps away from me. I scurry after him, carefully, hoping the floor doesn't have any weird lips or transitions that could trip me up. He walks over to the first set of glass doors—which are usually left propped open—and peers into the vestibule. The outer set of glass doors throws our ghostly reflections back at us.

"I need to get my bag," I say. "Could you aim the light over there?"

"Over where?" He turns around, and the glow from his phone hits me in the eyes. Squinting, I turn away.

"The teen section."

He snorts and starts to walk. "Looking for a vampire romance, were you?"

"No," I snap, which makes the lie all too obvious.

"Hey, I'm not judging."

"Sounds like you were."

"As long as they drink human blood and don't sparkle, it's fine by me."

"Oh, gee. I'm so glad I have your permission. And if you must know," I say, spotting my bag on the table in a puddle of blue illumination, "I'm only reading that crap for a class."

"Your teacher assigns young adult paranormal romances?"

"No. She assigned us to write a story in our least-favourite genre. I was just looking for inspiration." I grab my bag and slip the strap over my shoulder before plunging my hand inside. My whole body shudders with relief when my fingers find the phone within. Thank goodness.

The guy swings his phone away from me and aims it at the circulation desk. There's nobody there. I pull out my phone and check the time.

"I thought the library was open until nine," I say.

"It's supposed to be."

"It's only seven-thirty. Where is everyone?"

"Maybe they got sick and had to go find a place to puke."

"What's wrong with the bathroom?"

"You were in it."

"There are three stalls in there," I say, giving him a dirty look that I know he won't be able to see. "And it's one of two bathrooms." He turns back around with his light, and I quickly school my features into a neutral expression.

"I don't know, then. But we should probably go, too. I don't want to get blamed for that mess in the crapper."

"Shut up," I say. That just makes him laugh. "What's wrong with you?"

"Nothing. I guess I'm just not letting the stress of the situation get to me the same way you are."

I turn on my phone's light and shine it directly in his eyes. He closes them quickly and turns away. "Are you done being a prick?" I ask.

"I wasn't aware I was being one."

"Well, you are." I tilt the phone away from his face and head for the doors. I hear him follow, but I pretend I don't.

"Come on. You have to admit, this whole situation is pretty ridiculous. Who gets locked in a library?"

"We do, apparently," I mutter.

"Yeah, so it'll be a funny story to tell later." He's quiet for a few moments as he walks behind me. But then I hear him take in a breath to speak again. "I'm Lincoln, by the way."

"That's nice."

"And you are?"

"On my way home."

"Weird name."

"Oh, for fuck's sake."

"It's just that, when I tell this story later, I don't want to have to refer to you as Puke Girl. So—"

"Don't you dare." I sigh. "Fine. It's Sadie."

"Really?"

"Yes, really."

"Nice. Old school."

"I'm named after one of my great-grandmothers. Now, are you done being an asshole, or—" My breath catches in my throat as I peer out the glass doors. Quickly, I turn off the phone's light and grip the device in both hands. Lincoln turns off his light, too, and then we can see through the glass clearly without having to look through our reflections. He steps up beside me, so close to the glass that his breath fogs it a little.

"Holy shit," he whispers. "What is *that?*"

2

IN WHICH
THERE'S AN ARGUMENT
ABOUT CLIMATE CHANGE

Yeah, it's early March. But it wasn't that cold when I came in here. I'm just wearing a lightweight jacket. I didn't even bring a hat. So the sight outside makes zero sense, given the weather of just a couple of hours ago.

"Was it supposed to snow?" Lincoln asks.

"Not that I know of." I squint my eyes to try to see better. "I think that's the least of our problems."

"No kidding." He backs up a step and shakes his head. "Is that some sort of lightning?"

"Since when is lightning green? Looks more like an aurora to me." I watch the colours shift and swirl as they coalesce over the Italian restaurant across the street. Which is also dark. And I know for a fact that it should still be open because my parents took me there for my birthday dinner just a few weeks ago.

"Auroras don't produce snow," Lincoln annoyingly points out.

"Maybe they do now."

He snorts. "What? You think it's climate change?"

"What's your explanation?"

"Not that."

"Don't believe in it?"

He sighs. "I think there's a lot more to it than the superficial agendas the media pushes on us. In any case," he says before I can retort, "I'm pretty sure that changes in carbon concentrations and temperature fluctuations don't cause electric, green snowstorms." As if to emphasize his point, a gust of wind swirls a column of icy flakes against the outer doors. We can hear the sound even from where we're standing.

I turn away and look down at my phone. I try to bring up a browser, but then I notice I don't have any sort of internet connection. Zero bars. I'm holding a very expensive clock. "Great."

"What?"

"No phone service."

"Really?" He taps at his phone, and the light from the screen illuminates his frown. "Huh."

"You don't think this is weird?" My voice shakes. He looks up quickly and shakes his head.

"Relax. It's just a storm. It'll pass, and then we can go home."

"I'm not staying here with you."

He gives me a skeptical look that's emphasized by the shadows on his face. "Really? You're going to go out in *that?*"

"Maybe."

"It's your funeral."

"I thought you said it was just a storm."

"Yeah, with some sort of green electricity running through it. I wouldn't go out in the middle of a regular lightning storm, either. I'm not that stupid."

"And I am?"

"I don't know. Are you?"

"Fuck," I say before turning and storming back to the teen section, my phone held in front of me like a flashlight. I'm so over all of this. If I didn't have to write this stupid story—sorry, *novelette*—I'd probably be at home right now, watching this weird weather from the safety of my bedroom window. Grabbing the book I was looking at earlier, I let out a disgusted grunt and shove the stupid thing in my bag. The library's alarm might go off when I try to leave, but if the idiot librarians are going to lock their clients in, they can—

"Sadie?"

"What?" I snap, whirling around to face him. "Want to take another jab at my reading tastes?"

"Not if you're going to yell at me."

"I'm not yelling."

"You're getting close."

"Maybe if you weren't such an insufferable assho—"

"Hey. Whoa." He holds up his hands, one of which is still clutching his phone. "We just met. You don't even know me."

"I know enough."

"Yeah? So why am *I* in here?"

"How should I know? Maybe you're looking for porn."

He snorts. "Since when do libraries have porn? What's the Dewey Decimal number for that?"

"Shut up. I mean on the computer."

"You think they don't have that blocked?"

"How would I know? I've never looked it up."

"Neither have I."

"Right."

He shakes his head and walks over to plunk himself down in one of the chairs near the end of the shelf where I'm standing. The light disappears as he turns off his phone and slips it into his pocket, and then all I can see of his form is a shadowy blob.

"What are you doing?" I ask.

"Do you want to stand there for hours? We don't know how long that storm is going to be blowing, so—"

"I'm not staying here."

"Suit yourself." His shadow seems to elongate as he stretches out his legs. "See you."

"Asshole," I mutter under my breath. I aim my phone toward the doors and make my way over there. The first lock is easy enough. It's just a simple latch I need to turn. "Lock up after I leave, will you?"

"Who's going to break in?"

"Just do it." I let the glass door close behind me and shine the light on the second set of doors. The lock isn't as obvious; there's no latch. There's a keyhole on the inside, but that doesn't make a lot of sense (unless you're wanting to lock yourself *in*, which seems like a pretty pointless thing to do). I search the edges of the door, hoping to find something, but not spotting anything obvious. On the other side of the glass, the storm seems to have intensified. It's also a lot larger. In fact, it almost looks like it's surrounding the library; from where I'm standing, I can see the swirling clouds of snow, illuminated by ribbons of green, curving around us and out of view. The parking lot (which is completely empty) is already covered in a few inches of white powder. And I can barely see the buildings across the street. It takes a moment before I realize why: The streetlights have gone out.

I'm about to open one of the interior doors and ask Lincoln if the power is still on inside when a bit of movement catches my eye. It's over by the book-return chute. For a moment, I think it's something with wings, like a bat. Or a demon. Honestly, I'm so weirded out that I wouldn't be surprised if I start seeing things that don't actually exist. Taking a few deep breaths to calm my pounding heart, I edge sideways, trying to get a better view. Whatever it is, it's on the other side of the glass, so I'm fairly safe.

I hope.

The winged thing turns out to be a book. Some lazy person couldn't even be bothered to pull open the chute's door, so they just left it on the ground. In the middle of a snowstorm. That book is toast. It's lying open, splayed with shamelessness as it lets the wind play with its pages. One page in particular seems to bear the brunt of the gale, and it appears to stand up straight for a moment, caught between opposing gusts as snowflakes pock its surface.

I don't know why I'm staring at the stupid book. Maybe it's because I really don't want to go out there. Not that I could, since I still haven't figured out how to unlock the doors. Cold air is leaking between them, and I shiver as I stash my phone in my pocket so I can pull the zipper on my jacket higher. I'm still watching that page when a rip appears in the paper. My heart surges. I mean, I know it's just a book, but . . . it's a book. Tearing pages out of one is just wrong. (Unless it's some stupid vampire romance. If that's the case, maybe I'll give the wind a pass.)

A few moments later, the page tears away completely and goes soaring out into the night like a pale ghost. It's almost as if those green ribbons of electricity are sucking it in. *Maybe the storm's a voracious reader,* I think, my lips twisting in a wry smirk. But my amusement doesn't last long as I see a tendril of green reach out toward the page and seem to slap it. There's a flash of green, and something rather large tumbles from the sky.

"Lincoln!" I scream. "What the hell is going on?"

3

IN WHICH
THINGS START TO GET VERY, VERY WEIRD
AT THE LIBRARY

"What?" Lincoln shouts as he opens the inner door and practically tumbles into the vestibule. "What's wrong?"

"What is *that?*" My voice is too loud. My pointing finger shakes. I can't seem to blink.

He stares for a moment, then turns to me. "Um . . . that's a person, Sadie. Some idiot out in a storm."

"No, it's not," I say.

"Looks like a person to me."

I shake my head and turn back to the figure standing out in the swirling, green-tinged snow. The person looks just as bewildered as I feel. "They just . . ."

"What?"

"Appeared."

"Appeared?" His voice drips with skepticism.

"Yes, appeared. See that book?" I ask, pointing at it. It's still open, pages thrashing wildly in the wind.

"Yeah."

"One of the pages got torn out by the storm. It went flying, and then . . ."

"What?"

I wave my hand at the figure.

He snorts. "I think whatever made you puke is affecting your brain." With a shake of his head, he peers at the person, who's just sort of standing there, a dark shadow gazing at the swirling green storm. "We should invite them in."

"How do you propose getting the door open? I couldn't find a lock."

He reaches past me and pushes on the handle. A hiss of suction later, a flurry of snowflakes is pulled into the vestibule with us. "Just open it."

"How was I supposed to know that?" I snap. "Why would the librarians lock every door but that one?"

He's not even listening to me. The freezing air is almost unbearable, but he takes a step outside, holding the door open with one hand. "Hey!" The person turns. I still can't really make out any features. They're just a vague shape, lit from behind by the green glow. "Come inside before you freeze to death!"

The person doesn't need to be told twice. They hurry toward us, and when they're just a few steps away from the door, I can make out that it's a woman. Lincoln puts his hand on her arm and guides her inside before pulling the door closed. The vestibule is a little crowded with three people . . . especially since the woman is wearing this historical costume with a rather large skirt.

"My thanks," she says. Her voice carries a distinct English accent. She pulls her shawl more tightly around her shoulders, staring at me the whole time. I look down at myself, wondering if maybe I missed some puke splatter.

"What were you doing out there?" Lincoln asks. "Not a great night for a walk."

"It is quite a storm." The woman peers out through the glass. But then her gaze travels to the door itself, to the sleek metal handles and the plastic safety decals at around eye level. My gaze travels over to the book that's still flapping away in the wind.

"Lincoln," I whisper. "What book is that?"

"Huh? What book?"

"The one outside."

"How should I know? Does it matter?"

"It might."

He snorts. "I doubt it."

His sureness irks me, and I turn to the woman. "I'm Sadie," I say. "And you are?"

"Jane Elliott," she says after a moment of hesitation. "I'm pleased to make your acquaintance."

"Uh-huh. And why were you out there in that storm?"

Her expression becomes troubled. Her hair—which seems to have been braided and pinned up at one point—is dishevelled; limp strands hang into her eyes. She looks like a lost waif. I have a feeling she is. "I was travelling," she says, her gaze sweeping over me once more. "On the moor. There were no structures that I could see. In one moment, I was walking over rough, stony ground. In the next, I was surrounded by the storm."

"What storm?" Lincoln asks.

"That storm." She turns and gestures. "It is a strange one, is it not? I have never seen lightning in such a colour."

Lincoln turns to me with a quizzical look, and I realize that I can see it. The green ribbons have intensified and are bathing the whole scene in an eerie glow. "Method acting?" he asks.

"I doubt it," I mutter.

"Whatever. Let's get you in out of the cold," he says, pushing open the door to the library. The woman—who I'm pretty sure is not named Jane Elliott—walks in ahead of him. I stay where I am, my gaze fixed on the book outside.

It can't be, I think. *You've just read too many stories. How would that even work, anyway? It's impossible.* And yet, I can't really think of any other explanation. I *did* just watch "Jane Elliott" spark into existence out of a page torn from a book.

"Sadie?"

I turn and see Lincoln holding open the inner door. "This is weird," I say.

"No kidding. You should see the lighting in here. It's almost bright enough to read. Hope you don't mind the colour green."

I shake my head and turn back to the book. "I saw it."

He lets go of the door and comes to stand next to me. "You saw what?"

"Her. Jane. She just appeared."

"Yeah, well, the snow's pretty dense and—"

"Will you just shut up and listen to me for a sec? I saw the wind tear a page out of that book. It flew into the storm. There was a flash. And then Jane just dropped onto the parking lot."

He's quiet for a long moment. "You know how that sounds, right?"

"Yes, I know how that sounds. But that's what happened! Look at her." I turn and wave my hand toward the library. He's right; it *is* kind of green in there. "She's not from the twenty-first century. She's not from the twentieth century, either. And she's not some sort of actor. What would an actor be doing wandering around in the middle of the weirdest storm ever?"

"Fair point. So . . . who is she?"

"I think she's from the book."

He snorts.

"Shut up!"

"Oh, come on, Sadie."

"I *know* how it sounds. But you didn't see it. I did. So if you're just going to give me a hard time, you can . . ." My voice falters as he slams his hand against the door and pushes his way outside. "Lincoln!"

He waves me away as he marches over to the open book, his hair whipping wildly. When he reaches it, he picks it up, flips through a few pages—fighting the wind the whole time—and grabs a random one. I suck in a gasp as he tears it out, making eye contact with me through the glass.

"Asshole!" I shout, hoping he can hear me. I don't know if he can or not. He just snaps the book closed, tucks it under one arm, and marches back to the door. But he doesn't come inside. He stands there, feet planted, and raises the hand holding the page. I know what he's about to do, and my mind, like a social media carousel, flips through all the characters I know are in that book. He lets go of the page, and I watch, breathlessly, as it seems to be sucked straight into a vortex of green.

Nothing happens. He backs up a step until he's almost touching the door. My shoulders slump as embarrassment washes over me. *Of course nothing happened. What did you expect? When this is all over, you really need to see a doctor, because something is very wrong with—*

A verdant flash rips into the darkness, seeming to originate from the spot where the page disappeared. Another shape—this one smaller than the first—tumbles onto the snow. This one, however, doesn't land on its feet. It sprawls, arms and legs akimbo. Lincoln drops the book and rushes forward. I push open the door, only to be greeted by the biting cold.

"Hurry!" I say, but my voice is swallowed by the wind. I watch in disbelief as he runs to the figure and scoops it up into his arms. By the time he makes it back, his cheeks are flushed and dark.

"What the hell was that?" he practically shouts as he edges into the vestibule, kicking the book ahead of him. It skids across the floor, coming to rest against a side wall.

"I told you," I say, pulling the door closed. The storm fights me a little, but I manage to do it. The vestibule is suddenly a lot quieter. But it's still freezing, and the wide-eyed little girl that Lincoln's holding in his arms is only wearing a short-sleeved dress.

"Let me guess," he says. "These are book characters."

"As far as I can tell."

"And you know what book it is."

I look down at it. It's fallen face down, and the title isn't visible. "Yeah."

"Care to share?"

I turn to the little girl. *"Tu es Adèle?"*

Her eyes widen. *"Oui, mademoiselle."*

Lincoln frowns. "What?"

"It's French."

"I know that. And I understood what you said. But I still don't know what book they're from."

"Figures." I sigh and open the door to the library so he can carry Adèle inside. "Looks like you need to brush up on your Brontë."

4

IN WHICH
WE REALIZE THAT
THINGS ARE GETTING WORSE

"Okay, spill it," Lincoln says when Adèle is safely inside and reunited with Jane. They huddle together in the children's section near an oversized teddy bear that Adèle keeps casting nervous glances at. "Who are they, and what book are they from?"

"The kid is Adèle."

"Yeah, I know that."

"The woman is Jane Eyre."

"She said her name was Jane Elliott."

I roll my eyes. "It's an alias, dumbass. Jane Elliott is the name she used after she ran away from Mr. Rochester." I keep my voice low so she won't hear me. I have no idea how any of this works, but I don't want to make Jane's brain explode or something if I happen to reveal a spoiler. She probably doesn't have any knowledge of anything that happened after her flight across the moors.

"Jane Eyre?"

"Do you even know the story?"

"Give me the short version."

I shake my head. "It's not important. Besides, it's not like anybody's going to come looking for them."

"How do you know?"

"Are you going to go ripping more pages out of that poor book and feeding them to the storm?"

He snorts. "You make it sound like a devouring beast."

"Maybe it is. It's sure not a regular snowstorm."

With a glance over at the wall of windows on the far side of the room, his lips twist into a smirk. "Maybe it's a *brainstorm*."

"Whose?"

For some reason, that thought makes him go a bit rigid, like he's just considered something and now really regrets it. I sigh and pull out my phone again. Still no signal. The battery is getting a bit low, though, so I turn the device off completely. If we need the light later, I don't want to find myself with a dead battery.

Lincoln and I don't speak for a while. Even Jane and Adèle fall silent, and then all we can hear is the wind rattling the windows and whipping snowflakes against the glass. The library is fairly bright, thanks to the glowing ribbons that seem to be surrounding the building, so I try to make myself comfortable at one of the carrels and pull out the stupid vampire book. I don't really want to read it at all, but if I'm going to be stuck in here, at least I can get going on my writing assignment; it's one more thing I won't have to do later.

The book turns out to be annoyingly engaging, even though it's all kinds of stupid, and by the time I take a break to stretch, I'm startled to realize how noisy the room has gotten. The windows are rattling like crazy, and the snow—if you can even call it that now—sounds like beads flung at the glass by an angry hand. Watching the storm nervously, I close the book and stand up.

"Going somewhere?"

I blink and turn, only to find Lincoln leaning back in his chair in the next carrel. "How long have you been there?" I ask.

"Does it matter?" He laces his fingers behind his head and raises his eyebrows. The fact that I can see all that with perfect clarity tells me the green glow has intensified even more. When I turn and peer across the library, I can easily see Jane and Adèle. The child has her head on the woman's lap, her fists clutched around handfuls of skirt. I turn back to Lincoln with a frown.

"What are we going to do with them?"

"They're fine where they are."

I shake my head. "That's not what I'm talking about. *After* the storm."

"Maybe they won't be here."

"You think they'll disappear?"

"You think that's any less likely than fictional characters coming to life after throwing a few book pages into a creepy green snowstorm?"

I sigh and look down at the vampire book. The plastic cover catches the light and sends back nothing but a blank, green glare.

"Actually," he says, releasing his hands and sitting up a little straighter in his chair, "maybe we should move them."

"Why?"

He points at the window. I turn, but it's not really necessary. The rattle is becoming hard to ignore, and I can actually see the movement of the glass. It looks like it's warping at the same time as it's making that unearthly racket. Instinctively, I take a step back.

"Where would we put them?" I ask.

"Away from the windows." He twists around in his seat and peers upward. "Upstairs is probably best. The windows there are tiny. They'll hold up better."

I sigh. "You know what books are up there, right?"

"Graphic novels. So?"

"So, do you want to find out what happens when a couple of proper young ladies from the nineteenth century read about zombies, vampires, and alien genitalia?"

He snorts. "What do you think is going to happen? An implosion of the space-time continuum?"

"You don't know that won't happen. More likely, though, they'll just be traumatized for life. And what if they go back into their book and keep that knowledge? That's going to screw up one of the world's most famous classics."

With a shake of his head, he stands up. "That's a chance I'm willing to take. If the windows down here blow out, we could be looking at serious injury." He tilts his head and walks toward the children's section. "Hey, ladies! Let's get you out of the line of fire."

I'm not sure if Adèle understands what he means, but Jane seems to, and she doesn't ask any questions. I guess a window about to shatter in a storm is just as threatening to a time-travelling governess as it is to a twenty-first-century teenager. She takes Adèle by the hand, whispers something to her that I can't hear, and follows Lincoln as he leads them over to the stairs. When I look up, I can see the shadowy second level. It's true; the windows are smaller up there. Which means it's also pretty dark. Lincoln pulls out his phone on the landing halfway up and turns it on. I shake my head at the weirdness of the sight. *Oh, yeah. It's just some random cute guy I happened to get stuck in a library with, leading two fictional people up a staircase, in the dark, because the power's out due to some weird storm that glows green, eats book pages, and poops out characters.*

I snort before I can stop myself. Luckily, nobody seems to hear me over the rattling of the windows.

"Sadie, come on!" Lincoln calls.

"I'll be there in a sec."

"Why?"

"'Cause I have to pee. Do you mind?"

His chuckle floats down in the darkness. I leave the vampire book in the carrel and pull my bag from my shoulder while I'm at it. But I take my phone, because I don't particularly want to use a public bathroom when I can't see what I'm doing; the last thing I want to do is plunk my butt down on my own vomit.

The bathroom seems quiet after the cacophony in the library. I hold the phone awkwardly with one hand as I try to get my pants down and squat over the seat. I'm just about done when I hear footsteps.

"This may be a unisex bathroom, but there are two of them," I say. "Can I get a little privacy?"

"Sorry."

I gasp and nearly drop my phone on the floor. The deep, purring voice is definitely not Lincoln's. The one that shouts my name a moment later definitely is.

– 5 –

IN WHICH
I STUMBLE TOWARD A LOVE TRIANGLE WITH TWO EQUALLY ANNOYING BOYS

I may or may not dribble a little on the floor as I fumble to get my jeans back up. My heart pounds so loudly it almost hurts my ears. When I pull open the stall door and aim my phone out, two figures hold their hands up to block the light. One of them hisses.

"Get out!" I say, embarrassment and fear leaving me with very few words. When I lower the light a little, I can see Lincoln on the left, his eyes wide as he stares at the other person. It's hard to see much in the meagre light, but I can tell the person is a guy. He lowers his hand slowly, and when he sees me, he smiles. I can see *that*, not least because two very white, very sharp fangs catch the light. "What the . . . ?" I whisper.

"One of the windows blew out," Lincoln says, sounding out of breath. "Good thing you weren't still sitting—"

"Where the hell did he come from?"

"Hell, indeed," the guy purrs. I edge away from him, toward Lincoln, as my brain starts to put things together.

"Let me guess," I say. "The vampire book . . ."

"Flipped open and let the storm eat a page? Pretty much." Lincoln reaches out and takes my free hand. I let him. And then I let him pull me out of the bathroom and into the library, which sounds like the inside of a clothes dryer. Or what I imagine one might sound like if you happened to be inside while it was running. Shards of glass litter the carpet over by the carrels, and the green storm is lighting them up like they've been dipped in fluorescent paint.

"Are Jane and Adèle okay?" I ask.

"They're fine."

"They're in the dark."

"I thought you didn't want them reading any manga."

"I don't, but—"

"I left my phone."

I gape at him as he leads me toward the stairs, stepping into the feeble light cast from my phone. "You left Jane Eyre with a smartphone?"

"I told her it was a type of lantern. I also told her not to touch it. Think she's the obedient type?"

I honestly have no idea. Not when it comes to things like that, anyway. So I don't say anything, but just let him lead me up the stairs. Before we start to climb, I glance back and see the vampire—Gage, I guess . . . unless there's some other teenage vampire that comes along later in the story—staring at us from the bathroom doorway.

"How did he know I was in there?" I whisper.

"Where?"

"The bathroom. Did he just . . . pop into existence and then rush in there to disturb my peeing?"

That's met with a chuckle. I wrench my hand away and take the steps two at a time to pass him. When I reach the second floor, I notice it's a lot darker, at least back among the shelves. The view out over the railing is still lit with an eerie green, and I can see the vampire striding confidently across the floor, his shoes scattering shards of glass. I turn off my phone and shove it in my pocket. Then I use both hands to push my hair out of my eyes—the wind seems to be trying to work its way into every last corner of the library—and turn back to Lincoln, who's reached my side. He grips the railing and stares down at the paranormal teenager loping up the stairs.

"Do we need to worry about this?" he mutters.

"What? The storm?"

"Fang-boy."

"How should I know?"

"You read the book."

"I didn't *finish* it. How fast do you think I can read, anyway?"

He edges back as Gage reaches the top and steps closer to us. Well, to me. He doesn't even seem to notice Lincoln's here.

"Gage," the vampire says, with a smooth, cocky air that instantly makes me remember why I hate vampire romance books.

"I'm glad you know your own name," I say. My jab doesn't even seem to faze him. His lips curl in a smarmy grin, and he reaches out to run his finger over the edge of my jaw. The digit feels like a finger-shaped ice cube. I swat his hand away.

"Girls are supposed to like this?" Lincoln mutters, at which Gage shoots him a knowing grin. I edge toward the least annoying boy, keeping my gaze fixed on the vampire the whole time. In comparison, Lincoln's hand feels reassuringly warm when I slip my fingers into it.

"Not all of them." With a sigh, I nervously peel my gaze away from Gage and turn to Lincoln. His features are creased in a deep frown as he regards the otherworldly creature, who suddenly takes in a long breath as if he's smelling the most beautiful bouquet of flowers. I turn back to him with a raised eyebrow. "What's your problem?"

"Your scent is . . . intoxicating."

"She doesn't smell like anything," Lincoln says. I'm not sure whether to feel relieved or embarrassed. But I'm glad I remembered to wear deodorant this morning.

"I beg to differ."

"You have a nose like a dog or something?"

The vampire bares his fangs. Lincoln and I both take a step back, hitting the railing.

"Don't compare him to that," I whisper, leaning toward Lincoln's ear. "Vampires and werewolves are mortal enemies."

"Why?"

"I don't know. They just are."

"I thought you hated those books."

"I do."

"So how do you—"

"I had to read some to know I hated them. Right?"

He shrugs. "I guess." With an appraising look at Gage, he shakes his head slowly. "Is that how you knew Sadie was in the bathroom?"

The vampire blinks. "Books?"

"No. Your nose."

The gross smile that erupts on Gage's face is all the answer we need. Lincoln's reaction, I can do without.

"You smelled her *peeing?*" he asks, the words distorted by his amusement. My cheeks rush with so much heat that it kind of affects my brain, and before I know what I'm doing, I've wrenched my hand away and smacked him on the shoulder. Hard. "Ow!"

"Shut up!"

"What? Everybody pees."

"I don't," Gage says.

"Can we please not talk about this?" Pressing my palms against my temples, I close my eyes for a moment. The wind is still hissing, and the library is even colder than it was before. My eyes snap open as I remember. "Where're Jane and Adèle?"

"Back corner," Lincoln says, pointing to the shadowy area about as far away from the railing as you can get. There's a window there, but it's a small one, and not likely to break.

"They must be freezing."

"They're fictional."

"Shut up!" I hiss, casting a wary glance at Gage. But if Lincoln's words have registered, the vampire doesn't let it show.

"What?"

I grab the cute-but-stupid boy by the arm and drag him between the nearest shelves. It gets darker the farther we go, but it's not like there's anything to trip on in the stacks. "Don't say anything about that," I whisper, trying to keep my voice down, but worrying that our vampire guest might have super-sensitive hearing.

"About what?"

"Them. In relation to books."

"Why not? You think they don't know?"

"Are characters usually aware of their fictional status?"

"Maybe in reality they are."

I let out a soft groan. "Reality? Right. I think we left that behind a while ago."

"Well, we're both here, and alive, so—"

"Are we? How do you know we aren't dead?" My heart picks up its pace. Would it do that if I were dead? "Maybe I'm lying dead in the bathroom right now and—"

"Then why am I here?"

"I have no idea."

He chuckles. I feel like smacking him again, but I can't really see well enough to do so.

"You have to admit, this is *very* weird."

"Weird things happen every day," he says.

"Weird things like this?"

"Well . . . maybe not. But, until we know otherwise, we should operate under the assumption that this is all real."

"Meaning what?"

"Maybe we should think about protecting ourselves."

"From what? Teenage vampires?"

"You do realize he's probably a few hundred years old."

"Irrelevant," I say.

"In any case, yeah. Vampires. Or whatever might get puked out by the storm next."

"Like what?"

"If you can think of it, I'm sure there's a book in here that's got it. A swarm of bees. A pack of wolves. Hell, an invading army. It could be anyth—" He breaks off as I jerk and flail, accidentally hitting him.

"Hands off!" I roar, spinning around in the darkness. The movement pushes the vampire's icy hand away from the side of my neck.

"You should wear your hair up," he purrs. "A neck that lovely should never be covered."

"I'll wear my hair however I like," I say, glaring at his silhouette. All I can really see is the outline of his body, lit up from behind with green. "You keep your frigid fingers to yourself, or I'll snap them off."

"Sadie," Lincoln says.

"What?"

"Listen."

I do, stilling my breath so I can hear better. Beyond the whistle of the wind is a faint sound, just barely a whisper. For a moment, I can't really place it.

"Oh, crap," Lincoln says, pushing past me just as I figure out what it is we're hearing. I elbow the vampire in the ribs (which just jars my funny bone painfully, thanks to his rock-hard physique) and follow, joining the normal teenage boy at the railing a moment later. Down in the library, the floor is a mess, and it's not just because of the broken glass littering the floor. The magazine section seems to have thrown up, and glossy periodicals are scattered all over the space like dying birds. Double-page spreads flap, the sound carrying all the way up to the second floor. The wind grabs at the magazines, awkward fingers of breeze trying to get a good grip. The storm is hungry. And it's not going to stop until it's been fed.

As we watch the scene, one page begins to tear. I can hear it, but I don't see it until it twirls up into a draft and gets sucked outside into the snow. A moment later, a flash pricks the sky . . . and there's a huge thud as a shiny hatchback thumps into the garden right outside, its windows shattering. Lincoln and I turn to each other.

"Holy shit!"

6

IN WHICH
WE TRY TO FIGURE OUT
THE DEWEY DECIMAL SYSTEM

"That's a *car!*" I shout, just as Lincoln nearly screams, "A freaking *car!*"

"Yes, it's a car," Gage says, suddenly at my ear. "If you think that one's impressive, wait until you see my—"

"It must've been an ad," Lincoln says, waving his hand down toward the magazines that are still flapping in the wind.

"Or an article," I point out. "Maybe it was a magazine about cars."

"Whatever. But if we don't clean those up . . ."

"*Qu'est-ce que sais?*" a little voice asks. Lincoln startles and turns to find Adèle standing right next to him, gripping the railing and staring down into the messy library. Actually, no. She's staring at the car. A 21st-century hybrid that probably has GPS and heated seats.

"Where's your nanny?" he asks.

"Governess," I correct him, just as Jane steps from the shadows. She reaches out to take Adèle's hand from the railing, murmuring something softly in French that I don't catch. But the child doesn't want to go anywhere.

"*Non!*" she says, pulling away. "*C'est magnifique! La feuille est devenue une voiture.*"

"Shit," I say before I can stop myself.

"What?" Lincoln asks, whipping his head around to face me. "What did she say?"

"She saw it."

"What?"

"The page turn into the car."

"We all saw it."

"Yeah, but the rest of us aren't from . . ." I trail off as I see Jane staring at me, her brow creased in a slight frown. "Never mind."

Lincoln turns to the girl and the governess. "You two should wait back there," he says, pointing into the shadows. Jane nods, but Adèle stubbornly shakes her head and grasps the railing once more.

"*Je veux rester ici.*"

"Just let her stay," I say quietly. "What harm will it do now?"

Lincoln turns to me in disbelief. "Weren't you just telling me to shut up about them being fic—"

"Shut up!"

"Stop telling me to shut up. You've made up these weird rules, and you probably don't even have a reason for why. What's the worst that could happen if they figure out what they are? We're already trapped in a library with a vampire while some sort of sentient storm blows out windows, eats pages, and shits out hybrids."

"*Mon Dieu,*" Adèle whispers. "*Vous parlez comme les amis de maman.*"

I shake my head. "She said you talk like—"

"Yeah. I used a bad word. So sue me." He sighs heavily and stares down at the library floor. Magazine pages are still fluttering threateningly. "We better clean that up before we run into any more problems."

"What? It's just a bunch of ad-riddled magazines. Are you afraid of bottles of perfume popping into existence?"

"Kind of. If they break, it's going to stink in here."

"They'll break outside."

"You think the wind won't push the stench into the library?"

He's got a point. Casting a wary glance at the vampire—who's just standing there, looking like he's trying to decide what sort of spice rub to use on my neck—I head for the stairs.

"Stay up here," Lincoln says, though I'm not sure who the command is directed at. A moment later, though, I can only hear one set of footsteps following me.

We quickly scoop up all the magazines we can get our hands on, piling them into a stack in one of the carrels to protect them from the wind while we finish the job. There's still glass everywhere, so we have to be careful. The whole endeavour makes me nervous, and I pull out my phone and turn on the light so I can see whether I'm about to grab a magazine or slice my hand to ribbons on a piece of glass.

"Is that all of them?" Lincoln asks a few minutes later as he places one last magazine on top of the pile. I wave my phone over the area, not seeing anything other than the reflection of the light in the broken glass.

"I think so. Where should we put those? I don't want to leave them down here. It's too windy."

He makes a non-committal sort of noise.

"What?"

"Remember when I said maybe we should protect ourselves?"

"From what? Cars?" Peering out the broken window, I see the hybrid crouched in the garden. Shrubs are crushed under the wheels. All the windows are blown out . . . which is too bad, because a car might've made a decent shelter. Better than a freezing-cold library full of potential threats. But the thing is a write-off.

"I'm not worried about cars. But if any more characters—"

"The wind can't grab books. Most of them are tucked up on the shelves. I think we're safe."

"Where's the vampire book?"

"Uh . . ." Looking around, I spot the book. It's on the floor, spread open but upside down. Those pages aren't going anywhere. I scoop it up and turn it over. Some of the pages are bent, and one is missing altogether.

"Gage?" Lincoln asks.

"Looks like it." I snap the book closed. But I don't put it in my bag. I've had enough of that particular vampire. I return the book to the shelf. At this point, I don't even care about the stupid assignment. And if I'm dead after all . . . well, it doesn't really matter, does it?

"Are you familiar with the Dewey Decimal System?" Lincoln asks. I turn to him with a frown.

"Not very. Why?"

"Where would the books on weapons be?"

I blink. "Weapons? Are you kidding me?"

"What if the brainstorm eats a page with an army on it?"

"Then we're toast. Even if you had a cannon, I don't think you'd last long against a whole army."

He snorts. "I don't want a cannon. But don't you think we should have *some* sort of protection?" His gaze darts upward, almost like he's pointing. I raise an eyebrow.

"You want a wooden stake?"

"Seems kind of messy."

"Yeah, and unnecessary. I could probably incapacitate him with an earring."

"Huh?"

"They're silver."

"Whatever." He shakes his head. "What about a gun?"

"I think it'll take more than a gun to kill a vampire."

"Forget the vampire. I'm more worried about actual humans."

"Why? At least they're not immortal. If we need to shoot Gage, we're just going to end up with a pissed-off bloodsucker."

"We'll cross that bridge when we come to it." He turns to the non-fiction stacks. "So . . . any thoughts?"

"Maybe. But I really don't think this is a good idea."

"Why not?"

"You'll probably end up shooting me. Or yourself."

"Why would I do that?"

"Accidents happen."

"Exactly. We've had four pages accidentally fly into that storm, and now we've got Jane Eyre, Adèle, a vampire, and a freaking car."

"Adèle was on purpose," I point out.

"Whatever. That storm is hungry, and if it decides it wants to have another snack, I want to be prepared."

I stand there for a moment, my hair tickling my cheeks as it whips around my head. I can understand where he's coming from . . . but I'm also really wary about bringing a gun into an already dangerous situation.

"You keep it away from Adèle," I say.

"You think I'm going to shoot a kid?"

"No, I think a kid might shoot you. Or me. Or her governess. Honestly, I don't know, and I really don't want to find out. So just keep it away from her, okay?"

"I have to get it first." He waves his hand as if he wants me to lead the way. With a barely suppressed growl, I march toward the stacks, holding my phone out in front of me for light.

"I don't know exactly where the right section is," I say as I wave the phone over the rows of books in front of me. "Somewhere in the six-hundreds."

"You like to shoot?"

"Never done it."

"You like to read about it?"

"Hardly. I just remember seeing some gun books in that section when I was looking for something else." The blue glow looks cold on the spines, and I realize how much the temperature has dropped. "After we find your gun book, we should find something with kids' jackets in it. Adèle's got to be freezing."

"Yeah. We'll look. But first . . ." He leans closer so he can read the spines in the feeble light. "Is something wrong with your phone?"

"Probably. The battery's getting low. So hurry up."

He pulls out a book, flips through it, then slides it back onto the shelf. The second one gets the same treatment. But when he gets to the third book, he pauses on one of the pages. I hold the fading light closer, and I can see the black-and-white photograph of the handgun nestled among blocks of text.

"Will that work?"

"Probably."

"Good." I turn off the light and give him a shove back toward the storm-lit part of the library. "You get your gun. I'm going to go through those magazines and see if there are any kids' ones. There might be something for Adèle to wear."

"Just don't pick a page with an actual kid on it, or you'll be babysitting."

"We have a governess," I point out.

"You think Jane's going to be able to wrangle a twenty-first-century kid?" He chuckles as he absently thumbs the edges of the gun book's pages. "Actually, I might want to see that."

"One thing at a time," I say. I leave him at the window before returning to the carrel where we left the magazines. The shadows being what they are, though, I can't really see much. So I grab the whole stack and step into the light, crouching down and balancing the glossy periodicals on my knees while I flip through them.

"I'm going to do it," Lincoln says. I look up to find him gripping a page in his hand, ready to tear.

"So do it. You don't need my permission."

"I just don't want the flash to startle you."

I shake my head and turn back to the stack. A moment later, I hear a tearing sound. Then a flutter. And then there's a flash that makes me blink.

"Did it work?" I ask without looking up. But I guess it did because, out of the corner of my eye, I see him clamber outside through the blown-out window. He returns, and I look up to see a gun in his hand and a perplexed expression on his face.

"Got it."

"You look surprised."

"I wasn't sure it would actually work."

I snort. "Lincoln, we've watched three book characters and a car pop into existence. Why would this be any different?"

"I don't know." He looks down at the gun. "Maybe 'cause I actually wanted it to happen this time."

"Is it loaded?"

He shrugs and reaches over to put the gun book—which he's been holding this whole time—on the windowsill. As he turns the weapon over in his hands, I flinch.

"You better know what you're doing."

"I can figure it out. Besides, we've got a whole section full of books on the topic if I can't. I just need to—"

"*C'est magique! Moi aussi, je veux le faire!*"

We both turn and look up to find Adèle standing at the railing, a book in her hands.

"Shit," Lincoln says, and nearly drops the gun. "Shit!"

"No, Adèle!" I shout, just as the child gleefully rips out a handful of pages and flings them into the cavernous, glowing space. The wind whirls about her, fluttering the ribbons in her hair, before snatching the pages and sucking them outside with the sound of crumpling paper.

"Oh, god," Lincoln says, his voice shaking. "Was that a graphic novel?"

But I don't get a chance to answer him. The next instant, the world erupts in brilliant flashes, overloading my brain and making me twitch violently. I let the magazines fall to the floor as I slam my palms over my eyes. I'd need another set of hands to cover my ears, to block out the myriad thuds of what sounds like a thousand bodies dropping out of the sky.

That's when the groaning starts.

7

IN WHICH
WE FIND OUT
WHAT A ZOMBIE APOCALYPSE LOOKS LIKE

I abandon the magazines and get away from the window as quickly as I can. Lincoln's just standing there with a stupefied expression. The gun hangs, forgotten, in one hand.

"Come on!" I shout.

He shakes his head, seeming to come back into his body, and does sort of a double take as he sees the horde of corpses picking themselves up off the ground. They're scattered around the car, their filthy feet trampling what's left of the snow-covered gardens.

"What's going on?" Gage asks, his breath suddenly in my ear. I *hate* how he keeps doing that, but now really isn't the time to lodge a complaint.

"What does it look like?"

He shrugs, looking honestly perplexed. I guess his world doesn't have a lot of zombies. Or even books about them.

Books.

With a gasp, I turn and look up. Adèle's still standing there, the damaged graphic novel in one hand, her eyes wide as she stares at the horde outside the window. I don't know what she was expecting. A herd of unicorns?

"What do we do now?" Lincoln asks, drawing my attention back to him. He's staring out the window, a look of horror on his face. So far, the zombies are just sort of milling about. But the broken window is basically a huge hole in the side of the wall, and I know it won't be long before they'll try to come inside. That is, if they can climb over the two-foot wall under the opening.

"Stay quiet, for one thing," I say, keeping my voice low and my gaze on the zombies. "And try not to make sudden movements. They might not be able to see us if we stay still. Or maybe—" I break off suddenly as one of the zombies closest to the window lifts its chin and sniffs the air like an animal. "Shit," I whisper.

As if it's a flock of birds all working in unison, the horde starts to move toward the window as one, the sniffer in the lead. I scramble back, and Lincoln isn't far behind me. Gage stays right where he is, and though I have an urge to reach out and pull him after us, I don't. If he wants to get eaten by zombies, I'm not going to stand in his way.

The first few don't try to step over the wall. They just sort of fall into the gaping hole, landing face first on the floor with sick-sounding smacks. They don't even put their hands out to stop themselves. I start to hope that maybe they won't be able to get through after all. But the next group seems to be a little smarter. They crawl over their fallen comrades, tumbling into the library in a pile of groaning and slowly flailing limbs.

"Lincoln!" I shout, abandoning my resolve to keep quiet. It's not like it's going to help now.

"What?"

"Use the gun!"

As if he's just remembered, he raises the weapon and aims at a zombie that's struggling to stand. But all that comes out of the gun is a click.

"Are you *kidding* me?" I shriek.

"It's not loaded!"

"No shit!"

"Will you stop yelling? These things can—"

His shout is drowned out by an unearthly scream. I instinctively sprint away from the noise, cowering. He follows, though he probably doesn't even know why. We're both operating on reflexes at this point.

"Help!" Gage screams. He's got three zombies latched on to him: one with its hands around his head, another clawing at his leg . . . and a third with its teeth sunk into his side. He struggles to move, but he's trying to move toward us. Lincoln raises the gun again and tries to fire.

"There are no bullets, you idiot!" I shout.

He shakes his head and throws the gun into the shadows. Like, hard. As if it's the weapon's fault that the shit is hitting the fan. "Now what? If we don't do something, he's going to drag those things over . . ." He trails off as he looks over at where Gage was standing. All that's there now is a writhing pile of bodies. "Whoa."

"We have to get out of here."

"No argument."

"But we need to get Jane and Adèle out, too."

"Why? They might be safer up there. We don't know if zombies can climb stairs."

"And what if they can? Do you honestly want the death of one of literature's most famous heroines and her little charge on your conscience?"

"So . . . what? We take them and run? Where? We're surrounded." He throws out a hand to gesture to the window. More zombies are slowly oozing into the library. They're distracted a bit by the vampire feast that's going on down at the floor, but—

"Oh, my god," I whisper. "Gage."

"Yeah, he got himself eaten."

I shake my head. "No. He's a vampire."

"Not anymore."

I want to smack him again. "He's immortal, you idiot. And who the hell knows what he's going to come back as now?"

The colour seems to drain from Lincoln's face. At least, that's what it looks like, but it's really hard to tell in the green glow of the room. He stares at the writhing pile and shakes his head slowly.

"We need to do *something*," I say, more to myself than to anyone else. Lincoln might be cute, but I don't think he's going to be of much use in this situation. The gun might've helped—had it been loaded—but we would've run out of bullets eventually. Plus, we're not exactly experts on taking out zombies. We need to find . . .

"Adèle!" I shout, turning up to the railing once more. The child is still there. She hasn't moved. The book is still in her hands. The green glow highlights the tears streaming down her cheeks. *Where the hell is Jane?* I wonder. But I push the thought aside because, as much as I like her, Jane Eyre is probably not going to be able to help with zombies. "Drop the book!"

"*Je n'aime pas les monstres.*"

"I know. I don't like them, either." I raise my hands. "Let me have the book!"

She lets it fall as she turns away. It drops into my hands, and I fumble it a little but manage to catch it by one page. Of course it tears. Sucking in a breath, I hold it in place, careful not to let it go soaring out into the storm. And it's a good thing, too; its panels are absolutely teeming with zombies.

"What are you doing?" Lincoln asks. I shake my head as I begin to flip through the pages. "Sadie, what are—"

"Finding someone who knows what they're doing." I stop on a page with a promising illustration. The man is muscled. He's wearing an eye patch. The front of his shirt is open, showing off some unrealistic abs. But he's also got a couple of swords strapped to his belt. I grab the corner of the page and carefully tear it out, then check the other side. "Damn it."

"What?"

"More zombies."

"So don't throw that page."

I turn it around so he can see the picture of Sword Guy.

"What if he's some sort of villain?"

I shake my head. "That's a chance we'll have to take. Hopefully, he doesn't get taken out by the guys on the flip side before he can help us deal with our problem." My heart pounds as I lift the page into the air. We exchange a look. And I let the page go.

There's more than one flash (as I knew there would be), and the collective groaning gets a lot louder. I'd love to see if our potential saviour is outside, but there are too many zombies pouring through the window . . . and, as I peer over at the stairs, I see that a few have already made it there. My breath catches for a moment until I realize the stupid things don't have the coordination necessary to get to the second floor. I mean, they're trying, but all they end up doing is collecting in a pile that sort of claws at the steps. They might eventually make it upstairs . . . but it could take days.

"Adèle!" I shout. "Jane!"

The railing stays empty.

"Jane!"

"Sadie, we need to go."

I turn back to Lincoln, just as he grabs my arm. I'm about to pull away, but at that same instant I feel something cold and dry close around my other hand. I let out a scream and pull back, practically barrelling Lincoln over as I sprint into the stacks. I try to look at my hand, but it's too dark in here.

"Sadie!"

"Did it bite me?" I ask, stopping so suddenly that he runs into me, knocking me to the ground. I crawl forward on my hands and knees, aiming for the far end of the shelves. "Did it *bite me?*" My voice rises into a shriek.

"Let me see."

I shake my head and keep crawling, panic driving all sense from my body.

"Sadie, stop!"

With a sob, I lean down and rest my forehead on my hands. I feel Lincoln's knees hit the floor beside me.

"Did you feel it bite you?"

"No."

"Then it probably didn't."

"What if I turn into—"

"You won't."

"I might. And Gage might. And Adèle. And Jane, too."

"Zombie Jane Eyre?"

"It's not funny!"

"Who's laughing?" He puts his hand on my back. Somehow, that helps a little. "Look, these things are morons. Worse than morons. They can't climb stairs. They could barely climb over the windowsill. If we can just get somewhere they can't reach us . . ."

I sniff and look up at him. Or, I try to. He's just a shadowy blob. "Like where?"

"Um . . . on top of the shelves? Are these things bolted down?" He starts shuffling along to my left. I have no idea what he's doing. "I can't tell. Even if they aren't, I don't know if zombies would have the smarts to figure out that they'd need to push the shelves over to get at us."

He's probably right. Although, if enough of those things just run into a shelf, they might be able to knock it over.

Still, I don't see any other options.

Using the nearest shelf, I pull myself to my feet. My legs are shaking so bad. I'm not sure if I can do this.

But I do, using the shelves like a ladder until I pull myself up onto the top. The whole thing feels pretty solid, so it's entirely possible that the shelves are anchored to the floor somehow. And if they are . . .

"What do we do now?" I ask Lincoln when he's sitting next to me, legs safely tucked up out of the way of rotting fingers. He turns and looks toward the window. The light's better up here, and we can see the horde in all its rotting glory. A moment later, we also see something else fly into the air in a spray of blood that decorates the wall with dark spatter.

"Whoa," Lincoln breathes. "Was that a *head?*"

8

IN WHICH
WE REALIZE THAT EVEN EXPERTS
DON'T ALWAYS KNOW WHAT THEY'RE DOING

Yes, it was a head.

"I really hope Adèle didn't see that," Lincoln says.

"I really hope Jane didn't see that. She's from gothic romance . . . not horror."

He shakes his head and cranes his neck to try to see better. "I can't see that guy with the swords."

"Well, he's obviously in there somewhere. I don't think zombie heads just pop off for no reason."

"Some of them probably fall off," he says. "Being rotting corpses and all."

"That's disgusting."

He holds up his hands, still staring into the melee. "I don't write the books."

"I bet you read them, though."

"Why do you think that?"

"You weren't familiar with Jane Eyre. So I think it's safe to say you're not big on the classics."

"Hm."

"You had no idea where the gun books were, so you're probably not big on military fiction, either."

"So your conclusion is that I read zombie novels?"

"Zombie *graphic* novels."

He turns back to me, eyebrows raised. "Are you saying I'm so dumb that all I can handle are picture books?"

"You did get us an unloaded gun."

"If I'd had more time, I could've gotten some bullets to go in it."

I shake my head. "You're not dumb."

"Then why do you think I read graphic novels?"

"Shut up. When did I ever say that people who read graphic novels are dumb?"

He turns away with a grunt.

"You knew those books were upstairs," I say, my voice so low I'm not sure he hears me. "I just made a deduction. Am I wrong?"

He sighs and rubs his hand over his hair. Not that it makes a lot of difference with the wind still whipping about. "No."

"Okay. So can we *please* not spend our last moments arguing? I really don't want to die in a pissed-off state."

He reaches back without looking, finding my hand with his. "We're not going to die."

I snort. "You think this is survivable?"

"The storm has to end sometime. The *night* has to end sometime. Things will look better in the morning. And we might be able to see what's going on a little better." He squeezes my hand. "As a bonus, maybe the morning will also thin the horde by at least one."

I blink into the shadowy mass of groaning. "Gage?"

"Unless he's a sparkly vampire who can go out in the sun."

"I don't think he is." I frown as I try to remember what little I read of the book. "He . . . seemed to stay inside a lot. But he did go to school."

"Okay. So maybe he just needs direct sunlight. And maybe it won't actually kill him, but just weaken him enough that—"

"You're making a lot of assumptions. What if he's just a regular zombie? Maybe he can go out in the sun now."

"And maybe he can't. We'll find out in a few hours."

"If we last that long."

"Look, Sadie."

I wait for him to go on, but then I realize he wants me to literally look at something. I edge a little closer to him, still holding his hand, so I can peer past his shoulder. "What am I looking at?"

"Does it look as crowded out there as it did a few minutes ago?"

I shake my head slowly. He's right. It's not as crowded. It's also not quite as noisy. "Is Sword Guy killing them?"

"I guess." He chuckles. "Is that his name?"

"You tell me."

"I haven't read this one. I didn't recognize him at all."

"He obviously knows how to deal with zombies."

"Anyone who didn't wouldn't last long in a story like that." He pauses. "Actually, even the people who *do* know what they're doing don't always last."

"Great. What does that mean for us?"

"I have no idea. But we've made it this far, haven't we?"

I don't know how far we've made it. I don't know what time it is. My phone is somewhere in the library, but I doubt I'd be able to find it. I can't even remember where I left it.

But it's not like there's any lack of light in here now. The auroral storm is practically screaming outside. I edge closer to Lincoln. He seems to be shaking, but whether it's from the cold or from the situation, I couldn't say.

"Do you think Jane and Adèle are okay?" he asks. But before I can give him an answer, the library erupts in a continuous flash so bright that I can't stop the scream that twists out of me. He doesn't have any better luck.

"What was that?" I shout. "What the hell was—" And then I remember. The graphic novel is still on the floor. *Was* still on the floor. Although, with the explosion of light we just saw, I'm pretty sure the entire thing just got swallowed up by the storm. "Lincoln!"

But he can't hear me. The noise is deafening. Writhing shadows pour into the space. A few zombies have landed on the car, and they roll off, groaning, before struggling to their feet. Lincoln stands up, tugging on my hand until I do the same.

"What?"

"Let's go!" His voice is barely audible over the cacophony. "—room."

"What?"

He leans close to my ear, for a moment reminding me of Gage. "Bathroom."

"The doors don't lock."

"The stalls do."

I shake my head. It seems to me that the safest thing to do when you're confronted with a horde of zombies that can't climb is to stay well out of reach. The floor is the last place I want to be.

"Sadie, we have to." He turns and points. The stacks stretch in front of us—I count five rows of shelves—before the view drops into the darkness. "Hop across."

"If we fall, we're dead."

"So don't fall."

That's the least of our problems. After the last shelf, there's an empty space of about twenty feet that we'll need to cross. There aren't any zombies there now, but that's probably because they're so focused on what they can see . . . and that includes me and Lincoln standing up here. They're in the stacks now, reaching up with hungry groans. I edge out of the way of a hand, then stomp my foot down on the fingers clawing at the top of the shelf. They break away at the knuckles, leaving bits of the digits behind. The zombie doesn't even seem to notice.

"We can't stay here," Lincoln says, leaning close once more. "The shelves aren't that far apart. You can do it."

"I know I can," I snap. "I just don't know if that's the best option."

"I'm open to suggestions."

So am I. Unfortunately, I'm fresh out. I peer past him into the throbbing horde. It actually seems like the zombies are multiplying. I don't see any more flying heads. I guess Sword Guy—whoever he was—couldn't win against all that.

Lincoln lets go of my hand, and my heart surges in panic. I watch as he leaps lightly over to the next shelf. And then the next. He doesn't look back, seemingly expecting me to follow him. Like I have a choice. I don't want to stay up here by myself.

I kick away the finger bits so I don't slip on them and hold my breath as I make the first jump. It's easier than I would've thought, but I'm probably so full of adrenaline that I could vault over that car sitting outside in the garden right now. The zombies are really slow, not seeming to notice that their prey is escaping right over their heads. The noise gets marginally quieter as I make my way to the final shelf where Lincoln is waiting for me. When I reach him, he nods and starts to climb down to the floor. I don't even wait for him to finish; I just climb down beside him as quickly as I can.

When we reach the bottom, he turns to me and takes a breath. I hold my finger to my lips, and he clamps his mouth shut. As he edges forward to peer around the shelf, I hang back. I can't really see through the shelves. I don't really want to.

"Shit," he says, and turns back to grab my hand. I don't even have time to ask what's wrong before he pulls me out from behind the shelf and dashes across the open space. But I see it. A few of the zombies must've spotted us jumping across the shelves, because they're heading our way, slowly but inexorably.

Lincoln hits the bathroom door with a huge thump. Not that the noise matters, because a whole bunch of them have seen us come in here. It's pitch dark, and it still smells awful.

"Let's not hide in the one where I puked."

"It might throw them off the scent."

"I don't want to die surrounded by my own vomit!"

"Okay, okay." He moves forward into the darkness, towing me with him. I can hear his fingers trail on the stall doors. "Which one did you use?"

"The middle one. I think."

"Smells like it."

"Shut up, will you?"

He sighs. "I make stupid comments when I'm in intense situations, all right?"

"Yeah. You do."

His hand pulls away from mine. I stop with a gasp.

"Lincoln?" Holding my breath, I listen. I don't hear anything. Not from inside the bathroom, anyway. From the direction of the door comes an ominous, low-pitched roar, a hellish combination of howling wind and a thousand groans. "Lincoln? This isn't funny! Where are you?"

There's no answer. My heart hammers in my throat, and though I haven't eaten in hours, I feel like I might barf again. The smell in here certainly isn't helping. Desperately, I reach out and feel for the stalls. My fingers brush the cold metal. It's *really* cold. The whole room is freezing, almost as if the storm has been blowing in here all day, leaving snow-drifts around the toilets. I step forward. The floor feels slippery. And that's when I smell it, the scent like pennies clenched in a hot hand.

"Lincoln!" I scream, reaching forward and slamming my hands against the metal obstacle in front of me, which turns out to be a door that gives way. I try to brace myself to stop from falling, but my hands slide against the smooth surface. The dizzying darkness swallows me, and the world explodes in a flash—white this time—as my head smashes into something cold and hard.

9

IN WHICH
THE STORM REACHES
ITS CONCLUSION

Don't barf. Don't barf.

I gag and retch, pushing up quickly onto my hands and knees. But there's nothing left in my stomach. It's all in front of me, a puddle of puke and . . . blood. *Oh, my god. Am I dying?*

My head pounds, my teeth feel furry, and my throat is raw. Another fruitless heave is all my body can muster. I sit back on my heels, regarding the mess. The toilet seems to have been mostly spared. The walls and floor, on the other hand, look like modern art. I realize I've been lying on the floor of a public bathroom for goodness knows how long, but I don't even have the energy to be horrified. I pull off a section of one-ply toilet paper and swipe the scratchy stuff over my mouth. My lips feel like they're going to crack.

I push myself to my feet on shaking legs. My vision is a bit spotty, but . . . *The lights are on. Did Lincoln turn them on? Where is he?*

I toss the wad of paper into the toilet, flush, and open the stall door. Before I can take more than a step outside, though, I see him. Standing there with this horrified look on his face.

"Did you get bitten?" I ask. My throat feels like I've been gargling with battery acid.

He blinks a few times, looking utterly confused. "Huh?"

"Did they get in here? You disappeared."

With a shake of his head, he steps toward the sink and grabs a paper towel. My gaze sweeps over him, looking for any injuries. But I see none. He looks fine. He looks more than fine, actually. Before I can even think about what I'm doing, I launch myself at him and wrap him in a tight hug. He grunts in surprise.

"Are you okay?" I ask.

"I'm not the one with the head wound."

Frowning, I pull back. He turns to the sink and wets the paper towel. After squeezing it out, he brings it up to my forehead. I wince as the cool paper touches me. He dabs for a few seconds, then turns back to the flow of water to wet the towel again. I take the opportunity to glance in the mirror.

"What happened?" I ask, turning my aching head to examine the gash near my hairline. It looks like it's still bleeding. There's a trail of red down the side of my face and a dark spot on the shoulder of my jacket.

"Looks like you bashed your head good." His gentle fingers find my chin and turn my head back toward him. This time, he applies a little more pressure on the wound.

"Where did you go?" I ask. "Did the power come back on? Did the storm pass? What about the zombies?"

He lets out a short, awkward laugh, keeping his gaze trained on the hand that's holding the paper towel. "What?"

"The zombies."

"Zombies in the library? That's a new one."

"There are zombie books." My voice is small.

"Yeah. I think you might've read a few too many of those."

"Shut up. You're the one who reads those graphic novels."

His eyebrows rise. "How do you know that?"

"Stop playing games. We've just spent the last few hours feeding a sentient storm and watching it poop out zombies and a car and . . ." My voice falters as I see the look on his face.

"I think you hit your head pretty hard. You should probably go to the hospital and get checked out."

"I *can't*. The storm is—"

"What storm?"

"Some weird snowstorm. With green lightning. If you throw pages into it, the storm spits out what was on them."

He snorts. "Right."

"You saw it! You even did it. You made Adèle, and then a gun, but it didn't have any bullets so you threw it away, and then we couldn't fight the zombies so we—"

"Look," he says, tossing away the bloody paper towel and reaching for a clean one, which he folds and presses to my head. "I come in here to find you bleeding from your head, and you're rambling on about zombies and books and some weird storm, acting like you know me."

"I *do* know you!"

"Sorry to tell you this, but we've never met. I don't even think we go to the same school. I've never seen you before in my life."

Tears prickle behind my eyes, which only seems to make my growing headache worse. My words fall back into my ears, and I'm suddenly awash with embarrassment at how utterly stupid it all sounds. Zombies? Book-eating storms? He's right. I probably hit my head too hard, and now . . .

"Hey," he says. "It's okay. I'm sure you're a great person. I didn't mean . . . I just don't know you. That's all."

"You did know me." I shake my head. "And I knew you. Your name is—"

"Cash."

My disappointment makes me want to shut myself in a stall and have a little cry. "So it was all . . . just a dream?"

"Sounds like a pretty intense dream."

"It felt real."

"Sometimes dreams do."

With a sigh, I reach up and press my fingers over the paper towel, allowing him to let go. His gaze moves downward, and his nose wrinkles a little. I look down, carefully keeping the paper towel in place, and notice the specks and smears all over the front of my jacket. And then I remember that I hugged him like this.

"Just kill me now," I mutter.

He chuckles. "It's fine. What's a little puke?"

"It's not just that. You must think I'm totally insane."

"No, I think you're having a really bad day. You got sick and you hit your head. Why should I hold that against you?"

"Why should you care at all?"

He shrugs. "Because when I see someone in distress, it bothers me."

"So you follow them into the ladies' room?"

"It's a unisex bathroom," he says. "The library switched them over last year."

I press the paper towel a little more firmly against my head as I'm hit with a wave of déjà vu. The overly bright lights suddenly hurt my eyes. "I think . . . I should go home now."

"That's probably a good idea." He steps back, allowing me to access the door.

I grasp the handle, then pause. *What if it's all repeating? What if I open this door and the storm is back and it all happens again?* I look back at him with a frown.

He raises his eyebrows. "What's wrong?"

He doesn't believe me, so there's no point in saying anything. Besides, it doesn't *have* to happen the way it did before. If the storm is there, I can go out and grab that copy of *Jane Eyre* before the wind tears out any pages. I can put the magazines far away from the windows. If I can just make sure that storm doesn't eat anything . . .

"Should I call someone for you?" he asks, pulling his phone from his pocket. "I should call someone for you. I don't want you losing consciousness on your way home." He pauses, phone in hand. "Or I could give you a lift."

I open my mouth to tell him it's okay, that I can make it on my own . . . but I'm not sure that's true. I'm still feeling really weird, and I'm not sure if I have the strength to walk all the way. Still . . .

"You don't mind having a pukey girl in your car?"

"It's my brother's car."

I crack a little smile. "Nice."

"As long as you don't puke *in* the car, I don't think you'll do too much damage. Come on." He gestures to the door.

I want to refuse, but I'm so tired. I still don't have a book for my assignment; I don't want that stupid thing with Gage, though. Not now. So I just nod and pull open the door. The perfectly normal library greets me with the scent of books—new and old—and a stupid amount of noise coming from the kids' section. It's a good thing I'm leaving, because that would definitely make my headache worse.

Cash leads me outside. I glance at the book-return area, but there's nothing there. With a strange sense of relief, I follow the cute boy out into the evening. He leads me to his brother's car, which turns out to be a very familiar-looking hybrid. My feet scuff to a stop on the pavement. He turns with a frown.

"What's wrong?"

"This is your brother's car?"

"I know. Ridiculous, isn't it? It's like driving a virtue signal." He unlocks the doors with the remote. "Not that I'm complaining. A car is a car. When he goes away to medical school next year and leaves it to me, I'm not going to refuse, am I?"

I don't move. Slowly, I pull the paper towel from my forehead and peer at it in the light streaming down from the nearest lamppost.

"You coming?"

I point at my head. "Am I still bleeding?"

"Doesn't look like it. I still think you should get checked out, though." He opens the door and slides into the driver's seat. Strangely worried that he's just going to drive off and leave me behind, I hurry to join him. The interior of the car smells a bit like fries . . . or, at least, something fried. I pull the door closed and sink back into the seat.

"Can you take me home first?" I ask.

"Sure. Where's home?"

I tell him, then sit there in frozen terror when my dazed brain realizes what I've just done.

"You okay?" he asks. He still hasn't started the car. Maybe, if I'm quick, I can get out and make a run for it. I don't know how fast I can run right now, though. He'd probably catch me for sure, and then . . .

"I . . . Maybe I should just call my dad."

"Maybe. But I really don't want to leave you when you're looking like this." His gaze travels up to my forehead, and he winces. "You're bleeding again."

"Sorry."

"Don't be sorry. You're not doing it on purpose." He doesn't say anything for a few moments. Instead, he sits there, staring at me. It's so weird. I just went through the most intense night of my life with this guy, but . . . it *wasn't* this guy. I simply saw a stranger in the library, thought he was cute, and then stuck him into my concussion dream.

Or whatever that was.

"Can we go now?" I ask, pressing the scratchy paper towel against my skin.

"Not until you buckle up."

"Oh." My fingers fumble as I reach for the belt. He has to help me aim the two parts of the buckle together, I'm shaking so hard. But it clicks at last, and he starts the engine. I'm suddenly too tired to care whether I've just gotten into a car with a serial killer or not.

But he takes the most direct route to my house, and when we're about halfway there, I begin to relax. Closing my eyes, I let myself sink back in the seat.

"Did you at least get what you went for?"

"Huh?" My eyelids feel too heavy to move. So I don't even try.

"At the library. You must've been there for something specific, because nobody would go there just to hang out."

I swallow; my throat still feels like it was etched with acid. "Why not? Maybe I just like the library."

"Hey, I like libraries, too. But that branch smells funky."

"Sorry."

He's quiet for a moment, but then he laughs. "I meant in general. Not because you puked in it. Although, I'm sure that didn't help."

"I didn't get the book."

"What book?"

"Doesn't matter."

"We can go back and pick it up, if you want."

Slowly, I shake my head. Not a smart choice. The dizzying throb makes me suck in a breath. I open my eyes to see that we're just a block or so from home. I also see, swinging from the rearview mirror, a student parking placard. My exhausted gaze seems to be sucked toward one word in particular. Lunging forward, I grab the placard and twist it around.

"That's my brother's," he says. "I always forget to take it off when I'm driving his—"

"Dash Lincoln?" I whisper.

"Yeah." He lets out a grunt of laughter. "Cashel and Dashiell. Take it up with our parents."

"No." I twist the placard so he can see it. He glances at me, looking concerned.

"What?"

"Lincoln?"

"Yeah . . ."

"Your last name is Lincoln?"

"No relation to the president."

I swear and sit back in the seat a little too roughly for my aching head. "What the hell?"

"That's my question, too."

He has no idea what I'm talking about. And we're pulling up to my house. The lights are on, and both of my parents' cars are in the driveway. I just want to get inside, put some ice on my head, and lie down (if Mom will let me once she sees the gash), but I can't just leave it like this, can I?

When Cash stops the car in our driveway, I take a deep breath and turn to him. He looks right back at me, eyebrows raised in an expectant expression that's becoming comfortably familiar. *You better hope this is the last time you see him, because he's going to think you're completely nuts after you say what you're about to say.*

"Do you remember?" I ask quietly.

"Remember what?"

"The bathroom."

"Yeah, I remember the bathroom. You were on the floor."

"No . . . the first time."

His eyebrows rise even higher. Before I can overthink it, I take another deep breath and dive in.

"I was looking for a book. I have to write a novelette for this creative writing class I'm taking, and it has to be in a genre I don't like to read. So I was trying to get some inspiration by looking at the vampire books"—his lips twist in a smirk that I choose to ignore—"and I felt really sick, so I went to the bathroom to throw up. You followed me in there like a weirdo, and when we came out, the librarians had closed everything up and there was this weird snowstorm outside. With auroras."

"Auroras?"

"Something like that. You called it a brainstorm."

"I did?"

"We figured out that if you threw pages into the storm, it would make the things on those pages exist. So we got characters from *Jane Eyre* and a vampire and a car and a gun, and then Adèle threw half a graphic novel into the storm and caused a zombie horde to rampage the library, and we made it back to the bathroom and hid there . . ."

"Is that when I found you?"

I look down at my lap. Now that I'm saying it all out loud, it sounds like exactly what it is: a really weird dream caused by a blow to the head.

"How'd I know your name was Lincoln?" I ask, daring to lift my gaze to look at him.

"Lucky guess? Or maybe we actually have met somewhere before."

"I don't think so. I would've remembered your face."

"Why?"

"You're cute." My free hand slaps over my mouth, an instant too late. I close my eyes as I see his smile begin.

"Well, I'm flattered. But you *did* just hit your head pretty hard, so I'm not sure you're seeing straight." I feel something jostle at my hip, and I open my eyes to find him unbuckling my seatbelt. "Since both your hands are busy," he says. I quickly lower my hand from my mouth.

"Thanks for the ride." I fumble at the door handle. If I don't get out of this car soon, I'm afraid I might be sick again. Can extreme embarrassment cause vomiting? I don't particularly want to find out.

"You're welcome," he says, his voice almost getting lost in the sound of the door opening. I quickly get out on shaking legs and am about to slam the door when he shakes his head. "I don't think you need that book."

"What book?"

"The vampire book. I think you already have a much better story."

"Huh?"

"That thing you just told me about the crazy storm and the books. Write that."

"Oh. Yeah. Maybe."

He nods with a little smile. "I bet it'll be great. Anyway. Go take care of your head, okay? I'll see you around, Sadie." I take that as my cue to close the door.

It isn't until I'm standing inside the house, trying to take off my jacket while still holding the paper towel against my head, that I realize I never actually told Cash my name.

I think I might be sick again.

DREAM FLARE

1

IN WHICH
I MUST DEAL WITH
A PUKING POTATO

Nothing gets you out of bed faster than the sound of a dog about to puke.

I've retched twice by the time I disentangle myself from my sheet and flail out of bed. Even though I only had the one sheet on, I'm still drenched in sweat. The dry heaves aren't helping. Spud stands beside my closed bedroom door, alternately looking at me and at the door while shuddering as if he's cold. Which isn't possible, given the temperature of my room. The window is open, but I can already tell the day's going to be a hot one.

Great.

"Just a second!" I practically wail as Spud gags again. I wrench open the door, careful not to hit the dog with it. He trots out into the hallway, his gait jaunty even though he's still threatening to barf all over the floor. And, I mean, Mom and Dad *did* just get laminate flooring put in up here, so it's not like I'd have to clean Chihuahua puke out of the carpet. But . . . still. I don't exactly want to start off my day on my hands and knees with a bottle of spray cleaner and a roll of paper towels.

Spud hops down the stairs, rather impressively for a creature who's still heaving. I follow as quickly as I dare, peeling away from him in the foyer so I can grab his leash. And my shoes. Which, of course, are not where I left them, so I have to go searching. Dad's got this thing about shoes by the front door, so I know he's put them away somewhere. Unfortunately, I can't find them, and Spud's tiny retching noises are echoing throughout the hallway. I grab the first footwear I see—a pair of red jelly sandals that always give me terrible blisters—and tug them on, hopping down the hall as I fumble with the buckles. Spud scratches at the door, and I know that if I don't get him out soon, I'm going to have a mess. So I open the front door and let him squeeze outside while I finish fastening my shoes. Through the gap, I see him run to his favourite bush in Mom's garden and lift his leg.

"I thought you had to puke," I say, grabbing my keys from the table beside the door. My phone's there, too, and it's finished charging, so I unplug it and try to slip it into a non-existent pocket. Right. I'm wearing pyjama shorts.

Again. Great.

Spud finishes with the bush and goes sniffing along the edge of the garden. I call him back, and he comes right away, looking totally innocent with his buggy brown eyes.

"Well?"

He tilts his head with a little whine, like he often does when I ask him a question. It's like he wants to answer, but he knows he can't, and he knows I know he can't, so he can't figure out why I'm even asking.

"You gonna puke, or what?"

He looks toward the street. I sigh as I bend down and clip the leash to his collar.

"Fine. We'll walk. Might as well do it now before it gets hellish out here."

Not that it's that far off. It's not late—just after nine—but the sun is already heating the air to an uncomfortable degree. The house should be nice and miserable by the time we get back. Mom and Dad don't get it. They get in their air-conditioned cars and drive to their air-conditioned offices, ignoring the poor child they leave behind to swelter. Mom suggested I get a summer job washing dishes or something, but I really don't see how working in a hotter-than-hell kitchen would be an improvement.

Spud trots ahead of me, straining lightly at the leash, his stomach upset seemingly forgotten. It's not the first time he's magically been cured with the prospect of a walk. But these episodes aren't always false alarms. Better safe than sorry.

I turn off my phone so it doesn't warm up my hand too much, then just let Spud lead the way. Our neighbourhood is not the nicest place for walking, especially on a day like today. It's not that old, which means that the subdivision was basically denuded of trees when it was built. There's not much shade to speak of. But I also know that, a few blocks away, the houses are much older, and there are some beautiful tree-lined streets with plenty of shade. Spud seems to be having similar thoughts because, when we reach the corner, he automatically turns the way I was about to.

As if the day isn't miserable enough, the air is kind of thick and itchy. It's just smoke from wildfires in another part of the province, but if I didn't know any better, I would say those fires aren't that far off. The sky is free of clouds, but it's not really blue, either. It's sort of a hazy grey, heavy with smoke. My eyes will probably be burning by the time we get home.

Spud trots merrily along, pausing to sniff at a few things, but scampering ahead of me again before I need to tell him to get moving. His guts seem fine now. I wish I could say the same. The queasiness is still coiled in the pit of my stomach, ready to strike at the least provocation. Like, for example, if Spud actually does decide to puke.

It doesn't take long before we reach the shady streets. I've always loved this neighbourhood. I think the catchment boundary for the schools is a few blocks back, so I never went to school with any of the kids who live around here. Too bad.

In addition to lots of trees and their accompanying shade, this area also has proper sidewalks with boulevards. Spud trots right down the middle of the cracked cement pathway, tail straight up like a proud flag. I look up into the leaves. It's prettier on a day when the sun sparkles through them, but this is still nice.

My sandals are rubbing my feet the wrong way, and I know I'm going to have blisters by the time I get home. Unless I take the jellies off. But I really don't feel like stepping on something and having to go to the emergency room. It's summer vacation. I'm supposed to be relaxing.

Luckily, I spot something up ahead. One of the homeowners has put a bench out on the boulevard. It's made of wood, kind of rustic, but clean enough that I don't mind sitting down to give my burning feet a break. Spud doesn't really notice I've stopped until he reaches the end of the leash with a surprised tug. He looks back at me reproachfully.

"Deal with it. You dragged me out here. The least you can do is give me a chance to rest."

He lets out a sigh and wanders closer to my feet to give them a sniff. I wonder if he can smell blisters forming. Pulling my attention away from the dog, I glance up and spot something on the lawn directly across from where I'm sitting. It's a few feet back from the sidewalk, a cardboard box with the word "FREE" scrawled on the front in black marker. The addition of the quotation marks gives me pause.

"Is it free or not?" I mutter. I don't even know what it is, actually. Gritting my teeth, I stand up and hobble closer to have a look. When I peer into the box, I see a bunch of paperbacks. I crouch down, loop Spud's leash around my wrist, set my phone and keys on the grass, and start to paw through the box.

Unfortunately, there's nothing that interesting. Not to me, anyway. It looks like mostly high fantasy stuff. Dragons. Elves. Women with their boobs falling out of leather bustiers. I snort as I pull out a book from the bottom of the box and peer at the cover.

"*Dominating the Dragonyx,*" a voice reads from behind me. I startle a little and twist on the balls of my feet (which doesn't make my nascent blisters feel good at all), only to find Lincoln—no, wait . . . Cash—staring down at me. I blink.

"What are *you* doing here?" I ask. The question comes out embarrassingly accusatory. Shaking my head, I stand up. Cash's eyebrows are raised, possibly in amusement. He's kind of sweaty. But still cute. Annoyingly so.

"What does it look like?"

"Standing there, sweating."

He laughs. "Just out for a run. Before it gets too hot." He pulls the back of his wrist across his forehead, and I notice what he's got clasped in his hand.

"Walking an invisible dog?"

"Apparently. You haven't seen him around here, have you?"

"How would I, if he's invisible?"

With a smile, he turns and lets out an ear-splitting whistle. I wince.

"Warn me next time."

"Sorry." He's still staring off down the sidewalk, back the way Spud and I came. "William! Hurry up."

"Your dog's name is William?" I ask, unable to keep the smile off my face. He turns to me with a grin.

"Yeah. We tried calling him Bill for a while, but he didn't seem to like it." His attention is drawn to a medium-sized mutt with apparent ADHD who's zigzagging toward us. It's like everything—every blade of grass, every sidewalk crack, every pebble—must be investigated, and it must be done *now*. The dog doesn't even seem to realize Spud and I are standing here.

"Is he friendly?"

"Too friendly. If he tries to hump your leg, just push him off."

"What if he tries to hump Spud?"

"Spud?" He looks down at my dog, who just stares back up at him. "You named your dog Spud?"

"We can't name all the dogs William."

He laughs. "Didn't say we should." He crouches down and holds out his hand so Spud can sniff it. "But we shouldn't have to resort to naming them after root vegetables, either."

"He's not named after a root vegetable. Not exactly."

"Not exactly?"

"It's short for Spudley."

An amused snort is all I get. Spud seems to have decided that Cash is okay, because he's allowing a chin scratch.

"I wanted to name him Tater. Dad wanted to give him a human name. Like Dudley."

"Ah. The great compromise." He stands and looks around to see where William has ended up. The dog is getting cozy with the bushes, his leg lifted high. "William! Knock it off."

William finishes what he's doing and lopes off across the front lawns. With a shrug, Cash turns back to me.

"Shouldn't you have that thing on a leash?" I ask.

"Why? He knows his way home."

"Can he open doors, too?"

Cash frowns. I'm not sure why everything that comes out of my mouth around this guy seems to be drenched in snark. But I can tell he's noticed.

"Sorry," I say.

"For what?"

I shake my head. "I'm responding to you like . . ."

"Like what?"

"I don't know. Just forget it."

"Responding to me like what?"

I roll my eyes. "Like you're . . . someone else."

There's a pause. "Huh?"

"Like I said. Never mind."

He chuckles. "I don't know if I'd be able to pursue this line of questioning anyway. I have no idea what you're talking about."

"I have no idea, either."

With a smile, he points at something. I look down and realize I'm still holding that book. "Find something you want to read?"

"God, no."

"Really?"

"Yes, really," I snap, turning to toss the book back into the box.

"Dragons aren't your thing?"

"Not really. But it's the 'dominating' part that has me more worried."

"So . . . you don't like dragons. Or vampires. Or zombies."

I blink. "You remember that?"

"I remember you said something about having to write a story in a genre you didn't like to read, and something about vampires and zombies and Jane Eyre—"

"It was a dream. Or a brain injury."

He frowns. "How's your head?"

"Fine." Absently, I reach up to rub at the spot where my skull contacted the library toilet. "Sort of."

"Sort of?"

"I haven't felt right since then."

"Concussion?"

"The doctor didn't think so. But . . . I still get queasy. More than I should."

He nods sagely. "It takes time to heal from something like that."

"It's been months."

"It can take months." He stares off in the direction William disappeared, but he doesn't seem too concerned. When he turns back, all his attention is on me. "How'd your short story turn out?"

"Novelette," I correct him. "Twice as many words to be ripped apart with gusto."

"That bad?"

"I don't want to talk about it."

"I'm sorry." He reaches out and puts his hand on my arm. I just stare at it for a moment. He seems earnest enough, but I'm so taken aback by the gesture that I don't quite know what to say. So I just edge back a little. He takes the hint and drops his hand. "It sounded like a cool idea."

I shake my head. "Maybe you just have weird taste."

"Can I read it?"

"No!"

"Why not? Maybe, with my weird taste, I'll love it."

"You'd be the only one," I mutter.

"Come on. It can't be that bad."

"You weren't there. You didn't have to listen to the teacher read parts of it out loud for 'critique'"—I curl my fingers into air quotes—"and then sit there while everyone else wouldn't even look at me."

"Why wouldn't they look at you?"

"Vicarious embarrassment."

He lets out a short laugh. "I'm sure it wasn't that bad. Please, can I read it? Do you have a copy on your phone?"

"Yeah, but it'll take you hours to get through."

"I can speedread."

I regard him for a long moment. "If you think it sucks . . . don't tell me."

"Constructive criticism is important."

"Saying it sucks isn't constructive criticism."

A frown creases his features. "Okay, then, I promise I won't tell you if it sucks. I'll be more specific."

Might as well let him read it, I think. *What could he say that would be any worse than what that cottage-core pedant crowed in front of a dozen other people?* I grab my phone off the grass and find the file. "What's your number?"

He shakes his head and holds out his hand. "Let me read it now."

"I don't want to be here all day. I have things to do."

"What kind of things?"

"I have a life."

"I didn't say you didn't." His hand is still outstretched between us. He raises his eyebrows.

I slap the device onto his palm. "Fine. But read fast." I start to hobble back to the bench, then change my mind. I sit down on the grass—which is, thankfully, still cool, albeit kind of crispy where the sun has baked it—and unbuckle my sandals. My feet almost seem to scream in relief as I pull off the jellies.

"You've got blisters."

"Yeah."

"Plastic shoes will do that."

"No shit."

"You really shouldn't wear those to walk the dog."

I frown up at him. "Are you going to read, or are you just going to stand there and give me a hard time?"

"Tough choice," he says with a grin, but he heads over to the bench and sits down, stretching his legs halfway across the sidewalk as he leans back on the aged wood. Spud watches him, then lies down on the grass near my leg. I glance over at the box of books. I'm probably going to be here for a while. But since I really have no desire to read about dragons—or dominatrixes—I just check the area behind me for rocks, bugs, and dog poop, then lie down. Spud lets out a contented sigh. I wish I could relax the way he can. But my stomach still feels weird. The unexpected reunion probably didn't help.

Still, I might as well make up the lost minutes of sleep. It's not like anything's going to happen with Cash sitting just a few feet away.

I close my eyes and try to relax.

2

IN WHICH
WE DISCUSS
SO-CALLED LITERATURE

A noise startles me. I blink up into a rather beige sky, disoriented. For a moment, I think the sound must've been Spud puking. But then it comes again, and I realize it's not. I lift my head to see Cash coughing into his elbow. His other arm is stretched out to the side, still holding my phone.

"Is my story that bad?" I ask.

He shakes his head and barks out another cough. It sounds like it wants to come up from his toes. "Was it supposed to be this smoky today?"

I glance up at the sky again. It's no longer anything close to blue. And, now that he mentions it, my eyes are really starting to itch. Sitting up, I reach for my shoes. "Are you finished?"

"Almost." He turns back to my phone. I watch him, noticing that his eyes are a bit red. He almost looks like he's been crying, but I know it's just the smoke.

"How long was I asleep?" I ask, which just earns me a raised, wait-a-minute finger. I blow out a breath and arrange my sandals side by side. I have no desire to put them on. Spud is still lying in the same spot, which is surprising; he's not the most patient dog. But he seems pretty content. A quick glance around tells me that William is nowhere to be seen. Cash seems weirdly unworried about it.

"Okay," he says a couple of minutes later. He holds out my phone. I raise my eyebrows.

"Well?"

"You want to get out of here first?"

I snort. "We have to go somewhere special for you to tear it apart?"

"I'm not going to tear it apart. But I don't want to sit here breathing in woodsmoke all morning." He stands up from the bench, still holding my phone. With a groan, I haul myself to my feet. Spud takes that as his cue and stands up. As he shakes himself out, his collar tag jingles. "Probably not good for these guys to be breathing it in, either," Cash adds, frowning as he peers around.

"You should keep better track of your dog."

"He's fine. Probably just investigating something."

"Or digging up someone's garden."

"He's not that much of a digger. At least not of other people's yards."

"So he digs up *your* yard?"

"What's wrong with a little digging? It keeps him busy."

I shake my head. "I hope you don't approach raising children with the same attitude."

He laughs. "Wait . . . I have kids?"

"Your *future* kids," I say, giving him a dirty look. He just grins cheekily at me.

"Who's their mom?"

"I don't know. Your girlfriend?"

"I don't have one."

"I'm not surprised."

This seems to amuse him, though I don't know why. I'm being pretty rude.

"I haven't really had a close relationship with a girl since Lois," he says. "You would've liked her. She was more your style."

"What's that supposed to mean?"

"You kind of look alike."

I glare at him. He holds up both hands. One is still grasping my phone, so I march over there and snatch the device back from him. "I don't need to be compared to one of your exes, thanks."

He laughs. "My exes?"

"Yeah. I'm sure you have plenty."

"Why? 'Cause I'm cute?"

I'm about to retort with some comment about his ego when I remember what I said to him back in March when he gave me a ride home from the library. My cheeks get really hot. He just laughs again.

"Lois was our other dog, Sadie. Not an ex."

"And that comparison is better somehow?"

He shakes his head with a smile. "Come on. We've got air conditioning. And cold drinks. You look like you could use one."

"Why?"

"You're kind of red."

I let out a disgusted sort of grunt, but don't bother to correct him. Let him think the flushing is from the smoke and summer heat . . . and not from terminal embarrassment.

He waves his hand as he starts to walk. I look down at my phone—which is displaying the last lines of my story, so I know he actually did read it—then over at my sandals.

"How far is your house?" I ask. He turns around and walks backward for a few steps.

"A block or so. Why?"

That sounds a lot closer than my house. Which means I can probably leave my shoes off. With a sigh, I bend down to snag Spud's leash and my keys with the fingers of the hand that's holding the phone, and grab my sandals with the other hand. Then I walk gingerly down the sidewalk to where Cash is waiting.

"Watch your step."

"No. I think I'll try to find some broken glass to step in."

He frowns, but he doesn't say anything. As I fall into step (slowly) beside him, I feel a twinge of guilt.

"Sorry," I say quietly. "I'm not usually like this."

"Bitchy?"

"Tired," I snap.

"Partying until the wee hours?"

"Wee hours?" I repeat, casting a sideways glance at him. "Who talks like that?"

"I thought you liked old-timey language."

"In books. Coming out of modern teenage guys, it's just weird."

He grunts in amusement. "Fair enough." He's silent for a few steps. And then he takes a deep breath. "So . . . do you want my honest opinion about your story?"

"Sure. Why not? Can't be any worse than what's already been said."

"Why?" He shakes his head. "Okay. How about this: You tell me what this teacher said, and I'll tell you if she's full of crap or not."

"Is that how critiquing usually works?"

"I don't think there are any rules."

I let out a long sigh. "Fine. She said it was lazy."

"Well, you did name the main character after yourself."

"I changed *your* name."

He turns and gives me a funny look. "No, you didn't."

"Cash?"

"Lincoln," he says. I shrug. Maybe he's one of those guys who answers to his surname.

"Okay, *Lincoln.* First of all, I was going to change the names. But I ran out of time, and I was afraid that if I rushed it and didn't catch every instance of every name, I'd get chewed out for it."

"Probably."

"Second," I say, deciding to ignore his quip, "I think she was talking more about the storytelling."

"She thought it was lazy? How?"

"I didn't tie up all my loose ends. I just left Jane and Adèle upstairs, and the reader never finds out what happened to them."

"Maybe they got eaten by zombies. No . . . I bet they got turned into zombies! That's way better."

"So you write it," I snap. He turns to me, looking contrite.

"Sorry."

"At least someone is," I mutter. "That teacher was just getting started. Next, she chewed out my lack of a clear antagonist."

"I thought the storm was the antagonist."

"So did I. But she said it should've been a person. Maybe Gage."

"The vampire?" He makes a derisive noise. "That creep didn't need any more page time."

"He could've made a decent antagonist."

"You didn't need another one, really."

"That's what I thought, but . . ." Shrugging, I sigh. "If I'd just been allowed to write something in my favourite genre, I would've aced that assignment."

"So why didn't you?"

"Because on the first day of class, she had us all tell everyone what our favourite genre was."

"And yours is?"

"Contemporary fiction."

He frowns. "So why'd you incorporate *Jane Eyre* into your story?"

"It was contemporary fiction when it was written."

"Touché."

"I like historical fiction, too." I step around a suspicious-looking brown smear on the sidewalk, even though it's dried out and unlikely to transfer anything to my bare feet. "There was this other girl in the class. She loves all that shit I can't stand."

"Vampires? Werewolves?"

"Yeah. And screwing the vampires and werewolves."

"Shouldn't screwing a werewolf count as bestiality?"

"It should, but it doesn't. Anyway, she wrote this contemporary piece, and the teacher nearly crapped her pants over it."

He laughs. "In a good way?"

"Oh, yeah. It was a *masterpiece*, to hear her talk. But it wasn't even that great. The parts she read aloud were full of grammar problems and weird turns of phrase."

"Sometimes," he says slowly, "it's not really about how great the words are. It's about the emotion."

"I know that," I say, a little too harshly. "Believe me. And I know my story wasn't great from that standpoint."

"It was exciting."

"Yeah, but there was no chemistry between the characters."

He turns his head slightly, his eyebrow raised. "Was there supposed to be?"

My cheeks feel really warm again. I look down at Spud, who's obediently trotting along at my side.

"Maybe you can flesh that out in the sequel."

I shake my head, still watching the dog. "There's not going to be a sequel. I'm done. I suck at writing, so there's no point in wasting any more time on it."

"Whoa. You try something once, and because it's not perfect, you give up?"

"It's not *once*," I say, nearly spitting the last word. "I've been writing since I could hold a pencil. And before that, I dictated to my mom and she wrote down the words. But if I'm no good by now—"

"Who says you're no good?"

"That teacher. And the class agreed with her."

"Did they? Or were they just trying to suck up to her so they would stay on her good side?" He takes a deep breath. "Look, Sadie. Here's the honest-to-goodness truth: It's not terrible."

"Gee, thanks."

"I'm serious. The writing itself is really strong. The stuff that was pointed out isn't unfixable. Deal with those issues, and you could have a really cool story."

I shake my head. "It doesn't matter. I don't like zombies or vampires, anyway."

"That's not the point. You're ready to give up all of it based on one critique about a story in a genre that you don't even like. Do you know how crazy that sounds?"

"Why do you care so much?" I ask, peering at him with a frown. He bites his lip for a moment, lost in thought.

"It just pisses me off," he says at last, "when certain people discourage others from doing what they love."

"I didn't love writing that."

"But you love writing. And the circumstances when you were coming up with that story weren't the best, either, were they? You were puking, you had a head injury, and you had a deadline."

"So?"

"Not everybody works well under pressure. Imagine if you had plenty of time, and you weren't sick or bleeding, and you could write in whatever genre you wanted." He nods to himself. "I bet things would turn out really differently."

"We'll never know," I say, stumbling a little as I feel something sharp under one foot. "Ouch. Are we almost there?"

"Almost," he says, but his voice is a bit distant. I look up and spot what's gotten him so distracted. William is trotting toward us from a nearby backyard, head held high as he carries something long and shiny in his mouth.

"What the hell?" I say, trying not to laugh at the sight. The dog crosses the lawn and passes in front of us, close enough that I can make out the intricate detail on the golden sceptre. "Where did he get that?"

"Great. Another piece for his collection. William!" he barks, but at the sound of his person's voice, the dog takes off at a slow gallop.

"Your dog is a thief."

"Tell me about it. You should see the stash he's built up in the backyard."

"A stash of sceptres?"

"No. Just gold stuff. Bars. Lots of coins. I think there's even a crown in there."

"Really?"

He shakes his head and quickens his pace a little as he follows the dog. I hobble as fast as I can to keep up. "It's not real, obviously."

"Who has fake treasure just lying around?"

"No idea. My best guess is that they're movie props."

"Somebody's bound to be missing them."

"Yeah, well, I haven't figured out who yet."

"Maybe if you kept a better eye on your dog . . ."

"Yeah, yeah, yeah." He waves his hand and breaks into a jog. I don't know how he expects me to keep up, but then I notice he's heading for the house right in front of us. William's just disappearing around the side. I look down at Spud, who doesn't seem to need an invitation. He strains on his leash as if he wants to follow Cash. I move as quickly as I can, breathing a sigh of relief as I step onto the front lawn. There aren't any trees in the front yard, which means no shade, which also means that the grass is really yellow and dry. It scratches the soles of my feet as I crunch across it, but it's nowhere near as uncomfortable as my sandals would be.

Cash waits until I'm on the porch before he opens the door and steps inside. As I follow, I can feel the difference in the air right away. Inside the house, it's cool and dry, and the air doesn't seem weighed down with smoke. It's a welcome change.

He leaves his shoes on as he steps off the doormat and onto the tiles. I place my sandals beside the door, then look down at Spud.

"What should I do with him?" I ask.

"Release the hounds!"

"You sure?"

"Yeah. It's fine."

"What about William?"

"What about him?"

"Is he going to get all territorial and try to eat my dog?"

He snorts as he reaches past me and pushes the front door closed. A bit of smoky haze seems to get trapped in here with us. "He's a picky eater. Besides, he's pretty obsessed with his gold stash right now. He'll probably spend most of the day in the backyard, trying to bury coins in the flowerbeds." With a wave of his hand, he moves deeper into the house. I bend down and unclip Spud's leash. The dog just looks up at me questioningly.

"Be good," I whisper.

"I'm always good," Cash says.

"I wasn't talking to you."

He laughs. I deposit my keys and Spud's coiled-up leash on a little table beside the door, then hurry after him. We emerge into a brightly lit room. It's one of those open-concept spaces that incorporates a kitchen and a living area. Sort of between the two is a large dining table that's completely bare at the moment. The kitchen is at the front of the house, looking out over the street. The living area is at the back; through the tall windows on either side of a fireplace, I can see a spacious backyard. The tip of a jaunty tail bounces into view as William trots under the window, so close to the house that I can't see the entire dog.

"Pick your poison," Cash says, opening the shiny fridge. "We've got lemonade, pop, juice, or kombucha."

"Water's fine."

"You sure?"

When I nod, he reaches for a clear plastic bottle. "Tap water's fine," I clarify.

He makes a face. "We don't have a filter. It's kind of chlorine-y."

"Oh. I'll just have whatever you're having, then."

"I was going to have a kombucha."

Then it's my turn to make a face. He smiles, his amusement apparent. "What's wrong with kombucha?"

"Nothing," I say. "In theory. But I personally think it tastes like vinegar."

He snorts, but he gets out two glass bottles. He hands me one, and when I check the label, I see that it's some sort of pomegranate and berry juice. "That okay?" he asks.

"Yeah. Thanks."

He pops the lid of his vinegar drink and chugs a few gulps. "So . . . what's wrong with bottled water?"

"Do I really have to explain that?"

"I bet it has something to do with climate change."

I narrow my eyes at him. But he just laughs.

"I'm just teasing you."

"Do you really not know about how those huge companies go into small communities, basically steal their water, and then sell it back to them at a markup?"

"Actually, I did know that," he says, capping his drink and heading for the hallway. I frown and follow him. Spud follows me, his little nails clicking on the hard floors. "And that's why we only buy certain brands. *Not* the ones that screw people over."

I grunt. He leads us to the stairs and starts up them. I pause for a moment and look at Spud. He's not crazy about steps (and I can't blame him, given that he's only about as tall as one), but he follows Cash like a champ. With a shrug, I go after them.

It's kind of weird, being in Cash's house like this. I mean, it's only the second time I've met him, and now I'm in his house, drinking his juice, heading to his—

Are you seriously following a strange guy to his bedroom, Sadie? What's the matter with you?

– 3 –

IN WHICH WE SORT OF HAVE ANOTHER ARGUMENT ABOUT CLIMATE CHANGE

I hesitate at the top of the stairs. Cash and Spud have both disappeared into a room at the end of the hall, and I'm going to feel like a real dope if I stand here for too long, but something about this whole situation just feels . . . weird. Not wrong, really. Cash hasn't given me any indication that he's trouble. Annoying? Hell, yes. But he seems mostly harmless.

"Sadie?" he calls, and I startle a little. The juice in the bottle sloshes; I'm glad it's still capped.

"Yeah?"

"You coming?"

I don't have much of a choice, really. Not if I want my dog back. Because I know Spud's not going to come when I call him. Not when there are so many interesting things to sniff. Slowly, I make my way down the carpeted hall and step into the room at the end. Cash is lounging on a bed that looks suspiciously well made. My eyebrows rise before I can stop them.

"What?" he asks.

"Nothing." I turn and look around at the rest of the room. It's tidy, at least down near the floor. But the walls are nearly obliterated by all the things on them. Sketches. Lists. A few really rough comic book panels. Photos that look like they were printed from the internet.

"I promise, there's a method to the madness."

"Huh?" I grunt, turning to look at him. He waves his arm in a sweeping gesture, indicating the walls. "You writing a book or something?" I ask.

"Or something." He smiles and sits up, setting his bottle on the near-empty bedside table. "Graphic novel, actually."

"Yeah? Is it any good?"

He lets out a short laugh as he stands up. "You can be the first to read it when I get the rough draft done." Bending down, he scratches Spud behind the ears. The dog barely notices; he's totally obsessed with the edge of the comforter on the bed. Partly because that's the only thing he can really reach. "So . . . shall we continue?"

"Continue?" I repeat, staring at him blankly. He straightens up with a frown.

"With the critique."

"There's more?" My voice comes out as a groan.

"We don't have to."

"Good. Because I don't want to. It doesn't matter."

"Don't you want to improve?"

"In general, maybe. But I don't see how I'm going to get any better messing around with that piece of crap."

He looks stung, almost as if I've insulted something *he* wrote. "It's not crap, Sadie."

"Yeah, it is. Look, can we just forget about it?" Awkwardly uncapping the lid of my bottle as I hold my phone under one arm, I look out the window. The light is even weirder than before. There's a strange orange cast to the sky, and what looks like thunderclouds on the horizon. *Weird. There wasn't supposed to be any rain in the forecast.*

"You had some really cool plot elements in there," Cash says, drawing my attention back to him. I frown as I take a sip of the juice. It's sweet, but not in an unpleasant way. "That bit about the brainstorm taking the book pages and bringing to life whatever was on them? Pretty creative."

"Hooray for me."

His face twists in a weird sort of frown. "I wish *I* could come up with something like that."

"You're welcome to use it."

His frown deepens as I turn away to face the window. "Sadie—"

"What the hell?" I manage to choke out. My hands start to shake. I quickly put the bottle down on the nearest surface because I don't want to slosh dark red juice all over the place. "What's going on?"

He joins me at the window, a little too close for comfort, but I'm too freaked out to care. The darkness in the distance isn't quite so distant anymore, and what I thought were thunderclouds are actually something much, much worse.

"Whoa." His whisper seems loud in the quiet room. The only other thing I can hear is Spud's sniffing. Lucky thing is totally oblivious to the scenario that's unfolding outside.

"I have to go," I say, but before I can even turn around, Cash's hand is on my arm, gripping hard.

"Go where?"

"Home. And I need to call . . ." I trail off as I look at my phone. There's no signal.

"You can't go home," he says, gesturing at the window. At the wall of black smoke stretching across the land, probably just a few blocks away. Between me and my house. My heart drops into my stomach.

"Oh, my god."

"Where are your parents? At home?"

I shake my head. "At work. But—"

"Then they're fine."

But our house isn't. If I peer closely, I can see tongues of flame shooting up out of the bank of smoke and ash. The whole neighbourhood—and beyond—seems to be on fire. "What happened?" I say, more to myself than anyone else.

"No idea."

"The wildfires weren't *that* close, were they?"

He shakes his head. "Fires don't travel at hundreds of miles an hour. Not usually."

"Things change."

He snorts. "This is *not* climate change."

"How do you know? You're a comic nerd, not a scientist."

"Is that supposed to be an insult?"

I shake my head and turn back to my phone, just as a horrible thought occurs to me. "Oh, my god. Did somebody nuke us?"

"Who'd want to nuke Canada?"

"They wouldn't have to nuke Canada specifically. Just North America. We'd be—"

"No." He shakes his head and taps his finger against my phone. "That wouldn't be working at all. It would've been fried by the EMP."

"But there's no signal."

"Yeah, I'm not surprised." He gestures out the window. "I'm sure that fire took out a cell tower or two."

I turn away from the window. I can't look anymore. My mind is kind of in shock. At least, I figure that's what's going on, because I should be way more freaked out. Our house is gone. There's a wall of fire a couple of blocks away, getting closer every minute. And I'm stuck with—

"What do we do?" I ask, turning to face him. "We have to get out of here. If that fire comes any closer, we're toast."

"Literally."

"That's not funny!"

His mouth quirks in a weird expression. He almost looks amused, but I know that can't be it. I don't really feel like exploring the variations of how people react to stress, though. Instead, I bend down, grab Spud, and rush for the door.

"Wait!"

"No." I shake my head and continue walking. But Cash is right there a moment later, blocking the doorway. And that's all it takes. I burst into tears.

"Whoa. Sadie. It's fine." He holds up his hands, trying to look unthreatening, I guess, but it's too late. I just want to get out of here. I push him out of the way with the back of the hand that's holding the phone and step into the hallway, just as there's a godawful scream from outside.

"What the hell was that?" I shriek, my voice almost mimicking the sound we just heard. Cash shakes his head, his eyes wide. There's a thud, and then a crash. He runs back to his window.

"Holy shit." The awe in his breathy voice makes me want to scream.

I have to get out of here. Now. Before something even worse—

"You've got to see this."

I don't want to, my brain whimpers.

"Sadie!"

Slowly, I creep back into his room, coming to a stop beside him. Spud, maybe picking up on the tension in the room, has started to pant nervously. I hold him a little closer to my chest as I follow Cash's finger out the window. Out across the street. Over the trees we sheltered under just minutes ago. To the serpentine shape weaving its way through the billowing smoke.

I almost drop my dog.

"Holy shit!" I say, understanding at once why Cash said the same thing. I mean, it's not every day you see a forty-foot dragon laying waste to a bedroom community.

"Still think it was caused by climate change?"

"Shut up!" I shout, my shock leaving me completely unable to modulate my volume. "I never said it was. And what the hell is a dragon doing out there?" I shake my head and squeeze my eyes shut. But when I open them again and peer out, the view is the same. The dragon swoops over the treetops, many of which are now on fire, and blasts another spout of flame below it. "This can't be real."

"Looks pretty real to me."

"No . . ." I say, my mind starting to put the pieces together. "It's like before."

"Before?"

"In the library." I shake my head and swallow hard. My heart starts to slow its pace a little. "It's just a dream."

"It's not a dream," he says slowly. I turn to him with a frown. He looks back at me and raises his eyebrows. "How often do you realize you're dreaming while you're dreaming?"

I think about that for a moment. "Never," I admit. "But—"

"I've done it. And you know what usually happens when you realize you're dreaming?"

"What?"

"You wake up. It's frustrating as hell. Just when you realize you've got complete control . . ."

"You can't do anything with it."

"Exactly."

I shake my head. "Cash—"

"Lincoln."

"What?"

"My name's Lincoln."

"Whatever. What I was going to say is that dragons don't exist."

"Sure looks like they do."

"But they don't. So this has to be a dream."

"Does it?"

"What else would it be?"

"Do you want to discuss those theories now, or—"

"Right," I say, turning back to the impossible sight out the window. "We need to get out of here. You better know the neighbourhood well."

"Well enough."

"Is there a way out?"

"As of right now, yeah." He jerks his thumb to one side, still staring out the window. "A couple blocks that way, the street lets out on Golden Ave." The frown on his face deepens.

"What?"

"Does something seem weird to you?"

"Um, yeah," I say, adjusting Spud against me. I can feel his little heart beating fast under my fingers. "There's a dragon outside."

Lincoln—since that seems to be what he wants me to call him—shakes his head. "I'm not talking about the dragon."

"That's not weird enough for you?"

He finally turns away from the window to face me. "Where's everyone else?"

"Everyone else?" I echo, looking back out the window. From this angle, I can only see part of the street. But I can definitely see how empty it is. "Maybe they haven't noticed," I say slowly. My mind drifts back a few months in time. "It's the same."

"The same as what?"

"That night at the library. There was nobody else around then, either."

"There was a zombie horde."

"Doesn't count. I'm talking about *real* people."

"Yeah . . ." he says slowly, obviously not understanding what I'm getting at.

"This is a dream."

"It's not a dream." His response is so quick, it's almost like he knew what I was going to say. "Sadie, I promise. This is not a dream. But we should get out of here, anyway. Now."

"No shit," I say. Spud whines. I look down and notice that he's staring up and out the window, his bulbous little eyes wide. "Don't look," I say, quickly turning him away from the view of the dragon. Lincoln snorts. "You don't want to have to deal with him when he's freaked out," I snap. "Believe me."

"Why? Does he get snarly like his mom?"

"He gets diarrhea."

"Well, he can deal with that when we get outside." He glances out the window again, then does a double take. I feel my stomach sink into my feet.

"What now?" I ask, afraid to follow his gaze with my own. He heaves a deep sigh.

"Things are about to get a lot weirder," he says.

– 4 –

IN WHICH
WE LEARN ABOUT
FIRE SAFETY

Don't look. Don't look, I tell myself. But then I'm stupid enough to go and do it. I don't say anything, but just stare.

"There's one point against your dream theory," Lincoln says.

"Huh? Why?"

"Because we're not the only people here."

"We weren't the only people in the library dream, either. There was Jane and Adèle and Sword Guy—"

"Who were all characters from books. Not real people."

I snort, despite still being totally freaked out. "Since when do real people have hair made of fire?"

He squints. "I thought she was just a redhead."

"Get your eyes checked."

"Still," he says. "This isn't a dream. People don't share dreams."

"Maybe I'm just dreaming about you."

He turns to me, eyebrows raised. "How do you know I'm not dreaming about you?"

"I thought you said it wasn't a dream."

"It's not."

"So how would you be dreaming about me? For that matter, why would I have awareness in your dream?"

He doesn't seem to have an answer for that, even though he thinks he has an answer for everything. I turn back to the window and peer down at the strange woman on the street. She's facing away from us, so I can't see her face. But her hair—a fiery conglomeration highlighted by the dark asphalt behind her—is swaying in orange tendrils. I'm surprised it doesn't set her dress on fire. But her dress almost looks like it's made of flames, too. Blue, near where the fabric touches her body, then gold as the folds sway about her. There seems to be quite a bit of wind out there now. I've heard that large fires can create their own weather.

"What do we do?" I whisper.

"About what?"

"Her."

He shakes his head. "Tell her to get the hell out of here, if she values her life."

"I don't think she's afraid of fire."

"Anyone with an ounce of sense would be afraid of *that* one," he says, angling his chin out the window. The fire seems to be half a block away now. It's moving fast. Through the smoke, I can see the still-burning skeletons of the houses down the street. "Come on," he says, finally turning away from the window. He reaches out as if he's going to grab my arm, but I don't give him the chance. Keeping a tight grip on Spud, I back up. The closet doors rattle as I hit them. Deciding (wisely) that he better not try to touch me, Lincoln shakes his head and hurries for the hallway. I glance at the window and shudder at the sight of encroaching smoke and flames. Then I hurry after him.

His footsteps seem loud as he thunders down the stairs. So the sudden silence when he stops is jarring. I have no idea *why* he's stopped, and I wasn't expecting it, so I kind of end up nudging him from behind as I try not to stumble down the last couple of steps.

"What's the matter?" I ask. "I thought we needed to get out of—" My thought cuts off as I feel the weird heat in the foyer. And as my gaze follows his, I start to get it. Sort of. Because it doesn't make any sense. And yet, it's staring us in the face.

At least, I think she is. Staring us in the face, I mean. But it's hard to tell. I don't know how this weird woman even got in here, but there she is, standing just a few feet away. Up close, I can see that her hair is, in fact, made of fire. Sparks snap and twirl away from the swaying tendrils, overly loud in the closed space. The smell is toxic; it's almost like burning oil. I'm surprised I can't see any smoke, because the air feels thick. The weirdest part of the woman, though, isn't her fiery hair or her flame-licked dress or even her skin, which looks like black volcanic sand shot through with veins of molten rock (and, let's face it, that's all pretty weird). No, the part of her that's strangest of all is her face. Or lack of face. At first, I think there's just a blank space there, some weird trick of light that's allowing me to see right through her. But as she stands there, I realize I can see Lincoln and myself reflected in the surface of her face. It's a mirror, the reflective contours warped with the faint suggestion of facial features.

"Get back," Lincoln says, but so quietly that I wonder if the woman has even heard him at all. I don't realize he's talking to me until he turns around, and that's when I see the fear in his eyes.

"What?"

He reaches out and turns me around, and because I'm still standing on one of the steps, I don't have much room to work with. I stumble, dropping my phone so I can reach out to break my fall. "Leave it!" he whispers, the desperation so evident in his voice that my fear comes roaring back. I don't know where it's been, and I don't know why it's been kind of dormant even while seeing a flaming woman with a mirror face standing in an acquaintance's foyer. Maybe I'm just in shock. Or maybe my mind knows this really is a dream.

If that's the case, though, and I've realized it ... why am I not waking up?

I hurry up the stairs, and I can hear Lincoln's heavy footsteps right behind me. Spud is shaking against my chest, and that's kind of terrifying. Some Chihuahuas quiver like jelly all the time ... but Spud's not like that. If he's scared, there's a good reason.

I'm not sure where I'm supposed to go, so I just head back to Lincoln's room. As soon as we're inside, he closes the door quickly. And, I notice, very quietly. As the latch makes a soft click that causes him to wince, I take a deep breath. But before I can get anything out, he waves his hand at me. I clamp my lips together. He nudges me out of the way and heads for the closet. When he opens it up, I'm hit with a waft of gentle perfume, like from fabric softener. With a tilt of his head toward the closet, he raises his eyebrows at me. I shake my head. He gives me a look.

"I'm not getting into a closet with you!" I whisper, as loudly as I dare.

He holds a finger to his lips.

"She can't hear us. She's downstairs. Besides, you don't know if she's a threat."

He points to Spud, who's trembling like a little brown leaf. Then he reaches out and grabs my elbow. As he steers me toward the closet, I give him the dirtiest look I can muster.

"I'm not being part of your dirty dream, if that's what you're planning."

"Quiet," he whispers, finally daring to make a sound. I duck down so I can fit into the space under the hanging clothes; luckily, his closet doesn't have multi-level rods and shelves like mine does, so there's plenty of room. I'm crouching in a pile of shoes that don't smell anywhere near as pleasant as the clothes above me, and it's not exactly comfortable. A moment later, he joins me, pulling the louvred door closed. It lets out a tiny squeak, but nothing that anyone would be able to hear from downstairs.

"What's the plan?" I ask, keeping my voice as low as I can. "Hide in here all day?"

I can see him frowning as he leans forward to peer through the painted wooden slats. The faint lines of light from the swiftly dimming room paint a weird pattern across his features. "I don't know."

"You better know! This is your dream."

"It's not a dream." He pauses. "Wait. Why is it *my* dream?"

"Because you dragged me into a closet. I certainly wouldn't dream *that*."

He snorts softly. "You sure know how to make a guy feel special, Sadie."

"Shut up. I'm only in here to humour you. There's no reason to be hiding from—" The loud bang cuts me off and almost makes me scream. I slap my hand over my mouth. Spud, on the other hand, doesn't have as much luck keeping quiet. He lets out a tiny squeak and starts to struggle. And whine.

"Put him down," Lincoln whispers.

I feel like snapping at him, but I do as he suggests. Spud shakes himself out, causing his tag to jingle, but at least he doesn't whine again.

"Look."

I lean forward to try to see. The room is a little hard to make out. I can see that it's empty, though. "What am I looking at?"

"The door."

Right. Now that I look, I see that it's open. But I don't see anything that could've opened it. Frowning, I turn to Lincoln. "You closed it."

"Yeah. I did."

"Does it pop open on its own?"

"Nope. And not with enough force to cause a bang like that." He adjusts his awkward crouch. In the confined space, I can sort of smell him. Or maybe it's his shoes. In any case, it smells like sweaty-ass guy in here, and I don't know how long I want to put up with that. Even if this is just a dream.

"This is stupid," I say, reaching for the edge of the door. "If we stay in here, we'll be roasted when your house catches on fire. I don't want to burn to death, even in a dream."

"It's not a dream," he says absently, catching my wrist. "Trust me."

"Why should I trust—" I stop talking as he squeezes my arm. And then I see what he sees.

The woman is standing in the doorway, staring into the room. Well, she's facing into the room. And she obviously knows we're in here. I pull my hand back, slipping out of Lincoln's grasp, and slide it over my mouth, not trusting myself to stay quiet.

What the hell kind of dream is this? And since when do you have dreams where you're this aware that it's not real?

The woman's hair snapping and crackling is the only thing I can hear over the thumping of my own heart in my ears. And both of those sounds only get louder as she takes a silent step into the room, gliding as if she's not walking at all, but floating. I look at Lincoln, noticing that the pattern of light hitting his face has taken on some strange hues. Orange and blue. It's like an otherworldly fire has taken up residence in his bedroom.

I guess it has.

The closet door slides open, so quickly that I let out a squeak. Lincoln does, too, recoiling and falling back into his pile of shoes. His eyes are wide as he stares out into the room. I'm still hidden by the door (I hope), but he's right there, staring up into the face of . . . whoever she is.

What happens next is so fast that my brain can't really make sense of it. It almost looks like someone grabs Lincoln by the front of his shirt and forcibly yanks him to his feet, pulling him out of the closet and swinging him out of view. Despite my instinct to stay hidden, I lean forward so I can see around the edge of the door, just in time to see him slam backward into the wall as if propelled by an unseen force. I wince in sympathy, because I can see the pushpins around his head and shoulders, and I know that the ones poking into his back have to hurt. My gaze starts to drift over to the woman, and I notice her raised arm . . . at the same moment I spot a tiny movement down near the floor.

Spud trots out of the closet, his fear seemingly gone. I hold my breath as he wanders over to the woman to investigate. I don't dare make a sound, hoping that she just won't notice. Spud's a tiny guy, after all. It's not like he's going to lift his leg on her or anything, so he might just blend into the background.

"Sadie," Lincoln gasps. I whip my head back to him in disbelief. His eyes are wide, almost bugging out. Something seems to be holding him pinned to the wall. I guess it's the woman, but I have no idea how she's doing it because she's not even touching him. He gasps again. "Run."

The next thing out of his mouth is a scream. I draw back, stunned, as I watch what looks like a handprint blacken the front of his t-shirt. But it doesn't stop. As the fabric darkens and melts, I can see the skin beneath start to blister. My head shakes. I pull back into the closet, my eyes wide.

Wake up. Wake up. Wake up. This is just a dream. You have the power to stop it. So just wake up, damn it!

"Stop!" Lincoln screams. "Go!"

Spud's the one who listens, even though none of that contradictory message was meant for him. Startled by the command, he skitters out the door and into the hallway. Automatically, I jump up and sprint after him. Since I don't want to get anywhere near the woman, I end up jumping onto the bed and running across it, then take a flying leap to the floor. The walls rattle as I land. But I don't look back. I rush out into the hallway, just as a shrill alarm starts screaming above me. It takes a second for my panicked brain to register that it's a smoke detector.

"Spud!" I shout. But he's already out of view. I can hear barking coming from somewhere, but it's not the familiar yapping I'm used to. Whoever's barking is much larger. And pretty damn agitated. "Spud!" I shout again as I barrel down the stairs. "Come here!"

There's no response. No little dog comes running the way he should. Mind you, he's probably pretty freaked out by the whole situation. At the very least, he's picking up on my freaked-outness. And when he gets like this, he either gets the runs . . . or he runs.

I rush into the kitchen, scanning everything at ground level. But I don't see anything. Well, I don't see any dogs. What I do see is a massive shadow that flickers past the front windows.

Right. The dragon.

I stop for a moment and close my eyes. *A dragon, Sadie. If you needed any more proof that this is just a dream—*

A thundering noise makes me whirl around, my heart in my throat. I turn just in time to see Lincoln appear in the doorway. The front of his shirt is in shreds, and the skin within the burn mark is blistered and bleeding.

"Where is she?" I blurt out. He just shakes his head and rushes across the room. "Lincoln!"

"Let's go."

"Where? Are you okay?"

"I'm fine."

"You're not *fine*," I say. "Those look like third-degree burns."

He doesn't answer. He just grabs the knob on the door at the side of the room and turns it. Only then do I notice the movement at his feet . . . right as Spud squeezes through the gap and into the backyard.

"Spud!" I shriek, rushing over there and shoving Lincoln out of the way. He staggers aside with a grunt, but I can't stop. I throw myself through the opening and stagger into the smoke-filled morning, nearly coughing as the air chokes my lungs. The last I see of Spud is his white-tipped tail as he runs through the open gate and out into the neighbourhood.

– 5 –

IN WHICH
I FIND MYSELF
BACKED INTO A CORNER

"Spud!" My scream seems to hang in the thick air. I chase after the dog, out through the open gate, around the side of the house, toward the street. Down by the ground, the air is fairly clear, so I can just see the tiny figure in front of me, half a block down the sidewalk, his legs pumping as he runs. "Stop! Come! Heel!" He doesn't even know how to heel, but I'm desperate.

"Sadie, stop!"

I let out a choked sob as I watch Spud disappear around a hedge at the end of the street. "Spud!"

"He'll be fine," Lincoln says, coming to a stop next to me. He's breathing hard and sort of wheezing. But I don't care.

"He's *not* going to be fine!" I shout, shoving him hard in the shoulder. "He's a tiny little dog, and the neighbourhood is on fire. Or haven't you noticed?"

"Yeah. Exactly. He's a dog. Give him a little credit."

"What the hell are you talking about?"

"He's not going to run *into* a wall of fire, is he?"

I can feel my face twisting in a frustrated frown. "No," I say at last.

"No. Why do you think farmers let their horses loose when a wildfire's on the way? Animals have instincts. Pretty good ones." He glances to one side. Toward the fire. "Maybe better than ours."

"What are we going to do?" I say, my voice coming out in a wail. "And what the *hell* is going on here? Who was that woman? How did you get away from her?"

He starts to shrug, but the movement seems to pain him. He shakes his head instead. "She just disappeared."

"How?"

"Same way she just appeared in our house, I guess."

"That doesn't make any sense."

He raises his eyebrows at me.

"You still think this isn't a dream?" I ask.

"I know it's not."

"But—"

"Do you want to argue about this, or do you want to get someplace a little safer?"

"I'd rather be out here than stuck in a burning house."

"Really?" he says, and gingerly raises one hand to point. I turn to look . . . only to see a dark, serpentine shape weaving through the smoke.

"Oh, shit."

"Yeah." He turns and looks around us, as if searching for something. "We need a place to hide."

"I don't want to *hide* anywhere," I say. He blinks in surprise. His eyes are really red now. And watering. Either that, or he's crying. Honestly, with that awful-looking burn on his chest, it could be either.

"You want to take on a dragon?"

"Hell, no. But I don't want to be trapped when our hiding place catches on fire."

"So what do you suggest?" He tilts his chin down the street, away from the wall of flames and burning houses. "You want to try outrunning it?"

"The dragon?"

"The fire."

"We're not going to get stuck in some dead-end cul-de-sac, are we?"

He frowns. And I have my answer.

"Great. This is just great." My throat tightens. I'm sure it's partly from the smoke, but I'm also on the verge of tears myself. "My dog's probably going to die. *We* are going to die. And all because I can't wake up from this stupid—"

"It's not a dream," he says before I can finish the sentence.

"Will you stop saying that?" Waving my arm in a sweeping gesture, I glare at him through streaming eyes. "What part of this is compatible with reality, Lincoln? Go on. Tell me."

"I never said it wasn't unreal."

I just stare at him for a moment. "What the hell are you talking about?"

His lips press together so tightly they disappear.

"Spit it out. I don't have time for this."

"Yeah, you do." He reaches up and scratches his fingers through his hair. I feel a tight anger twist my guts.

"Enough bullshit. If you're not going to be helpful, I'm just going to . . ." But I can't think of a way to finish the threat. What am I going to do? Go home? It's kind of on fire. And all the escape routes appear to be blocked now. "Damn it!" I shout.

"Shh!" Lincoln hisses, but the sound is drowned out by an awful, nerve-scraping screech from above. And it's way too close for comfort. I turn and peer into the smoke . . . just as a jet of flames rips out of the haze and scorches a jagged scar across the asphalt, mere inches from where we're standing.

I can't move. My feet seem to be glued to the pavement. But Lincoln, somehow, isn't petrified by the sight of the impossible barrelling at him through the air. He grabs my hand and yanks me hard as he begins to run. My feet come unstuck, and I stumble after him, nearly losing my footing as we flail across the street. I can't really see much past the tall wooden fence, but I can see a rather large, leafy tree poking up beyond it. The branches offer a little bit of shade, which doesn't really matter right now (the sun can barely make it through all the smoke), but they also offer some cover, and I realize Lincoln's trying to keep us hidden. At least from things in the sky.

"A dragon is going to kill us," I say, the words coming out awfully calm, considering. But Lincoln shakes his head.

"No, it's not."

"What happens if I die in a dream? Will I die in real life?"

He snorts. "What do you think?" Still tugging on my hand, he leads me over to a gate in the fence.

"I might have a heart attack."

"You're a sixteen-year-old girl. I think it's pretty safe to assume that you can handle a scare without dropping dead."

"I'm seventeen," I say, but it seems irrelevant. He lets go of my hand so he can unlatch the gate and push it open.

"Come on."

"You want to get trapped when the dragon directs its fire in there?"

"It's not targeting the trees."

"What?" Turning, I peer back into the flaming neighbourhood. Most of the houses are ablaze now. But, curiously, I don't see many trees on fire.

"Only the trees close to structures are burning. This one's pretty far from the house. So if we stay here or go up—"

"I'm not in the mood for tree climbing."

"You don't have to climb the tree," he says, reaching for my hand again. I yank it away before he can touch me, and step through the gate. When I'm inside, I understand what he's talking about. The tree isn't just a tree; it's also the foundation for a treehouse.

"I'm not getting up there," I say as he closes the gate after us and comes to join me in staring up at the play structure.

"Why not? You just have to climb a ladder."

I turn to him in disbelief. "The dragon is burning *houses*. You think it's not going to burn this one?"

"It's pretty much hidden. You didn't even see it until I pointed it out."

"What about from above?"

"It's a leafy tree," he says, as if that makes all the difference. He steps toward the trunk, where six wooden boards have been affixed to it for a ladder. "It's as safe a place as any. As long as you stop yelling at me."

He has no idea how much I've been holding myself back already. But I don't say anything. I just watch as he climbs up and disappears through a square hole in the bottom of the structure. Stepping closer so I'm more safely under the canopy of branches and leaves, I try to peer upward through the hatch.

"Sadie." His hand appears, gesturing at me. I look around the yard. It's a fairly large one, and the tree is off by itself in a corner. The house is at least fifteen feet away from any branches. If it catches on fire, it'll probably spread to the tree eventually. But not right away. We might have time to escape.

I step to the trunk and look up into the hole, only to see Lincoln peering back down at me. "Remind me again why we didn't just go back inside your house if we're going to risk getting trapped in a burning building?"

"Because there's some crazy mirror-faced woman in there."

"I thought you said she disappeared."

"She did. But if she can do that, she can reappear at any time. Right?"

"What if she reappears in your stupid treehouse?"

"How would she know it's here?"

I roll my eyes. "It's not *invisible*. The leaves don't cover it completely."

"Yeah, but if she's not looking for it . . ."

"This seems like a terrible idea."

"So is taking shelter in a very visible house when we know for a fact that a dragon is roasting roofs."

Letting loose an angry sigh, I reach out and grasp the nearest board. It's rough, and it doesn't feel all that securely anchored to the tree. Still, I manage to make it up into the little space that smells of mold and sawdust. I crawl over to one of the walls and lean back against it, examining my hands. There's just enough hazy light coming in through the window (it has real glass and everything) for me to see what I'm doing.

"Pretty nice digs," Lincoln says. I pause from my examination of my hands to glare at him. He's leaning back against the wall opposite, but since the space is pretty small, the toes of his shoes are almost touching my feet. And I can smell him in here, too. He seems to be getting stinkier. Probably because he's sweating. A lot. His cheeks are slick with sweat, and his lips are almost white.

"Are you in pain?"

He gives me a look.

"How should I know what the characters in my dreams are feeling?"

"If this *were* one of your dreams, you should know, shouldn't you?"

"Not necessarily." I let my hands fall into my lap. I've got a few splinters stuck in them, but that doesn't seem like what I should be focusing on at the moment. "Sometimes dreams don't make sense."

"So how can this be a dream?"

"What do you mean?"

"It makes sense, doesn't it?"

I let out a snort. "Mirror-faced women with flaming hair and dragons flying around the neighbourhood? Yeah, Lincoln. Makes perfect sense."

"I'm not talking about plausibility. I'm talking about logic and continuity. Think about it."

"Why should I? None of this is going to matter when I wake up."

He blinks. A tear detaches from his eyelashes and rolls down his cheek. He swipes it away before I can comment on it. "You're not inspired for your next story?"

I let out a harsh laugh. "My next story? Why would I want to write a sequel to the most awful story of all time?"

"It wasn't awful."

I shake my head. "I'm done. I suck at writing, so—"

"Don't let one person tear down your dreams."

"But she was right. In a story like that, there should've been a better villain."

"So? You've got a better villain now."

"You?"

He laughs. Weakly. "I meant Blaze."

"Blaze?"

"It's as good a name as any."

I shake my head. "She looks more like a Mirror."

He blinks again, and his brow creases into a puzzled frown.

"What?" I ask.

"Nothing." He takes in a deep, pained-sounding breath and releases it with a sigh.

"Is there anything I can do?"

"Not unless you can make it rain so we can get out of here and get to a hospital."

"I think medical care is kind of unnecessary in a dream."

"Not a dream." He closes his eyes as he leans his head back against the wall.

"Well, I can't control the weather, so you'll just have to tough it out." I watch him for a few moments, noting the shaky rise and fall of his chest. Those burns really look awful. "Maybe if we'd gotten more rain this summer, the whole neighbourhood wouldn't be burning like this."

"Climate change?" he says without opening his eyes. His lips are twisting in a little smirk.

"What is your problem? Have you not noticed the weird weather recently?"

"Cloudy with a chance of dragons? Yeah. That's totally climate change."

"That's not what I'm talking about, and you know it."

"I know." He falls silent for a few moments. "And you know what I'm talking about, too."

"Yeah. You're a conspiracy theorist."

He shakes his head slowly against the wall. "You know that's just a term they made up to discredit people who ask too many uncomfortable questions."

"They?"

"You know."

Despite the fact that an argument like this is great for taking my mind off of what's going on outside (dragons and fire-haired women and all that), it's not really something I enjoy. "Why couldn't I have been stuck with someone *normal?*" I say, which just earns me a soft chuckle.

I can hear the fire. Actually, what I'm hearing is probably pieces of burning houses collapsing. Lots of thuds. Plenty of cracking and crackling. And the smoke is really starting to get to me. My throat tickles, and I know I'm going to start coughing soon. The haze seems to be creeping up through the hole in the floor, and there's really nowhere for it to go.

"Lincoln?" I whisper, wondering if he's still awake. Or alive. Because he looks kind of dead. The relief I feel when he opens his eyes makes me feel almost giddy . . . which doesn't make a lot of sense, considering I can't stand the guy and this is all just a dream. *You could kill him off,* I think. But something about that doesn't sit right with me. I guess I'm not that kind of person . . . even in a surreal, low-stakes environment like this one.

"What?"

"Do these windows open?"

"No idea." He closes his eyes again, and I think that's all I'm going to get out of him. But then he seems to rally, opening his eyes and sitting up a little straighter as he leans toward the window. "Why?"

"It's getting crazy smoky in here. Haven't you noticed?"

"Yeah." But his voice is absent. It's like he's half asleep. He reaches out and nudges the window with his hand. It doesn't move. "Nope."

"Does it slide?"

"Nope."

"Lincoln—"

"It doesn't open. It's a treehouse, Sadie."

"So what?" I snap. "If it's fancy enough to have a glass window, why is it inconceivable that it would open?"

He doesn't answer. He's peering out through the glass, a strange expression on his face.

"What? What is it?" My heart picks up its pace. "Is the tree on fire?"

"Mirror," he whispers, an instant before he pulls back violently, throwing himself against the wall. The window shatters with a deafening clatter, sending shards of glass sparkling into the air, highlighted by the ball of flames. I scream, but the noise is swallowed by the roar of the fire that's now raging up one wall of the treehouse.

6

IN WHICH
WE BOTH
END UP BLEEDING

"Whoa," Lincoln says, his breath coming in wheezing pants.

"What was that?" I shout. My voice seems to be stuck at top volume.

He shakes his head and waves his hand at the hole. "Go."

I look at the opening. Something makes me think that going down there is a really bad idea. Then again, staying here is a really bad idea, too, what with one wall on fire. Slowly, I lean toward the window and peer around the frame. Through a tunnel of dense leaves (the edges of which look kind of scorched), I can see the mirror-faced woman. She's standing in the middle of the street, her body angled in our direction. I jerk away from the window and flatten myself against the wall. "I'm not going down there."

"You want to stay in here and roast?"

"I'll wake up before I die."

With a grunt, he leans forward and touches the only part of me he can reach, which is my ankle. I recoil as a stupid little thought worms its way into my head: *I hope my leg stubble isn't too bad.*

"Don't touch me."

"Sadie," he says, still leaning forward, a pained expression on his features. "This is not a dream."

"Why the hell do you keep saying that?" I mutter.

"Because it's the truth."

"No, I'm asking why my brain keeps making one of my dream characters say that."

He lets out a pained sigh. "We need to get out of here. Go."

"So Mirror can get a cleaner shot at us?"

"What are you worried about if you think it's a dream?"

"I don't like nightmares, thanks." I look over at the hole, then lean forward to peer out the window again. Mirror's still there. But when I see her posture, a spike of adrenaline drives itself through my veins.

"What?" Lincoln whispers, as if he can tell something's wrong.

"I don't know."

"What's she doing?"

I shrug and shake my head. With what sounds like a groan of pain, he leans forward to join me in peering out the window at the strange woman on the street. One of her hands is raised high in the air, and she appears to be looking upward.

"That's not good," Lincoln says.

"Why? What is she even doing?"

He turns to me with a roll of his eyes. "What's in the sky?"

"A dragon. So?"

"So . . ."

I frown. "You think she's a dragon whisperer or something?"

"No idea. But given what we've already seen today, do you think we can rule it out?"

Damn it. He's probably right. But I'm not about to give him the satisfaction of knowing that. "So what's she whispering to it?" I ask.

I think the answer comes to us at the same time. We turn to each other, eyes wide . . . just as there's a massive thud on the roof over our heads.

"Shit!" Lincoln cries, and dives toward me, driving me to the floor. Unfortunately, there's still broken glass there, and I feel the sharp bites as the shards slice into my hands. A series of cracks rings out from above, and dust rains down as wood splinters and snaps. The fire, disturbed by the collapse, releases a blast of sparks that sting my skin.

"Get off me!" I wheeze, feeling the weight of his body press me down into the floorboards. I try not to move too much, painfully aware of the broken glass under me. But the weight doesn't lift. "Lincoln! You're—" My voice is drowned out by a terrifying animal shriek from above. My head snaps up to look, even though I know instantly what it is. And even if the sound hadn't made it clear what we're dealing with, the massive talons that drive themselves through the boards just inches from my face sure do.

"Move," Lincoln says, his command tight and sharp.

"I can't!"

"You have to. Get out of here. Out the hole."

"But—"

"Would you rather be crushed? Sadie, move!"

With a sob, I reach out and wrap my fingers around the edge of the hole. The dragon lets out another shriek, and all I want to do is throw my hands over my ears, but I can't pause to do that. The treehouse is little more than a nest of broken wood, glass shards, flames, and dragon, nestled in the branches of a tree that's slowly being devoured by flames. My hands are bleeding, leaving dark marks on the wood, but I barely feel anything. Not pain, anyway. I can sure feel the weight of Lincoln's body pressing down on me, though.

"I . . . can't," I say after a few seconds of fruitless tugging. "You need to get off me."

He grunts, and the weight shifts a little, but it doesn't ease much.

"Lincoln!"

He shifts again, then cries out. The sound sends a spike of panic through me.

"What's wrong?"

"Try again," he says, his voice strange. It's like he's trying to hold back a sob. "I'll try to . . ." He trails off, and I feel his body sort of wriggle to one side. Taking advantage of the slight easing of weight, I grasp the edge of the hole and pull myself with all I've got, my arms shaking. Once I manage to get my torso out from under him, it's easier. But I still don't have much room to work with, and it's an awkward sideways tumble out of the hatch. I land hard on the knobby roots of the tree, bashing my hip. The tree shudders above me, and I scramble back, looking up the whole time. I can't see much of the dragon, other than its tail whipping about, swishing through the leaves. The treehouse itself is a wreck, the walls collapsed and broken. The floor, the platform the whole thing rests on, seems to be the strongest part, and it's still holding up.

For now.

"Lincoln!" I whisper, then realize he won't be able to hear me over the sound of the approaching fire. So I call a little louder. "Lincoln!"

There's no answer. I stand up on shaking legs and peer up at the hole. It stays empty for so long that I start to panic as I remember the pain in his voice. Something's wrong. Something more than the burn on his chest (which is already pretty awful). I take a step toward the tree and am just about to reach for the ladder when I see a set of fingers curl around the edge of the hatch. My breath escapes in a relieved rush. It takes a few seconds for him to pull his upper body through the hole and reach for the ladder. Despite his best attempts, though, his exit from the treehouse is even clumsier than mine, and I stumble back to give him room. His rolling landing brings him to my feet, and he stares up at me, breathing hard, his brow creased in what looks like agony.

"What happened?" I ask.

He just groans and tries to sit up. When that proves to be too painful, he rolls over and pushes himself to his hands and knees before staggering to his feet. Before I can ask again, he grabs my hand and yanks me toward the gate.

Toward the street.

"Are you crazy?" My voice comes out in a shout. "She just tried to kill us, and you're going to drag us out there to let her finish the job?" Digging in my heels, I manage to bring him to a stop. Our hands feel slick where they're clasped together, and I remember I'm still bleeding.

"We have no other options," he says, angling his chin at the house behind us. I turn and look, only to see that the whole second floor is on fire. "It'll be fine. Come on."

I turn back to him in disbelief as he tugs me toward the gate. "What part of this is *fine?*"

"Trust me."

"Yeah, right." But I let him pull me out the gate. To my surprise, Mirror is no longer there. Even more surprising, Lincoln's house is still untouched. He pulls me in that direction before I can say anything else. At this point, I don't really care where we go, as long as it's not burning.

I can hear a dog barking as we approach, and that just reminds me of Spud. My eyes fill with tears as I remember my last glimpse of my best friend. As we make our way into the backyard, I see William. He looks really agitated, and when I turn to peer behind us, I realize why. He can see the dragon sitting in the ruins of the treehouse across the street.

If I were a dog, I'd probably be barking like crazy, too.

Lincoln slams the gate closed, and I almost tell him to open it again, just in case Spud comes back. But as soon as William can't see the dragon anymore, he gets quiet. Lincoln pulls me into the house through the side door. When we're inside, he lets out a pained breath.

"What happened in that treehouse?" I ask. "Are you okay?"

He lets go of my hand. I look down at it and see that my entire palm is smeared with red. A little moan escapes me.

"You're not going to faint, are you?" he asks.

I shake my head. He turns away and heads for the kitchen. My legs begin to tremble . . . and the next thing I know, I'm on the floor.

"Sadie?"

"Oh, god. Oh, my god." I curl my bloody hands into fists and press them against my temples. The stinging of the wounds is so clear, so sharp. *This isn't right. This isn't right. This isn't—*

"What's wrong?"

"This isn't a dream." My breath hitches, and I look up at him as my eyes let loose a flood of tears. "This isn't a dream!"

"That's what I've been trying to tell you."

"We're going to die!"

"I sure hope not." He limps closer and gets down on his knees, his uncontrolled descent thumping through the floor. "You're going to be fine."

"What about you?"

He winces a little, and my gaze jumps to his body, doing a quick check. The burn on his chest is still there, looking red and painful. I don't really see much else . . . until I peer around him and spot the back of his left calf.

"Oh, my god," I whisper, unable to tear my gaze away from the sight, even though it kind of makes me want to throw up. His leg is covered in blood, which isn't surprising, given that much of the flesh seems to have been ripped open. I'm finally able to pull my gaze up to his face. He gives me a rueful smile. "Did it bite you?" I ask.

"Nothing that exciting." He twists to look at his leg, shudders, then turns back to me. "I think it was part of the treehouse that did it. When the dragon sat on it, something impaled me in the leg."

"That's why you couldn't move."

"Pretty much." He reaches out and gently takes my wrists. My hands are still in fists, pressed against my head. It's like I've forgotten the position of all my body parts. "I wasn't trying to get any action with you. I promise."

"Gross."

His lips twist in the tiniest of smiles, and he nods at my hands. "Let me see."

I slowly uncurl my fingers. The cuts are still bleeding. As we watch, blood drips onto the floor. "I'm going to bleed to death."

"No, you're not."

"*You're* going to bleed to death."

He doesn't deny it, which scares me. I bite my lips together, hard, because I feel like I'm going to start crying and never be able to stop. When he sees my reaction, he lets go of my wrists and puts his hands on my cheeks instead. "We need to play it out."

I blink. "What? Play what out?"

"This scenario."

"But it's not a dream."

"I didn't say it was."

"Then what is it?" My voice shakes as I look into his eyes. They're kind. Gentle. Reassuring. Even though we're both bleeding like crazy, there's a dragon and its handler outside, and the whole neighbourhood is on fire. *Damn it. He's cute.*

Fuck, Sadie. What the hell is the matter with you? This is not *the time for that.*

"I promise I'll give you a full explanation," he says. "But not right now. Right now, we need to play it out so I don't die."

"What about me?"

"You're in no danger of dying."

"And you are?"

He strokes his thumbs against my cheeks before pulling away. With a groan of pain, he uses the edge of the dining table to haul himself to his feet. As he turns away to walk into the kitchen, I get a really good view of the back of his leg. And I retch.

"Remember what happened in the library?" he asks, leaning one hand on the counter as he uses the other to paw through a stack of mail and flyers. I frown as I stand up, not sure what he's getting at.

"When I hit my head and had some weird hallucination?"

"What if those two things weren't connected?"

I shake my head. "I don't understand."

"I know. If I were in your shoes, I probably wouldn't, either. And I wish I had time to—" He breaks off as he seems to find what he's looking for. Holding up the piece of paper triumphantly, he raises his eyebrows at me.

"What?"

"Where did that dragon come from?"

"How should I know?"

He rolls his eyes. "Sadie, where did the zombies come from?"

"A traumatic brain injury."

"Try again."

"What the hell are you talking about?"

He waves the piece of paper. "Remember the pages? And the storm?"

"Yeah . . . do you?"

A sly look crosses his features.

"You read about them. In my story." I shake my head. "What does that have to do with this situation, though? There's no storm. And no zombies."

"There's fire. And a dragon."

"Lincoln, there aren't any books involved in this—" I break off, my eyes going wide as I remember. "Holy shit."

"*Dominating the Dragonyx.*"

"How did that even happen?"

"A fire must've gotten to the box of books. After that . . ."

"Dragon apocalypse." I frown as I think of something. "Surely there are other characters in the books, though. So where are they?"

He stares at me for a moment, then shudders. I don't understand why until I think about it for a moment.

"Shit," I whisper. "They would've popped into existence *inside* the inferno, wouldn't they?"

"Probably."

I don't even want to think about it. I know those people aren't real, but . . . still. "Are dragons fireproof? And what about Mirror?" I ask before he can give me any sort of answer to the first question. "Is she a character, too?"

He shrugs. "Now we have something to work with."

"What do you mean? What are we supposed to do against a dragon?"

"We play it out."

"I don't know what that means."

"It means we work *with* the story . . . not against it."

"What story? I thought you said this wasn't a dream."

"It's not."

"Then what is it?" I ask with a frown. My heart shudders in panic as a thought occurs to me. "Is this hell? Did we die and—"

"Was the library incident hell?"

"At times."

He smiles a little. "Sadie, it's not hell."

"Then . . . a parallel dimension?"

"I guess you could say that." He shakes his head slowly. "That's not important right now. We can talk about that when I'm not bleeding all over the kitchen floor."

I look down as I step closer to him, noticing that the edge of his shoe is covered in blood, and it's dribbling over the sides into a puddle around his heel. "Maybe you should put some pressure on that."

"We need to deal with our pest problem first." He waves the paper.

"What are you thinking? Throw an ad for a machine gun into the fire and get ourselves some weapons?"

He laughs, the sound tight. "What kind of junk mail are you getting at your house?"

I peer at the piece of paper, then turn to him with a puzzled frown. "An engagement ring?"

"What do dragons love?"

"How should I know? I don't read that sort of book."

"Maybe you should."

When I glare at him, he just shakes his head.

"Dragons love bling. They're kind of like crows. Shiny things make them happy."

"So you think you're going to get yourself a ring and propose to the beast?"

"Something like that." He turns and peers out the window. The dragon isn't in the tree anymore. The tree itself is aflame. I lean forward so I can see up into the sky, and notice the dark shape circling above.

"How are you going to get close enough to give the dragon this ring without getting roasted? And how will giving it a ring even help?"

"It plays out the story. The dragon's a character, just like any other. It wants something. So we give it what it wants."

"To marry its handsome prince? Happily ever after? The end?"

"Now you're getting it."

"That's if I even believe you. You could be rambling from blood loss. How do I know that's what's going on here? We're trapped in some sort of story?"

"Not trapped."

"Okay, then, I want out."

"So play it out."

I shake my head. "What's the point? If it's not real—"

"I didn't say it wasn't real."

"So what happens if you die? Do you die in real life?"

"No. But there are other . . . consequences."

I snort. "Bullshit."

"What is?"

"All of this. I have no idea what's going on. I'm leaning toward some sort of hallucination. I must've hit my head again. And my brain made up this whole complicated scenario and stuck you in it for some reason, probably because I think you're cute, even though you're super annoying and I can't stand you, but I don't really have control over how my neurons are misfiring, do I?"

He blinks, as if stung. "You done?"

"Maybe you're slowly bleeding to death because I'm subconsciously trying to kill you off."

"I'm not ruling it out," he says, limping past me to reach for a cupboard door. He pulls it open and takes out a box of matches.

"What are you doing?"

"I'm not going to take the flyer out there and throw it into the inferno, am I?"

"Why not?"

"Dragon. Besides that, though, I want to be able to grab the ring without sustaining another life-threatening injury. Is that okay with you?"

"Yeah." My voice is small. His voice, on the other hand, was kind of harsh.

"Sorry," he says with a sigh. "I'm in a lot of pain here."

"I can see that."

"I hope so." He casts a quick glance at me before turning back to the matches. He strikes one, then raises it to the corner of the flyer while holding both over the sink.

"You do realize that this is a really weird thing to be doing, right? Trying to get a diamond ring by burning a flyer?"

He chuckles softly, pinching the burning paper between two fingers. "It's not the weirdest thing I've ever done."

"What was?"

"Incarnating a classic book character from a page of text and a glowing snowstorm."

"Aren't those equally weird?" I ask, then startle as the rest of the paper disappears with a flash of heat that I can feel on my skin. He jerks his hand back, just as something tiny and metallic clatters into the sink. "Whoa," I whisper.

"I'll say." He reaches in and plucks out the ring. It's a fancy one, too, shiny gold with a huge diamond in the middle. He holds it up between us. "Well? What do you say, Sadie? Are we doing this?"

7

IN WHICH
A PROPOSAL
IS ATTEMPTED

"We?" I say, staring at Lincoln in disbelief.

"Fine. *I'll* do it, since you're afraid of dragons."

"Who said I was afraid of dragons?"

He holds the ring out toward me with a shaking hand. Actually, his whole body is trembling, and he looks really pale. "Are you sure we shouldn't do something about your leg? The dragon proposal can wait."

"I really don't think it can." Swiping his shoulder against his face to wipe away some of the beads of sweat, he lets out a huge sigh. "I don't have much time here."

"So why are you worrying about some stupid dragon? It's not real."

"In this scenario, it's real enough."

"So if you die . . ."

"I die. But it'll be worse for you than for me."

I give him a funny look. "What the hell, Lincoln? You're talking about *dying*."

"I am." He looks at the ring that's still pinched between two fingers, then sort of tosses it and catches it in his hand. "No big deal."

"You," I say, "are not making any sense. I think you've lost too much blood." I glance down at his left foot. There's a puddle spreading around the base of his shoe. "I really think you should—"

"You need to trust me, okay?"

"Yeah, right. You won't even tell me what's going on."

"You know what's going on."

I shake my head. "Fine. But I don't know *why* it's happening, and you—"

"Where's the dragon now?"

"Huh?" Peering out the window, I crane my neck to try to see the sky. I don't see anything out of the ordinary, but then I spot the shadow moving across the heat-crisped lawn. "Still out there."

"Good." He takes a deep breath, then limps to the foyer. I can hear a squelching sound coming from his shoe, and it's enough to make my stomach quiver in warning. "Let's do this."

"Maybe . . . I should do it."

He pauses, his hand on the doorknob, and looks at me. "You want to?"

"No. But if you need to run, you won't be able to."

"I'm aware."

"So what if it turns down your gift and roasts you instead?"

"I don't think a dragon's going to refuse something like this," he says, uncurling his fingers to briefly display the ring. It's kind of gaudy, actually. But it is sparkly and shiny and all sorts of ostentatious. "I might get roasted anyway. Dragon etiquette probably isn't what we're used to."

I shake my head. "There has to be another way."

"Like what?"

"I don't know. But not . . . this."

His lips twist in a little smile. "I knew you cared."

"Shut up! I don't want to see *anyone* roasted alive. Even you."

He holds his clenched fist carefully in front of his chest and closes his eyes, looking super dramatic and heroic, and I kind of want to punch him in the face. But I manage to keep my hands to myself. He lets out a soft chuckle and turns back to the door.

"Lincoln—"

"You don't have to watch."

"I'm not going to. I just . . ."

He looks back at me and raises his eyebrows.

"I'll look after your dog for you."

He lets out a sharp laugh, then gasps as some sort of pain seems to hit him. "Don't worry about that. I appreciate it, but it's really not necessary."

"William doesn't need to eat?"

"He loves to eat. But once I do this, we're done."

"We're done?"

He shakes his head. "I mean, the scenario's done."

"And I'll wake up?"

"You're not asleep."

"I'm *something*," I say. "I'm certainly not awake. So if I'm not asleep, either . . ."

He turns away and twists the doorknob without offering any sort of explanation. As he steps outside, a huge shadow swipes over the front yard, and he looks up, shading his eyes from the dim sunlight. My eyes are watering, but it's not from the light. It's probably not from the smoke, either. I'm tired, I'm sore, I'm bleeding, I'm confused, and I'm annoyed. There's a good chance I'm crying.

Also, I really don't want to see Lincoln roasted to a crisp, even if this is some sort of dream. Or hallucination. Or brain injury.

Maybe I never recovered from hitting my head on the toilet. That was months ago, though. Wouldn't I have noticed other symptoms?

But . . . I do have other symptoms. The spaciness. The nausea. Something's not right.

So maybe this is all just something cooked up by my damaged brain cells and—

"Here we go," Lincoln says, snapping me out of my internal conversation with myself. I blink and focus on him, watching as he slowly waves the ring above him in sweeping arcs. I guess he's trying to get the diamond to catch the light. The shadow sweeps over him, darkening his features for a moment. But then it passes, and he follows something with his gaze, watching as it seems to move above the house. He lets his arm fall, his posture dejected.

"What's wrong?" I ask.

"I don't think the dragon can see it. It's too small."

"That's a huge diamond."

"Apparently not by dragon standards." He peers at the ring in his hand, frowning. "Maybe . . ."

"Maybe what?"

"We need more."

"Do you have more flyers?"

He shakes his head. "Mom's got some jewellery."

"Won't she miss it?"

He gives me a look, cocking one eyebrow. "Do you see her around here?"

"No . . . but if I gave my mom's jewellery to a dragon, she wouldn't be very happy about it."

"Even if you gave it away in a story?"

"What?"

He shakes his head. "Never mind. Just go upstairs and—" He breaks off as he looks up. At the same moment, I hear a massive thump on the roof. It's sort of like when crows are playing around on the shingles, but much, *much* louder. I duck instinctively. Lincoln's already hobbling back toward the door. I slam it shut.

In his face.

"Sadie!" His fists pound on the door. My heart pounds in my chest. *What the hell? Why did you do that?*

"I don't know!" I wail, backing away from the door as it flies open.

"You don't know what?" He sees my face and frowns. "What's wrong?"

"I'm sorry!"

"For what?"

I stare at him, my eyes wide. "You didn't notice?"

"That you slammed the door in my face, trapping me out there with a dragon? Yeah. I noticed." He moves past me to the stairs and starts to haul himself up them, giving me a great view of the back of his leg. Which doesn't even look like a leg anymore. It looks more like a piece of meat cut by a really unskilled butcher. I turn and retch, my hands on my knees. My bloody palms are sticky against my skin. "Sadie? You okay?"

"Yeah. Just . . . get the jewels."

He snorts. "You make it sound like she's got the Crown Jewels up there. It's mostly costume jewellery."

"Will that work?" I ask, daring to look up. I try to focus on the back of his head so I don't retch again.

"I don't see why not. I don't think dragons are jewellery appraisers. They probably just need it to *look* expensive." He reaches the top of the stairs and disappears into one of the rooms off the landing.

I consider going up there to help, but it would probably feel weird poking around in his parents' room, and besides, how many people does it take to grab a few pieces of jewellery? So I walk shakily to the stairs and sit down on the second one to wait. The front door is still open, giving me a front-row seat to view the approaching apocalypse. I can even see the treehouse across the street. Sort of. The tree's ablaze, and there's not much left of the treehouse itself other than a few broken pieces of wood. *And a good chunk of Lincoln's leg,* I think before I can stop myself. My mouth fills with saliva once more, and I only just manage not to gag.

"I never realized how little jewellery Mom has," his voice says a few minutes later. I crane my neck back to see him limping down the stairs, leaning heavily on the railing. His other hand is grasping something, but

I can't see what. "She has this nice gold pendant, but she's wearing it right now, so that doesn't help us."

"What did you find, then?"

He comes to a stop at the bottom and sort of falls back to sit beside me on the step. "Jesus, my leg hurts."

"Then maybe we should be paying attention to that and not trying to find bling for a dragon."

"Dealing with the dragon is how we deal with everything else." He opens his hand to show me what he found. There's a chain with a tiny gold locket, a simple pair of pearl earrings, and a silver necklace and pendant with two stones and a disc stamped with a couple of names: DASHIELL and CASHEL.

"Cashel."

"Dad gave her this for Christmas one year. It's basically costume jewellery, but it's shiny." He holds it up by the chain. The two stones glint in the light.

"Cash."

He puts the necklace back on his palm and pokes at one of the earrings. "I don't know if dragons like pearls, but—"

"Cash," I say again, gently taking his wrist. He turns to me slowly, his lips pressed together in a thin line. "You're Cash."

"Where do you think we should try this? I kind of want to keep the dragon away from the house. William is still in the backyard, so—"

"What about me?"

"You're smart enough to know not to antagonize a dragon." He clutches the jewellery in his fist and uses the other hand on the railing to haul himself to his feet. I frown up at him.

What was that all about? If this is all happening in my head . . . why is he being weird about his name?

"Is it because I guessed your last name before and now my brain won't let go of it?"

He turns slowly and gives me a funny look. "Huh?"

"Why do you want me to call you Lincoln?"

"Because . . . that's my name."

"No, it's not."

He snorts. "I'm pretty sure it is."

"It's your last name. But when I met you for the first time . . . I mean, after I hit my head . . ." With a sigh, I get to my feet. "You said your name was Cash."

He raises his eyebrows.

"Yeah. Great. And now my head is messing with me." I frown at him. "Lincoln . . ."

"What?"

I shake my head. I don't feel like playing games anymore. "Are you going to do this, or what? Because the sooner you do, the sooner I can be done with this whole shitshow."

"You're not enjoying yourself?"

"Should I be?"

"Well . . . if you were taking pleasure in my physical pain, I might be concerned I was in the company of a psychopath." His lips quirk. "But you have to admit, this is kind of exciting."

I gape at him. "Are you serious?"

"What? Dragons. Danger. Mirror. Magic." He opens his hand to display the jewellery, including the ring he managed to bring into existence with a flyer and a match. "You're basically living out a story. What's not to like?"

"I don't *like* those kinds of stories. I told you that."

"Maybe you do."

"I *don't*," I say, almost stomping my foot for emphasis. Luckily, I stop myself just in time. "I like real stories about real people. Not . . . whatever this shit is."

He shrugs. "So change it."

"Change what?"

"The story."

"How the hell am I supposed to do that?"

He shrugs. "You're a writer. You tell me."

"I'm not a writer. I was a deluded wannabe. I'll just stick to reading from now on and leave the writing to the people who are actually good at it."

His face gets so sad that I feel confused and angry all at once.

"Why do you even care?" I snap. "Who am I to you? We're just strangers who met in a library. You gave a pukey girl a ride home. That should've been the end of it."

"Then it would've been."

"Huh?"

"If that were supposed to be the end of it, it would've been. Maybe everything is happening the way it's supposed to."

"That's crap."

"Why?"

"It just is." I narrow my eyes at him. "Is this some new scam to lure unsuspecting women?"

He lets out a short laugh of disbelief. "Are you serious? Don't you think this is an awful lot of trouble to go to for a lie?"

"Maybe you're an obsessed stalker."

"If you want me to leave you alone after today, just say the word."

"I wanted you to leave me alone *today*, thanks."

"Yeah, well, I wasn't about to just jog on past without saying hello. I like to think I'm a little more polite than that." He almost sounds a bit annoyed.

Good.

"I'm going to go try this," he says, holding up the handful of jewellery. "Then I'll be out of your hair. Sound good?"

"Sounds great."

He stares at me for a moment, myriad tiny expressions flickering across his features so fast that I can't really tell what he's thinking. Overall, though, the impression I get is one of sadness. Which makes no sense, considering I've been kind of a bitch to him and he should be wanting to get rid of me by now.

When he finally turns away and limps out the open front door, I feel a strange twang of regret. But I don't say anything. I remain quiet as I go to stand in the doorway, watching him limp onto the lawn and turn around. He looks up at something on top of the house. I guess the dragon's still there. He opens his hand and angles it, trying to get the jewellery to catch the light.

"Here, dragon, dragon, dragon," he says softly. I snort under my breath.

"Maybe it responds better to dirty talk," I say. "Remember the book it came from?"

"Yeah. That's not going to happen." He frowns up at the roof.

"Is it working?"

"I can't tell."

"Can it even see that stuff?"

"I don't—" He breaks off. I don't even have time to scream before he's engulfed by a fireball. I stagger back into the foyer, eventually hitting the stairs and falling onto them.

Outside, Lincoln's fallen to the ground. But he's not dead. He's still moving, rolling to try to put out the flames. Unfortunately, the grass is so dry that it's catching fire all around him.

"Lincoln!" I shriek. *Help him! Do something!* But what am I supposed to do? If the dragon is willing to do that to someone offering a gift—

The agonized scream is what sends me running. At that moment, I don't care about the flames. I don't care about my own pain. I can't just watch this happen. And so I run out there, through the flames licking at my ankles. I grab him by the arm, stopping his frantic movement. His skin is already blistered and peeling. But I tug on the limb anyway.

"Get up! Stand up!"

He obeys me, staggering to his feet. I haul him down the lawn and onto the street, which is hard and unforgiving, but thankfully non-flammable. With a superhuman strength I wasn't aware I possessed, I throw him to the ground.

"Roll!"

He does, while I slap my hands against the stubborn flames on his shirt. Or what's left of it. Between Mirror and the dragon, there's not much fabric still intact. When the last stubborn flame is extinguished under my palms, I collapse onto my knees beside him, sobbing.

"Sadie."

I can't breathe. I try to suck in some deep breaths, but the air is too thick. My throat is too tight. I let out a strangled scream.

"Hey." A hand reaches for mine, pulling it from the pavement and closing around it. I blink through tears of pain and terror to see him looking at me. His face is badly burned, and I know those are the kind of injuries that are going to leave disfiguring scars.

"I'm sorry," I choke out.

"Not your fault. And you probably saved my life."

"You're not going to survive this."

He smiles a little. How can he smile? "You need to play it out."

"I *can't!* Look what happened to you when you tried."

"It's not my story."

"What?"

"You can do this." He squeezes my hand. It hurts. "You can do this, Sadie. Just . . . do it quick. I don't know how much longer I've got."

"You want to be alive to see me fail?"

He closes his eyes. "You're not going to fail. That's why . . ."

"That's why what?" I ask. But he doesn't respond. "Lincoln, that's why what?"

His hand relaxes. But he's still breathing. He's not dead . . . yet.

I turn and peer at the house. The sight of the dragon sitting up on the roof, like a giant bird in its nest, sends a spike of terror through me. Worse, the creature seems to be watching us. I look around desperately, trying to spot the jewellery. But Lincoln must've dropped it on the lawn, because I don't see it. And if it's there . . . well, it's gone. I'm not about to go searching through the flaming grass to find it.

The house isn't going to last much longer, for that matter. Once the fire on the lawn reaches the house itself, the building's toast.

"I don't know what to do!" I cry, turning back to the injured boy. "What do I do? You need to tell me. Before you die. Please!"

His eyelids flutter for a moment, but then he goes still again. I squeeze his hand and give it a gentle shake.

"Don't leave me."

He takes a slow breath. "I thought you wanted nothing to do with me."

My relief at hearing his voice almost drowns out the annoyance at his words. I decide to ignore them; I can be pissed off at the characters in my hallucination later. "I need you."

"No, you don't. You can figure this out."

"But I can't! I don't know anything about dragons, other than the fact that they like shiny things. And you already tried that, and it didn't work."

"It wasn't impressed with my offering."

"I don't have anything better."

He says nothing. I look back up at the dragon. It's still staring at us. I can hear it breathing from here, the sound like a roaring bellows. Beyond that, though, I hear something else.

Barking.

With a gasp, the idea comes to me. I lean closer to Lincoln, squeezing his hand to get his attention. "Where did William put that sceptre?"

A moan is all the response I get.

"Lincoln! You said he was burying his gold. Where?"

"Backyard."

"Yeah, I know that. But I don't have time to dig up the whole yard. Where, exactly?"

"It hurts." He sucks in a deep breath.

"Lincoln! Where?"

"Magnolia."

I don't wait for anything else. I pull my hand away from his sticky, blistered skin and jump to my feet. The front yard is fully ablaze now. I run down the street, feeling the eerie gaze of the dragon on me the whole time. My bare feet slap on the pavement as I turn and run up the driveway.

I hear the dragon take a breath.

And the world gets mighty hot.

8

IN WHICH
I TEAM UP WITH A DOG
TO SAVE THE DAY

I'm surprised my feet don't melt right into the driveway. Actually, I'm surprised I can still run. I guess adrenaline will do that to a person. And I'm full of it as I dive onto the ground, skinning my bloody and blistered palms on the aggregate surface. By some strange luck, the dragon avoids a direct hit. But I don't know if my luck is going to hold out much longer. I scramble to my feet and run the last few steps up the driveway before ducking around the side of the house. Everything feels hot against the soles of my bare feet, and I don't know if that's because it actually is or if it's because my feet have been burned.

I think it might be a little of both.

When I throw open the gate and stumble onto the crispy grass in the backyard, I spot William. He's standing in the middle of the space, looking up at the roof, digging in his paws and barking. His posture makes his position on the intruder pretty clear, and I can just imagine the translation: "Get off of our roof, you scaly shit!" To my great relief (and a bit of confusion), the dragon doesn't appear to be paying any attention to the dog. I take the opportunity.

"William!" I hiss. He doesn't seem to hear me. I'm going to have to be a little louder. "William!"

He stops barking and looks at me.

"Where's your . . . bone? The gold one."

He just tilts his head. I look around in desperation. The fence is lined with patches of garden, and there are shrubs and trees all over the place. *What the hell does a magnolia even look like at this time of year? I know it's not blooming right now, but beyond that . . .*

William resumes his guard-dog routine, and I know I'm not going to get any help from him. I'm on my own. So I get down on my hands and knees and start peering under things. If the dog's been burying his treasures, then the soil should be churned up a bit. At least, that's what I'm guessing. But it's really hard to tell with this garden because it's been taken care of pretty well. The soil looks fluffy and freshly watered, so I don't know where a dog might have dug. Frustrated, I sit back on my heels and close my eyes for a moment.

Think, Sadie. If you were a dog, where would you bury something?

I honestly have no idea. And since William can't talk, he can't tell me. I don't know if he would, anyway; he's too busy trying to defend his house from a dragon.

Wait a sec. Remember when you first got here? The dog was running around out here. Closer to the house.

I open my eyes and look over at the building. Through the windows, I can see flames. It looks like the fire has gotten inside the house. It's only a matter of time before it devours the whole thing. I need to be quick.

There's another strip of garden that runs along the back of the building itself. At one point, it bulges out into the yard a bit to accomodate some sort of ornamental tree. My gaze drifts down to the base of the trunk . . . and then over to the chunks of dirt flung into the nearby dry grass. Sucking in a gasp that actually burns my throat, I rush over and fall to my knees as I start to dig into the soil. The barking stops, and, a moment later, William's at my side. I'm afraid he's going to be angry that I'm messing with his stash. But then he starts to help.

"Good. Put your back into it," I say, watching as his front paws work like pistons, digging down into the dirt. It isn't too long before he hits something, since he didn't bury it that deep. He scratches at it with one paw. I work my fingers under the object and yank hard. The sceptre comes away from its cache easily, dumping a few cups' worth of dirt into my lap.

"Holy shit," I whisper as I feel the weight of the object in my hands. I peer closer, noticing the scratches and what look like tooth marks in the soft metal. "Is this real gold?" The dog doesn't answer. He's digging again. And I'm sure there's more. Lincoln said there was. But I don't know if we need it. I stand up, hefting the sceptre in both hands.

Now what? I think as I back into the middle of the yard and peer up at the dragon. It's still facing away from me. Maybe it's staring at Lincoln. Maybe it's roasted him again. I don't know. But I can't worry about that right now. I need to put an end to this, before it's too late.

Swallowing hard, fighting against my dry and scratchy throat, I lift the sceptre over my head. My arms shake, and it's not just from the weight of the thing. Lincoln might not be that concerned about dying in . . . whatever this is. But I am. Even if it's not real. I'm only seventeen, and I don't want to go through that yet.

Especially if it involves a lot of pain and screaming.

The dragon's tail swipes back and forth, dislodging a few shingles on the edge of the roof. I take a deep breath.

"Hey."

My voice isn't much more than a whisper. But I'm too terrified to get out any more than that. I close my eyes for a long moment. *You have to do this. Be brave. Lincoln's counting on you.*

"Hey." I open my eyes and glare up at the dragon. "Hey, you! Fire-breath! You lousy, overrated worm. You think you can just come in here and torch our neighbourhood? What the hell did we ever do to you?"

I regret opening my mouth at all as I see the dragon crane its neck in my direction. Its talons crunch on the roof as it turns around, swinging its tail. Wings open and flap once, as if to maintain balance. And then it's staring down at me, its malevolent eyes boring into my soul with the heat of a thousand dragon exhales. My arms tremble, but I keep the sceptre up where the dragon can see it.

"Is this what you want?"

In response, the creature lets out a tremendous shriek. So do I, and it's not out of fear. It's from pure ear pain.

"Shut up!" I shout. "Take the damn thing, then, and go back to your cave or your nest or wherever it is you came from."

It spreads its wings and takes to the air. I lower the sceptre as disappointment sinks over me. But it doesn't last long, and it turns into terror as I see the dragon circle back and come to land just a few feet away on the grass. Its tail swishes angrily, and half the fence at the back gets taken out in one blow. The creature lowers its head and seems to suck in a breath.

"Take it!" I scream, throwing the heavy sceptre away from me with all the strength I can muster. "Take it and leave! We don't want it."

As if to make a liar out of me, William lunges out of the garden, trying to grab the sceptre. I throw myself at him, falling to the ground but managing to snag his collar. He makes a whiny sort of yelp as he comes to a stop.

"Stay," I wheeze, trying to hold on. William's a lot bigger than Spud, and I'm not used to the power of a dog this size. He actually starts to drag me across the lawn before I manage to brace my knees under me and pull back.

And it's just in time.

The dragon takes a step forward. It's staring at the sceptre. I hold my breath, watching. William whines.

With an impossibly delicate movement, the dragon plucks the sceptre from the grass with two talons. It looks like the equivalent of me picking up a toothpick. But the dragon doesn't seem to care that the treasure is so relatively small. It brings the sceptre up to its eye and peers close, like a jeweller doing an appraisal. All that's missing is the loupe.

"Stay," I whisper to William, who's still trying to get away. He sits down with a grumble and stares up at the creature. I keep still, afraid that any sudden movement might set the dragon off again. Watching Lincoln get engulfed by a fireball was bad enough. I *really* don't want to have to watch that happen to his dog, too.

The dragon lets out a screech that startles me into a squeak and William into a yelp. It throws its wings wide and flaps hard, sending bits of dry grass and leaves swirling through the air. I close my eyes and turn my head away as hope burbles in my chest. *Did it really work? Is it over?* As the air becomes still again, I dare to open my eyes and look up. The dragon is high in the sky, heading in the direction of . . . its book? In the box on the street? I honestly have no idea. Letting my breath out in a rush, I let go of William's collar. He stares at me, tilting his head.

"Lincoln really needs to keep you on a leash."

He barks, as if in defiance.

"Yes, he does. If you hadn't stolen that dragon's property, none of this would've happened."

A snuffly snort is all the answer I get. My mind is whirling. *That sceptre was probably what the dragon was looking for this whole time!* I look over at the garden. There's got to be more buried there. But the dragon is satisfied for now, so I'm not going to push my luck. Still . . .

"Why isn't it over?" I whisper. I stand up slowly and nearly cry out at the pain in my feet. I stumble toward the gate, agonizingly aware of every blade of grass. When I look down, I note the blisters on my feet and ankles. The soles have to be even worse; I can barely stand. But I have to keep going. There must be something I still need to do.

The shrill yip makes my head snap up. I blink, sure I'm seeing things. But the mirage doesn't disappear. Spud stands just inside the open gate.

"Oh, my god. Spud! Come here."

But he doesn't. He turns and trots in the other direction. I stagger after him, not willing to lose sight of him again. I can't. I can't lose anyone else today.

I follow my dog along the side of the house and out to the driveway. The heat coming from the front yard and the flaming building is pretty intense; I'm surprised Spud ventured anywhere near it. I'm about to call out to him again, to make him stop, when I see where he's headed: to the figure lying in the street. A figure that is, somehow, still moving. But it's not a kind of movement that fills me with hope. It's more like a full-body spasm, as if he's writhing to escape the pain.

"Lincoln!" I shout as I hurry toward him. "The dragon has its treasure. It's gone. It's over."

I don't know if he hears me or not. Spud reaches him and tries to lick his face; the boy doesn't even seem to notice.

"It's going to be fine," I say, more to myself now. The driveway is so hot. I can almost hear the sizzle of my skin on the surface. Or is that just my imagination? My ears are ringing. Every nerve in my body seems to be screaming. I'm so exhausted that I just want to lie down beside Lincoln and sleep forever. *Why isn't it ending? He said it was my story. He said we had to play it out. And I did! But I'm still here. Why am I still here? Why won't this nightmare end?*

"Lincoln," I whisper as I step off the driveway and into the street. His burns look worse than I remember. The sounds that are coming out of him—breathy little moans that speak of unbearable agony—are something I know will be etched on my memory forever. Even when this nightmare ends. Even when—

My whole body jerks as if it's been hit with a thousand volts, and Lincoln is suddenly blocked from view. All I can see is the woman standing in front of me. All I can feel is the heat radiating from her volcanic skin, her flaming hair, her flickering dress. The mirrored surface that serves as her face seems to have its own magnetic pull, drawing my gaze there. But I don't want to look. *I don't want to look!*

"No," I say, shaking my head and keeping my gaze trained on the ground as I edge around her. The terrifying heat almost burns my skin. I rush over to Lincoln. Spud's just standing there now, looking confused and upset. He probably doesn't understand why his kisses weren't helping.

"Lincoln." I fall to my hands and knees beside him. He doesn't seem to notice I'm here. Tears are trickling through the landscape of blisters on his skin, shaken ever downward by the awful tremble that's moving through his body. I want to reach out and gather him into my arms, but I know that would only make the pain worse. I can't do anything except sit here and watch.

So I settle myself down on the ground, as close to him as I can get without touching. "It's okay," I say, even though it's definitely not. "You're going to be fine. You'll see. Help is coming."

Spud whines and takes a step closer to the boy's blistered face. I'm afraid he's going to try to lick him again, but he just stands there, staring at me, like he thinks I can fix this. My own tears start to flow, dripping over the bridge of my nose and onto the unforgiving pavement.

"I'm here, okay? Spud's here, too. You're not alone. Just hold on, okay? Just hold on . . ."

I get no response. I don't know if he can hear me or not. Letting myself roll onto my back, I stare up at the ugly, smoke-stained sky. A shadow flickers overhead.

"Fuck," I whisper, watching the dragon make a wide loop above Lincoln's burning house. But then something else catches my eye. I lift my head and look over at the mirror-faced woman, who has one arm raised high into the air. She looks like she's conducting an orchestra. Or maybe directing a plane in for a landing.

In the second it takes for me to realize what's about to happen, I have two thoughts. The first is: *I don't want to die.* The second is: *Please, make it quick.*

The dragon swoops around again, wings beating the flaming lawns into a fury of fire. As its body curls in our direction, I let my head fall back on the pavement.

"No."

It twists again and heads straight for us. The giant mouth opens. I can't move. Not even when I see the dripping flames shoot out toward us like an apocalyptic lasso.

But I do manage to scream.

A flash rips the world apart. I blink. My body suddenly feels light and soft. All my pain is gone. I blink again, realizing I'm lying on scratchy grass. Above me, the leaves hang silent in the still air. I lift my head and spot Spud lounging nearby in a patch of shade, panting slightly. Slowly, I move my gaze sideways to the boy sitting on the bench, holding my phone, his eyebrows raised in question.

Holy shit.

9

IN WHICH
I QUESTION
MY SANITY

I sit up quickly, trying to reorient myself. My feet are bare, but they're uninjured. Well, except for the nascent blisters from my jelly sandals. When I look at my hands, I see nothing but smooth palms. No burns. No cuts from broken glass. I turn and stare at the boy on the bench. He stares right back, as annoyingly cute as I remember. His t-shirt is intact. His left sneaker isn't half full of blood. He looks absolutely fine . . . if a little puzzled.

"You okay?" he asks.

"Yeah. Fine." I press my palms to my temples and take a few deep breaths.

"You don't look fine."

"I am."

"Forgive me if I don't believe you." He stands up. "It's too hot out here. Let's go get a drink."

I let my hands fall. "Where?"

"My house."

I just blink at him.

"We've got air conditioning."

"I know," I say, my voice coming out as a whisper. He frowns, then walks over and reaches out with his free hand to help me up. I stare at it, noting the smooth, unburned skin.

"Come on." He bends down and grabs my hand, not waiting for me to take his. I don't pull away, either. I just let him haul me to my feet. "You're probably dehydrated. Exercising in this weather probably wasn't a great idea."

"I wasn't exercising."

"He was," he says, waving my phone at Spud, whose leash is still looped around my wrist. I frown and bend over to pick up my keys and shoes.

"I think we should just go home," I say. He gets this dubious expression on his face. "What?"

"You think you'll make it without passing out? You're looking kind of pale."

I don't feel so great, either. Maybe he's right. Maybe I just need a nice, cold drink. There's no reason I should be feeling like this from a dream. I mean, I've had nightmares before, but they never made me feel like *this.*

"Okay," I say at last, and try to ignore the way his face sort of lights up. He goes and grabs William's leash from the bench, tilts his chin down the sidewalk, and sets off at a stroll. "Can I have my phone back?" I ask, falling into step beside him.

"I'm not finished reading your story yet."

"Doesn't matter. It's crap." I hold out my hand. He frowns as he places the device into it.

"Didn't seem like it, from what I read."

"Trust me. It is. The whole class thought so."

He makes some sort of dismissive noise in the back of his throat. "I doubt that."

I open my mouth to retort, then think about it for a moment. "There was this one guy who was really nice about it. Too nice."

"You think he was just being polite?"

"Either that, or he just didn't get it. He was, like, really old."

He laughs. "Older people sometimes have really good taste, Sadie. And they often don't have a problem saying what they think."

"You sound like him."

"Old?"

I shake my head. "No. He just said something similar. 'Life's too short for false flattery.' Something like that."

He makes a noncommittal sort of humming noise. "So what did this honest old dude think of your story? Did he tell you?"

"Yeah. He talked to me after class when all I wanted to do was get out of there and cry."

"And what did he say?"

I shrug. "He said it had promise. That my ideas are creative. And that I shouldn't listen to people who try to feel better about their own insecurities by tearing other people down."

"Did he mean the teacher?"

"I guess."

"So you'll believe this teacher—who sounds like a bit of a bitch, by the way—and not the guy who's giving you a compliment?" He shakes his head. "I don't know, Sadie. That doesn't make much sense to me."

He's right. It doesn't. "Shut up."

He laughs. "Nice. I'll chalk that up to the dehydration."

I let out a soft groan and rub the back of my hand over my forehead. "Sorry. It's . . . been a long day."

"It's not even ten o'clock in the morning."

I jerk, startled. Luckily, he doesn't notice.

We're just reaching the corner when a voice rings out from somewhere to our right.

"Damn it, Cash! Will you put your stupid dog on a leash already?" A moment later, William bounds out from around the side of a house. A pissed-looking girl follows him. When she sees us, she focuses her ire on the guy walking beside me.

"What'd he do this time?"

"Nothing. But he was getting ready to take a piss on Mom's roses."

"A little water couldn't hurt."

"Asshole," she mutters before turning and storming back into her yard.

"Nice to see you, too!" Cash calls after her. He turns to William, who's decided to join us like a good boy. He trots along ahead of us, head held high. It's just like before . . . except there's no sceptre in his jaws.

"Does he do that often?" I ask.

Cash lets out a grunt of laughter. "Every day. You know, I think Rachael likes me. Otherwise, she'd make sure that gate was closed and we wouldn't have to go through that every morning."

"She yells at you every morning?"

"Like I said . . . I think she likes me."

I peer at him sideways. "Do you like her?"

"Why?" He pokes me in the arm with his finger. I scowl and edge away. "Jealous?"

"Of what? Your nuisance dog? Or having to talk to you every morning?"

"Wow. You sure know how to make a guy—"

"Yeah, yeah. I know. Sorry."

"I know you are." He gestures ahead of us. A blast of déjà vu hits me really hard, and I almost stumble.

"Whoa."

"What?"

"That's your house?"

"It's not *that* impressive." He shakes his head as he leads me off the curb and across the street. "Yours is nicer."

I panic for a moment before remembering that he drove me home before. *Of course he knows what our house looks like.* But this whole situation is getting a bit weird. I don't like it. I rack my brain, trying to remember if I ever came down this way before. Did I go to a party at someone's house around here? Unlikely. The kids from this neighbourhood go to a different school.

"Cash?"

"Yeah?"

"Are you sure we've never met before?"

"You mean . . . before the library?"

"Yeah."

"Not that I can remember."

"Are you sure?"

"Pretty sure. We didn't go to the same school."

"Where do you go?"

He points in a vague sideways direction with his thumb. "Valley Heights. Go Cedars!"

"Oh."

"And I don't go there anymore. I graduated this year."

"Congratulations."

"You wouldn't say that if you saw my transcript." He shakes his head with a little smile.

"You don't *seem* that stupid."

That makes him laugh. And then he gently puts his hand on my arm as he steers me up the driveway. There's a car there now, that hybrid thingy I remember from when he drove me home a few months ago.

"Isn't that your brother's car?"

He nods. "He's in Thailand. Doing some backpacking with his girlfriend before he starts med school in August. And then the car's all mine."

"Yay."

"Hey, don't look a gift car in the mouth."

"Never. I'm just saying . . ."

"You insulting my baby?"

"Your baby?"

"I'm calling her Denise."

"Right . . ."

"What's wrong with Denise?"

"Why does your car need a name?"

"Because maybe if I name her, I'll bond with her. And then maybe I'll forget that I'm driving a big, shiny virtue signal." He pauses and angles his head back toward the car. "Sorry, Denise. No offence."

I can't help smiling a little, but I try not to let it show. He leads me up to the front door. William's still with us, waiting for Cash to open the door and let him in. I look down at Spud, who looks ready to jump inside at the first invitation. He always likes exploring other people's houses.

This is bizarre, I think as I step inside. The smell is familiar, for one thing. But, beyond that, the whole foyer is exactly as I remember it. The whole situation is eerily similar to what happened before, and as Cash closes the door behind me, I try for one last peek outside through the opening.

"Looking for something?" he asks.

Yeah. Dragons. I shake my head and keep my mouth shut, not wanting to sound like a lunatic. He just smiles and kicks off his shoes by the door. *Okay . . . so there's one thing that's different. But how was I supposed to know he lives in a shoe-free household?*

"You can take your potato off the leash," he says, hanging William's leash on a wall hook before striding away. I guess he expects me to follow him. Quickly, I dump my jellies beside his runners, place my phone and keys on the little table beside the door, and unclip Spud's leash. The dog shakes himself out and goes trotting after Cash like he owns the place. I follow a little more slowly, taking in my surroundings.

It's the same. But . . . that's impossible. I've never really been to this neighbourhood, let alone this house. How can I know what the inside looks like? As I come around the corner and emerge into a large space, the sense of familiarity and surprise sort of cancel each other out, and I'm left feeling a bit numb. The kitchen is as I remember. So is the rest of the room, including the living area at the back with its large windows overlooking the backyard. William's perched himself on the couch, sitting up like a fine gentleman.

"Get down," Cash says, somewhat wearily, as if he's had to use the same admonishment hundreds of times. "I don't want to have to vacuum the couch to cover your ass."

William just turns and rests his chin on the back of the cushion while he stares at Cash.

"Thank you for your cooperation." With a sigh, he turns to the fridge and yanks open the door. "Pick your poison. We've got . . ."

Lemonade, I think, the words in my head synching with the ones coming out of his mouth. *Pop. Juice.* I wait for the last option, but it never comes.

"No kombucha?"

"You like kombucha?"

I shake my head quickly. He raises an eyebrow, as if he thinks I'm totally weird.

"We do have it, but not everybody likes it." He pulls a couple of bottles out of the fridge. As he holds one out to me, I notice it's that pomegranate-berry thing I had before.

In the freaking dream.

"Thanks," I manage to get out, taking the drink with a shaking hand. I watch as he pops the top of his kombucha and takes a swig. I can smell the vinegary scent from where I'm standing.

"You're welcome. Now, drink something before you shrivel up."

I uncap the bottle and take a gulp. The sweet liquid feels so good going down. I chug half the bottle, not really realizing how thirsty I actually was. My mouth still feels dry, though.

"How long was I asleep?" I ask. He's right in the middle of another sip, so he just raises his eyebrows before swallowing and answering.

"You were sleeping?"

"I must've been." I shake my head and look out the kitchen window. The sky is still hazy, but there are no dark clouds of smoke on the horizon. And no dragons.

He shrugs. "Quick nap. I was only reading for a couple of minutes before you sat up, looking totally confused."

"I had a bad dream. No, actually, I had a nightmare."

"I'm not sure that's possible."

I snort. "You think I'm incapable of dreaming?"

"No. I'm just questioning whether that's actually what happened. It takes longer than that for the body to get into a sleep state where it can have nightmares." He takes another sip, watching me closely. It's almost like he wants me to say more. To tell him all about what just happened.

Or maybe I'm just projecting because I really want to tell *someone*.

"Maybe I'm going crazy."

"Maybe." He smiles and waves his hand over toward the living area. "Want to talk about it?"

I nod sheepishly. He walks over to the couch and grabs William—who's still sitting there—by the collar to haul him off. I walk closer, passing the dining table. It doesn't look like much dining's been going on there lately, though; it's almost completely smothered in paper. When I peer a little closer, I see that the sheets are covered in drawings. And words. It looks like these are rough sketches for a comic book. Remembering the ephemera tacked up all over Lincoln's bedroom walls, I frown and lean in for a better look, setting my bottle down on one of the only clear spots on the table.

"Are these yours?" I ask, already knowing what the answer will be.

"Just something I'm working on. I kind of needed the space to lay everything out." He chuckles softly. "Mom can't wait to get her table back."

My gaze is stopped by something in one of the panels. I lean closer, trying to read the scrawled words that accompany it. My body starts to feel a little cold. I snatch up the page so I can read it better.

"Careful. I just got the pages in the right order."

"You should number them," I say absently, my gaze frantically skimming across the paper as my heart begins to hammer. The drawings are rough, but I can see the skill in them. The characters are instantly recognizable, too . . . especially the woman with the blank face surrounded by wisps of cloud-like hair.

"Yeah, I probably should," he says lightly, as if my entire reality hasn't just been upended. I turn to him, still holding the page. It's fluttering like a leaf in my shaking hands.

"What is this?" I whisper.

"A chapter of my graphic novel."

"No. What is *this?*" The page flutters as I shake it at him. He sort of winces.

"Careful. That's my only copy."

"Satori and Linus?"

"Yeah . . . no good? I'm not the best at naming characters."

"Mirror."

He screws up his nose. "I wasn't sure about that one, either. Sometimes an obvious name is best, but . . ."

I turn back to the table. It's all there. The library. The storm. I lean over, following the panels across the table. The zombies are there, too, blinking into existence when Linus throws the pages of a comic book into the maelstrom. "This isn't right."

Cash snorts. "It's fiction."

"No . . . it's my story." I turn my gaze to look at him. "It's my dream."

"It's not a dream."

I've heard him—or a version of him—say those words so many times now. But this time, when I'm standing in his house (which I'm already familiar with, even though I've never been in it), drinking his juice (which he already offered me once before), staring at the pages of a graphic novel that pretty accurately records what happened at the library three months ago . . . I get really scared. The page crumples in my hands.

"Sadie, be careful with—"

"Who the hell are you?" I say. My throat feels so dry. I desperately want something to drink. My gaze drifts over to the half-empty bottle on the table. "Did you drug me?"

"What?" He sets his kombucha on the coffee table and stands up. "Why would I drug you?"

"Then what is this?" I shout, waving the paper at him. "How do you know all of this?"

"You told me."

"I didn't give you all the details. And I never told you about Mirror. She wasn't even in the first dream!"

"It's not a dream."

"Stop saying that!"

"I will when you stop saying it is. It's not a dream, Sadie."

I take a step back. Something in his expression is really freaking me out. He looks contrite. Sad. A little desperate.

"What did you give me?" I whisper.

"Nothing. I swear, I did not drug you." He presses his hand over his chest and lowers his head a little so he can stare intently into my eyes. "I promised you I'd explain everything. But I never got a chance before . . ."

"Before what?"

"You're going to freak out."

I swallow hard. "Why?"

"Because when I tell you what stopped me, your whole worldview is going to shift."

Shaking my head, I back toward the foyer. I'm still holding the page. His gaze flicks to it, then back to my face.

"Sadie, please." He holds out his hand. "Let me explain."

"This is mine." My voice is small. A frown creases his features. "Huh?"

"This is *my* story. *My* idea. You just took it."

"I thought this wasn't the sort of thing you wanted to write."

"That doesn't mean you can just come along and take it!"

He holds up both hands, his eyes wide. "I'm sorry. I didn't—"

"You didn't mean to rip off my idea?"

His hands fall to his sides. "You said I was welcome to it."

"I only said that today!" I shout, just as the flash of realization hits me like a dragon's belch. My head starts to shake. "You can't know that."

His lips press together, disappearing entirely.

"How can you know that?"

He closes his eyes. "I totally fucked this up," he whispers under his breath.

"You fucked something up." I look at the paper in my hands. I'm trembling so hard I can barely read the words. Turning away, I let it fall.

"Sadie—"

"I don't want to hear it."

"I promised you an explanation. But then the dragon . . ."

My eyes widen. I turn back around to face him. He shakes his head.

"I'm sorry, Sadie. I'm sorry you had to see that. Sometimes these things get away from us, and—"

"What things?" I say. My voice is comically high, like I've inhaled helium. "What the hell are you talking about?"

"The dragon. When it roasted me. I never got a chance to—"

"I've gone insane?" The statement comes out sounding like a question. "It must be from the brain damage." I work my fingers into my hair as I clutch my head. "Is any of this real? Or am I strapped in a bed some-where, drooling and—"

"You're right here," he says softly, stepping forward as he reaches out to touch my arm. I pull back so violently that he winces.

"Stay away from me! Just stay away!" The command tapers into sobs. "None of this is real. I'm losing my mind, and you're enabling my delusions."

His eyes are wide. "I'm not."

"That's what a figment of my imagination would say. Are you even real? Is this house even real?" Turning, I stagger to the foyer. I just want to go home. Back to my room, where I can curl up in my bed and sleep until Mom and Dad get home. And then they can take me to some insti-tution and have me committed, because I've obviously lost my grip on reality. But before I can go too far, Cash is right there in front of me. I slam my hands into his chest, right where Mirror burned her handprint into his flesh. He staggers back.

"Sadie—"

"Stop talking to me! Stop trying to be my friend. Stop trying to get me into bed."

He lets out a little cough. "Excuse me?"

"Is this some sick new tactic for seducing women? Make me think I'm insane, and then you're there to hold my hand and pick up the pieces while I try to claw my way back into reality?"

He looks appalled. "No!"

"Then why would you do this? Why would you take my story?"

"You didn't want it."

"It still wasn't yours to take!" My voice catches.

"How did I take it?" he asks, his voice infuriatingly calm. I shake my head.

"You . . . just did. You wrote about it."

"How did I even know about it?"

"I told you. In the car."

"You told me the basics about the zombies and the storm." He takes a step closer. I stay where I am, even though all I want to do is back away, because backing away will just take me farther into his house. I'm trapped. "You didn't tell me anything about the dragon, Sadie. So how do I know about it?"

"I'm hallucinating. I'm probably still lying on the grass, having some sort of medical episode. Or maybe I died, and this is . . . this is hell."

"And I'm in it? Thanks a lot." His mouth twists in a sad smile. "I'm sorry. I should've handled this better. But, I promise you, you're not having a medical episode. You're not dead. You're standing in my house, trying to make sense of something that doesn't make any sense. Believe me, I get it."

"No, you don't. You don't get it. You're not the one who's lost their mind." I close my eyes and feel the tears detach and roll down my cheeks. "Please. I just want to go home."

I hear him sigh. His bare soles shuffle on the floor as he moves away from me. I wipe my eyes and open them to find my path to the front door clear. "Spud! Come here."

He trots obediently out of the kitchen. I grab his leash and clip it on. I stick my blistered feet into my jellies and buckle them up. I snatch my phone and keys from the little table beside the door.

And I leave.

So many questions swirl in my head as I limp my way toward home. With each new one, I have to remind myself that there's no question that can't be answered the same way: I've lost my mind.

There's no such thing as dragons. Or zombies. Or mirror-faced women. Quite frankly, I have my doubts as to whether Cash is even real. Maybe I didn't get a ride home from the library at all. Maybe I walked, existing in a brain-damaged daze the whole time.

That would explain a lot.

When I pass the house with the box of books, I cast my gaze over the dry lawn, as if I might see something there. Myself, maybe, a shimmering mirage. But maybe I never even lay down. Maybe I just zoned out when I took Spud for a walk, and I've been wandering around in some sort of pathological trance state ever since.

I make a note to get Mom to make a doctor's appointment.

There's something very wrong with me.

MIND QUAKE

1

IN WHICH
AN ANNOYING HALLUCINATION
RETURNS

Maybe I should've just done the extra-credit assignment instead of the camping trip. At least then I wouldn't be trudging up the side of a mountain, getting blisters in weird places, and feeling like I'm going to puke.

Okay, so it's not that bad. The doctor said I should be good to go if I take things slow ... which I am. Luckily, I have an understanding teacher and a hiking partner who doesn't mind me stopping to smell the roses.

Or stopping to breathe heavily and try not to puke up that last granola bar.

"You doing okay?" Djanet asks. I just nod and keep my eyes on the trail in front of us. It's true: I am doing okay at the moment. But if I do anything to break my stride, that could change. "I think there's a place to rest up ahead," she adds. "And a place to pee. Thank god."

"We're surrounded by woods," I say, daring a few words. She gives me a skeptical sideways glance.

"Yeah, and about a million hikers. I don't want an audience."

The trees surrounding the trail look pretty dense to me. I'm sure you might be able to see someone if they were to tramp in there and squat in the woods, but you probably wouldn't be able to tell what they were doing. I don't say anything, though. It's hard enough just to breathe. Djanet's the one with asthma (which is why she's stuck with my sorry, slow ass), but she seems to be handling the hike better than me. I haven't even seen her pull out her inhaler yet.

The trail is steep as it winds through the trees, full of switchbacks and worn smooth by thousands of hiking boots. We pass quite a few day hikers going the other way, which is pretty annoying considering how early in the day it is; they must've gotten started at the crack of dawn to be coming back down already. The trail is kind of narrow in spots, so it's a tight squeeze. I try to tuck my arms in to let the others pass. It's not like I can angle my body with the giant backpack strapped to my shoulders.

When we finally get past a group of loud, touristy seniors (seriously, is everyone a faster hiker than me?), the trail widens a little and we're able to walk side by side again. I don't know Djanet very well, but she seems nice enough. And our speeds seem to be a pretty good match, which is a relief.

"I can't wait to get the camp stove set up," she says. "A girl can only take so much trail mix."

"Didn't you eat a real breakfast a few hours ago?"

"Yeah, but we're burning a lot of calories here. And my stomach wants something . . . real."

"Trail mix is real."

"Something hot," she clarifies, edging sideways as a young man in a tight-fitting t-shirt jogs past us up the trail. He doesn't have any sort of gear with him, so he's probably just out for a run. "Like that," Djanet says under her breath. I glance at her and notice she's staring after him.

"You'd have to catch him first. I don't think you could."

She laughs. "Oh, well. This trip isn't supposed to be fun, anyway, is it?"

I shrug. "Unless your idea of fun is cataloguing scree slopes and calculating glacial melt."

"Crap. That reminds me. I forgot my calculator."

"Can't you use your phone?"

"I don't have the right app. And I forgot to download it before we came out to the middle of nowhere."

"You might be able to get a signal," I say. "I've seen a few people on their phones."

"Probably just checking to see if there's a signal at all." She sighs. "Guess I'll have to do that part of the assignment when I get home."

I don't know why she doesn't just ask to borrow my phone. Maybe she figures we don't know each other well enough or something.

"You want to stop?" she asks. I frown . . . but then I notice the way my feet are sort of shuffling.

"No. I'm okay."

"You're really pale."

I'm really nauseated. Swallowing a mouthful of saliva, I shake my head. "I just need to sit for a minute. Have a drink."

She nods. "It's just up there."

I lift my gaze to the brightness ahead of us. The trees thin out, and, a few steps later, I can see the clearing. My feet, in their brand new hiking boots, practically scream in relief, and it's all I can do not to join them.

We're not the only ones here, but it's not crowded by any means. The clearing looks sort of like a picnic area. There are four wooden tables with benches near the centre of the space. An information kiosk stands off to one side, its trail map behind Plexiglas. On the far side of the clearing are a couple of small buildings that look worryingly like outhouses.

Djanet marches over to one of the tables and hauls the backpack from her shoulders. She plunks it on the bench, leaning it against the table itself. I follow her over there, a little more slowly. A groan escapes my lips as I unclip my own backpack and swing it from my shoulders. It lands with a thump on the dusty ground.

"Sit down and have a snack," she says absently as she rummages in one of the pockets on her pack. She pulls out a small packet and zips the compartment back up. "Anti-bacterial wipes," she says, even though I didn't ask. "It's like a horror movie in there, so be prepared."

"Great." I let out a long grunt as I sink onto the bench.

"Watch my stuff?"

I nod, and she hurries off to brave the toilets. I pull my legs over the bench so I can sit properly, and lean my elbows on the table. I'm tempted to put my head down, too, but I know that if I do that, I'll probably fall asleep . . . and with my luck, someone would come along and steal both our backpacks.

My head feels weird. It's like that spaciness I had after I hit my head on the library toilet is back. It hasn't been that bad the last few months, so I thought my brain was finally starting to heal.

Maybe not.

Still, I haven't had any other weird symptoms like seeing book characters come to life, zombies destroy a library, a dragon torch a neighbourhood, or a cute-but-annoying boy invade my altered states of consciousness and steal my story ideas. I think the counselling has helped. I mean . . . not with the brain injury itself. But at least now I know that none of those hallucinations were real. That's kind of a relief. Cashel Lincoln, that incredibly detailed figment of my imagination, was really starting to mess with my head.

Now that I'm sitting down, I feel a little less queasy. I lean over and pull my water bottle from its pocket, unscrew the lid, and take a few long gulps. The electrolyte mix I added this morning makes the liquid taste like lemons. It's refreshing. Even though it's the third weekend in September, it's still pretty warm. I'm probably going to want to take my sweatshirt off before we get going again. For now, though, as the sweat is starting to make me feel a bit damp and cool, I think I'll leave it on.

The trail passes along one side of the clearing, and most people don't even bother to stop. I watch them, half twisted around, one elbow on the table, and wonder what it must be like to just go on a hike and not have to worry about whether you're going to leave your breakfast behind in some bushes. I mean . . . I used to know what it was like. But ever since March, I haven't felt quite right. I'm starting to forget what "right" even feels like.

Djanet seems to be taking an awfully long time. Either there was a line at the toilet, or she needed to do more than just pee. Not that I mind waiting. It gives me more time to rest my feet. They're burning already, and I know we're not even halfway to the campsite. I bet the rest of our group is already up there, claiming their spots and setting up their tents, stringing up their food in the trees so the bears don't get it. I wonder how much insurance the school has to have that the geography teacher is allowed to take a bunch of seniors into bear country every year.

I wonder if anyone has ever been mauled.

With a snort, I smile wryly. I'm pretty sure we would've heard about an incident like *that*.

The variety of people on the trail is pretty impressive. Most of them are going up—like we are—which makes sense. There are groups of obvious tourists in matching t-shirts and hats. And there are more than a few couples, some of them carrying as much gear as we are, so they must be planning on staying a few days. I even see some families with kids. There's a lot of whining emanating from one of them.

At the moment, feeling as crappy as I do, I totally get it.

I turn back to my bottle and take another swig. As I place it on the table and turn back to the trail, my heart flops in my chest like a dying fish. I squeeze my eyes shut for a few seconds.

It's not real. Just breathe, okay? It's not real. Your brain's still healing. It's not real.

I crack open one eye. But the stupid hallucination remains. And it starts to walk over to the tables. Quickly, I turn away and lean my head against my hand. I really wish my hair wasn't in a ponytail, because maybe then I could use it to hide my face.

What is wrong with you? You're hiding from a figment of your own imagination!

"Hurry up," I whisper, staring toward the toilets. I don't see any sign of Djanet, though. And then, the view is blocked as a figure steps right into my line of sight. I let out a groan.

"Nice to see you, too," Cash says.

"Go away," I mutter.

"What?"

I turn my gaze upward. He's just standing there, cute as ever, with that expectant expression he does with his raised eyebrows. "You're not real."

He lets out a short laugh. "Excuse me?"

"You're not real." I narrow my eyes at him. "I've just spent the last three months trying to get you out of my head."

"Why?"

"Because you're not real."

His expression darkens into a frown as he steps over the bench and sits down across from me. I shake my head and cap my bottle. The last thing I need right now is to slip back into this delusion.

"Why do you think that?" he asks, his voice gentle.

I sigh impatiently. "I'm not doing this."

"What?"

"Talking to imaginary people."

"No, you're talking to a real person."

"That's what an imaginary person would say."

"Why?"

"To screw with me."

He lets out a long breath. "Sadie, I know it looks like that. I messed up. Big time. But, I promise, I'm not screwing with you."

"You're here, aren't you?"

"Yeah. Hiking."

"What a coincidence."

"Sometimes a coincidence is just that." He frowns at Djanet's backpack. "Are you camping?"

"Maybe."

"By yourself?"

I snort. "Yeah, that sounds totally safe."

He just raises his eyebrows.

"School trip," I say. "Geography class."

"Where's the rest of the class?"

"Probably at the campsite. I can't keep up."

"Why not?"

"Shut up! You already know, so why are you even asking?"

He looks taken aback. "How would I know?"

"You're an imaginary person that my damaged brain cooked up," I say, leaning forward and lowering my voice. "So you already know the whole story."

His eyebrows rise.

"Could you please just . . . not be here?" Maybe, if I ask nicely, my brain will cooperate and he'll vanish. Or walk off down the trail. Honestly, I don't care which.

"Are you okay? You look—"

"Yeah. Pale. I know." I shake my head. "I was *fine* until you showed up. Maybe I need to try those meds after all . . ."

"What meds?" he asks, looking alarmed.

I fix him with a dark glare. "For the imaginary people I keep seeing."

"You're still seeing Mirror?"

"What? No! I'm seeing you."

"I assure you, I'm not imaginary." He reaches across the table and lays his fingers gently against my wrist. The touch certainly *feels* real. Then again, so did everything in my last hallucination: the heat on my skin from the fire, the cuts on my hands from the broken glass in the treehouse, the burns on my feet and ankles from running across the flaming lawn. Cash's fingers are steady as they rest against my skin. They're even warm.

My brain is really good at this.

"If you value your life," Djanet says, "do *not* go in there." She hurries back to the table, still clutching her packet of wipes. I stare at her in desperation, using her like my only anchor to reality. She busies herself returning the wipes to the zipped pocket, then squeezes onto the bench between me and her backpack. My eyes are wide—I probably look totally deranged—but I keep staring at her, hoping she'll keep talking. Maybe that will jar me out of my delusion.

"Are you the culprit?" Cash asks, a playful smirk on his lips. He's staring right at Djanet. He sees her. But—

"Yeah, right," she says, turning at the sound of his voice and staring directly at him.

My throat lets out an involuntary squeak.

"What wrong?" Djanet asks. She lifts her t-shirt toward her nose and gives it a sniff. "Did I drag the smell back with me?"

"You can see him?" I say, my gaze flipping back and forth between the two of them. Cash has this knowing smile on his face that makes me want to scream.

"Who? Him?" She jabs her index finger in his direction.

"Told you," Cash says.

"Told her what?" Djanet asks.

"That I was real."

She lets out a short laugh. "Why wouldn't you be real?"

I grab my head in both hands and lean my elbows heavily against the table, staring at Cash. His smile gets a little wider. I narrow my eyes.

"It's happening again," I mutter.

"No, it's not." He shakes his head, then reaches his hand across the table toward my companion. "I'm Cash."

"Djanet," she says, giving his hand a quick shake. Then she gives me a glance as if to say, "What's up with this weirdo?"

Cash laughs. "Sorry. That was a little old-fashioned, wasn't it?"

"A bit," Djanet says, but she doesn't seem offended. "So, how do you two know each other? You don't go to our school."

Cash looks at me, as if he's expecting me to answer. But I want to see how he's going to explain. Actually, I want to see how my brain is going to make this fictional guy explain to the imagined version of the girl sitting beside me.

"We . . ." he begins.

"One night stand?" Djanet suggests, holding up her hands. "Say no more. None of my business."

I let go of my head and turn to her in disbelief. "What is wrong with you?"

They both laugh. *Great. My hallucinations are ganging up on me.*

"Nothing like that," Cash says at last. He fixes me with a soft look. "I gave Sadie a ride home from the library earlier this year. She wasn't feeling well."

"Oh." Djanet's voice is full of disappointment. I feel kind of let down, too. The explanation is a bit mundane. And it's perfectly sensible.

My brain is boring.

"Are you on a class trip, too?" Djanet asks. "Or is it just our teacher who's brave enough to take a bunch of teenagers into the woods?"

He smiles. "Just a regular weekend camping trip for me."

"By yourself?"

His gaze shifts in my direction. "No . . . with my girlfriend."

Why should I care, Cash? You think my imaginary enemy's imaginary girlfriend is going to make me jealous?

Djanet peers around the clearing. "She in the toilets?"

"No. We agreed to meet here, then head up to the campsite together." He gestures over at one of the other tables, and I notice a stuffed backpack lying on the bench.

"You didn't want to do the whole hike together?"

"No," I say, drawing the attention of both in my direction. "He wanted an excuse to meet me here."

"Yeah?" he says, an amused smile quirking his lips. "Why's that?"

"To annoy me."

He laughs. I can feel Djanet staring at me. She probably thinks I've lost my mind.

She doesn't realize I really have.

"Actually," Cash says, "meeting you here was purely coincidental. I swear. Rachael has to cut the trip short 'cause she's got an early shift on Monday morning. So we drove ourselves in our own cars." He shrugs. "I just felt like getting an early start."

"Sure you did," I mutter. Djanet nudges me in the ribs with her elbow. I give her a dirty look before turning back to Cash. "Look at that! Here we both are. You've said hello. Now, can you please just . . ."

"Yeah. Of course." He nods and stands up, pulling his legs out from the bench. "Nice to meet you, Djanet. See you around, Sadie?"

"God, I hope not."

He just smiles and heads over to his backpack. But he doesn't pick it up or put it on. He nudges it aside so he's got enough room to lie down along the length of the bench, his knees bent over one end so his feet can rest on the ground. It looks like he's going to squeeze in a nap before Rachael gets here.

Djanet leans close to my ear.

"What the hell happened between you two?"

"Nothing," I say, because that's the truth. Nothing happened. Nothing real, anyway.

"He's cute."

"Shut up! He'll hear you."

"So? You don't think he knows?"

"I'm sure he does. So he doesn't need to hear it from you."

She lets out an amused grunt. "Why do you hate this guy so much?"

"I don't *hate* him. He's just . . . not compatible with my sanity."

She draws back a little to give me a funny look. "What the hell does *that* mean?" Her gaze shifts to the boy on the bench. He's got one arm thrown over his eyes, shading them from the sun. "Is he an abusive asshole or something?"

I shake my head. Cash may be a lot of things, but he's not that. In fact, he's one of the gentlest people I know.

It's too bad he doesn't actually exist in the real world.

Enough, I think. *I need to wake up. Or pull myself out of this. The last thing I need right now is one of these episodes. I'm sure Mr. McFadden doesn't want to deal with a psychiatric crisis this weekend.* I close my eyes and take in a few deep breaths, focusing on the sensory input coming in. I hear Djanet breathing. The soft sound of breeze in the trees. Faint voices coming from the trail. I smell the forest. The dusty dirt under our feet. A faint whiff of the toilets. I feel the time-smoothed table under my fingers. My butt sitting on the hard bench. The ache in my toes from walking in too-new hiking boots. When I feel good and grounded, I dare to open one eye. Cash is still lying on his bench.

"Damn it."

"What?" Djanet asks.

"Nothing. I'm just tired."

"Well, I'm not carrying you the rest of the way, so don't get any ideas."

"I wouldn't dream of asking."

She laughs, reaching for her backpack. She pulls out her phone, turns on the device, and sets it in front of her. I can see the startup screen with its spinning circle. "Want to take a nap?" she asks.

I snort. "We don't have time for that."

"Sure, we do. A power nap. Fifteen minutes. Then we'll head out. We should be able to get up there before it gets dark."

"I hope so. I don't want to stumble into any bears in the darkness."

"You and me both." She picks up her phone and starts tapping at the screen. "Wow. So that's what a crappy signal looks like."

"Will you be able to download that app you needed?"

"I'll try." She leans her elbows on the table and stares at the device. I try to adjust my butt (this stupid bench is really hard) before draping my upper body over the tabletop. I turn my head away as I rest it on my hands, closing my eyes against the bright day.

I'll try to have a quick nap. Maybe, when I wake up, my brain will have reset and Cash will be gone.

"Sadie."

"What?" My voice comes out in a groggy groan. "You're the one who told me to take a nap."

"No, I didn't."

2

IN WHICH
I FIND OUT I'VE HAD
A TEENAGE STALKER

It takes a moment for the voice to register. It's not Djanet. I open my eyes. At least, I think I do. But everything is dark. Too dark. I sit up like a shot, my heart pounding. In this moment, I'm convinced I've somehow gone completely blind.

"Whoa. It's okay," Cash says, his vague form silhouetted in front of me in the extremely faint light. I look up, only to see the Milky Way spread out over our heads like a bucket of spilled paint.

"What the hell?"

"Not hell. And not a dream."

I let my gaze fall. It's hard to focus on him; he's just a shadow. "What?"

"You were going to say it's just a dream."

"If it's not . . . then what is it? I certainly didn't sleep for hours. Djanet would've woken me." *Djanet. Where is she?* I look around in desperation, my eyes straining against the darkness. I don't see anything, so I reach out to where her backpack was sitting. All I find is an empty bench.

"She's not here," he says.

"No kidding. Where is she?"

"Right where you left her."

"Like hell she is." I slap the empty bench so he can hear it, even if he can't see it. "She's gone. Her backpack's gone, too."

"Do you want me to explain?"

"Explain what? That this is another dream?"

"It's not a dream."

I stand up, pressing my hands on the table for balance, and manage to step over the bench without falling. "Hallucination, then."

"It's not that, either."

"Then what is it?"

"A Reverie," he says, and the blunt delivery of his answer shocks me into silence for a moment.

"What's that?"

"I told you I would explain, and I will. But we need to get going."

I let out a short laugh. "Go where? It's pitch dark out there, and we're not exactly dressed for night hiking." Now that I've mentioned it, I realize I'm cold. The temperature isn't anywhere near freezing, but it's still not sweatshirt-and-shorts weather. Not in the middle of the night.

His shadow shifts, and then there's a scraping noise. A moment later, a warm glow blooms on a nearby table as a lantern comes to life. The light illuminates the front of his form. He's dressed the same as before, too, in a t-shirt and shorts.

"Aren't you cold?" I ask.

"Just a little."

"Why didn't you bring a jacket?"

"I did."

"So . . ." I begin, but then an awful realization hits. I turn and search the shadows for my backpack. But I don't see anything. I bend down and sweep my hands over the area. In desperation, I get on my hands and knees, crawling in the dirt as I pat at the ground. "Where is it?"

"Maybe someone stole our bags."

"Both of them? At once? When they probably have their own to carry as well?" Standing up, I brush my hands off on my shorts.

"Could be bandits."

"Are you serious? Backpack bandits?"

"It's more probable than bears."

"Who said bears stole them?"

"Hey, this is your Reverie. I don't know *what* you're going to do with it. We could be going into a full-on Goldilocks scenario here."

"Goldilocks was the thief, not the bears," I say, trying to wrap my head around his words. "What do you mean it's my Reverie? What the hell is a Reverie?"

He picks up the lantern. As the light swings, the shadows shift, making me feel a little dizzy. "What does it sound like?"

"A dream," I say, then shake my head quickly. "But you keep saying it's not a dream."

"It's not. You're not asleep."

"Right. My brain is just misfiring all over the place. Am I lying somewhere right now, peeing my pants while I moan incoherently?"

Even in the dim light, I can see the quirk of his eyebrow. "Did that happen before?"

"Before?"

"With your other Reveries."

I blink at him. "You mean . . . with the zombies and the dragon?"

"You catch on quick." He holds the lantern out in front of him, as if pointing the way. "Let's go. We can talk on the way."

"On the way to what?"

"The end."

I cough. "Excuse me?"

He lets out a humourless chuckle. "Sorry. Bad choice of words. I should've said 'the ending.'"

"Okay, the ending of what?"

"You coming?"

A frustrated sigh escapes me. "I guess I have to, don't I?"

"You don't *have* to. But it won't be much fun if you quit before you've even started."

"Are Reveries supposed to be fun?"

"Yes."

"Then I didn't do them right."

He laughs. "You did fine. But they're more fun when you know what they are . . . and what they aren't."

"They aren't dreams. I get it."

"Do you?"

"Not really, but you keep saying it, so . . ."

He smiles, his features striking in the golden lantern light. Then he starts to walk, heading in the direction of the toilets. I scurry to catch up, edging around the tables while I still have enough light to see them. When I reach his side, I peer ahead of us, noticing that the small buildings are no longer there. Neither is the smell.

"What the . . . ?" I whisper. "Where did they go?"

"Just go with it."

"But—"

"Think of it as my gift to you. The destinking of the night."

"Cash—"

"Lincoln."

"Okay," I say, grabbing his arm and bringing him to a stop. "What the hell is this thing with your name? Your first name is Cash, right? So why do you keep telling me to call you Lincoln?"

"It's a touchstone." He peers at me in the swaying golden light. "It's supposed to be like a signpost. So you know you're in the Reverie."

"Why would that help? I don't even know what a Reverie is!"

"I know. That's my fault. I sort of screwed this up." He smiles ruefully. "Not even 'sort of.' But, to be fair, I'm new at this."

"New at what? Messing with girls you barely know?"

"I know you better than you think, Sadie."

I shake my head. "That sounds totally creepy. You've only known me since March."

"Technically, yes."

My eyes widen. "Are you saying you've been stalking me?"

"No." He sighs and runs his fingers through his hair. "Okay. Let's try starting from the beginning."

"The library?"

"No. Before that."

My heart's picking up its pace again. I'm not sure I want to hear his answer to my next question. "How long before that? When is the beginning?"

His mouth twists in a little grimace. "Around five years ago. Give or take."

"What the hell?" I whisper.

"Sorry."

I blink at him in the darkness. "You're *sorry*? You're basically admitting that you've been stalking a teenage girl for the last five years, and all you can say is you're sorry?"

"First of all, I haven't been stalking you. Not exactly."

"'Not exactly' still isn't great."

He shakes his head and starts to walk again. If I don't want to be left behind in the darkness, I have no choice but to follow him. "I was just a kid myself. And it wasn't . . . It wasn't like I was actively watching you. Not back then."

"Why did you need to be watching me at all?"

"Because I'm your Cicerone."

"Um . . . I don't know what that is."

"I didn't either. Basically, I'm your tour guide through the Reverie."

I frown. "So you're . . . like a sandman?"

"No, because that would imply sleep and dreaming." He's quiet for a few paces as he seems to gather his thoughts. "A closer comparison might be a muse."

I snort. "You're my muse?"

His gaze shifts toward me. "You don't want one? I thought you wanted to be a writer."

"Maybe. Before."

"Sadie, are you still letting that so-called teacher live rent-free in your head?"

"She made some good points."

He switches the lantern to his other hand. "Wish you'd thought up a lantern that didn't weigh so much," he mutters.

"What does that mean? I didn't think any of this up. Why would I?"

"Because a Reverie is a place for writers to explore and experiment."

I frown as I think back to the half-finished graphic novel on the dining table. "Maybe . . . *you* thought it up."

He shakes his head. "It's not my Reverie. It's yours."

"So you have no control here? Then what's the point?"

"I do have some control. Ciceroni would be pretty useless otherwise."

I let out a groan. "This makes no sense."

"I know. I'm not explaining it very well."

"Yeah. You suck at exposition."

He laughs. "That's why I prefer graphic novels. A picture's worth a thousand words, right? I don't have to do much to explain something other than draw it."

"Okay . . . so, if you were going to draw this so I could understand it, what would it look like?"

His smile is illuminated by the glow in front of him. "Good question." He nudges me with his elbow, forcing me to take a step to the side. I look down, noticing the shadowy root I almost tripped on.

"Do you know this place?"

"I'm familiar with it."

"But you said it was my Reverie."

"It is. Just like the one with the zombies and the one with the dragon."

I shake my head. "I can guarantee that I would *not* have included zombies and dragons."

"No?"

"No. You must've put them in the dream and—"

"Not a dream."

"Right. Sorry. You must've put them in the Reverie. Because I sure as hell didn't."

He says nothing. When I look up at his face, I see the little smirk.

"Explain it, then," I snap. "I still don't know what the hell is going on here."

"A Reverie is like a dream," he says. "Except you're not asleep. It's more like a daydream. But more intense. And there are rules."

"What kind of rules?"

"Rules about how they end, mostly."

"And how's that? Death?"

He chuckles. "Not usually."

"I'm glad you found getting flambéed so funny."

"I'm not laughing at that. I'm laughing at the fact that you managed to get to that level of intensity in your second Reverie. You know how long it was before I was experiencing anything more than just wandering around, asking people about the weather?"

I frown. "You have Reveries?"

"I do."

"And you have a Ciceroni?"

"Cicerone. Singular. You only get one."

"That doesn't answer my question."

"Yeah, I have one."

I feel my stomach drop as a thought occurs to me. "It's me, isn't it? Is that why you said you've been stalking me for the last five years?"

He grunts in amusement. "No, Sadie, it's not you. Actually, you've met my Cicerone."

"Where?"

"Your writing class."

My jaw drops. "The teacher?"

His laughter shakes the lantern, causing the shadows around us to sway crazily. "No, not her. Thank god."

"Then who?"

"Ritch."

I frown as I try to remember. "The nice old guy?"

He nods with a smile. "That's him."

"How long have you known him?"

"Technically, since I was thirteen. But I didn't meet him in person until a couple of years ago."

"Wait," I say, shaking my head slowly to try to clear it. "What do you mean? How did you know him if you hadn't met him?"

He switches the lantern back to his other hand. "We met in dreams."

"I thought you said Reveries weren't dreams!"

"They're not. But sometimes the connection between Ciceroni and their charges is first made in the dream state."

I blink. "Were you in my dreams?"

The smile that tweaks at his lips is all the answer I need.

"Gross! Are you serious?"

"What?"

"So I'm just supposed to be okay with some guy invading a young girl's dreams?"

"I'm only a year older than you. And there was never anything . . ."

"Dirty?"

"I was going to say 'inappropriate,' but that works, too." He shakes his head. "I was mostly just observing. Sometimes I interacted with you. Said hello. Little things like that."

"I don't remember anything."

"They weren't really memorable interactions. Not like what Ritch did the first time I encountered him in a dream."

"Why? What did he do?"

"Basically came right out and explained everything. Spectacularly, I might add. Gave himself wings and came soaring out of the sky, when I was just sitting in the middle of the school rugby field playing with a pack of puppies."

I snort. "You expect me to believe that's what teenage boys dream about?"

He turns to me with an amused lift of his eyebrows. "What do you think they dream about?"

"I don't know. Isn't it pretty much sex after you hit puberty?"

"Nice, Sadie."

"Isn't it?"

"No. So, there I was, playing with these puppies, and this massive angel comes swooping out of the sky. He lands right in front of me, and all the dogs go running over to him, so I kind of had to pay attention."

"What did he say?"

He clears his throat and lifts his free hand in a dramatic swoop. "'Cashel Lincoln! You have been chosen.'"

I grunt. "Seriously?"

"He does have a flair for the dramatic."

"What were you chosen for?"

He gives me a sideways glance.

"For me?"

He nods. "But I didn't know that yet. He had to convince me that he wasn't just a weird dream brought on by too many energy drinks."

"And then?"

"Then what?"

"Then what did he say?"

"He told me I had great things to share with the world, and that I could have a Cicerone if I wanted. The only catch?"

"You had to be a Cicerone for someone else?" I guess.

"Exactly."

"And that's where I come in."

"It is."

"Why me?"

"You want to be a writer."

"I *did*. But so do a lot of twelve-year-old girls. Why did you choose me?"

"I didn't. We're sort of . . . assigned."

"Based on what? And who does the assigning?"

He shakes his head slowly. "I'm still not entirely clear on that."

"Then how did you know to target me?"

"Target?"

"Whatever."

"Ritch gave me your name. We were already connected, though. When I entered into the agreement with Ritch, that's when I started dreaming about you . . . and finding myself in your dreams."

I frown as I stare at the dark trail ahead of us. It just seems to go on and on, with no end in sight. "How did Ritch know about me?"

"I'm not sure. There's some sort of hierarchical structure in the Reverie system. Ritch is higher than I am."

"Obviously."

"Beyond that . . . I know there's some sort of council orchestrating all this, but I've never met them, and Ritch won't give me a straight answer when I ask more pointed questions." The frustration is evident in his voice. I can't really blame him. Even though he knows more about this than I do, he's still being kept in the dark about some things. And I know how annoying *that* can be.

"Okay," I say slowly. "So, let me see if I've got this straight. This is a Reverie. You're my Cicerone. Ritch is *your* Cicerone."

"Right."

"So where is he?"

He shakes his head. "This is your Reverie, not mine. Besides, Ciceroni don't always show up in physical form as a major character. Sometimes they just tweak the Reverie."

"Why?"

"To provide inspiration. That's kind of the whole point."

"Inspiration for what?"

"Stories."

I frown. "So what did you tweak?"

"When?"

"Let's start with the first time. I thought you said throwing the pages into the storm was my idea."

"It was. Most of that Reverie was all you. My contribution was the storm and the after-hours library. You came up with everything else. I just went along for the ride."

"Jane Eyre? Adèle? Gage? The zombies? Sword Guy?"

"All you."

"Bullshit. I don't even *like* fantasy."

"And yet, you came up with a pretty neat premise."

"What about the dragon Reverie?" I ask. "You must've done more there."

"Why?"

"Because it was so violent."

He lets out a grunt of amusement. "Maybe you have issues."

"Shut up! I wouldn't make a dragon attack someone on purpose. And I wouldn't come up with a mirror-faced woman in the first place."

"Mirror was my idea, actually. I created her for my graphic novel."

"The one about the zombies?"

"Yeah."

"The one where you stole the idea from me?"

"I thought you said I was welcome to it."

I fold my arms across my chest and trudge along in silence.

"The dragon and the firestorm came from you," he says slowly, almost as if he's afraid I'm going to snap and bite his head off.

"The dragon that nearly killed you."

He nods. "I'm not taking it personally."

"Maybe you should."

His laugh comes out in a sharp bark. "Really?"

"I never asked for this."

"Neither did I. But who am I to look a gift horse in the mouth?"

I turn to him in disbelief. "How is this a gift?"

He stares right back at me, as if in confusion. "How is it not? We've basically got our own private muses. Someone we can explore our ideas with. It's kind of like having a beta reader, except they can actually step into the story with us. Then we can figure out what works and what doesn't."

"None of this is working for me."

"Yeah, I noticed." He shakes his head. "You know that's why you've been feeling like crap for the last few months, right?"

I jerk in surprise. "What?"

"You fought it from the beginning. You're still fighting it."

"Fighting it how?"

"You didn't want to write that story for your class, did you?" He shakes his head. "That was bad timing on my part. Ritch thought you could use the help, and he figured it would be an easy way to start."

"Why?"

"Because you *had* to write that story. If I'd just popped in with a Reverie when you weren't on a deadline, you might've dismissed me."

"Not if you'd told me who you were and what was going on. Isn't it against the rules to do what you did?"

He shakes his head. "There are no specific rules about that. We can make contact however we like. In hindsight, yeah, I wish I'd chosen a different tactic. But it's not like I knew what I was doing at that point, either. I was just so excited to start working with you properly. I didn't really stop to think about what would happen if you weren't as open to the whole Reverie thing as I was."

"You could've told me during the dragon Reverie."

"I know. But . . . again, crappy timing. By the time I got around to it, you were already freaked out. And then I kind of freaked out, and I didn't know what to say to make it right."

I sigh. "I don't think there's anything you could've said to make it right." We walk for a few steps in silence before I work up the courage to ask the question that's been niggling at me for the last few minutes. "So, are you saying that . . . I'm not crazy?"

"You're not crazy. No crazier than me, anyway."

"And I'm not sick?"

He shakes his head. "The dizziness and nausea happen when you fight the oncoming Reverie."

"But I didn't even know I was fighting it!"

"You didn't want to write that first story in that genre, did you?"

"Well . . . no."

"So there was resistance. It happens."

"You talk like you've seen this sort of thing before."

"Ritch has told me plenty of stories."

"How does *he* know? I thought you only get one Cicerone."

"You do. But a Cicerone can have more than one charge. You think Ritch just sat around for decades, waiting for me? He's been doing this a long time."

I chew on my lip as I let the information sink in. "What happens when he dies?"

"You mean . . . to my connection with him?"

"Yeah."

"It's broken, I guess."

"Looks like you got ripped off, then."

"How?"

"You've potentially got, like, five more decades to live."

"I'm only living to sixty-eight?"

"I'm just saying. Ritch is *old*. He'll be gone long before you. Then what?"

He shrugs a little, causing the lantern to sway. "Then I guess I'm on my own. At least on that side of things. But I hope to have done a bunch of

Reveries with Ritch before that happens. And I'll still have my own charges."

"Yeah, right," I mutter.

"What?"

I turn to glare at him. "You think I want this? Do I even have a choice?"

He's quiet for a few seconds. Then he takes a deep breath. "Yes. You have a choice."

"Okay, then tell me what I need to do to get out of this stupid Reverie. Tell me what I need to do to get you to leave me alone."

He comes to a stop, holding the lantern out in front of us. It's still swinging a bit. Finally, he turns to me with a frown. "Do you hate me that much?"

"I don't hate you. I just don't want to waste my time wandering around fictional landscapes with you when I'm not even going to write anymore. What's the point?"

"A little fun?" His gaze seems to pierce the darkness as he stares at me. "Friendship?"

I sigh. "Lincoln, we never would've been friends in real life, so—"

"Why not?"

"Because you're cute." I don't realize what's coming out of my mouth until it's already hanging in the air between us. As my cheeks rush with heat, I look down at the ground, and I realize how close to him I've been standing. I take a little step back.

"What does that have to do with anything?" he asks, his voice gentle. At least he's not laughing.

"I don't know what it was like at your school, but at my school, the pretty people ran in different circles."

"Pretty people?" he says, and even though I'm not looking at him, I know his eyebrows are high.

I shrug. "They didn't exactly hang out with the bookish types."

"Looks and smarts aren't mutually exclusive."

"They were there."

"Sadie, you fall into both groups."

I don't think my cheeks could get any hotter. I know he's just being nice, but that doesn't help the blushing. Good thing it's dark out here.

"Sounds like a real fun school," he says. "And just in case you've forgotten, I'm a comic nerd. Remember?"

I draw my shoulders up a little as I remember when I called him that. He sighs.

"Maybe us being friends would've been a long shot. But it wouldn't have been because you weren't pretty, or because you like to read kissing books—"

"Hey!"

"I'm just saying. If anything, it would've been the age difference."

I let out an amused grunt. "One year?"

"Do you have a lot of friends in grade eleven?"

"I don't have many friends, period." I finally dare to pull my gaze from the ground and look at him. The lantern light is casting weird shadows on his face, making him look much older. When he gives me a sad smile, it's almost like I'm getting a glimpse of what he'll look like in forty years.

"I can't force you," he says. "But I want you to be sure."

"About what?"

"Severing our connection."

I blink. "We can sever it?"

"Yes. But it can't be undone, so I want you to be sure."

My heart's kind of pounding. And as much as I want to say, "Yes, let's sever this thing right now!" there's a part of me that's hesitant. Maybe I just don't want to disappoint him. He's staring at me with this look that's part resignation, part sadness, and part regret.

"Let me propose something," he says at last, when I still haven't opened my mouth in far too long.

"Okay."

"Finish this Reverie with me. Have fun with it. Let it play out to the end. If you still want to break the connection . . . that's fine. I'll accept your decision. But I want you to give this Reverie a chance." He lifts his eyebrows in a cheeky little expression. "I think you'll like it."

"Why?"

"You'll see."

3

IN WHICH
THE INFODUMP
COMES TO AN END

I never actually agreed to do this, but I didn't say no, either. So we continue on into the darkness, in silence, the trusty lantern our only light in a shadowy world. In our island of illumination, time seems to come to a standstill. I don't even know how long we've been walking (although, judging by how my feet feel . . . it's been a while). The woods around us are weirdly quiet, but that's also kind of reassuring. If I were hearing snapping twigs and rustling leaves, I'd be freaking out and thinking about bears.

Stop thinking about bears! If Lincoln's right and this is your Reverie, then you might actually bring them into existence. So, stop it. Think about something else. Think about Spud. Or William. Remember that sceptre he had, and how it turned out to be part of a dragon's hoard?

I shake my head, admonishing myself yet again. The last thing we need right now is a dragon burning down the forest around us.

"Lincoln?"

"Yeah?"

"What happens if I'm afraid of something?"

He glances at me before switching the lantern to his other hand, shaking out the free one. "You face your fear, I guess."

"No, I mean . . . if I'm afraid of bears, am I going to make one appear?"

"Are you afraid of bears?"

"Will you just answer the question?"

He shakes his head. "I mean, it's possible. But now that you know you're in a Reverie, there's less chance for accidental bear creation."

"Is that the same as accidental dragon creation?"

"Pretty much." He smiles. "But you were just using that trick again.

Page into the wind: book character. Page into the fire: book character. There's no wind or fire around here, so I think we're safe for the moment."

I frown. "Elements."

"What?"

"Classical elements. Air, fire, earth, and water."

"Is that the theme you're going with?"

I turn to him. "Is that what I'm doing?"

"You tell me."

With a sigh, I shake my head. "I don't even know how that would work. How do you throw a page into the earth?"

"I don't know. Throw it into a hole?"

I suck in a quick breath. "Or bury it."

"See? You know what to do."

"In case you haven't noticed, we aren't exactly awash in books here. Even if I'd had one in my backpack, that's gone, so . . ."

"I used a flyer for the ring."

"Do you see any junk mail just lying around?"

He chuckles. "Fair enough. We'll have to wait to test your theory."

"Wait for what? And where the hell are we going? Are you going to make me walk all night?"

He comes to a stop. "Right. We should get some rest."

I snort. "Where? We're in the middle of the woods. We don't have a tent or sleeping bags. Neither of us are dressed for this, and if we stop moving, we're going to get really cold, really fast."

He sighs, but he doesn't say anything as he peers into the trees to our right.

"What's going on in the real world?" I ask. He turns back to me, eyebrows high.

"The real world?"

"Yeah. Is Djanet trying to wake me up?"

He shakes his head. "She probably hasn't noticed anything's going on with you at all. Time is different here."

"Different how?"

"It's . . . expanded. A second out there is around an hour in a Reverie. A minute out there is a few days in here."

I gape at him. "You're kidding."

"How else would it work? If time ran the same in both places, there would be reports of people falling into weird comas for days at a time." He shakes his head again. "Did you know that you can have a Reverie standing up? You don't even have to worry about keeling over. That's how quick it can be, at least from the body's perspective. The mind, on the other hand, is working like crazy."

"What happens if someone tries to pull a person out of a Reverie? Like, what happens if Djanet tries to wake me up?"

"Like I said, she probably hasn't even noticed you're in here. You're not actually asleep, for one thing. And, from her perspective, it's only been a few seconds."

"Huh."

"If she *did* try to get your attention . . . I don't know. Maybe you'd just come out of the Reverie. No big deal. Unless you were having an awesome time. Then it would be kind of annoying."

I grunt. "I've yet to have an awesome time."

"Then let's get some rest. Because I can promise you that tomorrow is going to be a lot more interesting. And you won't want to miss it."

I don't relish the thought of resting anywhere in these creepy, dark woods, but he's the one holding the lantern, so I don't have much of a choice other than to follow him as he steps off the trail and picks his way into the shadowy brush. It's mostly evergreens here, but there are a few deciduous trees. It's too early for the leaves to have fallen, so the forest floor isn't too loud and rustly as we make our way across it. He seems to be heading for a large tree in front of us. When I get closer, though, I see that it's actually two trees that have sort of grown together down by the base. He bends down and brushes away some forest debris to make a clear spot for the lantern. Then he gets himself settled, leaning back against the trunk.

"You're not serious," I say.

"What's wrong with this spot?"

"It's a tree. Not exactly a comfortable pillow."

"You'd be surprised." He folds his arms around himself as he raises his eyebrows expectantly at me. I let out a harsh sigh and join him. As I nestle back against the tree, I'm struck by how comfortable it is. It's almost like the trunk is just the right shape for my body.

It's annoying when he's right.

"We should turn the lantern down to save fuel," he says.

"We'll freeze."

"It's not giving off that much heat. If we stay close to each—"

"I'm not snuggling, if that's what you're getting at."

He laughs. "Dang it."

"I can't tell if you're joking or not."

"I'm only half joking. We don't have to snuggle. But the closer we stay to each other, the more comfortable it'll be." He leans forward and does something to the lantern. The flame shortens and dims, but it doesn't go out. As he leans back against the tree again, he starts writhing to pull his arms inside his t-shirt.

"We can share my sweatshirt," I say, and when he turns to me with raised eyebrows, I can just make out the expression in the dim light.

"I thought you didn't want to get that close."

"Not at the same time," I say. "We can have it in shifts."

He shakes his head. "It's okay. Dawn's not too far away. Once we get moving again, I'll be fine."

"You're already shivering."

"Yeah, 'cause it's cold out here. But I don't want *you* to get too uncomfortable. Not when I'm trying to sell you on the positives of Reveries. Kind of hard to do that when it's a miserable experience."

"You think this has been fun so far?"

"No, it's been an info dump. But it was necessary. And now that that's out of the way, we can have a good time."

I lean my head against the tree and tilt it back a little. The stars are just visible between the treetops. "You never did tell me how to sever the connection."

"And I'm not going to. Not right now. I'm afraid you might do something you'll regret."

"Of course you are."

"Can you blame me? Are you saying that, if I told you right this second, you wouldn't just do it?"

"So you're holding me hostage?"

He lets out a groan. "Damn it. I really suck at this, don't I?"

The edge in his voice stops me from speaking the word that was about to come out of my mouth. He sounds frustrated . . . and I don't think it's just with me.

"Never mind," I say. "Let's just do this stupid thing. You can tell me later. And then . . ."

"And then you can sever the connection. I won't stop you."

"That's fair."

"But I want you to give this a fair shot, okay? No half-assing it."

"When have I ever half-assed one of these things? I was all in."

"Yeah, but you didn't know what was going on. Now you do. And you don't really want to be here."

I sigh. "I promise I'll give it a fair shot." Holding out my crooked pinky finger, I turn to him. He just stares at me for a moment before wiggling awkwardly. One hand emerges from his sleeve. As our fingers curl around each other, he gives me a little smile.

"And *I* promise to make it an experience you'll never forget."

"Great."

He laughs and tucks himself back into his shirt. "Just get some rest. We'll get going when it gets light enough."

"How long?"

"Not too long." He jerks his chin to the side. I can see faint silhouettes of the trees in that direction. Must be east.

"Shouldn't we keep moving?"

"You're not tired?"

I am. And my feet hurt. But I'm also cold, and getting colder the longer we sit here.

"Just rest," he says, tilting his head back against the tree and closing his eyes.

I sigh and look at the lantern. The glow is a promise of warmth, but, unfortunately, I can't feel anything. The only heat I can feel is that coming from Lincoln's body beside me. I edge a little closer until our sides are touching. And then I can feel him shivering.

"This means nothing," I say as I lean into him and slip one arm around his body. As I pull myself against him, I can feel our warmth start to meld a bit. He doesn't say anything, even when I rest my head on his shoulder and close my eyes.

I think warm thoughts and will the sun to hurry up and rise.

A loud chirp startles me, and my eyes pop open. For a moment, I'm disoriented. *Where the hell am I?* I wonder, peering around the woods. I can see everything now, although it's not really bright in here. Sunlight sparkles in shafts off to one side as the morning sun lifts into the sky. One hand is clutched around a wad of fabric, and I lift my head from the body it's been resting against. Lincoln smiles a little.

"You okay?" he asks.

"Yeah. Why wouldn't I be?"

He nods and starts wriggling around, getting his arms through his sleeves. I notice the goosebumps on his skin, and the hairs on his arms standing on end.

"Sorry," I say.

"For what?"

"I was going to give you my sweatshirt."

He shakes his head. "Don't worry about it." His attention turns to the lantern in front of us. It's not glowing at all now.

"Did you turn it off?"

"Must've run out of fuel." He braces his hands on the trunk behind us and pushes himself to his feet. "Don't worry about it."

"Won't we need it?"

"This Reverie shouldn't last that long. It'll be over before tonight. I don't want to overwhelm you." He stretches his arms above his head, working out the kinks.

"Too late for that," I mutter.

He drops his arms to his sides and frowns down at me. "We haven't even done anything yet."

"Yeah, other than have an infodump about Reveries. And I *still* don't really understand them."

"It took me a while to sort everything out, too."

I slowly get to my feet, then brush off the back of my shorts. "How come you got such a head start?"

"Because I was only thirteen when I became your Cicerone, and I'd only just found out about the whole thing myself." He tilts his head as he regards me. I quickly reach up and try to smooth down the escaped hairs from my ponytail. But my hair is a mess. I pull out the elastic and try to comb the strands with my fingers. "Ritch advised against contacting you directly right away," he goes on as I struggle to redo my hair as neatly as I can without a hairbrush. "So I was in observation mode for a long time."

"Five years."

"Yeah. And I still wasn't ready, despite what Ritch seems to think."

"How many years do you need?"

He snorts. "Apparently more than five."

"You know, maybe you're not as useless as you think. You just need to get better at picking your moments."

"Thanks?"

I give him a little smile. That's all I can seem to muster. I do feel a bit better after resting, though. I don't know what's going to happen today, but I feel like I'm ready for it. Especially now that I know none of it's real. It's just a story. Sort of like some weird-ass virtual reality game.

We leave the lantern behind as we make our way back to the path. We don't need it, and it looks kind of heavy. Once I get moving, I start to warm up a bit, even though I'm feeling damp and chilled after spending hours in the cold, dark woods. Lincoln stays at a bit of a distance as we walk so he can swing his arms and jump up and down.

"You look like an absolute lunatic," I say.

"I'm just warming up."

"Are you speaking literally or figuratively?"

He lets out a short grunt of laughter. "Both. But this is your Reverie," he says as I groan. "I'm just here to . . ."

"What?"

"Tweak the narrative. Help you out if you get stuck."

I shake my head. "You created this, didn't you? I'm kind of at the mercy of your weirdness."

"Hmm . . . a compliment?"

"Hardly."

He chuckles. "I haven't done much, Sadie. Other than changing the time of day. The overall setting was already here, so you went with it."

"How is *that* exciting?"

"That's where my tweaks will come in." He laces his fingers together and stretches his arms above his head. "But I'll just be following your lead."

I frown. "What am I supposed to do?"

"Whatever you want. Judging by that lantern, I'd say you're leaning toward some sort of historical fiction story."

"We're not exactly dressed for it," I say, regarding his moisture-wicking t-shirt and cutting-edge hiking boots.

He snorts. "That's an easy fix. But I'll let you figure it out."

"Easy? Do you see any tailors or haberdashers around here?"

He raises his eyebrows.

"What?" I snap.

"This is your *Reverie.*"

"Whatever," I mutter, falling silent as we continue to trudge through the trees. He finishes his frenetic warm-up and falls into step beside me.

"You do seem to have a penchant for empty liminal spaces."

"Huh?"

"There's nothing wrong with that. It could totally work in horror or some sort of paranormal thriller. But you probably don't want to get too comfortable with that. It's going to make your job harder."

"Why?"

"Without a fleshed-out cast of characters, it'll be more difficult to create conflict. You're pretty much limited to the protagonist versus her environment. Or herself."

"Or the protagonist versus her annoying companion."

"Enemies to lovers?"

I swat him on the arm before I can stop myself.

"I'm just teasing you, Sadie. Although, that *is* a really popular trope . . ."

"Not going to happen."

He holds up his hands. "Hey, I didn't say it should."

"So when does this thing start?" I ask, folding my arms across my chest. "Because wandering around in the woods all day is not very exciting."

"It's your Reverie."

"So?"

"So . . . if it's boring, that's on you."

"Then what's the point of your presence?"

He shakes his head. "Do you really want me to take over?"

"Are you allowed to?"

"If you give me permission, yeah. But that's not what today is supposed to be about."

I sigh. "I suck at writing. So maybe you *should* just take over. Otherwise, we're going to—" The noise causes me to break off. I come to a stop and stare at him. "Did you hear that?"

"Yeah." He peers ahead of us. It's a little brighter up there. "Come on."

"Are you serious?" I ask as I watch him jog off ahead of me. "You hear a mysterious noise, and you go running toward it?"

He laughs. "Just go with it!" he calls over his shoulder before taking off at a full run.

"Go with what?" I mutter. But I guess I won't find out if I hang back here by myself, so I run after him.

As the trees thin out, the day seems to get a lot brighter. The woods are still all around us, but I can see that a road has been cut through the forest. The trail deposits me onto it, and I stagger a little on the uneven surface. *Cobblestones? Who puts a cobblestone road out in the middle of nowhere?* Lincoln turned to the left when he reached the road, and now I can see him about fifty feet away, just standing there. Something about his posture looks odd, and I immediately get a bad feeling. I rush over to him as quickly as I dare, mindful of the stones under my boots.

"What is it?" I ask when I reach him. He holds up one hand, as if he wants me to be quiet, and I realize he's listening. I don't hear anything other than my laboured breathing after our run. "Lincoln—"

"Shh," he hisses. And, just then, I hear . . . something. I turn to him with a frown.

"What is that?" I whisper, but he doesn't stick around to answer me. He hurries forward, rounding a rather tight curve. I follow more slowly, not at all sure I want to find out what made that weird noise. Maybe because I already suspect what it might be.

And I'm not wrong. When I round the curve myself and take in the scene in front of me, I feel my stomach sink.

So much for a fun day, I think as I step closer.

4

IN WHICH
WE GO THROUGH
A DEAD MAN'S BELONGINGS

Lincoln's already crouched down in front of the sprawled figure. It's a middle-aged man, and he's lying face down on the stones, like he fell there and couldn't get up. As he lets out an awful keening sound, I realize that's what we heard from the trail.

"What's wrong?" I ask. Lincoln shakes his head and reaches forward to grab the man's arm. As he starts to roll the guy onto his back, I notice the clothes. Despite the fact that he's out here on the mountain with us, the guy's not dressed for hiking. In fact, he looks like he'd be more at home in the city. He's wearing some sort of wool suit: trousers and a jacket. A newsboy cap is still on his head, so I can't see much of his hair, but what I can see is shot through with white. As Lincoln manages to roll him over, I see the dark stain on the middle of his white shirt, sort of centred between a pair of suspenders.

"Whoa," Lincoln mutters. He leans forward, into the man's line of sight. "Hey. Talk to me. What happened?"

Another awful wail is the only response. I shudder and wrap my arms around my middle.

Lincoln gently slaps the guy's cheek. "Who did this?"

The man coughs, and I don't think he's going to answer. But then, on the back of a moan, come some words. "It doesn't matter."

"Like hell it doesn't," Lincoln says. His gaze moves to the man's bloody shirt. A moment later, he's got his hands pressed against it. The man doesn't even seem to notice.

"Mechanism," he says. His teeth are bloody. I look away.

"What mechanism?" Lincoln asks. "Was this some sort of accident?"

"No. Bag."

"Sadie."

I turn at the sound of my name to find Lincoln looking at me, his eyebrows raised.

"Get his bag."

"What bag?" I say, but then I see it. It's lying on the side of the road, just a few feet away from the man, half buried in dirt and leaves. I hurry over to it—giving the wounded man a wide berth—and crouch down. The canvas messenger bag is filthy, and when I pull at the strap, I can feel there's something really heavy inside.

"What do we do with the bag?" Lincoln asks, his voice kind of loud considering there's no other noise to cut through. But when I turn back to look, I see the man's eyelids fluttering wildly, and I realize Lincoln's trying to keep his attention. "Hey! We've got your bag. What do we do with it?"

The man takes a deep breath. It sounds wet and gurgly, and I almost gag. "Mechanism."

"Yeah, the mechanism." Lincoln jerks his chin at me. I turn to the bag and flip open the flap. It reminds me a bit of my school bag. In other words, it's a mess. There are loose papers, a pair of leather gloves, a book, and a pipe. Everything seems to be covered in some sort of dried leaf debris. Tobacco? I'm not sure. I pull out everything I can, trying to get to the heavy object at the bottom of the bag. It's wrapped in cloth and tied with a piece of twine. As I lift it out, I glance over at Lincoln. He nods and turns back to the man. "What's the mechanism for?"

The man shudders. "Guard post. Everlea Bend. War."

"What war?" I say, feeling my eyes go wide. I turn to Lincoln. "You never said anything about a war!"

He ignores me and bends closer. The man's eyes have closed. He's still breathing, though; I can hear the awful sound. "What do we need to do?" Lincoln asks.

"Take it to—" The final word is a garbled mess. He tries again, but I still can't catch it. Then he coughs. Lincoln winces as blood sprays into the air. "Stop those damn . . ." But he never finishes the thought. His body goes still as his breathing comes to a final halt, and all the muscles in his face relax. A deep frown creases Lincoln's features as he slowly lifts his bloody hands from the man's midsection.

"Are you serious?" My voice is an angry rasp. "This is supposed to be fun?"

He stares at his hands. "Isn't it?" he says absently.

"Not for that poor guy."

"He's not real."

I stand up, still holding the heavy, cloth-wrapped object. "It's real enough."

He shakes his head. "Don't beat yourself up over it."

"Who said I was?" I say, staring at him in disbelief. "This was *your* idea."

"What was?"

"Him. The blood. This stupid mechanism thingy." I lift it in both hands. "Oh, yeah, and we've got a war to deal with, but we don't even know who the enemy is because this guy conveniently goes and dies right before he can tell us."

Lincoln stands up, holding his bloody hands out to the sides like he doesn't want them coming anywhere near his body. "I don't think that's the important part here, Sadie."

"Then what is?"

He gestures to the dead man. "Somebody shot him, and I'm guessing it had something to do with that mechanism."

I look down at the bundle in my hands. "The mechanism that's now in our possession."

"Exactly."

"This is just great." I let the stupid thing fall onto the bag and all the spread-out crap that was in it. It thuds heavily as it lands on the gloves. Lincoln winces.

"Careful with that."

"Why? It's solid."

"Yeah, and it's also valuable. It sounds like it might save lives."

I shake my head. "What does a guard post have to do with a mechanism?"

"No idea. But maybe there's something in his stuff that will explain it." He frowns down at his hands. "I don't suppose you want to find us a stream or something. This is nasty."

"You're the one who stuck your hands on a gunshot wound. What good did you think that would do? He's been bleeding for a while, and it's not like we're close to a hospital. He was a goner, no matter what."

"I'm sorry that my first instinct was to try to save his life."

There's a harsh edge to his voice that cuts deep. I look down at the dead man, then at his belongings. A weird twinge of guilt hits me in the stomach, right where that bullet started the poor guy on his march to the end. I turn back to Lincoln. "Did I do this?"

He closes his eyes for a moment as he lets out a long breath. "It's fine. Don't worry about it."

"But I just killed a man!"

"You killed off a character. That's not necessarily a bad thing."

"Then why do you sound so pissed off?"

"I'm not."

"Lincoln—"

"I'm not pissed off, Sadie. I'm disappointed."

I blink. "Why?"

"Because you said you wouldn't half-ass this. But you're not even trying."

"I followed you into the woods. I watched you make a futile attempt to save some guy's life. What else am I supposed to do? Cry over a fictional stranger?"

"That would be a start."

I shake my head. "Not going to happen."

"Why not? Don't you ever get attached to characters so much that you cry when something bad happens to them?"

"Sometimes. But I didn't even know this guy. You want me to write him a eulogy?"

He sighs and shakes his head. "Get the mechanism. Grab all his other stuff, too."

"Why?"

"We might need it."

"For what?"

He just gives me a look. With a grumble, I bend down and grab the mechanism. I place it into the bag first, letting it settle at the bottom, before I stuff all the other crap back inside. When I stand back up, hauling the bag by the strap, I realize how heavy the thing is.

"This is going to make me a target, isn't it?" I ask.

"It might."

"Then maybe you should carry it."

He snorts. "Nice, Sadie."

"What? I don't want to get shot."

"You're not going to get shot. Not unless you really want to get shot." He raises his eyebrows. "Do you?"

"Will it bring this Reverie to an end?"

"Is hanging out with me really that bad?"

"It's not *great*," I mutter. But I don't ask him to hold the bag again. I lift the strap over my head and settle it across my body. The weight of the mechanism is heavy against my hip.

"Let's go," he says, tilting his head along the cobblestone road. "We don't know if he was being followed. I'd rather put some distance between that mechanism and whoever wants it so bad."

"How do you know we're not going to run straight into them if we go that way?"

He gestures to the dead man. "Judging by the way he fell, I'd say he was coming from the other direction."

I turn and look back along the road, almost expecting to see a battalion of gun-wielding soldiers rounding the bend. *Stop it,* I admonish myself. *Do you* want *that to happen?* I really do not, so I turn back to Lincoln and start walking down the road. It feels wrong to leave the guy's body there like that, but if he's being followed, we really don't have time to stop and have a funeral.

The day's getting brighter all the time. The sky is a brilliant blue, and the woods surrounding the road are awash in birdsong. It's pleasant. Well, except for the fact that I don't want to be here. And that I'm stuck with a guy who's bloody and kind of pissed off. He won't come right out and say it, but I know he is.

What does he expect? This isn't my idea of fun. Maybe he likes blood and guts and zombies— Shit. There better not be zombies. Or dragons.

"Lincoln," I say as we start up a slight incline. He's still got his bloody hands curled into fists, held away from his shorts so he doesn't get himself too dirty. He glances at me, then turns his gaze back to the road.

"Yeah?"

"Where are we going?"

He shrugs.

"If you're going to be like that—"

"Sadie, I honestly don't know. We're just following the road. Seeing where it leads."

"But you must have some idea what's going on here."

"Why should I? It's your Reverie."

I shake my head. "Last time . . . with the dragon . . . you created the setting. I sure didn't."

"You mean my house?"

"Yeah. I certainly didn't do that."

He nods. "I built a replica of it in your Reverie. But that was just the scenery. You came up with the story."

"Really? I came up with your stupid dog stealing real gold from a dragon, causing the scaly bastard to go on a rampage? And you said you created Mirror."

"Fair enough. I stuck her in there."

"Why?"

"To see what you would do." He turns to me with a frown. "But the dragon storyline was yours."

"Yeah, right."

"Believe me or don't." He shrugs. "That won't change the truth."

"And what's the truth, Lincoln?" My voice comes out sharp. "Okay, maybe I'm not crazy. Maybe all this stuff about Cicerones—"

"Ciceroni."

"That sounds like a type of pasta."

He smiles. "I know."

"Maybe all that stuff is true, and we're just in this giant simulation."

"Are you talking about the Reverie or life in general?"

I just blink at him. He shrugs.

"What? You're not versed in simulation theory?"

"You believe some weird things."

"I've experienced some weird things. I can't exactly live my life in denial about other strange stuff that might be true." He comes to a stop as we reach the top of the rise. Over to our right, through a frame of trees, a stunning sight stretches out before us. I step a little closer to the edge of the road and just stand there for a moment, taking it all in.

"Wow."

"My thoughts exactly," he says, stepping up beside me, though I notice he's careful to keep his grody hands to himself.

Below us stretches a verdant mountain valley, its steep sides covered in trees. At the bottom, winding like a shimmering ribbon over the green velvet landscape, is a river. And off in the distance, its roofs sparkling in the morning sunlight, is a small town perched on the riverbank against a mountain backdrop.

"Come on," I say, turning to Lincoln. "You must be doing this."

"Doing what?"

"Creating this."

He shakes his head. "Why must it be me?"

"Because I couldn't come up with something like this."

"Says who?"

I open my mouth, then close it again.

"Have a little faith in your abilities, Sadie." He steps back from the edge of the road as he turns away from the view. "Look."

I pull my gaze away from the gorgeous valley and turn to the left. When I see what he's looking at, I suck in a breath.

"Are those . . . people?" I ask.

He chuckles. "You sound surprised."

"Well, we don't usually see many." I peer down at the tiny figures moving about. From up here, they look like ants. They're milling about in front of a building. It takes a few moments of squinting before I figure out that it's a train station. "Are we going down there?"

"Why wouldn't we?"

"For one thing, you're covered in blood."

"Maybe there's a bathroom."

"You think so? Judging by the way the dead guy was dressed, I'm not so sure. And that's another potential problem."

"What?"

"The way we're dressed." If I squint a little harder, I can just make out the two distinct types of silhouettes. "I think the women are wearing long skirts."

"Hm," he says, and when I turn to him, he's staring at my legs. My very bare legs, clad only in shorts. "We might stand out a little."

"You think?"

He grunts in amusement. "Could be fun. Want to go scandalize some prudes?"

"Not if it's going to get us killed."

"Why would it get us killed?"

"Thrown in jail, then. And spending the rest of this Reverie stuck in a cell does *not* sound like fun."

"You're having fun now?"

"Not yet."

He shakes his head with a smile, then waves his hand in front of us. "Come on. Maybe there's a stream or something on the way. At least I'll be able to wash my hands. A clean weirdo in hiking boots will probably attract less attention than a bloody one."

It doesn't take very long for me to realize there aren't any streams, though. The road winds down along the side of the hill, with some hairpin turns that must be a bitch to try to manoeuvre a wagon through. My knees are starting to get sore from the beating they're getting as we go downhill. *Never mind the turns. How do you keep a wagon from building up so much speed that it just goes sailing off the side of the mountain?*

We don't say anything as we walk, for which I'm glad. I'm not even sure what to say. I'm not happy about this situation . . . but it could be worse. The weather is good, the air is invigorating, and there don't appear to be any supernatural creatures around. And I've been checking the sky. It's just a clear—and empty—blue expanse capping the tree-covered hillsides that surround us.

The road eventually levels out a bit, right as it makes one last turn and heads toward the station. The surface under our feet changes from cobblestones to wood as we make our way over a short bridge. I stay well away from the edge, because I can see that the gully we're traversing is scarily deep. Lincoln, though, veers toward the side to peer into the depths.

"Well, there's our stream."

"Go right ahead," I say, hurrying to get to the other side and back onto the solidity of the stones. He chuckles and jogs to catch up with me. As we step off the bridge, I glance over at the building. There are a lot more people there now, some sitting on benches, others just standing around.

They're all staring at us.

"Good morrow!" Lincoln says, raising one bloody hand to wave. I grab his elbow and yank his arm down.

"What are you doing?"

"Being friendly. Why?"

"You look like a friendly serial killer."

He grunts, amused. "They probably just think I'm wearing gloves."

"I doubt it." I glance over at the people. Nobody has answered his greeting. They're just gawking at us. I notice a couple of women lean their heads together, mouths hidden behind hands. "Great."

"What?"

"We'll be the talk of the town."

"Hardly. It's not like we've got green skin and tentacles."

I turn to him, my eyes wide. "Don't you dare."

He holds up his hands. "I wouldn't dream of it."

"Let's find some water," I say, watching his hands fall back to his sides. The blood looks dry now, but it's still really obvious. "Do you think there's running water in the station?"

His eyebrows rise. "Do you?"

"It doesn't matter what I think," I snap, watching as his eyebrows move a little higher. "Fine. Whatever. But I have no idea."

"Want to find out?"

"Not really." I glance at the people once more, then turn my attention to the road. It passes the station building before heading off into the trees. But I can see a bare patch behind the building itself, like the ground has been worn down. For some reason, I want to go check it out. And I have no idea why.

"Let's take a break and regroup," he says, striding down the road toward the spot I was just looking at. I gape after him.

"Are you a psychic now?"

He glances back at me with a frown. "What?"

"Never mind." I hurry after him, holding the bag so it doesn't thump too much against my hip. When we reach the quasi-driveway, it's easier to see what's behind the building. And it's not much. The space is pretty empty, except for some piles of discarded junk and a few wooden crates. The crates look like they've been sitting there for a while. Tucked behind one of them, though, almost invisible from the road, is something that twigs recognition right away.

"Yes!" Lincoln says, hurrying over to the old-fashioned pump. It's painted a dark green (or, it was at one time, but a lot of the paint is flaking off) and comes up to my waist. He reaches for the handle, then stops.

"What are you waiting for?" I ask.

"It's going to take more than just a bit of a rinse to get my hands clean." He looks around, then seems to spot something. As he pulls the moldy old bucket from a pile of trash, he glances at me. "A little help?"

"You're the one who stuck his hands on some dying guy," I say, but when he gives me a look, I sigh and step forward to grasp the pump handle. The ground is too uneven for the bucket to sit on it, so he holds the vessel up under the spout while I start to pump. The metal lets out a few squeaks that set my teeth on edge. I grasp the handle with both hands and put my weight into it. Finally, after a few pumps, clear water starts to gush out. A bit of it splashes on my bare legs. It's freezing.

When the bucket's about a quarter full, he pulls it away. I let go of the handle with a sigh of relief and watch as he crouches down on the ground, finding a flat spot to place the bucket. He plunges his hands in, sucking in a breath as he does.

"Whoa. Cold."

"It's probably from a well."

"Probably." He swishes his hands in the water, then begins scrubbing them against each other. "While I'm doing this, maybe you should look at what else is in that bag."

"Why?"

"So we have a little more to go on. We don't know what this mechanism does, or why Everlea Bend needs it. We don't even know about the war."

"Maybe the less we know, the better." I clutch the bag's strap. "People have gotten killed for knowing too much."

"In real life, maybe. But this is a Reverie. It's a story. Some things we *need* to know. Otherwise . . ."

"Otherwise what?"

He shrugs. "Things will get boring."

I snort. "That's not a very good reason to go poking your nose where it doesn't belong."

"In stories it is."

Letting out a frustrated groan, I march over to one of the crates and perch on the edge. I pull the bag onto the surface beside me, then open up the flap and peer inside. All the papers I stuffed back in are a bit crumpled now. I grab a handful and try to smooth them out on the crate.

"What did you find?" he asks, raising his voice to be heard over the swishing and splashing.

"Newspaper clippings." I pick one up and turn it over, searching for any sort of date. I don't see one. What I do see, though, is a lot of text.

Tiny text. And black-and-white drawings. "When did they start using photos in newspapers?"

"No idea. Why?"

"It's just drawings."

He chuckles. "I guess you don't know the answer to that question, either."

"Shut up."

"What are the drawings of?" he asks, ignoring my snark.

"Soldiers," I say, peering at one of the pages. My gaze moves down to read the accompanying text. "'The siege of the border town of Wildermede has lasted now for twenty-two days. As provisions wear thin, the mayor and council have requested aid from the federal government. Such aid has, so far, been withheld, as resources are needed in the east.'"

"Sounds ominous," he says. "What else?"

I shake my head and paw through the clippings. "'Airship service to all Star Cities has now been suspended. The transport companies can no longer guarantee the safety of passengers and crew. Therefore, out of an abundance of caution—'"

"Hold on. Airship service?"

"That's what it says." I hold up the clipping to show him. "There's even a picture."

"I see that." He pulls his hands out of the bucket, holds them out to his sides, and shakes them vigorously. Then he stands up and walks over to join me.

"Don't touch!" I say as I see him reach his dripping fingers toward the paper.

"Sorry." He juts his chin at the bag. "Wasn't there a book?"

Nodding, I plunge my hand back into the bag and pull out the thick volume. It's a softcover, which, now that I think about it, seems odd for a book from this time period. I turn it over to read the title. "Oh."

"What?"

"It's a catalogue." I frown as I read the ornate text on the front. "*J. R. Livingston and Sons: Fine Apparel for Gentlemen and Ladies.*"

He points a wet finger at something in the upper left corner. I suck in a breath.

"We're in eighteen ninety-four?"

"Looks like it. Or thereabouts. We don't know how current this catalogue is."

I shake my head slowly. "What war was going on here in the eighteen-nineties?"

"None that I know of. But it's fiction, Sadie."

"Right," I say absently, flipping open the catalogue. The pages are full of ornate drawings showing various articles of clothing.

"You know what this means, right?"

"That I created some historically inaccurate Reverie because I don't know what I'm doing?"

He shakes his head. "There's no reason a Reverie has to be historically accurate. Especially if it's steampunk."

I cough and stare up at him. "It's what?"

"Steampunk. The airship thing was a dead giveaway. The date pretty much confirms it."

"But . . . they really did use airships back then, right?"

"Not on the kind of scale that article is implying. And not so much on this side of the country. I think it was more of an east coast thing. Travelling back and forth between North America and Europe."

I turn back to the catalogue, feeling annoyed. "Great."

"What?"

"Another genre I don't like."

He lets out a sigh. "You don't seem to like much."

"So sue me." I flip through a few more pages, then close the catalogue. He clears his throat. "What now?" I snap.

"We should order something."

"Huh?"

"From the catalogue."

I frown at him. "How would that work? It'll probably take weeks for anything to arrive. What are we supposed to do? Just hang around here waiting for our packages?"

"Find something you want," he says, as if I haven't just pointed out the very obvious flaw in his plan.

"Are you serious?"

"Yes, I'm serious. It's worth a try."

"What is?"

"Remember what you said about the elements?"

"Vaguely."

He rolls his eyes. "Pick a page. Bury it. See what happens."

I open my mouth to retort, but find I don't have a comeback.

"It's logical to think it might work. It worked with the storm. It worked with the fire. It might work with the earth."

"How do you know it's not water we're dealing with?"

"Do you see any water around here?"

I point at the bucket.

"Only one way to find out, then." He juts his chin at the catalogue. "Pick something. If we want to fit in, we'll need something else to wear."

The only reason I start to flip through the catalogue again is that I figure the sooner he tries his stupid little experiment, the sooner we can change the subject and start concentrating on more important things. Like the war that's apparently raging all around us. My fingers pause, hovering over an illustration of a woman in a simple outfit. She's wearing a long wool skirt with a high-collared blouse tucked into it. I can just see her boots peeking out from under the skirt. Without thinking too much about it, I tear the page carefully from the binding and hold it out to him.

"You sure?"

"What's wrong with it?"

"Doesn't look very comfortable."

"Nothing was very comfortable for women back then. Back . . . now. Whatever. And I'm probably going to need a corset to fit into this stupid outfit, so just shut up and do your thing."

"My thing?" He shakes his head. "This trick with the pages was your—"

"My idea. Yeah, yeah, yeah." I set the catalogue on the pile of newspaper clippings and slide off the crate.

"Better check the back," he says.

"Why?"

"Because we don't want any surprises."

With that less-than-reassuring thought, I flip the page over. "It's just another page of clothes. I don't need more than one set."

"Is there a pen or pencil in that bag? Something you can use to scribble out the stuff you don't want?"

"Would that even work?"

He shrugs.

"Not helpful."

"Hey, this page thing is your creation. I should be asking *you* questions like that."

I narrow my eyes at him. Annoyingly, this only seems to cause amusement. So I try to ignore his infuriating expression while I look around at the junk stored behind the station. I soon find what I'm looking for in an old metal bucket. I dig through the ashes until I find a piece of charred . . . something. Wood? It's hard to tell. Bracing the page face down on the crate, I rub the black surface over the paper, obliterating pretty much everything printed on that side. When I'm done, I loosely crumple up the paper as I march over to the bucket. But then I just stand there.

"What are you waiting for?" he asks.

"I don't want to get too close. What if the clothes just sort of explode out of the bucket?"

He snorts. "You think you're going to get impaled on a stocking?"

"No, but . . ." Sighing, I turn back to the bucket. I take a deep breath, open my hand, and let the crumpled paper fall. It floats on the surface of the water.

"Maybe it needs to be submerged."

"I'm not sticking my hands into a bucket of bloody water."

He shakes his head, but he steps closer and crouches down to poke his finger at the crumpled wad until it's somewhat submerged. But nothing happens. He straightens up with a grunt, pulling the sodden scrap with him. "Guess we'll have to try burying it," he says, handing over the disgusting piece of paper.

The dirt right behind the station is too hard to do any digging, so we move away from the building and into the trees until we find some softer soil. Lincoln uses his hands to carve out a small divot in the loam while I stand there with the dripping page, pinching one corner between two fingers. The paper is looking a little pinker than I remember.

"Stick it in there," he says when he's got a small depression scooped out. I let the page drop, and it lands with a wet-sounding plop. He quickly covers it over with the dirt he just dug up.

"How long do we give it?" I ask.

He shrugs. "We got the ring pretty quick when I burned the flyer in my sink, so—" He stops talking as a muffled *whump* shakes the ground under our feet. At the same instant, the dirt sort of jumps, almost like there's something down there trying to escape a grave.

5

IN WHICH
WE MISS THE TRAIN
WHILE PLAYING DRESS-UP

I take an alarmed step back from the disturbed pile of soil. Lincoln just laughs.

"Awesome!" As he begins pawing away at the dirt, I shake my head. *This is impossible. That should* not *have worked. And yet . . . you did see a ring pop into existence with a similar trick. Why should you be surprised?*

I feel my eyes getting wider as he brushes the dirt away from a couple of cloth-wrapped parcels. The one on top is larger and flatter than the mechanism, and seems to weigh a lot less when he pulls it from the earth. He stands up and hands it to me. I just stare at it.

"Well? You going to open it?"

"How?"

"Undo the string," he says, thinking I'm asking how to open the thing . . . not how it's suddenly existing in my hands, against all the known laws of the universe.

I gingerly pull on one end, and the bow unties. I unwrap the cloth to find a bundle of neatly folded clothing. There's a blouse and a long skirt. I turn to Lincoln, my eyes wide.

"You look surprised," he says.

"Aren't you?"

He shakes his head. "I've seen weirder." He jogs back toward the station. I want to ask him where he's going and why he's just leaving me standing here in the woods holding an impossible outfit, but he's coming back soon enough, catalogue and charcoal in hand. "Want some underwear?"

"I have underwear."

"Probably not the right underwear." When I glare at him, he laughs. "Oh, come on, Sadie. No half-assing, remember?"

"How is wanting to wear my own underwear half-assing?"

"Don't you want the full experience of living in the nineteenth century?"

"Not really," I mutter. "I'd rather read about it and live vicariously through characters."

He gives me a funny look. "But you have the opportunity to actually *be* those characters."

I shake my head. "I'm not into steampunk."

"Could've fooled me."

"Steampunk and historical fiction are *not* the same thing," I say, my voice coming out sharp.

"I know that."

"Then what's your—"

He holds up one hand. "Never mind, then. But we're here, we've got the catalogue, and the Reverie's still going. Might as well take advantage of it."

"Go ahead," I say as I see him flip through the pages. He tears out one, awkwardly scribbles over the back, then keeps going. "How many clothes do we need? We're only here for today. Right?"

He doesn't answer, but he does find another suitable page before closing the catalogue and placing it on top of the folded clothes in my hands. He crouches down and removes the other parcel from the hole before replacing it with the two pages and covering them with dirt.

"What's in the other package?" I ask, but before he can even answer, there's another earth-trembling thump. This time, I know what it is, so I don't startle.

But it's still extremely weird.

"Probably your boots," he says, brushing the dirt away from the new packages that have appeared just under the surface. There are three there this time. He scoops them out of the hole, grabs the one he set aside before, and nods his head toward the station. "Come on. Let's get changed."

"Shouldn't we stay in the trees to do that?"

"Do you see anyone prowling around back here?"

"No," I admit.

"Do you see any windows on the back of the building?"

"No."

"Do you really want to get changed in the woods and end up with dirt and twigs in your britches?"

"I'm not wearing britches. I'm wearing panties. And they're staying on," I say quickly, because I can see he's about to give me some annoying retort.

"Hey, it's up to you." He starts to pick his way out of the trees. I frown, but I follow. I'd feel pretty stupid getting changed in the woods all by myself. And since I'm definitely keeping my underwear on, it's not like he's going to get a great view of anything.

The second package from the first page trick does turn out to be a pair of women's boots. And they're just my size. Everything turns out to be my size, in fact. Including the undergarments, which Lincoln must've sneakily thrown into the second batch. Along with the cream-coloured stockings, there's a pair of white underpants that look more like Bermuda shorts, a sleeveless chemise, and a thing with laces that I know right away is a corset. I hold it up with two fingers, the same way I did the bloody catalogue page.

"Are you serious?" I ask.

"What?" He pauses in what he's doing, his own pair of underpants in hand. His are a lot more streamlined, in contrast to the boxers he's stripped down to.

"Okay, first of all, warn me before you whip those off to change. We don't know each other well enough for me to see . . . all that."

"'All that'?" he echoes, looking amused.

"Second, I'm not wearing a corset."

"Why not? Didn't most ladies wear them in this time period?"

"Yeah, but that's not the point. I've never worn one. It's going to be uncomfortable."

"A little discomfort might be good. Makes the experience more real."

"That's easy for you to say, wearing what you get to wear."

He raises his eyebrows. "You want me to wear the corset?"

"Shut up."

He chuckles and gestures over to the folded trousers that are sitting on the crate. "I'm serious. We can trade. But once you feel those things, you might change your mind."

"Huh?"

"They're rough wool trousers."

"So what? My skirt is made of wool."

"You've got the benefit of underpants and stockings that cover your entire legs." He shrugs. "I'm serious. We can trade if you want to."

"Do you *want* to stand out like a sore thumb? Besides, we don't know what the laws are here. We might get arrested."

His eyebrows rise. "For wearing each other's clothes?"

"Okay . . . *you* might get arrested. I don't think men dressing in drag was that acceptable in eighteen ninety-four."

"Fair point." He regards the corset. "I can help you put it on."

"I'm not wearing it."

"You think you'll get that skirt done up if you don't?"

I let out a growl of displeasure, because I suspect he might be right. Tossing the corset on the crate, I start to peel off my clothes. We get dressed in silence, aside from a few breath-holding grunts on my part as I try to get the skirt buttoned up. It's fine over my butt, but the waist is weirdly tight. Finally, I give up and reach for the corset.

"You're going to have to help me with this."

"I figured," he says, slipping the second suspender over his shoulder. He's already mostly dressed, other than his shoes. In the cream button-up shirt, dark trousers, and suspenders, he looks like an extra from a movie.

I get the corset positioned around my middle and turn around so he can access the laces.

"You should probably take that bra off," he observes.

"Not happening."

"Doesn't it have a wire? Once I start pulling on these laces, that's really going to hurt."

"It's a sports bra. It doesn't have a wire." I snort. "You think I go hiking in my fancy underwire push-up?"

"I'm not a bra expert."

"Sure you're not. Don't you have a girlfriend?"

He doesn't say anything. I look back at him over my shoulder.

"Or do you?" I say as I start to get a weird sensation in my stomach. The corset's not done up yet, so it can't be that. *Damn it, Sadie. That better not be hope.*

"Yeah. I do," he says. He shakes his head.

"Are you going to tell her about this?"

He blinks. "Should I?"

"Um . . . yeah. If she finds out one day, she's going to be pretty angry that you were hanging out with some other girl."

"Why would she be angry?" He tilts his head. "All you've done is snark at me. It's not like we're . . ."

"What?"

He shrugs. "Friends. We're definitely not more than that. Right?"

"Right."

"So what would she have to be angry about? Besides, how would she find out?"

I'm about to say that she might wonder why he looks like he's sleeping so much, but then I remember what he said about the time differences. It's probably only been a few seconds since he lay down on that bench. Honestly, who would know that we've been traipsing through the mountains, getting roped into some weird delivery as part of the war effort, and dressing in really uncomfortable costumes?

I sigh and turn away. "Just lace it up. My bra's staying on," I add before he can say anything.

After what seems like a lifetime of tugging, I'm feeling really grateful that I was born in the twenty-first century and not the nineteenth. My bra feels kind of bunched under the corset, but I'm not about to tell him to undo the thing so I can take it off. I can barely breathe, anyway; I'm probably not going to want to do much talking at all until the Reverie is over and I'm back in my sweatshirt and shorts.

But the stupid corset does make the skirt fit better. I manage to do up the buttons. And then I have to undo them again while I put on the blouse, do up *those* buttons, and tuck it into the skirt. By the time I'm finished, I feel like a trussed-up turkey.

"Maybe you should do something with your hair," Lincoln says, perching comfortably on the crate beside me and watching as I struggle to try to get the stockings on. I've done this all out of order, and now I can't even bend over. I toss one at him with a growl of frustration.

"My hair's fine."

"A ponytail is a bit modern, don't you think?"

"Well, I don't know how to do a Gibson Girl hairdo, if that's what you're getting at."

He shakes his head as he absently runs the stocking through his fingers. "No need to go that far. A braid should be fine."

I sigh as I pull the elastic from my hair. "Fine. I'll do that. You put my stockings on."

"You sure?"

"Yes, I'm sure. This skirt is scratchy as hell. I'm already starting to itch." I'm pretty sure I should have a petticoat or something, but I don't want to spend any more time on this ridiculous game of dress-up. I remain silent as I slip the elastic around my wrist, then start to braid my hair. He stands up and crouches down in front of me. As he pushes up my skirt, looking unsure, he glances up.

"Don't bite my head off."

"Why would I?"

"For touching you. And I don't think I can manage this without touching you."

I shake my head a little. "I give you permission to put my stupid socks on."

He laughs softly and starts gathering up the stocking so he can slip it over my left foot. "Thank you." He actually gets it on pretty quick, and without any questionable touch, so I start to relax and just concentrate on the strands of hair in my hands. "You know," he says, "I bet the train goes right into Everlea Bend."

"What train?"

"The one that stops at this station." He gathers up the other stocking. "There are people waiting, so it's probably coming soon."

"As long as it's reliable."

"True. And there is a war going on. Who knows if that's had any effect on public transportation?"

"Public transportation?"

"What? It is, isn't it?"

"I guess. I just usually think of buses and subways when I hear that term."

He smiles and finishes, pulling my skirt back over my legs before he stands up. "Guess I'll probably need to put your boots on for you, too."

I sigh. "I feel like a toddler."

"You're not. You're just not very good at figuring out what order you need to get dressed in."

"It's not as much of an issue in our time," I point out, just as I reach the end of the braid. I slip the elastic from my wrist and wind it around the tapered point of hair.

"You should probably put on your underwear first, no matter what time period you're in."

"No shit."

He chuckles. "Hand me a boot."

I reach for one of the pair that's sitting beside me, but before I can even hand it to him, I hear a sound. He hears it, too, and peers over to my left. "What is it?" I ask.

"Just the train."

I shove the boot at him. "Then hurry up! I don't want to miss it. And you still need to put yours on, too. They're not going to let you on with bare feet."

"We've got plenty of time," he says, crouching down so he can slip the boot onto my foot. It doesn't feel right, though.

"Did you put it on the wrong foot?"

"I don't know. Maybe." He slips it off and tries it on the other foot. It's still a bit uncomfortable, but it doesn't feel as wrong. "Better?"

"Marginally." I perk my ears, trying to listen. Above the hiss of the engine and the rumble of wheels, I can hear more voices now, too. Those are easier to hear a moment later, after a final hiss of steam. "Hurry up!"

"Give me a sec." He slips on the second boot, frowning at my feet. "How am I supposed to do up these buttons?"

"You probably need a button hook."

"What the hell is a button hook?"

"What does it sound like? It's a hook for doing up buttons. You slip it through the buttonhole, grab the button, and pull."

He sighs. "I didn't know we'd need one." His gaze drifts to the catalogue. "Think they have one in there?"

"Lincoln, we don't have time."

"We have plenty of time. It'll take a while for passengers to get off and new ones to get on."

"If we miss the train . . ."

"What? You'll have to spend more time with me?" His mouth is twitching. I resist the urge to smack that smile off his face.

"I thought you wanted me to take this seriously!"

"I do."

"Then why can't I be worried about missing the train?"

"We're not going to miss the train."

"We are if we keep arguing about it." I reach for the catalogue. "You put on your boots. I'll try to find a page with button hooks."

He doesn't argue. He grabs his boots (which are the lace-up kind . . . lucky bastard) and shoves them onto his feet. I flip quickly through the catalogue, but so much of what's in it is unfamiliar to me, and I'm not exactly sure what I'm looking for. I don't even know what a button hook looks like up close. Pausing, I lift my feet and peer at them. The boots *might* stay on without doing the buttons up, but if we have to walk a long way once we get to Everlea Bend . . .

"Find what you're looking for?" Lincoln asks, straightening up. I shake my head and let my legs fall. The backs of my heels hit the crate with a bang.

"I can probably wear them like this."

"What if we need to run?"

"We better not have to."

He shrugs. "Hey, it's your Reverie. Judging by past experience, I think we can safely assume that there will be some sort of running for our lives."

"Assume all you like," I say. "But I know what this is now. So I'm not going to let anything like that happen."

"Anything like what?" His eyebrows are rising again. He's enjoying this whole thing a little too much.

"Dragons. Zombie hordes. Or other things we'd need to run from."

"Still. I don't know how quickly you can walk in those."

"So I'll take them off if I need to," I say, sliding from the crate. I take a couple of experimental steps. The boots slip a little around my heels. "Can we go now? Or are you going to—" The shrill whistle cuts me off. Lincoln's eyes grow a little wider. He grabs my hand and starts to run, nearly yanking me off my feet and out of my boots. The dropped catalogue flutters to the ground behind us.

By the time we make it around to the other side of the building, I know we've screwed up. The caboose is already about twenty feet beyond the platform. Lincoln comes to a stop and lets go of my hand, staring after the retreating train.

"Shit," he says, the uncouth exclamation coming out rather loud. But there's nobody around to hear it. The passengers are all gone from the platform. "Think we can catch up?"

"Huh?" I say, turning to him for a moment, then looking back at the train. "Yeah, right."

He walks over to the nearest bench and sits down. But he sits like a twenty-first century teenager, knees spread wide. It doesn't look quite right with the outfit. "Okay . . . we need to regroup." He runs his fingers through his hair and stares after the train. It's pretty small now, and most of it has disappeared around a bend.

"Why? This is stupid. Can't we just end it and call it a day?"

He stares at me. "Is that *really* what you want?"

"I thought that was obvious."

With a deep sigh, he leans back against the bench.

"Catching the train wouldn't have helped, anyway," I say.

"Why not?"

I gesture to myself. "Notice anything?"

He frowns. I roll my eyes.

"I don't have the mechanism. You hauled me out here so fast, I didn't think to grab it."

He lets his head fall back with a groan. "I hope they don't take my licence for this."

"There's a Cicerone licence?"

"No. But maybe there should be. And a test to qualify for it. It would weed out the incompetents like me."

I look at him sitting there, so disappointed. In himself, maybe. In me, probably. *But I never asked for any of this! Why should I feel guilty? He's the one who barged into my life, bringing all the crazy shit with him.*

Slowly, so I don't lose a boot, I walk over and sit down beside him. I open my mouth to say something, but just then, someone comes out of the building. It appears to be the stationmaster. I nudge Lincoln in the arm, and he twists around to have a look.

"Excuse me," he says.

The stationmaster looks over at us, then shakes his head. "You've missed it."

"We know," Lincoln says. "When's the next train?"

"Not until tomorrow." He bends down to pick up a dropped newspaper. What he sees on the front obviously doesn't please him, because he shakes his head again. "Damn warmongers."

"Tomorrow?" I say, turning to Lincoln. "Can we *please* end this? I'm not spending another night here."

"Sorry, miss," the stationmaster says. "I'm afraid we don't allow anyone on the platform overnight."

I'm not sure what he's talking about for a moment. Then I realize he thought I was talking about sleeping on the platform. *Yeah . . . that's not going to happen.*

Lincoln stands up. "How far is Everlea Bend from here?"

"Half an hour."

"Is that all?" I ask, getting to my feet.

"By train," Lincoln says. The stationmaster nods, and I feel my hopes fall into my stupid, loose boots.

"There's been talk of closing this station down. We're so close to Everlea Bend as it is."

"Not close enough," I mutter.

"True enough, miss." He tucks the folded newspaper under his arm and turns to the station door. Keys jingle as he locks it.

"Where are you going?" Lincoln asks. "It's the middle of the day."

"As I said, the next train isn't until tomorrow."

"What about one coming the other way?"

He nods. "Passengers get on here in the morning. They disembark in the evening. I have nothing to do with that."

Lincoln turns to me with a raised eyebrow.

"What?"

"Is this how you think train stations work?"

"Shut up," I hiss. "I am so done. So you need to tell me how to—"

"Good day to you, then," he says loudly, addressing the stationmaster. The man nods, pockets his keys, and strides away toward the road.

"Lincoln!"

"Get the mechanism. We'll have to walk."

"I'm not walking anywhere. I told you, I'm done."

"Get the mechanism," he says again. "I'll tell you everything you want to know while we walk."

I narrow my eyes at him. Then, with a growl, I whirl around and storm away, heading to the back of the building where I left the bag. My boots flop precariously.

"If you're going to make me do this, I'm getting a button hook."

But when I get to the back of the station . . . I'm just so tired. I don't want to do this anymore. I mean, I didn't want to do any of this in the first place. But Lincoln's got this weird insistence on making me follow through with this Reverie. Maybe he thinks it'll be good for me or something.

Presumptuous dick.

I grab the bag and slip the strap over my head. Then I stuff everything back inside, including the catalogue. I think about trying to fit our clothes, which are just lying where we discarded them, but figure that'll be more hassle than it's worth. Still . . .

I kick off the uncomfortable 1890s boots. Then I try to pick up my hiking boots. I have no illusions about putting them on myself, and that just annoys me. Lincoln's going to have to help.

Stupid corset.

But it turns out that I can't even pick up the damn things. Not by bending over. I try crouching beside them instead, and manage to get low enough to pick them up.

"Having problems?" Lincoln asks. I shake my head and keep it turned away.

"I'm fine."

"Want some help?"

"Not if you're going to bitch at me about half-assing it. I don't care about historically accurate footwear, okay? If I'm going to be walking for hours, I want to wear something I can actually walk in. Besides, nobody's going to see my feet, anyway. This stupid skirt is basically a giant road duster." I grab a handful of fabric and give it a little shake. The hem is already filthy.

"I won't say a word," he says, and gestures to the crate. I tiptoe over in my stockings and sit so he can help me put on the hiking boots. To my surprise, he stays silent the whole time. No quips. No jokes. Not a single annoying word comes out of his mouth. I watch as his fingers adeptly tighten the laces and tie the bows. When he's done, he stands back up and raises his eyebrows.

"Let's just do this," I say, sliding from the crate. My feet probably won't fare *that* much better in these (I'm still breaking them in, after all), but at least I won't have to worry about losing them if we have to run.

We better not have to run.

6

IN WHICH
A FLASH
FORETELLS DISASTER

As if in silent agreement, we walk back to the front of the station. Instead of heading for the platform, though, we step onto the tracks and start to walk. I guess we both have the same idea. This is probably the most direct route to Everlea Bend. And there won't be a train sneaking up behind us, if the stationmaster is to be believed. The only thing we really have to worry about is the train making the return trip . . . but we'll be able to see that one coming.

When we go around the first bend, it's like walking into another world. Out of sight of the station, it's so . . . still. Sure, there are birds and what-not in the trees around us, but the isolation is almost making my skin crawl. The iron rails on either side of our path are the only sign that the world isn't completely uninhabited. I tilt my head back and look up into the clear blue sky, taking a deep breath while I do so. Aside from a slight whiff of creosote from the railway ties, I can't really smell much else.

"We going to talk?" Lincoln asks. I glance sideways at him.

"Depends."

He shakes his head. "We'll talk about whatever you want to talk about. Whatever you want to know. Just ask."

"You haven't exactly been forthcoming up to this point. *Now* you want to talk?"

He gives a quick nod, then focuses on the railway ties under his boots. "You're not enjoying yourself."

"No kidding. This is *boring.*"

"Boring?"

"Yes, boring," I repeat, because I kind of can't believe the puzzlement in his tone of voice. "All we've done is walk through the woods, get dressed in some really uncomfortable clothes, and miss a train."

"My clothes aren't uncomfortable."

I come to a stop, my hiking boots scuffing on the wooden tie beneath them. "Are you serious? What's the matter with you?"

He sighs heavily and stops a few feet away before turning back to me. "I'm sorry, Sadie. This isn't going the way I thought it would."

"Maybe because I don't want to be here at all! Nobody ever asked me if I wanted this. And now you won't even tell me how to get out of it."

"I can if you want me to."

"Hello? Yes, I want you to tell me!"

"Okay." He sounds a bit sheepish. I realize that the confidence he usually has is gone, blown out and away like the air from a deflated balloon.

"Okay." I fold my arms across my chest. It almost feels like hugging a rigid robot, what with the corset and all. "So? How does this end?"

"There are three ways to end a Reverie," he says, turning and starting to walk down the tracks again. I don't see why we can't just have this conversation here, but it's not worth arguing about. The more I can keep him talking, the sooner I can find a way out of this; being a little farther along the track isn't going to matter. I jog to catch up, the heavy skirt swinging around my ankles.

"Only three?" I ask.

"Isn't that enough?"

"What are they?"

He stares off into the woods beside us, as if he can't bring himself to look at me. It's almost like he's about to tell me a dirty secret. "The first way is to return to the place it all started."

I frown. "The place it all started? You mean . . . the library?"

"Not quite. In that case, it was the library bathroom specifically. That's where the Reverie started. And when we ran back in there while being chased by the zombies, that's where it ended."

I shake my head. "So why didn't it end when I peed?"

"Huh?"

"I went into the bathroom to pee, remember? Gage followed me in there."

"You have to be in the *exact* same place. Which means—"

"I had to end up in the same barf-decorated stall." My nose wrinkles as I remember. "Okay. What are the other two ways to end a Reverie?"

"The second way—my favourite way—is to simply finish it."

I frown. "Finish it?"

"There's usually a goal. This is like living a story, right? So what's the goal here?"

"Get the mechanism to Everlea Bend."

"Exactly."

"So this will end when we get there?"

"If we get the mechanism into the right hands. Yeah, it should."

I chew my lip as I mull this information over. "So . . . in the Reverie with the dragon, that's what happened? I finished the story?"

"I don't think so. The Reverie didn't end right away when you gave the dragon its gold, did it?"

I think back, frowning. "No. But that doesn't make sense."

"Maybe it does. Maybe you had to give *all* the gold back, not just one piece of it."

"So why did the Reverie end?" I ask, just as the answer comes to me. I turn to him, my eyes wide. "What's the third way?"

"You've already figured it out."

"Death?"

He shakes his head. "Not quite. Impending, unavoidable death is enough to end a Reverie."

"So why didn't it end when you got roasted? That wasn't survivable, was it?"

"It was your Reverie, Sadie. So it had to be *your* death. Not the Cicerone's."

He's looking away again, and I get the feeling there's something more to this. Something he's not telling me.

I'm not sure if I want to know what that is.

We walk in silence for a while. Maybe an hour. I honestly don't know because I don't have a watch. Briefly, I mull over making one; after all, I still have the catalogue, and there might be something like that in it. But would a watch even be set to the right time when we pulled it out of the ground?

The tracks seem to be sloping ever so slightly downward. It's not like I can feel it in my knees or anything, but I can tell the track's not going uphill, and it doesn't seem to be perfectly flat. It hugs the side of the hills, curling through the valley like an iron snake. A weird itch of disappointment is bugging me, and I realize it would've been kind of fun to ride the old-fashioned train. Not much we can do about that now, though.

The woods on our right start to thin out a bit. They seem to be on a bit of a slope. Between the trunks, I can see a lot more light as if there's a clear area beyond. I can also hear something. It's faint, but it's definitely there. I stop for a moment so I can listen without the sound of my own footsteps. Lincoln stops a moment later and looks back at me with a frown.

"Do you hear that?" I whisper. He listens for a moment, then nods.

"Sounds like a river."

"Where?"

He waves his hand. "Probably down in the valley."

"Wish we had a map," I say, heaving a sigh. He gives me a funny look.

"You sure there's not one in that bag?"

"I didn't see one."

"Maybe you should check again."

I roll my eyes. "It's not just going to *appear* there."

"How do you know?"

"Isn't that against the rules?"

He lets out a sigh that sounds rather frustrated. "Sadie, maybe you just didn't notice it before. It could be among all those newspaper clippings."

With a shake of my head, I open the flap, plunge my hand into the bag, and grab the loose papers. Just to show him he's wrong. But, of course, as I start to sort through them, I feel my cheeks warm with embarrassment.

"Find something?"

"Shut up," I say. "It might not even be for this area."

He steps closer so he can peer at the map in my hands. It's not a full map, though; it looks more like a page torn out of a book, then torn in half. I peer at the tiny print.

"Everlea Bend," he says, jabbing his finger at a dot near the middle of the scrap.

"I can read."

He traces his finger along a solid, winding line that runs from the northwest to the south, making a wide curve right near the dot. "This is probably the river."

"It's not the railway line?"

He shakes his head. "I think that's this one." He moves his finger to a bristly-looking line that runs directly from the dot itself. "Everlea Bend is the end of the line."

"So where does that put us?" I ask, tilting the paper to try to read it better. "And why is the writing so damn small?"

"Need glasses?"

"No," I snap. "Is it too much to ask to have a readable map?"

He shrugs. "It's your map."

I open my mouth to retort, but he jabs his finger at the map again.

"There's the station," he says, indicating an even smaller (if that's possible) dot marked as Wind Crossing.

"How do you know?"

"It's the only one on the map."

"Whatever." I stuff the papers back into the bag. "So we're not even halfway there."

"Looks like it."

I sigh. "Wouldn't it be faster to just go back?"

"Go . . . back?"

"To the beginning. The picnic tables at the rest area."

He frowns. "We walked for hours last night. And a few more this morning. We might only be halfway to Everlea Bend from the station, but we're definitely more than halfway there from the rest area."

"Fuck!" I shout, which seems to startle him. And that kind of startles me, since he's usually pretty unflappable. "How do I get out of this stupid—"

"I told you."

"I'm not going to kill myself. Even in here."

"Then you'll just have to play it out."

I take a step toward him, fists clenched. "You presumptuous asshole. What made you think you could just come into my life—no, hijack my life—with this bullshit? I never asked for this!"

"Neither did I."

"But you're going along with it, aren't you? Trying to be some sort of weird mentor-muse, when all I want is for you to leave me the hell alone!"

He presses his lips together and looks away.

"Sure, this Reverie will end. But then you'll be back with another and another and another. Won't you?"

He doesn't say anything. I shove him in the shoulders. He stumbles back, catching his heel on the track. It's a wonder he doesn't fall.

"Tell me how to break the connection between us. Now!"

He takes a deep breath. I brace myself for more evasions, more excuses, as he opens his mouth.

"Kill me."

I'm about to retort when I realize what he just said. My mouth snaps closed, and I stare at him for a moment. "What?"

"You have to kill me off. If the Cicerone dies in the Reverie, the connection is broken."

"For good?"

He nods. But he keeps his lips pressed together. It almost looks like he's trying not to cry.

"Damn it," I say. I storm past him down the track. A moment later, I hear him jog to catch up.

"Sadie, I thought you wanted to know—"

"What good does that do me?" I say. "I'm not going to *kill* you."

"Don't you want to?"

"Shut up." Pressing my palms to my temples, I take a few deep breaths. "That is so messed up."

"A Cicerone's death is not usually a conscious choice."

I drop my hands and turn to him with a scowl. "So how are you still walking around?"

"Maybe you don't actually want to break the connection."

"I do."

"Consciously, yeah. But subconsciously?"

It takes all I have in me not to let out a scream of frustration.

He doesn't say anything else for a long time. Neither do I. I guess there's this unspoken agreement that we're going to finish this thing. Get to Everlea Bend. Deliver the mechanism. There really are no other options at this point.

No other great ones, anyway.

The slope doesn't get much steeper, but the track itself straightens out for a while. Up ahead, I can see a hill that seems to fall right across the track. It isn't until we get a little closer and I squint that I can see the mouth of the tunnel.

"Great," I mutter.

"Claustrophobic?"

"Not particularly. But we don't know what's in there."

He snorts. "It's a train tunnel, not a serial killer's basement."

"It's dark," I say, choosing to ignore his comment, even though it totally creeps me out. "The visibility is terrible. What if we fall into a hole?"

"Wouldn't the train fall into that hole?"

"Not necessarily. It runs on the tracks. We're walking on railroad ties and dirt. If there's suddenly no dirt . . ."

He shakes his head. "I don't know where you got this weird idea about tunnels with pits in them."

"I'm just being careful. I don't know what could happen in this stupid Reverie."

He clears his throat and looks away, seemingly stung.

"It's not like you created it."

"I sowed the seeds."

I open my mouth, then close it again. I just don't know what to say to this guy anymore. And I don't know why I should feel guilty at all. He forced himself into *my* life . . . not the other way round.

Turning my gaze back to the hill in front of us, I peer up at the treed hillside. It's actually a good thing there's a tunnel, because it would be a bitch to have to climb over this hill. It's more like a mountain spine, really. The trees thin out near the top, and it's mostly rocks up there. Down closer to where we are, the hillside is a mass of trunks and roots and fallen logs. Something flashes between the trees, and I blink. A moment later, though, I trip on a stupid railroad tie and nearly go sprawling. Lincoln catches my elbow.

"Careful."

I jerk away. "I don't need to be told."

His eyebrow rises.

"Fine," I snap. "I'll be careful." My gaze moves upward again, to where I saw the flash. There's nothing there now. Although, if it was something metal catching the light, the angle might not be right to see it anymore. "Did you see it?"

"See what?"

"Just . . . I don't know. A flash."

"Like from a camera?"

"No. Like something reflecting off metal."

He comes to a stop and peers up at the hillside. "I don't see anything." With a shake of his head, he starts walking again. "Could be something to do with the railway."

"Like what?" I ask, jogging to catch up.

"I don't know. A railway signal? It's right above the tunnel."

He's probably right. Although, I'm not sure why I would stick that into the Reverie. That's kind of random.

The mouth of the tunnel gets larger and larger, and, as we approach, it doesn't look quite as dark as it did before. I mean, it's still pretty dark in there, but some light manages to illuminate the path for around fifteen feet or so. From this distance, I can also see a bit of a glow at the other end; the tunnel seems to curve as it goes through the hill, which is why we can't just see straight through to the other side.

We get to the threshold, and Lincoln stops. I stop beside him. The air in front of us is cold; I can feel it through the sleeves of my blouse.

"Well?" I say.

"You going to be all right in there?"

I scowl. "What do you think is going to happen?"

"I don't know. But if you freak yourself out and curl up in a corner, I'm not carrying you the rest of the way."

"Why not?" I demand. He stares at me like I should already know the answer.

"You'd probably clobber me if I tried to pick you up."

I sigh heavily. "I'm not going to end up a babbling mess in the corner. I didn't do that when the dragon was roasting you, did I? Or when the zombies were chasing us?"

"Sadie, you weren't exactly in brave mode, either."

"Only 'cause I had no clue what was going on. Thanks to you." I shake my head and step forward. "Let's just do this. I don't want to get stuck out in the woods after dark."

"We'd still be following the track," he says absently.

"You think bears can't follow a track?"

"You put bears in the Reverie?"

I shake my head. "I honestly don't know what I might've put in here. Most of it was apparently subconscious."

"Well, that's reassuring."

"Shut up. You're the one who dragged me in here, so . . ."

He sighs heavily, but he follows me into the tunnel. It's really not very wide, considering a train has to run through it. As we walk, I start to feel the weight of the whole mountain looming above us. I mean . . . it's just my imagination, but it's still not a great feeling. And it sure doesn't get any better as the light fades and we can no longer see the track in front of us.

"Hold up," Lincoln says. His shadowy form seems to stop.

"What?"

"One of us is going to trip."

"No kidding."

A moment later, I feel something on my arm. I flinch before I realize it's just his hand. "Move over."

"To where?" I ask, stumbling in the dark. I reach out my other hand, and my fingers soon brush a cold, rough surface.

"The ties don't extend all the way across. It'll be easier to walk here. Plus, we can follow the wall."

That doesn't sound like the worst idea, so I don't bother trying to think up any snark. I just walk forward, trailing my fingers against the wall. The ground does seem a little more even under my feet. It's just gravelly dirt, but there doesn't appear to be anything to trip us. It's kind of a relief. I realize all my muscles are really taut; I'm wound up like a spring.

I can't wait for this stupid thing to be over.

We walk in silence, listening to the soles of our boots crunch and echo in the still air. The tunnel's curve isn't apparent under my touch, but after a while, I can see a brightening up ahead as the light from outside illuminates the tunnel wall in front of us. A sliver of light finally appears, and we can see the end.

"Sadie," Lincoln begins, "I never meant for it to be like—"

"Yeah, you did. You just didn't think about whether I wanted this or not."

There's a pause. "How was I supposed to know you wouldn't?"

"What? Are most people glad to have some annoying person barge into their lives and force them into some weird-ass virtual reality?"

"Actually, yeah."

I chew on my lip. "Well . . . I guess I'm not like most people."

"No. You're not."

I come to a stop and whirl around to face him. There's just enough light that I can see the expression on his face. He looks surprised for a moment. But then that expression sort of fades into something that looks more like resignation.

"I don't want to fight with you," he says before I can get any words out. "I'm just . . . sorry. Okay?"

"That's a shitty apology."

"I didn't know I'd have to apologize for offering you an experience many writers can only dream of."

"Well, I'm not a writer."

"Yes, you are."

"Stop telling me what I am!" I shout. My voice echoes around us, bouncing off the rounded ceiling. "You don't even *know* me. You think you do because you stalked me in my dreams, but that's just—" I break off, my heart in my throat. I can't tell if I'm trembling or if the ground is. When I realize it's not me, I suck in a gasp of panic. "What's going on?" I whisper, just as I start to hear what sounds like handfuls of pebbles being scattered against a sidewalk.

"Shit," Lincoln says. He steps forward, reaching out to turn me around. But I don't need to be told. "Run!"

I don't need to be told that, either. I just do it. The noise in the tunnel grows, and it sounds like the mountain is waking up with a cranky groan. The ground pitches under us, and I keep falling against the wall. Up ahead, the view finally opens up. The sight of the trees and sky—and even the tops of buildings down in what must be Everlea Bend—should fill me with relief, but the earthquake rumbling through the mountain makes that impossible. There's a massive crash behind us, and I feel the blast of air on the back of my neck.

Oh, my god. Is the tunnel collapsing?

It's now bright enough that I can see the floor of the tunnel, so I pull my hand away from the wall and run to the middle of the space. I really don't like the sound the walls are making.

We burst out into the sunlight. The track stretches ahead, and I can see that it starts to really make its descent toward the town. On our right is a treed hill that slopes downward. On our left is a rocky hillside that looks like it was partially carved away to make room for the train tracks. There are trees on its upper slopes, and they're swaying like crazy.

"Keep going!" Lincoln says, grabbing my hand as he runs past me, his long legs and his apparent panic making him forget that I'm quite a bit shorter and also wearing a heavy wool skirt. But I don't pull away. I hold on tight, letting him pull me along as rocks and dirt shower down from the hillside above us.

I don't really see what happens. It's just out of the corner of my eye.

The next moment, the view looks like it's sliding, as if someone's swiping a picture across a phone screen. The noise isn't nearly as loud as I would've expected. But the violence of this act of nature is terrifying as the landslide hits us.

The last thing I hear from Lincoln is a swear. I hold on tight to his hand as the dirt and rocks tumble us like some sort of perverse washing machine. But it's no use. We can't hold on against that, and an instant later I find myself alone, rolling and spinning as I'm pushed into the trees. It's a wonder I don't hit my head on any trunks. It's a further wonder I don't get buried. A mouthful of dirt very quickly teaches me to keep my lips closed. I reach out with both hands, trying to grab at something to stop my slide. Boulders slam into trees all around me, splintering bark and taking a few of them down with mighty creaks and crashes. And I ride on top of the wave, inexplicably, impossibly, until the insane momentum slows. I reach out and manage to snag a branch, bringing my body to a shoulder-wrenching stop.

7

IN WHICH
I FIND OUT HOW TWISTED
THE SUBCONSCIOUS CAN BE

The feeling of dirt in my teeth makes me want to retch. But my body is too tense to do even that. I squeeze my fingers around the branch, daring to lift my head to look back up the slope. It doesn't look anything like a forest floor anymore. It's covered in dirt and rocks. A few pebbles are still bouncing down toward me, tapping like marbles. But there's another noise, too. Some sort of hiss. At first, I think it's just my ears. But it seems to be coming from behind me. Still holding the branch for security, I crane my neck and peer back. The trees thin out just past my feet, and I can't see much. It looks like the land just drops away. To . . . what?

The river? Remember the map. Did the train tracks come that close to the river?

I turn back to the hillside. "Lincoln?"

There's no answer. I'm kind of afraid to move, certain I'm going to set off another landslide if I try. But it's not like I can just lie here all day, working the dirt out of my teeth.

My hands are filthy and covered in bleeding scratches. I let go with one of them so I can reach up and touch whatever it is that's tickling my temple. Of course, my fingers come back red.

"Great." My groan seems so loud in the still air. I swipe at the wound that must be there, then very carefully let go of the branch with my other hand. Nothing happens. I press both hands into the dirt and haul myself to my feet. The stupid corset digs into my bruised body, causing me to grunt. Amazingly, the bag is still hanging at my hip, the weight of the mechanism letting me know it didn't fall out during my chaotic tumble. "Lincoln!" I shout, then strain my ears to listen for an answer.

Maybe he got knocked out. He probably surfed that dirt wave down the hillside, too. But if his head hit a tree . . .

"Lincoln!" My cries grow more desperate. I start to pick my way back up the hill. The dirt slips under my hiking boots, sending small cascades down the slope behind me. But my movement doesn't seem to be enough to trigger another actual landslide. I use the smaller trunks that are still standing to pull myself forward, aiming for the tracks . . . or where I guess they might've been, because they're probably buried now. Or destroyed. In any case, the evening train is *not* going to be able to get through.

I wonder if they know. What if they don't, and they try to drive that train up here? Will they be able to stop in time? Or will they derail and—

I shake my head. *One problem at a time,* I remind myself. *First, find Lincoln.*

As I crawl up the last few feet and out of the trees, I can see the mouth of the tunnel. Well, the top of it, anyway. The rest is buried. Huge boulders are scattered throughout the area, some resting where the tracks should be. It's probably going to take some dynamite to get rid of them, because a few are almost as tall as me. I stumble on the dirt and smaller rocks, scanning the area, my despair growing. Turning, I look back down the hillside. From this angle, I can clearly see the damage. It looks like about a third of the trees got taken out.

"Lincoln?" My voice is tiny as the view blurs. I wrap my arms around my middle and close my eyes. *I didn't want this. I didn't want this. Did I really—*

A small sound makes me start. I whirl around and scan the pile of dirt at the mouth of the tunnel. But I don't see anything.

"Lincoln?"

Again, the sound. It's so faint, but it's definitely there. And it's coming from behind me. Down the hill. I take a hesitant step, hoping the sound will come again and not wanting to drown it out with my footfalls. For some reason, I feel like I'm being pulled toward one of the still-standing trees. Or maybe the massive boulder that's come to rest beside it. I don't know why; I just follow my instinct and move closer.

And I hear it again.

"Lincoln." I hurry forward, making sure to stay uphill from that massive rock, because I have no idea how stable this hillside is. Probably not very. The noise gets louder as I approach. But I still can't see anything. I round the tree and peer down at the ground. And that's when I can make out the noise.

"Sadie."

It's muffled. But it's definitely my name. I look down at the dirt and spot what looks like something heaving just underneath the surface. Sort of like when we buried the pages, only not as sudden. I fall to my knees and claw at the dirt where I saw the movement. As I clear away a few inches of soil and rocks, a filthy hand comes into view. I grasp it, and it gives mine a weak squeeze.

"You're okay," I wheeze. "You're going to be okay." I let go of his hand and start clawing at the dirt around where I figure his head must be. I'm a little bit off, and I uncover a shoulder first. But that gives me my bearings, and it's only a few more desperate digs with my hands before I unearth the back of his head. His hair is caked with blood and dirt, so I'm careful as I finish pulling the earth away. He stirs, lifting his head a little to turn it toward me. I'm relieved to see that his face hasn't been totally mangled. He still looks awful, though. Through the dirt ground into his skin and the scratches on his cheeks and forehead, I can see that his lips are white.

"Tell me how you really feel," he says, then lets out a pained groan as he closes his eyes.

"What?"

"Are you okay?"

I nod, but he can't see that. "Yes," I say. "Are you?"

His face contorts in an expression that's halfway between amusement and agony. "Does it look like it?"

"You're lucky you didn't smash your head on a tree," I say, moving to pull the dirt away from his back. But then I stop. I don't know how I didn't notice it before. Maybe my brain's half offline or something. Gently, I press my fingers against his back, moving them down his spine . . . until they're blocked by the massive boulder. "Oh, my god."

He opens his eyes and blinks quickly, as if to clear the dirt from his eyelashes. "Sadie, you need to go. You have to finish this."

I turn to him in disbelief. "You want me to leave you here? Crushed under a rock?"

"Is that what happened?" He tries to twist his neck to look back, but he can't seem to move much. He gives up with a sigh and settles his ear back against the ground.

"Does it hurt?"

"I can't feel my legs."

"That wasn't what I asked." I bite my lip and look at the boulder. It's just over four feet high. I don't even want to think about how much it weighs. Even if I could somehow get it off of him . . . what would I find underneath?

"You need to finish the Reverie," he says. "Now."

"But—"

"Sadie, I don't know how much longer I've got. But if I die before you finish, that's it. The connection will be broken."

I don't say anything.

"If you really wanted me dead, that landslide would've taken me out."

"It did."

"No. I mean . . . completely."

The view blurs, then clears as the tears detach and run down my cheeks. I wipe them away with the back of one hand while I reach for his exposed hand with the other. "I can't."

"Yes, you can. Just follow the tracks the rest of the way. You're almost there."

I squeeze his hand and don't say anything. His breathing is laboured, each noisy inhale a scratch on my soul. *You little bitch. Are you really going to do this? Sure, it's not real, but are you really willing to sit here and watch him die? Even in a Reverie?*

"Sadie," he says, his voice choked.

"I can't," I say again. "I never wanted this."

"Then why was I assigned to you?"

I sniff up a wad of snot and look down at his face. He seems to be having a hard time keeping his eyes open. "What do you mean?"

"It's true. You didn't ask for this. You didn't know to ask. But you wanted it. I wouldn't be here with you if you didn't."

I shake my head. "Tell yourself whatever you want. I don't want a Cicerone. I don't want the Reveries. I don't even want to be a writer anymore, so this is all pointless. Worse than pointless," I say, my gaze drawn once more to where his body disappears under the boulder.

"So give it some meaning. Take the mechanism. Finish the Reverie."

"But you'll never leave me alone!" My voice rises into a wail, and I'm aware of how petty and spoiled I sound when I'm not the one lying with my pelvis crushed under a massive rock. "You'll just keep popping into my life, and I can't even fight it without getting sick and wanting to puke. That's not fair!"

He lets out a pained sigh and gives up fighting his eyelids. "I'm not changing your mind, am I?"

"Get them to assign you to someone else."

"I don't want to be someone else's Cicerone."

"Don't say that." I shake my head. I want to pull my hand away, but he's got a tight grip on it. Plus, I'm already rejecting him. Pulling a bit of comfort away from a dying boy seems unnecessarily cruel. "Find someone else. Someone who actually wants this. You'll have all sorts of adventures together, and it'll be great because you'll both want it."

"You wanted it." His voice is little more than a whisper. I shake my head again, then turn away. It's going to be hard enough when I feel his life leave him; I don't want to have to see it, too. But when I register what's looming above us on the unstable hillside, I squeeze his hand so hard that he lets out a little grunt.

We just stare at each other. At least, I *think* she's staring at me, but, with that face, it's hard to tell. Like before, it's just a shiny, silvered surface with only the slightest of contours that suggest features. Unlike before, though, that mask is surrounded by a much more primal form. Her hair looks like the fine underground roots of trees, twisting and turning as if searching for nutrients in the air. Her skin is filthy bark, her clothes little more than a shroud of decaying leaves. As I stare at her blank face, I can feel something radiating off of her, some sort of ancient energy, terrible and awesome all at once.

I remember the flash in the trees before we entered the tunnel. Hot anger courses through me as I glare up at the preternatural bitch.

"What did we ever do to you?" I say, raising my voice as loud as I dare. There's no reaction that I can see, so I'm not even sure if she heard me. "Just leave us alone!"

"Sadie," Lincoln whispers. "What . . . ?"

"Mirror," I say. His hand tightens on mine. "I didn't do this. She did." I shake my head and pull my gaze away from the horrible earth spirit so I can look down at him. "You created her. This is your—" But I have no time to finish the thought. My attention snaps back to the woman as I see her start to move out of the corner of my eye. She raises her arms high. My heart sinks in the opposite direction.

It starts slowly, just like it did before. The trees tremble, causing their leaves to whisper. The dirt starts to shift. Small rocks bounce down the hillside toward us. And Mirror begins to glide. She doesn't even seem to touch the ground, but the dirt is sliding rapidly from beneath her feet, anyway. Lincoln digs his fingers into my hand, so hard that I almost cry out.

"Don't let her win," he says, his voice full of hot desperation. He releases my hand and turns his head away, toward the tree it's come to rest beside. I stare at him in horror, but I don't even have a chance to say anything before a rather large rock smacks into my arm with a blow that goes straight to the bone. I stagger to my feet, but the ground is already sliding out from under me. I look up at Mirror. She's frozen in this horrible pose, arms up and out as if she's commanding all the forces of nature. With a suddenness that makes me suck in a breath, she throws her arms down to her sides.

And the hillside gives way.

A wave of dirt surges through the trees, submerging half the boulder and burying Lincoln almost instantly. I fall back as the wall of soil and debris hits me. Like before, I seem to end up surfing on top of the wave, tumbling and rolling and filling my boots with dirt. But, unlike before, I'm not quite as lucky. I slam, ribcage first, into a tree, and I feel something crack. When I scream, my mouth fills with decay. I can't stop this. It hurts too much to try to grab anything.

And then there's . . . nothing. It takes me a moment to realize I've been swept off some sort of cliff. Out in the open air, surrounded by falling dirt and rocks and leaves, the world seems peaceful once more. I twist and try to look down, seeing the river rush up scarily fast. I squeeze my eyes shut.

Impending, unavoidable death, I remind myself. *This is it. You're almost out. This is almost over. For good this time.*

I brace myself for the jolt back to reality.

– 8 –

IN WHICH
I FIND MYSELF ALONE
IN A STRANGE LAND

My body slams into the frigid water, but it feels more like I've slammed through a concrete wall. I try to suck in a breath to scream, but only water floods my mouth. The skirt grabs my legs, and my boots might as well be made of cement. I pull at the water with my hands, fighting against the weight of everything on me . . . including the bag containing the mechanism, which seems determined to drag me to the bottom of the swift-moving river.

When my head emerges, sputtering and choking, I look up instinctively, worrying about what might be about to rain down on me from above. But the current has already carried me a good distance. Upstream, I can see debris—dirt, rocks, even entire trees—still pouring over the edge of the cliff. The river itself is a mess; I'm surrounded by all kinds of flotsam, and the water is a muddy beige as it carries me away from . . .

Don't think about him. Not right now. You need to survive this and finish the Reverie.

I wave my arms through the water, trying to twist around so I can see where I'm being carried. A tree floats past, bumping against me with painful force. I push away from it, terrified of getting caught on its branches and dragged under. From this vantage point, I can see that I'm coming up on Everlea Bend. Fast. I guess the river doesn't run northwest to south; it runs from the south to the northwest. And I'm heading straight for the town nestled in its curve.

Unfortunately, I don't see anywhere to get out of the water. Buildings have been built right up to the shoreline, their foundations licked by the rushing river. There's an old-fashioned water wheel jutting out into the flow, but I can't see any way of using that to my advantage. I float past, frustrated.

If I don't do something soon, I'm going to bypass the town entirely. Already, the rail bridge is approaching at a dizzying speed. Beyond that . . . I don't know where I might end up. For all I know, there could be a waterfall around the next bend. That would probably mean a quick death.

Then again, that's what I thought about being swept off a cliff by a landslide.

As I get closer to the bridge, I can see that there's a bit of empty shore beneath. It's not much—and it's heavy with vegetation—but it might be my only chance. So I strike out for it, swimming perpendicular to the current, cursing the stupid old-timey outfit. Cursing the stupid modern boots even more. I could probably move better without them on, but I don't have time to try to get them off . . . and besides, I don't know how much walking I'm going to have to do once I get out of the river. I don't particularly want to do it in my stockings.

My toes touch the bottom soon enough, but the current is still scarily strong. I keep swimming as much as I can until I'm able to break free from the force and get my legs solidly under me. As I wade out of the waist-deep water, my skirt tugs menacingly on my hips, like it's threatening to go down . . . and take my underwear with it. I grab handfuls of wool and hold it up as I crash through the weeds and rushes. By the time I collapse onto my knees, I'm sobbing.

Wasn't this what I wanted? The connection is broken now. Lincoln didn't survive that. He's probably coming out of the Reverie on that bench back at the rest area, wondering how he got assigned as a Cicerone to such a horrible person. I swipe at my cheeks with both hands, then look down at them. Despite being in the river, my skin is still dirty, and a dark substance is caked under my fingernails. My hands are covered in scratches, too. I'm sure much of me is; my body is stinging like crazy. And where it's not stinging, it's aching. As I let out a hitching sob, my ribs let me know that I need to calm down.

Fuck. Now I know why people say broken ribs hurt so much. Gently probing the area with my hand makes me suck in a breath. The least that stupid corset could've done was protect me a little.

Who knows? Maybe it did, and I'd be looking at a punctured lung otherwise.

I don't think that's what I'm dealing with here. It hurts to breathe, but that's understandable. Wiping my tears away again, I look around. I'm just to the south of the bridge, close enough to see the rivets on its girders. I stand up slowly on violently trembling legs, wondering what to do next.

I guess the first thing to do is find the guard post. Whoever's there will probably know what to do with the mechanism, so I can pass it off to them. Hopefully, that will be enough to finish the Reverie. If it's not . . .

"Damn it, Lincoln," I wheeze, taking a few halting steps through the weeds. "You drag me in here and then *ditch* me?"

I can imagine his raised eyebrows as he waits for me to process what I just said.

"Mirror is your creation, not mine," I go on. "So don't you dare blame me for that gruesome death. That's on you."

Here I am, bloodied and broken and miserable, talking to a dead guy. I might've wondered if he could hear me somehow, being connected and all. But with that connection broken, I'm painfully aware that I'm really just talking to myself. Trying to make sense of this whole thing that doesn't make any sense, but that has me trapped in its grip nonetheless.

The weeds give way to a low stone wall. I clamber onto it, then stand up, finding myself on a cobblestone street. I pause there for a moment, trying to catch my breath. There's not much activity around where I'm standing—I don't think I've been noticed yet—but that's probably a good thing. I must look awful. I can hear my clothes dripping onto the stones, and the stinging cuts all over my body make me well aware that I look pretty beat up. With a ginger sigh, I gather up as much of the skirt as I can and try to wring it out.

The garment feels a lot lighter after a few well-placed squeezes. The blouse is plastered to my arms, but there's not much I can do about that. It's not that thick, though, and it should dry out soon enough.

I have no idea which way to go to find the guard post, so I decide to just start walking until I find someone I can ask. The river seems to have coughed me up on the outskirts of town, so I aim myself toward where the buildings are the densest.

It becomes pretty obvious that I *have* been noticed when people start giving me a really wide berth. At first, I'm insulted. Do I not look like I could use a little help? But then I remind myself that these people are at war, and they've just found this weird-ass girl limping through their town, bloody and soaked and somehow still dirty even after that spin cycle in the river. For all they know, I could be a spy. A really inept one. But maybe pretending to need help is exactly what a spy would do to get more information.

How should I know? I don't read spy novels.

Damn it. Lincoln's right. My reading tastes *are* kind of limited, aren't they?

After watching the tenth person nearly trip over themselves trying to get as far away from me as the narrow street will allow, I come to a stop. *Maybe I should just go back to the river. I can jump in and let it carry me away. Even if there aren't any waterfalls, I'll eventually get exhausted and slip beneath the surface. Then this whole sorry mess will be over.*

For some reason, though, I can't bring myself to do it. It feels like adding extra insult to injury. My stupid Reverie already killed Lincoln off. If I don't at least *try* to finish this . . .

I shake my head. *Why do I even care what he thinks? He forced this on me, not the other way round. I don't owe him anyth—*

"You lost?"

I blink and break out of my internal conversation. Peering in the direction of the voice, I find a little girl staring back at me. She's young—maybe eight or so—with straight, dark hair pulled back into a braid that's hanging over one shoulder. I would've thought someone her age would be wearing her hair in tumbling ringlets, but her hairstyle doesn't look much different than mine. She regards me with her dark eyes, letting her gaze travel from my head all the way down to my boots. She doesn't seem to care if I catch her staring.

"Kind of," I say. She frowns, still looking at my feet. I look down, noticing that the long skirt has sort of caught on one of the boots, leaving the front half of it exposed. I quickly grab a handful of wet wool and shake it over the offending footwear.

"Where'd you get those boots?"

"Um . . ." I say, not quite sure how to explain. Finally, I just decide to go with the truth. "They were made in China."

"China!" Her eyes light up as her gaze finally returns to my face. She stands up from the doorstep where she's been sitting and hurries closer. I kind of want to run, but I realize how silly that would look. She's just a little kid. "Have you ever been to China?"

"No."

"Then where'd you get the boots?"

"They were imported." I turn and look down the street, as if I might see something—or someone—that could help me. "Do you know where the guard post is?"

She makes a funny noise, sort of like an amused, snorting giggle. I turn back to her with a frown. "Everybody knows where the guard posts are," she says. "You must be new in town."

"Pretty new," I admit.

"How come you're all wet?"

"I came by river."

She laughs. "You're supposed to use the bridge, silly!"

"I didn't have much of a choice."

Her dark eyes are alight as she looks up at me. A moment later, she sticks out her hand, as if she wants me to shake it. "Sadie," she says.

"Huh?" I grunt, taken aback for a moment. *How the heck does she know my name?*

"Sadie," she repeats. "That's my name."

I resist the urge to roll my eyes. "Of course it is," I mutter.

Undeterred, she keeps her hand hovering between us. "And now you're supposed to tell me *your* name."

"Riley," I say, the name just popping out. *Hey, if Lincoln can use his last name, why can't I?*

"Riley?" She tilts her head. "That's a funny name for a girl."

"Thanks."

She just laughs and reaches out to grab my hand so she can shake it. *She's not forward at all,* I think.

"Could you show me the way to the guard post?"

"How come?"

"I need to . . ." Trailing off, I frown down at her. Sure, she's just a kid. But who knows what a spy might look like? I don't want to screw this up. If I don't actually finish the Reverie, I might be stuck here for a while.

I realize there are some questions I really should've asked Lincoln before that stupid mirror-faced bitch went and killed him. There's a lot I still don't know—and likely never will—and some of that information would probably be useful right about now.

"You should talk to Gerald," Sadie says. She switches her grip on me to her other hand before starting to pull me down the street.

"Who's Gerald?"

"He's like my dad."

"Yeah, but *who* is he? What does he do?"

"Oh. He takes the night shift at the northern post."

"Won't he be asleep now?"

"Nah. He's in the tavern."

Great, I think. *So I have to deal with some guard with a drinking problem.* Shaking my head, I grab my skirt with my free hand and try to hold it up a little. It's still kind of wet—and therefore kind of heavy—and it's really dragging on my hips. "You said . . . the northern post? There's more than one?"

Sadie laughs. "You really *are* new in town, aren't you, Riley?"

"Yeah." I let out a sigh.

"Don't worry," she says. "There're only two posts."

Which one needs the mechanism, though? I wonder. I don't really want to ask (and I'm not sure a child like Sadie would know, anyway), but I realize I'm going to have to gather some information. And I need to do it in a way that's not going to get me into trouble. As the thought of getting thrown into some dank, rat-infested prison—unable to deliver the mechanism and finish the Reverie—washes over me, I shudder.

"You cold?" Sadie asks.

I shake my head. "Not really."

"There's a nice fire in the tavern. Sometimes Hube lets me sit beside it, but only if there aren't too many customers."

"Hube?" I ask, praying I've heard her right and the name doesn't actually start with a P. She nods.

"Yeah. His name's Hubert, but we just call him Hube."

"Okay."

She tilts her head up at me. "How old are you, Riley?"

"How old do you think I am?"

She twists her lips like she's thinking hard. "You're dressed like Auntie Hortense. But I don't think you're *that* old."

"I'm probably not."

"Are you forty?"

I'm not sure whether to be offended or burst out laughing. Or maybe cry. *How bad do I look?* I wonder. I haven't seen my own reflection, so I have no idea.

"Thirty?" Sadie guesses again, her voice unsure.

"I'm seventeen," I say.

"Oh."

"How old are you?"

"Eleven," she says. I blink at her in surprise.

"Really?"

She nods sadly. "Auntie Hortense says I'm just a wee speck." She shrugs. "I don't mind. People think I'm younger, so they say things in front of me because they think I don't understand."

"What kinds of things?" I ask slowly, keeping my gaze on the top of her shiny, dark head.

"Things about the war. I don't understand *all* of it, mind, but I understand a lot. More than Auntie Hortense. When I try to ask her about certain things, she says a lady should mind her own business and stay out of the affairs of men." She squeezes my hand and leans a little closer. "I think that just means that she doesn't know the answer."

"I think you're probably right," I say.

She drags me sideways, jerking my arm, and I nearly trip on the cobblestones. The door to the building lets out a squeak and a jingle of bells as she pushes it open. Inside, it's dank and rather dark. And smoky. I cough, feeling my eyes instantly start to water from the haze I can see hanging in the air. The place isn't crowded, but every man in here seems to be smoking something: a pipe, a cigar, a hand-rolled cigarette. I'm probably getting lung cancer as we speak.

"Gerald!" Sadie bellows, causing me to jump and a few nearby men to glare at us in annoyance. I give her hand a shake, and she turns to me with a frown.

"Not so loud."

"He's a bit hard of hearing. 'Specially when he's been drinking." Her face blossoms in a smile. "Auntie Hortense says he's got liquor ears."

I don't really care what her aunt says. I just want the men to stop staring at us. Well, at me. I'm not even sure if it's because of the state of me, or if it's because I'm the only woman in here.

"Come on," Sadie says, dragging me closer to the bar. She clambers onto a smooth wooden stool and slaps her hand on the counter. "Afternoon, Hube!"

The man—who I assume is Hube—turns around, and I suck in a breath. He's got to be one of the most gorgeous men I've ever seen. Tall, dark, and handsome, with smoky green eyes that seem to want to bore into the soul. The only thing kind of wrecking the effect is the hairstyle, an overly combed mass of curls that looks a bit greasy and continues down into ridiculous mutton-chop sideburns. But those eyes . . .

"Out," he says, letting go of the glass he's drying with a cloth to point at the door.

"But—" Sadie begins, but he cuts her off with a smouldering glare that I would not want to argue with.

"You don't need to be in here. The weather's fine."

She shakes her head. "That's not why we're here, Hube."

His gaze turns to me. I feel myself shrink under it. *Damn, he's hot. Too bad his name rhymes with pubic hair.*

"Hi," I manage to get out. His well-groomed eyebrows rise a little.

"Afternoon, ma'am."

Sadie laughs. "She's only seventeen. Not much younger than you!"

Hube's expression darkens, as if he doesn't want to be reminded of his age. It's hard to place. He might only be a couple of years older than me. Sure, he's working in a tavern, but this place probably doesn't have the sort of underage drinking laws that we do.

Does it?

This is so weird. This is all in my head, right? These people are my cre-ations. All of this place is. So if I want to finish the Reverie, do I just . . . finish it? Grasping the strap of the bag crossing my body, I lift my chin and stare that devastatingly handsome figment of my imagination right in the eye.

"I need to find the guard post," I say.

"Which one?"

"That's none of your business."

One eyebrow rises. "Then how do you think you'll be findin' it?"

"Tell me where they both are."

"Why?"

Sadie shakes her head. "She won't tell me much, either, Hube. I think maybe it's a secret."

Hube's eyes narrow ever so slightly. *Damn it,* I think.

"I'm no spy."

"That's what a spy would say." He sets down the glass and tosses the damp cloth over his shoulder.

"Do I look like a spy to you?" Holding my arms out to the sides, I raise my eyebrows.

"You look like you were attacked by a salmon."

My eyes widen. "How big are the salmon around here?"

He chuckles and shakes his head. "Not that big. But I can think of no reason a young woman would be all scratched up *and* soaked to the bone other than a fight with a mighty salmon."

I'm pretty sure he's teasing me. And I'd like to let him. But I'm already really tired of this Reverie and just want it to be over. Besides, how crappy of a person would I be to start flirting with this guy right after losing Lincoln?

"Sadie said I need to talk to Gerald," I say, stepping a little closer to the bar, hoping he'll see the desperation. "Please. It's a matter of . . . national security."

"National security?"

"You're at war, aren't you?"

"Not personally." His eyebrows pull into a frown that somehow makes him look even more handsome. "What's your business in Everlea Bend?"

This is not going well. Trying to fly under the radar isn't working. Maybe it's time for a more direct approach.

"I have . . . something."

"Yes?"

"Something you need."

"That I need?"

"Not you. The town. The guard post. Gerald. I don't know." I sigh. "Can I *please* just talk to him?"

"No."

I turn on my heel and start toward the door. "Then I'm afraid—"

"You can't talk to him because he's not here."

I stop and turn back around. "Where is he?"

"I wouldn't know. Maybe he drank himself into a stupor."

Sadie nods sagely. "The war is hard on men."

"War is hard on everyone," I snap. She looks a little shocked, but she doesn't say anything.

"Where do you come from, ma'am?" Hube asks slowly.

"The name's Riley. And I come from . . . very far away."

"Very far away," he repeats.

"Yes. And I was tasked with an urgent errand. So if you can't point me to Gerald, at least point me to the guard posts so I can—" A strange sound makes me pause. It cuts through the air outside, sneaking into the tavern through every crack and ill-fitting window frame. The other men go rigid, their eyes wide as they look at each other. "What is that?" I whisper.

"Air raid siren," Sadie says, her eyes just as wide as everyone else's.

"Comin' from the south!" a man at a nearby table shouts, jumping to his feet and knocking over his chair. "Them bastards be circlin' us now!"

"Circling?" I repeat, looking to Sadie for an explanation. But it's Hube who answers.

"Our enemies come from the north."

I feel my eyebrows twist into a frown of confusion. "Who the hell are your enemies?"

But he doesn't get a chance to say anything. A crash outside shudders the walls. I feel the rumble come up through my feet. Hube practically leaps over the bar, swipes Sadie from the stool, and bolts through a doorway. The room erupts in chaos as the rest of the men try to follow.

– 9 –

IN WHICH
EVERYTHING
ENDS

"Where are you going?" I shout, trying to stay upright as a bunch of panicked, alcohol-scented men push and crowd past me. But nobody answers. I'm left standing in the middle of the empty tavern. The only thing I can hear is the crackle of the fire, the wail of the siren, and the beating of my own heart.

Okay, now would be a great time to come up with a brilliant idea. Unless you want to be buried in the rubble of this place.

Frowning, I hurry to the back of the space where a couple of grimy windows look out onto a dim alley. I try to peer out, but I can't see much. There's nobody out there (they're probably all taking shelter, like I should be), and I don't see anything above us. Mind you, I can't see very much of the sky, but I would think something big enough to warrant the siren should be large enough to see.

Shouldn't it?

"Riley!" Sadie shouts, and I turn to see her gripping the doorframe, her other hand waving frantically at me. Something yanks her back an instant later, just as a colossal thump and roar shakes me to my knees. I dive under the nearest table as glasses rattle and topple, spilling their contents over the floor before they join the mess with a shattering of glass.

What is wrong with me? Why is my brain coming up with this shit? I cling to a table leg and peer toward the doorway. I can hear the people in the other room, talking softly, and one childish voice rising above it all. I'm tempted to just try to make a run for it, but now that I've created these people—including an innocent kid—I don't feel right just leaving them here to their fate.

Taking a few deep breaths, I try to calm my pounding heart. I'm not going to be much good to anybody if I don't calm down so I can think. If I want to finish this Reverie, I need to get the mechanism into the right hands. Problem is, I don't know whose hands those are. Gerald's? Maybe. But if this mechanism is something to do with the guard post, I might be too late. Everlea Bend is already under attack.

Maybe if we hadn't spent so much time at the train station trying to get all historically accurate, we would've made it here in time. And Lincoln would still be alive, so I'd have someone to bounce ideas off of. He understands these Reveries way better than I do. I mean . . . he should. It sounds like he's been having his own for years.

A prickle of jealousy surprises me. But why should I even care? And why would I even want to be part of a system that assigns a thirteen-year-old newbie as a Cicerone? I missed out on five years of learning because Lincoln was too young (or inexperienced) to really help me out with this.

My fingernails are digging into the wood of the table leg. *Calm the hell down. You don't want any part of this, remember? It doesn't help to be jealous. Just finish and get out of here.*

I barely suppress a groan as I think about coming out of the Reverie back at the rest area. I've still got a whole weekend of camping to get through with my geography class. Great. All I want to do is go home and sleep.

Stupid Lincoln. I mean Cash. Whatever.

"Let go!" I hear a little voice say, and a moment later, Sadie stumbles into the room. I suck in a gasp, sure that, in the next instant, a bomb's going to rip through the ceiling and blast the place into splinters. When that doesn't happen, I shake my head.

"Get down," I order, then hold out my hand toward her. She frowns and tilts her head back, as if listening. The siren has stopped (when did that happen?), and the silence hangs heavy in the space.

"Maybe they're gone," she says.

"Bloody unlikely." Hube appears at the doorway, looking shaken. He jerks his head, sending a flop of greasy curls out of his smouldering eyes. "They'll be comin' back for another round, if it's anythin' like last time."

"Last time?" I echo. "This has happened before?"

"Happens once a week," another man says, stepping back into the room. He looks at the spilled ale on the floor with an expression of regret. "Like clockwork," he adds with a sigh. "Ever since the—"

He breaks off as Hube turns and smacks a hand over his mouth. I blink, taken aback.

"Watch your tongue. You don't know who might be listenin'."

Sadie's nervously clutching the skirt of her dress, her gaze darting between the man and me. Carefully, I pull myself from under the table, trying to avoid the broken glass.

"*I'm* listening," I say. "Ever since what?"

The man's eyes are wide. But with Hube's hand still firmly over his mouth, he can't say a word. I sigh. Enough is enough. I reach into the bag and pull out the mechanism. It's still wrapped in its cloth, but that doesn't stop Sadie from letting out an excited squeak.

"You brought it!"

"You know what this is?"

"Course I do. Gerald told me—"

"Sadie!" Hube barks, cutting her off. She shakes her head and steps closer to me, peering at the lumpy bundle.

"We *need* that."

"We needed it five minutes ago," Hube says, finally letting his hand drop from the man's mouth. He frowns at the mechanism in my hands. "You could've said somethin'."

"I didn't know who I could trust. I don't even know what this is or what it does."

"Then how'd it end up in your possession?"

"Some guy died and left it to me."

His unfairly gorgeous eyes narrow for a moment.

"I didn't *kill* him."

"I didn't say you did." He shakes his head, then turns to Sadie. "You best get her to Gerald, then."

"Thank you," I say, though I don't really mean it. "If you'd just told me where he was when I walked in here, we could've avoided—"

"We wouldn't have avoided anythin'. That siren came from the southern post."

I look down at the bundle. "What is this for, anyway?"

"The posts' turrets can turn. A proper sweep of a hundred-eighty degrees."

"And if they can't turn?"

"Then we can't see who's comin' to kill us. And we can't fire on them with the guns." He jerks his chiselled jaw at the mechanism. "The one at the northern post broke. Gerald's been waitin' on that for weeks."

"Come on," Sadie says, grabbing my wrist. She starts to pull me to the door, but Hube steps in front of us.

"We haven't heard the all-clear yet."

"The guards probably forgot again."

I snort. "That's professional of them."

Hube gives me a dark look before turning back to Sadie. "Do you even know where Gerald is at this moment?"

"No. But Auntie Hortense says he's always in one of two places: the tavern or the whorehouse."

"Shit," I say, and the word seems to startle all of them. I don't really care. "You're going to take me to a whorehouse?"

"That's probably where he is," she says slowly.

"It's the middle of the day."

She frowns. "Why does that matter?"

I close my eyes. *What next?* I think. *Am I going to have to go undercover as a prostitute to try to finish this damn thing?* "I better not," I mutter.

"You better not what?" Sadie asks. Shaking my head, I open my eyes.

"Take me to Gerald. Wherever he is. I don't care." I put the mechanism back in the bag. I am *so* ready to get rid of the stupid thing.

Sadie leads me outside, and Hube doesn't try to stop us. Out in the street, other people are starting to survey the damage. It doesn't look like any nearby buildings got hit, which is surprising, given the explosion that rattled the tavern. In fact, the town looks curiously intact for being under attack once a week. *Plot hole?* I wonder, darkly amused.

"We can't see the northern post from this street," Sadie says. "But the southern post is down there." She points. I turn and follow her finger, peering up at something on the side of the hill, just as she slowly lowers her arm.

"Is it supposed to let off smoke like that?" I ask, staring at the small, dark blotch jutting from the edge of the hillside.

"No." Her voice sounds close to tears. She turns and looks up at me, but her gaze is drawn to something past my shoulder. Her eyes go wide. The people around us seem to notice the same thing, because there's a sudden silence. I turn around, my heart sinking into my toes.

A massive airship is floating above, a dark cloud in the otherwise-pristine sky. It's not directly over the town—it's sort of drifting closer to the steep mountainside that skirts the eastern edge—but it's still menacing enough. It's some sort of zeppelin, dark green with a golden gondola that hangs underneath like deadly fruit. In the sudden silence of the town, I can hear the hiss of steam, the buzz of a propeller, and the slight grinding of gears in its fins and rudder.

"Should we be out here?" I ask, because this certainly doesn't seem like an "all-clear" situation. Just the opposite, in fact. If they drop a bomb on us when we're standing in the street . . . No. I shake my head. They're not actually over us, so we're probably safe enough for now. I turn back to Sadie. "Take me to Gerald."

"It doesn't matter now!" she wails. And, with that, the reality of the situation crashes over me like a wave of dirt. With the northern post out of commission, the town was more vulnerable than it should've been. Everlea Bend was attacked, and it's because I failed.

"Damn it," I say. My head shakes as a hot rage builds up in my core. "Damn it!"

Sadie starts to cry. I can't really blame her. This is her home, and it's just been bombed by . . . I still don't know who they are. Honestly, I don't care anymore. *I just want this to end. Why won't it end? Stupid Lincoln and his stupid Reveries. Where are you now, you lousy Cicerone? You never told me what happens if I get stuck in one of these things!*

"No!" someone shouts, and even though the sentiment is a perfect fit for what I'm feeling at this moment, I know they're not in my head. They're talking about something else.

Something worse.

I look up, just in time to see the hillside directly under the airship seem to explode. A huge cloud of smoke and dirt bursts from the mountain. But it's not the only one. There's a second explosion. A third. A fourth. It takes a few seconds for the sound to carry down the mountainside.

Sadie edges up beside me and grabs my arm. My gaze is fixed on the smoking slope. On the trees that seem to be sliding downward. On the massive wall of earth—as wide as half of Everlea Bend itself—that detaches and starts to roar toward us.

"Oh, god," I whisper. Resignation sweeps over me. Sadie starts to scream and pull on my arm. People around us panic, running into buildings as if they're hastily choosing their own tombs. Death is coming. And this time, there's no escape.

"No!" Sadie screams, with one last mighty tug to try to get me to move. But it's no use. We can't outrun *that*.

The building in front of us explodes as the wall of earth and rocks and trees hits it. I turn and curl myself over Sadie's little form, a futile attempt to shield her with my body. "I'm sorry," I whisper as the mountainside hits me in the back with a terrifying thump.

I let out a little huff of air. *Not again*, I think. *How am I still alive? How do I get out of this . . .* It takes a moment for me to realize that I don't feel like I've just been hit by half a mountain. In fact, I feel really good. The stinging in my skin is gone. My feet aren't aching so much. I can take a deep breath without pain.

Tears spring to my eyes. Tears of relief, yeah. But of anger, too. *That was supposed to be fun?*

My head is still resting on my arms on the picnic table, just like I remember. I keep my eyes closed as I try to compose myself. If I'm being honest, though, I don't really want to have to see Lincoln—I mean Cash—right now. I wouldn't know what to say. "Sorry I left you buried under a landslide" seems kind of inadequate.

I just sit and let myself readjust to reality. I think Djanet's still beside me; I can hear the little scuffing movements of her boots under the table. She doesn't seem to be in any rush to get going, so I'm just going to take a moment. To breathe. To reassure myself that I really am back in the real world. I'm pretty sure I am. There's more noise than there would be in the ruins of a town where everyone's just been killed. I can hear voices as people chat on the nearby path. Birds are chirping in the surrounding trees. My lungs are breathing and my heart is thumping . . . which would probably not be happening if I'd just been hit by a landslide.

It's over, I think, but I'm almost afraid to let myself go there. It's as if it might suddenly not be true, and I'll find myself still tied to Cash somehow, a prisoner that keeps getting sucked into Reverie after Reverie. But . . . it's different this time. Lincoln wouldn't have survived his landslide, any more than I survived mine. I was killed, so the Reverie ended. He was killed, and the connection was broken.

So why am I not happier about it? Maybe I will be, in time, when the memory of what happened isn't still so fresh. Certain scenes from the Reverie—certain sensations—seem to be etched on my mind, and it's going to take a while to move past them. It's sort of like a nightmare; the feeling of dread is always the worst when you first wake up. All you can think about is the guy crushed under a massive rock, his hair caked with dirt and blood. Or the screaming little girl as you curl your body around her just as it all ends.

Tears prickle behind my eyes, and I'm not even sure why. Is it for the Reverie and what happened in there? Is it anger that I had to go through it in the first place? Or is it simply relief because it's over?

I take a deep breath and blow it out slowly. It's going to start getting awkward soon if I let this "nap" go on for too long. So I open my eyes and slowly raise my head, pretending like I'm just the right amount of groggy. Djanet doesn't even look up from her phone.

"Short nap," she observes.

"I . . . guess."

"You ready to go?"

"I am if you are."

She nods absently, but she doesn't put her phone away. I take the opportunity to glance over at the next table. It's empty. My heart seizes a little, but then I remember. *He died, right? He got out hours before you did.* But . . . the way time works in those things, he wouldn't have packed up his stuff and left the rest area hours ago. I haven't had my head down on the table for hours, either.

"When did he leave?" I ask.

She doesn't answer.

"Djanet."

"Huh? What?" She frowns at her phone. "Stupid thing won't install . . ."

"When did Cash leave?"

She shakes her head. "I don't know. A few seconds ago? Why?"

That's all? Wow . . . time really is warped in there. I pull my legs out from the bench and stand up. I would've expected to be shaky, but I don't feel much different than when we hiked up here. A little more rested, actually. I peer in the direction of the trail, then glance at Djanet. "I'll be right back."

"Hold your breath."

I frown as I hurry away, and it takes a few seconds of thinking about it for me to realize she thinks I'm making a toilet run. She doesn't seem to notice I'm not, though. It doesn't really matter; I'll only be gone a minute or so. At least, if I'm able to catch up.

My steady jog takes me through the twists and turns of the path. It's fairly flat in this section, which means I make good progress, and soon enough I see figures on the trail ahead of me. One figure in particular. The sight of the back of his head, uninjured and relatively clean, fills me with so much relief that I feel a stupid smile spread over my face. I break into a run.

He turns around at the sound of my footfalls the instant before I barrel into him, wrapping my arms around his neck in a desperate hug. I don't even know what's come over me. I should be yelling at him. I should be giving him hell for creating Mirror, getting himself killed, and leaving me in an unsolvable puzzle. Well, I guess it *was* solvable . . . but death is a pretty high price to pay for a win. I close my eyes as I rest my chin on his shoulder, revelling in the warmth of life in his body.

It isn't until he gently takes my arms and pulls them from his neck that I realize he hasn't been hugging me back. He pushes me away, carefully, a perplexed expression on his face. My heart sinks into my hiking boots.

"I . . ." My tongue doesn't seem to know what to do. What's the protocol in a situation like this? Do I apologize? Does he apologize to me? My gaze drifts over to the side, and, for the first time, I notice the girl who's standing there. She's around my age—maybe a little older—but the sour expression on her face looks like it might fit on either a child or a bitchy old woman. Actually, she's a bit familiar. I frown as I try to place her. It takes a moment before I realize that I *have* seen her before. Months ago. When I was heading to Cash's house after a morning of confusion and dragons. A much more recent conversation steps forward in my mind, and I feel a rush of heat blast through my cheeks.

The girlfriend.

"I . . ." I begin again. Cash is just standing there, waiting for me to say something, leaving me to try to explain why I'm acting like a weirdo, hugging strange guys in the woods. There's no recognition in his expression. *Nice act*, I think. *Unless . . . it's not.* The connection has been broken, after all. And he never said what would happen. Not exactly. I just assumed that would mean no more Reveries.

But maybe it's more than that.

I take a step backward. Rachael is still watching me, warily. Like she's afraid I might maul her man with another hug. I turn back to Cash and look him right in the eye. He raises his eyebrows ever so slightly.

"Sorry," I whisper. "I'm sorry. I . . . thought you were someone else."

"No harm done," he says slowly. A tiny smile tweaks the corners of his mouth.

"Yeah, but . . . I'm *sorry*."

"It's fine." He watches me for a moment, then turns to Rachael. She hooks her thumbs under the straps of her backpack and starts to walk down the trail once more. He hesitates, turning back to me.

"I'm sorry," I mouth. He frowns, seemingly confused, before giving me a quick nod and following his girlfriend. I just stand there like an idiot until they go around the next bend and disappear into the trees.

My chest is tight as I walk back to the rest area. This time, I know it's anger. But it's not at Cash.

I'm angry at myself.

Wasn't this what I wanted? Wasn't this *exactly* what I wanted? Wasn't this what I bitched at him about through much of that last Reverie, probably making it a miserable experience for him until the Reverie itself took him out?

The connection is broken. I no longer have a Cicerone.

Well, I didn't need one anyway. I didn't even *want* one.

This is what I wanted.

I stop as the trail blurs. *Keep it together. You don't want to have to explain this to Djanet. Besides, how could you ever explain it? You can't even explain it to yourself.*

A few deep breaths push the shaky feeling in my chest away. I wipe my eyes, swallow the lump in my throat, and square my shoulders.

Then I walk back to my classmate, just a normal high school senior on a class trip, ready to do our geography project.

HEAD RUSH

1

IN WHICH
THERE'S A SURPRISE REUNION
IN THE FOOD COURT

The mall's food court is loud enough to make my ears ring. I wouldn't have thought it would be this busy; Christmas is still a couple of weeks away. But it looks like everyone had the same idea I did: Get the shopping done early.

I take a sip of cola, then go back for another bite of pizza. The chairs in here are not exactly comfortable, and my butt's sort of falling asleep. They probably do that on purpose, forcing shoppers to get back out there and spend more money. I wouldn't mind spending more time where I am, though. Aside from the noise, it's kind of great. It smells amazing, and there's so much going on. As I watch the people come and go from the space, carrying trays with a global assortment of foods, I can't help but wonder about their lives. Is that harried-looking mom with the two preschoolers going to snap and start yelling if they don't stop that incessant whining? Will that group of teen boys actually do any shopping today, or are they only here for the sandwiches? Is that lovey-dovey act from the couple two tables away even real?

I smirk a little as I take another bite of pizza, still watching them. The guy is feeding the girl a forkful of noodles. All I can think of is a baby bird getting a meal of worms.

"Is this seat taken?" a voice asks. I blink and pull my attention away from the weird vignette so I can nod and let whoever it is swipe the other chair at my tiny table. But when I look up at the owner of the voice, I nearly choke on my mouthful of mozzarella and dough.

"What?" It's all I can manage to get out. Cash's eyebrows rise in that familiar expression he has, sort of a silent, expectant question.

"Is this seat taken, or . . . ?"

I shake my head. My eyes are wide, and I must look a bit weird, because he frowns.

"Everything okay?"

Carefully, I set the remnants of my pizza back on the paper plate and reach for the already-stained napkin. He's still standing there, waiting for an answer. I take another sip of my drink to try to force down the lump of pizza in my throat. But before I can say anything, he plunks his tray on the table, pulls out the chair, and sits down.

"Busy in here today," he says as he starts to pull the paper off some sort of wrap. I stare at his fingers, desperately trying to figure out what to say. He glances up at me with a smile, just before he takes a bite.

"I thought you wanted the chair."

His nose wrinkles, and he makes an amused little grunt. "You want me to move?"

I shake my head quickly. Automatically. He raises his eyebrows again.

"Because I can, if you want me to."

"No, it's okay. I'm almost done, anyway." I grab my pizza, which is mostly crust at this point, and tear off as big of a bite as I can. But my mouth doesn't seem to be producing saliva anymore, so it's like chewing on a sock.

"Oh." His expression falls a little.

I'm totally confused. When we broke the connection back in September, he didn't seem to recognize me afterward. And I haven't heard from him since. The dizzy spells are gone. So is the nausea. My daydreams have been pretty normal . . . and pretty bland. No more Reveries. No more Lincoln. But that's the way I like it.

So why do I have this weird hope fluttering around in my chest?

"Doing some Christmas shopping?" he asks.

I shake my head. Then I nod. "Yeah. Trying to."

"I hear you. It's all a bit much." He takes another bite of his wrap. A few chickpeas bounce out and land on the tray. "A word of warning: Stay far away from Santa's Workshop, or you'll be sorry."

"Santa's Workshop?" I repeat, blinking like an idiot.

"Yeah." He gestures with one hand, out toward the rest of the mall. "They've got it set up down in the south atrium. It actually looks pretty cool. But you definitely don't want to go down there during business hours."

"How would I go down there during non-business hours?"

"Maybe you know someone who works in the mall."

"I don't."

"Sure, you do." He lets go of his wrap with one hand to pull at the edge of his open button-down shirt, flipping it over to reveal a plastic name tag. My eyes go wide.

"Lincoln?" I whisper, unable to believe what I'm seeing etched into the blue plastic. Suddenly, I don't feel so great. I drop the crust on the plate, noticing that my hand is shaking. *This can't be happening. The connection was broken. But if that's his name . . . How can I be in another Reverie?* "It's not fair!" I blurt out.

"Yeah, I know. It said 'Cash' at first, but then customers thought I was just the cashier." He shrugs, looking amused. "I don't mind if they call me Lincoln."

"Yeah, but . . ." My mind races. How do I even try to make sense of this? I can't just bring up the Reveries and the name thing. If he doesn't remember me, he's going to think I'm totally weird. And he probably still has Reveries with his own Cicerone, so then he'll want to know how I know about all that stuff . . .

I grab my drink, suck down a few fizzy gulps, and place it on the tray as I stand. He looks up, startled.

"Are you—"

"I'm fine," I snap. "I just . . . need to go."

His face sinks into disappointment, but I can tell he's trying not to let it show too much. He picks at the wrap's paper, pulling more of it aside. "Okay. See you later, Sadie."

I jerk so hard, the tray nearly ends up on the floor. "You *remember* me?"

He snorts, and his mouth twitches in a smile. "You think I'd just plunk myself down and start a conversation with a complete stranger?"

"Shit," I whisper, sinking back onto the ass-punishing chair.

"The girl who created zombies, dragons, and corsets out of magical book pages is kind of hard to forget."

"Be quiet!" I hiss, looking around us nervously.

"You think anyone can hear properly over all this noise?"

"I can hear you."

"Because you're sitting less than two feet away." He seems to relax a little as he takes another bite of his wrap. "Nobody's that interested in random conversations in a food court."

"I am."

"That's because you're a writer." He shrugs and swallows. "It comes with the territory."

The automatic denial starts to bubble up the back of my throat, but I push it down.

"Speaking of writing—"

"No," I say, shaking my head. "I want to know what happened."

"When?"

"After the last Reverie. It was like . . . you didn't even know me."

He winces a little, but doesn't say anything as he goes in for another bite.

"The connection was broken when you died. I thought . . ."

"You thought I wouldn't remember you?"

I shrug. "I had no idea. But you had this blank look on your face after I hugged you, so . . ."

He shakes his head and sets the wrap down on the tray so he can reach for the bottle of water sitting next to it. "I've made a lot of mistakes, Sadie."

"Huh?"

The plastic cap cracks as he twists it open. He takes a few gulps, then sets the bottle back down before looking me straight in the eye. "I'm sorry."

"For what?"

He smiles a little. "Do you really need to ask?"

"Kind of. There are a lot of things you should be apologizing for."

"I know. And it's been pointed out to me."

"By who?"

"Ritch." He sighs and picks up his wrap again. "Making contact with you . . . I mean, *how* to make contact with you was always my choice. And I had this whole plan set up."

"What kind of a plan?" I ask, my voice sounding way more suspicious than I intend.

"A grand one. An epic one." He shakes his head. "That's what happens when you give teenage guys free rein with this sort of thing."

"Why didn't Ritch help you?"

"Believe me, he tried. He offered plenty of advice. But I chose to ignore it."

"Advice like what?"

"Be up front about the whole Reverie thing from the beginning. Start small. Get your permission."

I snort. "Fail."

"I know." He shakes his head. "I guess I just had this idea about how things were going to be. I'm a writer, too, you know. Those sorts of grandiose ideas come with the territory."

Nodding slowly, I pick at the piece of pizza crust. "How's your graphic novel coming?"

"It's not," he says. I blink in surprise, partly because of the quickness of his answer.

"I thought it was almost done."

He shakes his head. "I didn't feel right continuing with it. It's not my story."

"Sure, it is."

"Not the best parts. Those came from you."

"So what? It's not like I'm ever going to try to publish anything in that genre."

His lips twist in a sad little smile. There's a fleck of sauce at the corner of his mouth, but I don't bother mentioning it.

"I'm serious," I say. "If you want the page-magic thing, go ahead and use it. You have my permission."

He nods, staring at the wrap in his hands. "Thanks. But . . . it wouldn't feel right."

"Why not?"

He turns his gaze to mine. "You came up with that during our first Reverie together. And a lot of that story . . . It was *our* story."

I shrug, feeling rather awkward.

"I don't know if you noticed, but I was really into it."

"Yeah, I noticed. You were freaking out, even though you must've known what was going on."

He nods. "I was playing a part. Lincoln. I thought that would be a cool way to do things. Make them more intense. You'd get better inspiration for your stories if you thought it was all real . . ."

"So you let me be traumatized by zombies? You thought watching you get burned alive would inspire me to write a masterpiece?"

"When you put it that way . . ."

I sigh. "You realize it was just as intense when I knew what was going on. Especially once your stupid Mirror character showed up."

He nods, takes another bite (even though it looks like he's lost his appetite), and raises his eyebrows. "What happened while I was dead?"

"In the last Reverie, you mean?"

"Yeah. After she brought half the hillside down on me."

I stare at him, aghast. "You know what happened?"

"I do remember the second landslide. Lucky me." He smiles ruefully.

"I'm sorry," I breathe.

"That one's kind of on me. I created Mirror, after all."

The way he's talking about it, almost like he's discussing the weather, makes me feel a little queasy. *Sunny with a chance of being squished by a rock.*

"Did you make it to Everlea Bend?" he asks, breaking me out of some pretty grim thoughts. "Did you deliver the mechanism?"

"It's a long story."

"And you're the only one who can tell it."

I lean back against the metal spindles of the chair. But when that proves to be too uncomfortable, I just shift the tray forward a little so I can rest my forearms on the table. "The landslide swept me off a cliff and into the river. That carried me right to the edge of town."

"So what was the mechanism for?"

"I don't know, exactly. Something to do with the guard post and gun turrets. Hube expl—"

"Hube?" he repeats, his eyes lighting up in amusement. "And I thought I was bad at naming characters."

"Short for Hubert," I say. "Shut up." I don't bother mentioning the little girl that my brain apparently named after myself. That's just cringeworthy.

He chuckles. "So you finished the Reverie."

"No. I died."

The amusement fades from his expression. "What?"

"I got there too late. While I was in Everlea Bend—and before I could deliver the mechanism—it was attacked by an airship."

"Attacked how?"

"Explosives were dropped on the hillside above the town." I shrug. "So I died pretty much the same way you did: under a wave of dirt and rocks."

"Shit, Sadie. I'm sorry."

"I didn't feel much."

"I know. I'm still sorry." He abandons his half-eaten wrap on the tray and fixes me with a gentle stare. "Really. For everything. Up to and including pretending I didn't know you after."

"It's fine. You were with Rachael, so . . ."

"But that's not why I acted the way I did."

"She didn't think it was weird that some random girl just ran up and hugged her boyfriend in the woods?"

He smiles. "I'm sure she did."

"Sorry."

He goes back to his wrap and takes another bite. Now the fleck of dressing is joined by a smear on his chin. I take a breath to say something, but he grabs the napkin from my tray and quickly wipes his mouth.

"Ew. That's used."

"What? You're pretty clean."

In spite of myself, I have to choke back a little laugh. He grins as he crumples the napkin and drops it on his own tray. "Never mind Rachael. We broke up last month, anyway."

"Oh."

"Don't you want to know why?"

My cheeks start to get warm. I shrug casually. "She believes in climate change?"

He snorts so hard he has to drop his wrap and reach for his water. After a long gulp, he clears his throat and fixes me with an appraising look. "Is this our running joke?"

"Climate change isn't a joke."

He sighs. "Sadie, I never said I didn't believe in climate change. It's a real thing. It's the politicization of it that I can't stand." After another swig of water, he sets the bottle back down. "And, no, it had nothing to do with that."

"She doesn't like vegetarians?"

He blinks. "Vegan, actually. How'd you know?"

I gesture at the wrap. "Kind of a weird choice when you have the wonderful world of meat surrounding you."

"Well, it wasn't that, either."

"Then I guess it must be because you let it slip that you stalk teenage girls in their dreams."

He gives me a dark look. It doesn't seem quite right on him somehow. "I wasn't *stalking* you. And the encounters didn't happen very often."

"How often?" I demand.

He studies the shreds of lettuce spilling out of the top of the wrap. "I don't know. Maybe once or twice a year, at first."

"At first? Meaning . . . it was more frequent after that?"

He sighs. "I just wanted to get to know you. Before I swooped in and hit you with all this Reverie stuff. I barely understood everything myself, and I was being assigned as a Cicerone to someone else. It was . . . a lot."

"Sounds like a pretty stupid system to me."

"What is?"

"The whole Cicerone thing. What happens if a little kid gets a Cicerone? Do they expect five-year-olds to turn around and act as virtual-reality tour guides?"

He shakes his head. "Nobody gets—or becomes—a Cicerone until after puberty. At least, that's what Ritch would have me believe."

"You don't believe him?"

"I have no reason *not* to. I guess it makes sense. Little kids can be creative, but they don't always have the language skills to become really good storytellers yet. So what would be the point of the Reverie system?"

"System?"

"There's got to be one. I didn't pick you myself."

"So who assigned us?"

He shrugs and goes in for another bite of wrap. There's not much left in the paper wrapper, other than a wad of folded tortilla. "Probably the Council. Does it matter?"

"Kind of. How did you know to come to me? I thought you didn't have any contact with the Council."

"Ritch pointed me in the right direction."

I snort. "The right direction. Sorry to have to tell you this, but—"

"I know, I know. You don't want a Cicerone. Believe me, I get it now."

For some reason, his words sting. I sigh and grab my cola to take a sip. The ice is melting, though, creating a watered-down drink that's not very appealing.

"So," he says, his voice bright again, "having fun at the mall?"

"Sure."

"Love eating pizza while sitting in a space that sounds like the depths of hell and smells like farts?"

"I don't know what your farts smell like, but . . ."

He chuckles. "Guess you don't mind the sensory overload."

"It's . . . interesting."

"The sensory overload?"

"The people. The setting." I look around, taking in the chaos. "There's a lot going on."

"I'll say."

I shake my head. "I'm doing some . . . quasi-shopping."

An eyebrow rises. "What the hell is quasi-shopping?"

"It's when your dad breaks his leg snowboarding, and you have to go to the mall to scope out the potential gifts he wants to buy for your mom so he can buy them online later. Before they're all out of stock."

"Ah." He finally abandons the wrapper on the tray and reaches for the balled-up napkin. "So you're like an executive assistant."

I snort. He just smiles.

"Where do you work?" I ask.

"The nerd store."

"There's a nerd store?"

He shakes his head. "Phantasmazine."

"The comic book store up on the second floor?"

He straightens up a little. "I'll have you know that we sell a lot more than comic books. We've got video games, board games, dice sets—"

"Nerd store. Got it."

He grins as he grabs his water bottle. "Maybe your mom would like a nice, limited edition orc brooch."

"I doubt it."

"It's gold plated."

"Maybe you should get it for William for Christmas."

He laughs. "Right."

"What? He likes gold."

"That was just something I stuck into the Reverie. After seeing that dragon-kink paperback you were looking at, I figured you might subconsciously throw some dragons into the mix. So I wanted to give the Reverie a goal." He pauses, his water bottle halfway to his mouth. "You realize that my dog doesn't actually hoard gold, right?"

"What does he hoard, then?"

"Socks. He prefer's Dash's, though, so he's going through withdrawal at the moment." He takes a quick sip, then caps the bottle. "How's your little potato dog?"

"Fine. That reminds me, though. I said I'd pick up some kibble while I was out."

He raises an eyebrow. "You know that stuff's terrible for dogs."

"What do you feed William? Tofu steak?"

"I'm sure he wouldn't refuse it." He stands up, startling me a little with the suddenness of the movement. "I gotta get back."

"Okay." I nod, feeling oddly disappointed. And, for some reason, a little bit nauseated. I suck down a mouthful of watery cola, hoping it will help.

"Have fun," he says, giving me a little salute with his bottle. "And remember what I said about Santa's Workshop."

"Stay away from the elves?"

"Something like that." He smiles. "It was nice to see you again, Sadie."

My tongue feels dry. I wiggle it around a little, hoping it'll come unstuck. But when it does, I still don't know what to say. Honestly, I don't even know what to think right now. So I just nod. He returns the gesture as he leaves, weaving his way between the tables to deposit his tray near the recycling station.

Relax. It's over. See? No big deal. You can handle running into a cute guy once every few months, right?

I nod again, as if I'm answering myself. It's not like he could possibly have been trying to engineer an encounter this time. I mean . . . he works here, for goodness sake. Now that I know, though, I might avoid the food court during lunchtime.

I take my own tray, still bearing the pizza crust and half a cup of watery soda, over to the recycling station and leave it there. As I make my way into the mall, I pull out my phone to check the time. It's just after one-thirty. I still have to pick up Spud's food, and of course the store that carries it is not in the mall. Plus, it closes at three. So I need to finish up this errand for Dad and get out of here as quickly as I can. Stuffing my phone in my pocket, I quicken my pace, careful not to bump into anyone in the crowded space.

But something's not right. I know that before I've gone past fewer than half a dozen stores. *Damn it. Was the tomato sauce rotten? Maybe the cheese turned.* I feel myself start to get sweaty under my jacket. I quickly unzip it all the way, but that doesn't help much. The whole mall feels like it's about a million degrees. My cheeks are probably bright red; at least, it feels like they are. Making a quick u-turn, I head back toward the food court.

The walls of the short hallway that leads to the bathrooms seem to be wiggling. I clench my fists and keep my lips tightly clamped. I'm not sure what's about to happen. Vomiting? Diarrhea? Fainting? Honestly, it feels like it could be any of those options. Or all three at once.

Which would mean embarrassment of apocalyptic proportions.

I push my way into the ladies' room, only to be hit by a wallop of soapy perfume. I quickly start breathing through my mouth as I head over to one of the free sinks. I'm not the only one in here, but the room isn't full, either. Most of the toilets are free, if I need them.

I'm not sure what I need.

I edge my way in between a young teenager applying lip gloss and a mother who's helping her little girl wash her hands. A glance in the mirror shows me that I look absolutely awful. Like I'm carrying some fatal disease. I definitely wouldn't want to be anywhere near me right now. For some reason, all I can think about is that I hope I didn't look this bad a few minutes ago when I was talking with Cash.

Jesus, Sadie. Why do you even care?

I turn on the cold water and plunge my hands into the flow. When they're good and chilled, I press them onto my cheeks. I know it looks weird, but I don't really care. Projectile vomiting the length of the bathroom would probably look weirder. If this is what's going to prevent that, then so be it.

I notice the mother looking at me. Warily. Rather than ask what's wrong, though, she just takes her daughter's dripping hand and hauls her over to the paper towel dispenser. I close my eyes and grip the edge of the sink, even though it's probably crawling with bacteria and goodness knows what else.

The next thing I hear is a collective gasp and a childish squeal. Even through my closed eyelids, I can tell that the room has gone dark.

2

IN WHICH
A PERSISTENT ANNOYANCE
UPENDS MY LIFE YET AGAIN

"Seriously?" someone says. A moment later, there's a flare of bluish light as a phone comes to life. I can see it reflected in the mirror as Lip Gloss Girl lifts it a little higher.

"Mommy . . ." The kid sounds like she's on the verge of panic. I brace myself, knowing that a kid's scream in this sort of space will probably be an eardrum-killer.

"It's okay," Lip Gloss Girl says, aiming her phone a little lower. "The power just went out. That's all." She has this tone to her voice that makes me think she's had a lot of practice dealing with ramped-up little kids. "Let's get out of here. I bet it's brighter in the mall."

The kid doesn't say anything. Her mom finishes drying her hands—roughly—with the paper towel. I realize I'm still gripping the sink. The wave of nausea seems to have passed, though I'm still a bit shaky. It's probably just adrenaline from the surprise of the lights going out. I let go, then give my hands a quick rinse. Lip Gloss Girl is waiting by the door, her phone held high to illuminate the space.

"Anyone else in here?" she calls, directing her voice over to the stalls. "I'm going to take the light, so . . ."

"Just a second, love," a voice says. A moment later, the sound of a toilet flushing roars through the space, and a stall door opens. An older woman steps out and heads for the sinks. She doesn't really look like the sort of person who frequents a lot of malls. Farmers' markets, maybe. Her white hair is pulled back on the sides into tapering braids, and she's wearing what looks like a cloak over her long skirt. Her boots actually jingle with each step. As she stands beside me at the sink the mother and daughter just vacated, I catch a whiff of something. It's not pot. Incense, maybe? I can't quite place it.

I realize I'm still just standing here with dripping hands. My stomach might be recovered, but my brain doesn't seem to be. I hurry to grab a couple of paper towels, then dry my hands with the scratchy squares. When they're as dry as I can get them, I pull out my phone and turn on the light. The bathroom gets a little brighter.

"We good?" Lip Gloss Girl asks. Nobody objects, so the mom grabs another paper towel and uses it to grasp the door handle. A moment later, the five of us are standing in the hallway. My heart starts pounding.

This isn't right.

"Why is it so dark?" I ask, more to myself than to anyone else. It's not even two o'clock in the afternoon, for goodness sake. The mall is full of skylights (including in the food court), and it's not cloudy outside. It definitely shouldn't be this dark. Unless some of those skylights got covered with Christmas decorations. Maybe I just didn't notice. Well, I wouldn't, if all the lights in the mall were on. I take a few deep breaths to try to calm myself.

"Mommy," the kid says again. She's clinging to her mom's hand as we walk slowly down the hallway toward the food court, which looks like a gaping abyss of darkness. I hold my phone a little higher, frowning as I try to peer into the space.

This is definitely not right.

"Where'd everyone go?" I ask. Lip Gloss Girl, the mom, and the cloaked woman all turn to look at me. I suddenly feel like I've asked the dumbest question in the world.

"Krampus took them," the little girl whimpers. Our attention all shifts to her, just as her mother lets out a deep sigh.

"Harper, enough."

"But Tyler said—"

"Tyler shouldn't have let you watch that movie. He's in big trouble."

Harper doesn't say anything. She just clings to her mom as we emerge into the weirdly silent food court. As I peer into the space, I can see that the power's not actually out. There are bits of light here and there. Drink machines are lit up. A few tiny lights blink in the kitchens. But it's like everyone just closed up shop and left.

It takes me a moment to realize that my head is slowly moving back and forth, like an automatic denial. I pull my phone where I can see it and turn off the light app so I can check the time.

"Shit."

The mom clears her throat. But I'm too panicked by what I see to care. Besides, I'm sure the kid has heard worse if she's been watching horror movies.

"What is it?" the cloaked woman asks.

I shake my head in disbelief, even though I *can* believe it. I just don't understand it. "It's eleven-fifteen."

Nobody says anything. They're probably wondering what the hell is going on, and how a trip to the bathroom somehow caused time travel. My hands shake as I grip my phone. My first instinct is to call someone. Cash, preferably. He's the only one I know of who might know what's going on. But when I look at the signal strength, my heart sinks.

"Of course," I mutter.

"What?" Lip Gloss Girl asks.

"Does your phone have a signal?"

The space gets quite a bit darker as she turns off the light so she can check. "Nope," she says a moment later. "And my battery's about to die. Great." She sighs. I reengage my light and shine it in her direction.

"You don't think it's a bit weird?" I ask.

"What? A power outage?"

"The power's not out. The lights are just off."

She shrugs.

"It's late at night," I say.

"So?"

"So, what time was it when you went into the bathroom?"

She gives me a blank look. I groan internally. *Sadie, you moron. She's just a character in a Reverie. She probably doesn't even realize anything's wrong with the timeline. You really are terrible at this.*

"What the *hell* is going on?" I mutter, stepping away from the group and toward the mall. I hear their footsteps as they try to keep up. Great. I'm somehow stuck in another one of these things, and now I've got a posse. I hope I'm not supposed to be responsible for these people; that didn't go very well last time.

"I'm Emmeline," Lip Gloss Girl says, suddenly at my side.

"Riley," I mutter. *Hey, it's a Reverie. Why not?*

"I'm Harper," the little kid says. Emmeline glances back at her with a smile.

"Yeah, we know."

"Mommy's name is Jessica."

The mom sighs. "Thank you, Harper."

"And you?" Emmeline says, glancing over at the cloaked woman who's walking briskly on my other side.

"Rainraven."

Jesus, Sadie. Are you serious?

"Okay," Emmeline says. "So . . . what are we doing, exactly?"

"Can we go see Santa now?" Harper asks.

"I think he's probably gone home for the day," Emmeline says.

"To the North Pole?"

"Yeah. He has to feed his reindeer, right?"

"No. The elves do that." The way she says it makes it sound like that fact should be totally obvious.

"The elves are pretty busy building toys right now. It's nice that Santa wants to help out with the reindeer, isn't it?"

"Yeah." There's a little sigh. "Mommy, can we come back and see him tomorrow?"

"We'll see," Jessica says, in that way moms do. It's totally obvious she's hoping Harper will forget.

Fat chance of that.

"Riley?" Emmeline says, pulling my attention back to her. I glance her way, only to find her staring at me with an expectant expression, her eyebrows raised. It reminds me so much of Cash that, for a moment, I wonder if he has a long-lost little sister he just never told me about.

"What?"

"What are we doing? 'Cause I don't think wandering around the mall until your battery runs out counts as a plan."

"Do we need a plan?"

She lets out a short laugh. "Probably, yeah. I don't think my bus runs this late, so I have no way to get home."

"Nobody can give you a ride?"

"You think that if I call my parents to come and pick me up from a closed mall, they're not going to have questions?"

"We all have questions."

"I have a nine o'clock curfew. Let's just say I don't want to get grounded until next year."

"So you're going to stay here all night?" I ask, somewhat amused by her lack of reasoning. But she just shrugs.

"Why not? It might be kind of cool, actually."

"Everything's closed."

She shakes her head. "No, it's not."

I frown and aim my phone at the store to our right. It's dark in there, too, though I can see a few pinpricks of light that are probably from the cash register and the security system. But the metal grate that should be pulled over the entrance is nowhere to be seen. In fact, all the stores seem to be the same. It's like someone did a really half-assed job of closing up the mall.

Or maybe I'm just doing a really half-assed job of this Reverie.

That's impossible. You shouldn't even be having *a Reverie. The connection is broken. You haven't seen Cash for months, so . . .*

"Damn it," I say, then brace myself for Jessica's grunt of disapproval.

"What?" Emmeline asks.

"Never mind." Focusing the light ahead of us, I shake my head. "Let's go get some answers."

The escalator is still and silent, so we walk up in single file, gripping the rubbery railing for safety because my phone isn't enough to illuminate the climb for everyone at once. When we're all at the top, I shine the light around the space, trying to orient myself. I've passed Phantasmazine plenty of times (though I've never gone in), so I know where it is. But the mall looks disorientingly unfamiliar in the darkness. The skylights over our heads are just as dark as everything else . . . and there's a weird noise coming from them. I peer upward, listening at the same time.

"Is that rain?" Jessica asks.

I shake my head. I honestly don't know. When I came into the mall, the day was sunny . . . and freezing. If anything, it should be snowing.

"Let's look on the bright side," Rainraven says. "We're not out in that."

"Yeah," Emmeline says. "Things could totally be worse." She walks ahead, into the darkness.

"Where are you going?" I call after her.

"You coming?"

I sigh. She's going in the right direction, in any case. But I'm not sure if I feel comfortable leading these people farther into a darkened mall. I seem to have become a sort of leader; I'm the one with the light, after all. Glancing at the other three, I shrug. "Let's go, then."

Emmeline waits for us, then falls into step beside Rainraven, leaving me to lead the group, phone held high to illuminate our way. It's making me really nervous. I don't know what my brain might be planning next, but I'll probably be the first one of the group to experience it if I'm out in front. My eyes feel like they're going to roll right out of my skull, I'm scanning the darkness so hard. And I'm shaking, too. It's not that it's cold in here—it isn't, which is weird, given the silence; I don't hear any sort of heating system running. I'm just freaking out.

Who wouldn't be?

All the glowing signs over the store entrances are off, so we're almost at Phantasmazine by the time I can make out the lumpy shape of the word. As I shine my light toward the gaping hole, a new thought occurs to me, and I almost swear again. (Jessica's going to get really tired of me if I keep that up.)

Why would he be here? Seriously, Sadie. The rest of the mall is abandoned. Why would Cash be sitting in a dark store, waiting around for you?

I come to a stop. Shaking my head, I let the light fall to the floor.

"What's wrong?" Emmeline asks.

"I don't know." I press one fist to my temple and close my eyes for a moment. "I don't even know—"

"Sadie?"

My eyes snap open, and I whip the phone upward, just in time to see a figure emerge out of the darkness. He sidles forward, into the light, his posture strange. It isn't until he gets closer that I can see he's brandishing a sword. Beside me, Jessica swears (I knew she had it in her) and grabs Harper by the arm, pulling the kid back. Cash lets the point of the sword fall to the floor, where it makes a fairly realistic clanging noise.

"You sell *swords*?" I ask. The sound of my voice seems to confirm something to him, because he rushes forward. The next thing I know, I'm swept up in a one-armed hug.

"What the hell is going on?" he whispers, his breath warm against my ear. I pull back, trying to illuminate his face while simultaneously trying not to shine the light right in his eyes.

"The connection was broken," I say. "Right?"

"As far as I know. I died in that landslide, so . . ."

"So this doesn't make any sense." I sigh and look down at the sword. "Seriously. Is that real?"

"Apparently. Most of the ones we sell are plastic, but . . ." He lifts the weapon, letting it catch the light. The blade seems to be etched with a fancy design, and the hilt has some sort of fiery jewel set in it. "Twenty-nine ninety-five, plus tax." He shakes his head.

"Never mind the sword," I say. "Why are we in a Reverie? How is that even possible?"

"I don't know." He frowns at the sword, as if it might give him the answers he seeks. But it's just a piece of metal. He lowers it to his side, then looks around at my companions. His expression doesn't really change . . . until he gets to the one who's slipped into the gloom of the store to peer at the shadowy shelves. "Hey!" His voice is suddenly loud. Jessica flinches as Cash strides back into the store and leans close to Rainraven. "What is this?" he whispers, though in the silence of the space, it's easy enough to make out every word.

"Hello, love."

"Seriously?" His voice is tight, hissing through his teeth. I don't think I've ever seen him like this before. I'm not sure if I like it. Especially since he's my anchor in these Reveries. If *he* doesn't know what's going on . . .

Or does he?

"Lincoln," I say. He whips his head in my direction as I walk over to where he's standing with the cloaked woman. His usually placid features are creased in a deep frown that's accentuated by the bluish glow from my phone.

"Exactly," he says. He turns back to Rainraven. "Spill it. Sadie broke the connection. So what are we doing here?"

The woman smiles enigmatically with an exaggerated shrug of her shoulders and moves away from us. Lincoln swears under his breath.

"Try not to do that," I whisper. "There's a little kid here."

"Yeah. I noticed." He lets out a deep sigh and peers after Rainraven. "Unbelievable."

"You going to tell me what's going on? Or is this another secret you're going to keep from me until we're both being eaten by Krampus or something?"

"Krampus?" He shakes his head. "Shit, Sadie. You better not."

"Call me Riley."

"Your last name?"

"How the hell do you know that?"

He gives me a dark look.

"Right. I forgot you were a stalker."

"And you seem to have forgotten that we have a mutual friend."

"Huh?"

"Ritch."

"How does he know my last name?"

"Probably from that writing class you were both in. He didn't tell me until after that, so he probably didn't know your last name at first, either."

I sigh and shake my head. "Is there a way you can call him up right now? You need to ask him what the hell is going on."

"I already did."

"What?" Peering at him in the darkness, I frown. I don't see any phone. It's so dark in here that, if he had one, he'd be using it for light. He shakes his head and gestures the point of the sword over toward Rainraven, who's examining a cluster of figurines in a glass case.

"Some answers would be nice," he says, directing the words in her direction.

"They would, wouldn't they?" she says.

I shake my head. "I don't get it."

He steps closer and leans toward my ear. "Rainraven is one of Ritch's . . . characters."

I draw back in surprise. "What?"

"No. Not characters." He shakes his head. "Avatars."

"What?"

"Avatars," he repeats.

"Since when are avatars involved in Reveries? Why don't you use them?"

"I do. Just not when I'm working with you."

"Why not?"

"I wanted you to be able to recognize me easily."

"Okay, but why don't *I* use them?"

He stares at me. "You want to skip straight from beginner level to advanced? I didn't use an avatar until I was sixteen." With a wave of his hand in Rainraven's direction, he shakes his head. "Ritch, on the other hand, always uses them."

I turn to the cloaked woman. "Shit."

"Yeah."

"So why won't she—he—tell you what's going on?"

"Because he's not going to break character."

I frown. "If he doesn't break character, how do you know that Rainraven is one of his avatars?"

"A couple of reasons. The main one being: He told me. Outside the Reverie." With a shake of his head, he steps back into the shadows. When I lift the phone, I see that he's putting the sword back on some sort of fancy wooden stand.

"What if we need that?"

"What we need," he says, turning back to me as he starts to roll up the sleeves of his button-down shirt, "is to end the Reverie. It shouldn't even be happening, and I don't want to know what'll happen if we mess something up in here."

My heart quickens a little at the thought. "What would we mess up?"

"I don't know. Based on past experience with you, though . . ."

"Excuse me?"

He shakes his head as he gives his second sleeve a final tug, settling it just below his elbow. "I'm just saying. Let's finish it."

"How? We don't even know what we're supposed to do. It's not like we can finish the story."

"There are two other ways to end a Reverie, remember?"

"What do you suggest? Killing me with that sword?"

His expression morphs into something that looks like disappointed horror. "I wouldn't do that."

"Yeah, I know. But I don't think I'd be able to kill myself with it."

He sighs and looks around. "And we're already at the beginning."

"What?"

"The beginning. Where we started."

"No," I say, suddenly understanding. "We're where *you* started."

He blinks, as if the same thought has just occurred to him. "Where did you start?"

"The bathroom."

A snort escapes him.

"Shut up. I felt like I was going to puke. And now I know why." I glare at him. "Did meeting you in the food court trigger this?"

"I don't see why it should have. The connection was broken."

"So you didn't just barge your way into my head and make me—"

"I'm not making you do anything, Sa—Riley." He shakes his head. "Sorry."

"Don't worry about getting used to it," I say, turning on my heel and facing the darkened mall. I can just make out Jessica and Harper huddled on a bench in the middle of the concourse. Emmeline is on the other side of the space, peering into another store, though she doesn't seem brave enough to actually venture inside. I consider taking them with me, but figure it'll be faster if I just do this myself.

"Riley?" Lincoln's voice says. "What are you—"

"Ending this," I say before turning and jogging back to the motionless escalator, my phone held high to light my way.

3

IN WHICH
WE REALIZE THAT
IT'S NOT ALL ABOUT ME

I make it downstairs and back to the food court in no time, though not without a lot of startling and jumping. The bouncing light from my phone casts shadows all over the place—on the benches, on the darkened directory kiosks, on the store signs that loom above my head—and I keep thinking I'm seeing things that aren't there. I hear some of them, too, though it's probably just the sound of my jacket rustling or the voices of the others carrying from upstairs. The mall is kind of a giant echo chamber; my footsteps seem to run away from me before bouncing back to my ears, slightly out of sync.

The hallway off the food court is scarily dark, but it lights up quite a bit when I shine my phone down it. I hurry toward the ladies' room and reach out for the door. As my hand presses against the metal rectangle, I'm expecting the door to give and swing into the bathroom. When it doesn't, I end up sort of crumpling against the hard surface, my phone banging against it with a loud clunk.

"What the hell?" I groan. I pull back, then push again. The door doesn't budge. "Are you *serious?*" My voice rises into a desperate wail. I put my shoulder against the door and lean into it. Nothing. Aiming my phone at the edge, I spot the lock. And the keyhole. "Damn it!" My shout is loud in the echoing space. "Damn it, damn it, damn it!"

I whirl around and lean back against the immovable door, breathing hard. My fingers fumble at the collar of my sweater, pulling it away from my throat. I feel sick again . . . but not like I did before. I don't think I'm going to throw up.

I think I might be having a heart attack.

I slide down the door, landing with a thud on my butt as tears blur my view of the dark hallway. *God damn it, Lincoln! If you hadn't forced your way into my life with these stupid Reveries, none of this would be happening right now!* My heart feels like it's pounding in my throat. The sweating has started again. The light from my phone is shaking as I try (and fail) to keep my hands still.

I have to get out of here. Now.

Shaking my head, I haul myself to my feet and rush down the hallway toward the food court, brandishing my phone in front of me like a priest wielding a crucifix against a demon. As my winter boots pound on the hard floor, they kick up such a racket that I'm sure the others can hear me from all the way upstairs. I barrel into the darkness . . . and run straight into a shadowy figure. My phone goes flying into the food court, clattering on the floor. But I almost don't hear it over my echoing scream.

"Whoa. It's me." Lincoln's voice edges out of the darkness. I can only see the outlines of his form, but that's enough. I strike out with both hands, managing to land a blow. "Ow. Riley—"

"Don't call me that!" I screech. "I don't want any part of this shitshow. I never did. I *told* you that, and you just keep coming and coming, and now I'll *never* get rid of you!"

He doesn't say anything. He doesn't even move. I can hear my own breathing, shaky and chaotic, and the sound of my heart hammering in my ears. The next thing I know, I'm enveloped in an embrace. I'm too tired, too scared to fight it. But I'm not too tired and scared to burst into tears.

I know I'm probably getting his shirt all wet and snotty. I can feel his name tag digging into my shoulder where it's pressed between us. It's one of the most uncomfortable hugs I've ever had in my life. But, for some strange reason that I couldn't articulate if I tried, I don't want him to let go. Not yet.

"It's going to be okay," he says, gently tightening his arms.

"How? We're trapped in here."

"Trapped?"

"The bathroom door's locked. I can't get in." I sniff hard. The sound is disgusting. "I can't get back to the beginning."

He sighs. I feel it travel all the way through him. "I don't know if that would make any difference, anyway." He lets go of me and steps back. I still can't see him very well. I take the opportunity to swipe my wrist under my nose.

"What do you mean?"

I hear him step away. A moment later, a bluish light seems to float as he picks up my phone. Somehow, it's still on, even after its crash. I guess that case Mom and Dad got me for my birthday really *is* shock-absorbent. "Here," he says, handing the phone back to me. I take it, keeping the light directed upward so I can sort of see his face.

"What do you mean?" I ask again. "Why wouldn't getting into the bathroom make a difference? Isn't that how you end a Reverie? Go back to the beginning?"

"Yeah. And that should work."

"So what—"

"I died."

"Yeah . . ."

"The connection was broken."

I just raise my eyebrows at him, waiting for him to spit out more than a few words at a time.

He sighs. "I don't think this is your Reverie, Sadie. It can't be."

"If it's not mine, then whose is it?" I ask, an instant before the answer hits me. I frown at him, mirroring his expression. "It's yours?"

"I think so. That's the only thing that makes any sort of sense."

"That's why Ritch—I mean Rainraven—is here."

He nods. "That's my assumption."

"Then why am *I* here?"

"I honestly have no idea. And Rainraven's not giving me any answers." He shakes his head. "God, I hate that avatar. And he knows it. Pretentious, woke, virtue-signalling hippie wannabe . . ."

"Jeez, Lincoln. Tell me how you really feel."

He snorts. "I just did." Peering back into the mall, he sighs. "We should get back to them. If Rainraven's involved, there's probably some sort of weird story in play. I don't want to get back there and find your friends knee-deep in some narrative that we're too late to figure out."

"They're not my friends," I say. "And how do you know if that's really Ritch? If this is your Reverie . . . couldn't you just be imagining that character?"

"It's possible."

"Couldn't you just be imagining me?"

He turns back to me, eyebrows high. "You think you're a figment of my imagination?"

He's got a point. I grip my phone and look out into the mall. "What if we can't get out?" My voice is so tiny, I'm not sure if he can hear me. But then he sighs again.

"We can."

"How?"

"I don't know. Figure out how to finish the story, I guess."

"Or die trying?" I say, turning back to face him. He's wearing a really weird expression. "What?"

"What if we've . . ." He trails off, shaking his head. "Never mind."

"What were you going to say?"

"Nothing."

"No, it's not nothing. We need all the help we can get, so if you have any ideas—"

"I'm still working on it."

"Great. That's super helpful."

"Would you rather I lied and made something up?"

"No," I say, not sure whether to be disappointed or annoyed with him. Maybe I'll just be both.

"It was just a thought. And it wouldn't help us get out of here. All we know for sure right now is that I'm the one who needs to die if that's the way we choose to end the Reverie."

"So what are you waiting for?"

He snorts. "Nice, Sadie."

"What? You've done it before."

"So have you. And it's unpleasant, so I'd rather not have to do it again unless there's no other option."

"Great. So we're trapped here because you want to live forever." My voice comes out sounding petulant. *Shut up, Sadie. You sound like a spoiled brat. You do realize what you're asking him to do, right?*

"Not forever."

"Not technically. Yeah, my body's still standing in the ladies' room. But my mind . . . We could spend months in here."

"Okay. I promise you right now that I'm not going to let it go on for months. If this isn't over by the time the sun comes up, I'll fall on that stupid souvenir sword upstairs." He holds out his hand as if he wants me to shake it. "Deal?"

"What happens if I die instead?"

His expression falls into a frown. He doesn't move his hand; it's still hanging in the space between us.

"What?" I say.

"What if this is a second chance?"

"I never asked for a second chance."

"Maybe not. But you might have one." He leans down a little more so he can look me right in the eye. "Were you even the tiniest bit disappointed when we broke the connection before?"

No, I think. But the word doesn't seem to want to cross my lips. It doesn't dare come out.

It knows it's a lie.

"I messed up," he says. "I know that. And I'm really sorry, Sadie. But maybe we can give it another try. And this time . . ."

"You'll actually listen to what I want?"

"Yeah." He shakes his head. "I mean . . . it won't be quite the same. You won't have control like you did before."

"Way to sell it, Lincoln."

"I'm just saying. If this is my Reverie—"

"That's what I'm worried about. There could be anything lurking in this mall."

He snorts and finally lets his hand drop. "Like what?"

"Oh, I don't know. Zombies. Dragons. Mirror-faced women who command the forces of nature—"

"Shit," he blurts out, interrupting me.

"What?"

"Air, fire, earth, and—"

"Water," I finish for him. He's fallen silent. I angle the phone's light so I can see his face better. He looks a little freaked out. "What's wrong?"

"Nothing."

I sigh. "If we're going to do this, you need to be completely honest with me. Don't pretend to be afraid of things, because that just freaks me out."

"I'm not pretending, Sadie." He shakes his head. "I'm really not a fan of water."

"You don't bathe?"

"Deep water," he clarifies.

"Can you swim?"

"Reluctantly."

"Then relax. Besides, the only water I know of is in the fountain at the west end of the mall. And that's barely deep enough to soak your ankles."

"It's raining."

"Are you afraid of rain?"

"No, but . . ."

"But what?"

He shakes his head. "Sadie, this is a Reverie. My Reverie. Anything could happen. The mall could flood."

"So that still wouldn't be deep water." I adjust my grip on the phone, causing the shadow on his face to bend. "And if it's *your* Reverie, water shouldn't even be an issue. The element thing was *my* brain's stupid idea."

"Mirror was my idea, and look where that got us."

"Jesus, Lincoln. Are you serious? That's not helping."

"Sorry." He sighs and pushes his hand through his hair. "Let's just work through this slowly. We'll go back to Phantasmazine and get the others. Maybe Rainraven will have some brilliant ideas about what to do next."

"She better. I don't want to just wander around this mall for the next twelve hours."

"It better not be twelve hours." He sighs and steps away from the light. "But you're right. We're certainly getting nowhere just standing here like—" He breaks off suddenly and comes to a stop, his shoes squeaking on the floor. "Did you hear that?"

I did. I scurry closer to him, pressing my phone against my chest to block the light. He grabs my arm and pulls me back into the hallway leading to the bathrooms. We huddle there in the inky shadows and watch as a golden light emerges from the far side of the food court and starts to bounce lazily through the darkness. The glow is accompanied by a number of voices.

Male voices.

Shit, Lincoln. Where are you taking this Reverie?

The glow—which reminds me an awful lot of the one cast by the old-fashioned lantern in my last Reverie—illuminates three figures. I can see scruffy hair. I can see beards. I can see eye patches. The light even catches on a shiny metal hook that seems to be a replacement for one of the men's hands. I cast a sideways glance at Lincoln, but I can't see much. I lean closer to his ear.

"Seriously?" I whisper.

"What?"

"Pretty stereotypical, aren't they? And why are they wearing their eye patches in the dark?"

"To hide their missing eyes," he says, as if that should be obvious.

"That wasn't why pirates— Never mind." I shake my head and turn my attention back to the three men who are roaming slowly through the food court. They don't seem to notice their surroundings, which is odd; surely three stereotypical 18th-century men would have opinions about glowing vending machines. I can't quite make out what they're saying from here, but they seem to be in a pretty good mood.

"We need to get back to the others," Lincoln whispers.

"No kidding. But those guys will notice."

"They're going to notice if they go all the way around the food court and spot us standing here."

"You should've brought the sword."

"Yeah, well, I didn't." He nudges me with his arm. "Come on."

"How are we supposed to see where we're going?"

"Use your phone."

"They'll see us!"

"Maybe not."

"Lincoln, I'm not going to—" I break off as he pushes me backward, into the hallway. "What are you doing?" I hiss.

"We'll hide in the bathroom. Just until they're gone."

"It's locked."

"Did you try the men's room?"

"No, but why would it be unlocked when the ladies' room isn't?"

"Reverie," he says, as if that explains it all. I turn around so I don't lose my balance in the dark and peer into the gloom. Daring to let loose the light from my phone, I spot a second door around six feet past the one I already tried. Lincoln grabs my hand (as if I'm going to stick around when a trio of pirates is searching the food court) and hauls me down there. He pushes his way through the door, which opens with a squeak. I hold my breath as he pulls me inside.

As soon as the door is closed behind us, I wrench out of his grasp and shine the light around the space. The smell is much the same—soap and disinfectant and damp paper towels—but the urinals along the far wall make it clear that this is an entirely different bathroom. Still, the light switch should be in a similar spot. I wave my phone over the wall near the door and spy what I'm looking for. But before I can do anything, Lincoln grabs my wrist.

"Don't. They'll see the glow under the door."

"So we're just supposed to stand here in the dark?"

"For now."

I sigh. He lets go of me, and I turn away from the light switch. There isn't even any place to sit down in here. Well, other than the toilets. But that wouldn't exactly be comfortable.

"If this is my Reverie," he mutters to himself, "where's the touchstone?"

"What?"

"The touchstone. The name."

I blink at him in the darkness. "She's upstairs."

He shakes his head. "Ritch always tells me his avatar's name. It's our signal to start."

"He did tell you, didn't he?"

"No. He told you." He sighs. "I don't get it. This shouldn't be happening in the first place."

"Why not? He's your Cicerone."

"That's not how it works with me and him. He'll pop into a daydream and introduce himself. It's how he asks if I'm up for a Reverie."

I shoot him a dark look. "So he needs your consent."

"I know, I know. I screwed up, okay? Like I told you earlier: I had no idea what I was doing."

"Maybe he's just giving you a taste of your own medicine."

"Maybe. But even if that's the case, it doesn't explain why you're here."

"In the mall?"

"In the Reverie. In *my* Reverie."

The puzzlement in his voice isn't reassuring at all. I angle the phone a bit, trying to see his expression. His eyebrows are pinched into a deep frown. *Good. Now you know how I felt when you barged into my head and—*

I jump as a toilet flushes, the sound a sibilant roar in the small space. Lincoln actually yelps. Then he skitters back toward the door, shielding me with his body and arms.

– 4 –

IN WHICH
WE FIND OUT THERE ARE SOME STRANGE
THINGS TO WORRY ABOUT IN THE MALL

"Who's there?" Lincoln demands. His voice actually cracks a little. I grab the back of his shirt and clutch the fabric in my fist. I can't see anything past him—his body would block any light from my phone, anyway—but I do hear a stall door squeak open. That noise is followed by a tapping sound and a few footsteps . . . and a rather unpleasant smell.

"Might want to clear out," a male voice says. A moment later, I hear water running in one of the sinks. When that stops, Lincoln takes a deep breath.

"We'll take our chances with the funk." He straightens up and reaches back, fumbling to find me. I let go of his shirt and grab his hand.

"Can't take the pre-Christmas chaos?" the guy asks.

"Not quite." Lincoln's quiet for a moment. He seems to be considering his next words carefully. "Haven't you noticed anything odd?"

"Odd? Well, it does smell strange in here, but I had that spicy squid last night, so I'm not surprised."

"I was talking about the lights."

"I'm afraid I wouldn't know anything about that."

Lincoln grunts and lets go of my hand. Heart pounding, I peek around his shoulder. I don't see much of anything until I carefully aim the phone toward the voice. As the shadow comes into view, I start to make sense of what I'm seeing. The guy—who looks like he's in his 20s, with a raggedy beard and a man bun—grasps the long cane in his fingers and walks over to the paper towel dispenser with a confidence that makes me think he's done this before. He even manages to toss the crumpled towel into the trash on the first try.

"Would you mind grabbing the door for me? You never know what's crawling on those handles."

"I'm afraid we can't let you do that," Lincoln says. The guy raises his eyebrows, and my phone's light catches him in the eyes. They don't look quite right, somehow. He doesn't even blink.

"And why is that?"

"Pirates."

"Lincoln!" I hiss, whacking him in the shoulder. "Shut up."

The guy grunts. "Pirates? That's . . . interesting."

"What am I supposed to tell him is out there?" Lincoln asks, craning his neck to look at me.

"Not *that.*"

He sighs and turns back to the guy. "It's a long story. We're just waiting until it's safe to go out."

"Fair enough." The guy nods. "I'm Farley."

"Lincoln. And this is—"

"Riley," I say quickly. I don't want this Farley guy knowing my real name, even if he *is* just a figment of Lincoln's imagination.

"Nice to meet you." His nose wrinkles. "Sorry about the stink."

"I've smelled worse," Lincoln says. "Hell, I've made worse."

I roll my eyes.

"So, how long do we need to wait?" Farley asks.

"Yeah, Lincoln," I say, my annoyance clear in my voice. "How long do we have to stay in here?"

"I'll go out and check in a few minutes."

"And then what?"

He shrugs. "How should I know?"

"Shouldn't you be better at this by now?"

He twists to frown at me. "This is uncharted territory. I don't know what the hell Ritch is doing, but it's not something we ever did before. It isn't even something we *discussed* before."

"Great. Lucky me."

He shakes his head. "There's no reason the usual rules wouldn't apply. So . . . the best thing to do is try to play it out."

"You know, I thought I was done with all this."

"I thought so, too. Apparently, someone else has other ideas."

Farley's just standing there, listening, and I realize our conversation probably sounds pretty weird. He's got his cane in both hands, the tip pressed to the floor between the toes of his heavy boots. I lean closer to Lincoln so I can whisper in his ear.

"What if he's the touchstone?"

"Huh?" He turns to try to look at me. "What?"

"He introduced himself. So—"

"Ritch's avatar is still upstairs. At least, I hope she is."

"Maybe he switched to this one."

He shakes his head. "That's not how he does it. At least, that's not how he's ever done it before. That wouldn't make much sense, anyway. Characters just appearing and disappearing randomly? How would there be any story continuity?"

"Do the characters have to exist when you're not around them?"

"Technically, no. But what happens if they all end up in the same place? As far as I know, we can only embody one avatar at once."

I sigh. "So much for that theory."

"It's not a *bad* theory," he says. "It's just not how it works." He edges to the side, nudging me out of the way so he can grab the door handle. "Can you hide that light for a sec? I'm going to take a peek."

I press the surface of the phone against my sweater, blocking out most of the light. I hear the door squeak a little as Lincoln slowly pulls it open. The space beyond is so dark, I can't see anything at all. I can only assume he's sticking his head out to have a look.

"Let's go," he whispers a moment later. I frown into the darkness.

"How do you know they're gone?"

"I can't see any light from their lantern. And I can't hear anything, either. They probably went out into the mall."

"Oh, that's reassuring. Isn't that where we're going?"

"What else do you suggest? If we want to finish this story, we need to go *somewhere*. We can't just stand in a funky bathroom all day.

"Again," Farley says, "I'm sorry about that."

"Everybody poops," Lincoln says absently, and if I weren't dealing with pirates and the suddenly changing rules of someone else's Reverie, I might actually be amused enough to laugh. "I've got the door open," he says, directing his voice back into the dark bathroom. "You want to go first?"

I keep the phone's light hidden, so I hear rather than see Farley approach.

I feel him pass me, the warmth of his body and the tapping of his cane the only indication he's there.

"Thanks," he says when he's out in the hallway.

"Riley?" Lincoln says. I can almost see those expectant eyebrows. With a sigh, I sidle through the doorway. The door squeaks shut behind me, and a hand falls gently against my arm. "Can we have a little light?"

"I don't want them to see us."

"They're going to hear us coming, anyway, if they're out there."

He's got a point, especially now that we've got Farley. I slowly pull the phone from my chest and aim the light down the hallway ahead of us. Farley's already walking slowly toward the food court, his cane sliding in short, tapping arcs in front of him. Lincoln and I follow, stepping into the pool of bluish glow that lights our way.

The food court looks—and sounds—deserted when we get back to it. The sliding glass doors that line the entrance vestibule separate the dark mall from the even darker night. As I'm looking over there, though, there's a sudden white flash that makes me jump. I hold my breath, waiting for the rumble. I don't have to wait very long.

"Sounds like the storm's getting worse," Lincoln whispers.

"To keep us from going outside?"

He turns to me with a frown. "You want to go outside?"

"What if we have to?"

"I'm pretty sure we're supposed to play out the Reverie in here."

"The food court?"

"The mall." He frowns into the nearest takeout place. "Wonder if we'll be able to find anything to eat if we get hungry."

I let out a grunt. "We better not be here long enough for that."

"You never know."

"What's the longest Reverie you've ever had?"

"Two days."

"Two *days?*" I say, my voice coming out in a squeak.

"That's less than a minute, remember?"

"Where were you?"

"History class."

"Did anyone notice?"

"Yeah. But they just thought I was zoned out. That wasn't unusual with that particular teacher." He turns and looks around. "Where did Farley go?"

I lift the light and shine it in a wide arc, trying to see the tall shadow. I spot him heading for the doors.

"Farley!" Lincoln says, in a whisper-yell that still manages to echo enough to make me wince. But the guy doesn't stop, so Lincoln jogs after him. Deciding I really don't want to be standing by myself if the pirates come back, I hurry to follow.

By the time I catch up to them, they're both standing in front of the glass doors. On any other day, those doors would be sliding open automatically to let us through. But I'm kind of glad they aren't doing that right now. The floor of the vestibule glistens wetly as I shine my light through the glass. And it's no mystery as to why: About two feet of water is lapping against the outer doors. It almost seems like there's some sort of tide; the waves are slapping at the glass, sending squirts of water through the gaps.

"Whoa," Lincoln whispers. He takes a step back. "We probably shouldn't be standing here."

"What's wrong?" Farley asks. He's gripping his cane and almost looks like he's staring out into the night. "The doors didn't open."

"We don't want them to open," Lincoln says. "There's a bit of a flooding issue out there."

"A bit?" I say, watching a wave splash against the outer doors. Another flash cuts through the night, silhouetting . . . something. "What the hell was that?"

"Turn off the light," Lincoln says, his voice nearly getting drowned out by the rumble of thunder. I slap the device against my chest once more, peering out into the darkness as I let my eyes adjust to the meagre glow coming in through the glass. The three of us wait in silence; the only thing I can hear is the tapering growl of thunder, followed by our breathing. I can feel the chill coming from the glass, though, and I shudder.

When the next flash of lightning comes, none of us say a word. Lincoln and I turn and look at each other, our expressions shadowy mirrors of surprise.

"You have *got* to be kidding me," I finally say.

"What?"

"A pirate ship? What the hell is it doing in the mall's parking lot?"

"Maybe it ran aground."

I snort. "On what? An SUV? Plus, we're nowhere near the coast."

"It's a twenty-minute drive."

"Yeah. By road. How the hell would a ship get all the way out here?"

"If there's flooding . . ."

"Lincoln, do you have any idea how deep a ship's hull is? You can't sail one of those through floodwater that would barely take out a basement."

"It's obviously deeper than that. A lot deeper."

I stare at him in disbelief. "Didn't you just tell me that you're afraid of deep water? Are you *trying* to torture yourself?"

"Apparently." He shakes his head and turns to Farley. "We should get away from these doors. If they give—*when* they give—this place is going to flood."

Farley sighs. "I suppose my ride won't be coming anytime soon."

"Not unless it's a hovercraft."

The man lets out a bemused grunt and rearranges his cane in his hand. He turns and heads off around the perimeter of the food court, skirting the large seating area in the middle. He's obviously been here before. I turn to Lincoln as I release my phone from my front. When I shine the light toward him, I can clearly see the look of distress on his face.

"Are you sure you're not just playing a character?" I ask.

"What?"

"Pretending to be freaked out."

He shakes his head. "I'm not pretending."

"You're scaring me."

"Sorry." He takes a deep breath and lets it out slowly. "Sometimes it's hard *not* to get too into this. We're perfectly safe. It's just . . ."

"Yeah. I know. Believe me, I know." I chew on my lip as I watch him. He looks away, out into the wet night, almost as if he can't help but stare at the source of his terror.

You're going to regret this, I think as I reach out and gently take his hand. He turns to me in surprise. "Let's play it out," I say.

"I'm sorry."

"I know."

"You never wanted this, and I—"

"Shut up. We're here now, so we might as well make the most of it. Maybe you'll even get some ideas that'll help you write another graphic novel."

His eyebrows rise. The familiar expression buoys me with relief. "With pirates?"

"Why not? You apparently like them."

He smirks. "Not really."

"Then what's with the galleon double-parked by the nail spa?"

With a smile, he starts to walk. I hold tight to his hand, even though my mind is telling me to let go. It feels too nice.

We hang back and walk slowly, letting Farley lead the way. When he reaches the far side of the round space where it opens up into the mall, he makes a smooth turn and strides into the darkness. Lincoln and I exchange a look, but we keep walking.

"Where's he going?" I whisper.

"No idea."

"You created him."

"Not consciously."

I turn to him in surprise. "But—"

"You didn't consciously create any of the stuff in your Reveries, did you? I mean, other than my death."

"That wasn't a conscious choice," I snap, the sudden annoyance feeling all too familiar. "Do you think I *wanted* to flail around all by myself for the rest of that Reverie? I had no idea what I was supposed to do."

"Yes, you did."

"Well, I didn't do it very well. I died, remember?"

He nods slowly. "Try not to do that in here, okay?"

"What do you think's going to happen in a mall? I'll get impaled on a mannequin or something?"

"There are pirates in here with us, remember?"

"So they're murderous pirates? Nice."

"I don't know what they are. Not yet. And I hope we won't have to find out."

"But we probably will, won't we?"

"Probably."

I sigh and fall silent. The cold glow from my phone lights our path and the backs of Farley's ankles. I keep it trained straight ahead, too afraid to shine it to either side, just in case I see something—or someone—I really don't want to see.

We make it back to the escalator without incident—and without telling Farley anything about where we're going. But he just grasps the railing in one hand and his cane in the other, and carefully makes his way up the stationary metal steps. Lincoln and I wait at the bottom.

"You think Rainraven will still be there when we get back?" I ask.

He shrugs. "I don't see why she wouldn't be. I'm actually more concerned about the others."

"Why?"

"They're wildcards. I have no idea who they are or what their function is supposed to be in the story."

"I think Harper's function is to freak us out with stories about Krampus." I shine the light upward; Farley's almost made it to the top. "There better not be a Krampus in this story."

"No guarantees."

"Great."

He grunts. "My Reveries usually have more of a theme. Krampus *and* pirates? That's getting a little . . . eclectic."

"Do other people's Reveries usually have a theme?"

"The good ones do. Otherwise, they're just blinged-out dreams with no logic or continuity."

"Guess that means my first one was a dud."

"Why?"

"Jane Eyre and zombies?"

He chuckles. "Okay, but they both came from the same source, remember? They were tied together by your idea of the pages and the elements."

I guess he has a point. Still, that was one weird Reverie.

"Wish we could do that now," he says, almost to himself.

"Do what?"

"Throw pages into water and get what we need."

"What would you get?"

He shrugs. "I don't know. I'm just saying. If we do end up needing something, it would be nice to have a way to get it." He stares upward. I follow his gaze. Farley must've made it to the top, because he's nowhere to be seen. I step toward the escalator, trying to let go of Lincoln's hand so I can use the railing. But his fingers tighten on mine. I stop and look back, frowning.

"What?"

"Do you hear that?"

I hold my breath for a moment, listening. I'm about to tell him I don't hear anything at all when the sound comes again. The hairs on the back of my neck stand at attention.

"Come on," he says, pulling on my hand and tugging me away from the escalator . . . and toward the faint screaming.

"Are you crazy? Since when do we run *toward* blood-curdling screams? I thought we were trying not to die here!"

"We have to play it out. And if this is part of it . . ."

"I don't particularly feel like dying today."

"I don't particularly want you to die today. If you do . . ."

"What?"

"The connection will be broken."

I shake my head. "It was already supposed to be broken!"

"It is. But . . . what if this is a second chance?"

"A second chance?" I echo. A weird little bubble of hope burbles in my chest. *Stop it, Sadie. Do you really want to go back to those months of nausea and feeling like you were crazy?*

"Yeah. I have a theory."

"Great."

He ignores me and goes on. "This is obviously my Reverie because Ritch is here."

"Obviously."

"Okay. Then why are *you* here?"

"Because you aren't finished messing with me?"

"I'm not messing with you. Not anymore." He rounds a corner and pulls me into an even darker hallway. I didn't think that was possible. I raise my arm, trying to make the light carry farther ahead of us. The screams are getting louder . . . and also more echoey. "I died when Mirror buried me under half a hillside. So our connection—with me being your Cicerone—was broken."

"Yeah. I get that part."

"I've had Reveries with Ritch since then. And you've never played a part in them. So something's different here." He squeezes my hand. "I think . . . maybe . . ."

"Maybe what? Spit it out."

He sighs. "Maybe you're my Cicerone."

"I thought you only got one."

"That's what I thought, too. But Ritch is old, so maybe he's auditioning replacements or something."

"Wouldn't someone have told me? Wouldn't someone have *asked* me? Or do all you Ciceroni-Reverie people just ignore consent altogether?"

His silence sounds . . . stung. He tightens his grip on my hand as we walk into the darkness, ever closer to those creepy screams.

"Maybe that's what's going on," I say, though I don't really want to entertain the possibility at all. "But how does knowing that help us now?"

"It doesn't. Not really. But it does *warn* us."

"About what?"

"Not to let you die. Because if you're the Cicerone—"

"—then my death will break the connection," I say. "Again."

"I know you said you never wanted this. But was there ever a moment, after Mirror took me out, that you regretted breaking the connection?"

"*I* didn't break the connection," I snap, choosing to ignore his question for the moment. "Mirror did. There was nothing I could've done. Your lower half was smashed to a pulp. Even if I could've gotten that boulder off you—"

"I know. Sorry." He walks in silence for a few steps. And then, "Did you regret the connection getting broken?"

I don't say anything. The screams are becoming more spaced out. I'm not sure if that's a good thing or a bad thing. Lincoln glances at me as we emerge into an open space. It takes a moment before I realize where we are. Usually, the atrium would be filled by the sound of rushing water. But the fountain appears to be turned off, and I can't hear anything.

That is, until another scream makes me jump.

I quickly whip my phone against my body, but there's already enough light in here, coming from the golden lantern that's sitting on the edge of the fountain, for me to see what's going on. Two people—a man and a woman—appear to be cornered. At their backs is the gaping darkness of a store. I think it might be the outdoor outfitter. The couple doesn't seem to want to go any farther into the darkness . . . but they can't exactly go anywhere else, thanks to the three men standing in a semicircle in front of them. I didn't notice it before, but the pirates have swords. And those weapons are pointed at the terrified couple.

Still, I'm not sure why we heard so much screaming. Not until one of the pirates lunges forward, swinging his shining blade toward the man. The guy jumps back with a grunt of pain, and the woman screams again.

"Stop! Please, stop! What do you want?" She lets out a sob. The man cradles his arm against his chest. I really don't want to know what kind of injury he has. But, judging by the woman's reaction, it's pretty bad. Lincoln squeezes my hand so hard that I turn to him. He gestures with his chin, and I look down at the ground. A trail of dark spots follows the couple into the store. I shake my head, too frozen with fear to do anything else.

"Tell us where it be!" one of the pirates bellows. He's the one in the middle, wearing a fancy tricorn hat, and he's at just the right angle for me to make out the eye patch covering one eye. He can't see us, at least.

"We don't know what you want!" the injured man grinds out. He almost sounds like he's holding his breath. Bending over his arm, which he's still got pressed against his stomach, he grunts. "Believe me, we'd tell you if—"

"Where be the treasure?" another pirate, the one who slashed at the man, shrieks. He sounds hysterical. "We be needin' our booty! Arr!"

If there wasn't blood involved, it would almost be funny. Lincoln's idea of pirates is pretty comical . . . although he is a graphic novel fan, and those things can be a little over the top. I glance at him, only to see a horrified look of amusement on his face.

"What treasure?" the woman asks, her voice tight with panic. "We don't know of any—"

"It was stolen from us," the third pirate says. I guess, by process of elimination, it's the one with the hook for a hand, though he's far enough away that I can't really see him that well past his companions. "So if you'll kindly tell us—"

"Arr!" the crazy slasher pirate screams. I jump. Lincoln lets out a snort.

And all five of them turn in our direction.

5

IN WHICH
THE REVERIE
STARTS TO GET A LITTLE DAMP

The pirates might only have four eyes and five hands between them . . . but their legs work just fine. Lincoln nearly yanks my arm out of its socket as he pulls me back the way we came, but I know, even before we've gone more than a few steps, that we're in major trouble. Something heavy—something huge—hits me in the back, and I go down hard, Lincoln's hand slipping from mine as I fall.

I scream and squirm and try to get out from under the weight that smells like old fish, stale beer, and a body that hasn't been properly washed in a few decades. But it's no use. I'm just not strong enough. I look up, just as two figures sprint past, their shoes slapping on the hard floor.

"Arr!" the guy on top of me screams. He manages to grab my wrists and pin them to the floor. "Them curs be gettin' away!"

I hear a nearby grunt, and I turn my head to find Lincoln a few feet from me, pinned under his own pirate. "Maybe if you didn't call them names," he says, his voice tight, "they would've told you what you wanted to know."

The pirate—the one wearing the fancy hat and eye patch—reaches for his dropped sword. A moment later, the sound of the hard handle hitting Lincoln's skull reverberates through the space.

"No!" I shout. "Stop it!"

That gets me my own blow to the side of the head. It feels like it's just from a fist.

Lucky me.

"I'm fine, Riley." Lincoln closes his eyes for a moment as he rests his head against the smooth tile floor. But he doesn't get to rest for long. The pirate who's got him pinned gets off him, grabs him by the back of his shirts, and hauls him to stand. I hear him choke a little before he manages to get his feet under him.

"Who be ye?" the pirate asks. "Ye be the ones what pilfered our treasure?"

"No," Lincoln says. "But maybe we can help you find it."

"Arr," my pirate says. "Ye'll steal it."

"What would I want with your treasure?"

"Everybody be wantin' our treasure," the hatted pirate says.

"We don't even know what your treasure is. So how could we have stolen it?"

They're both silent for a moment, as if they're mulling that over. They don't strike me as particularly bright, so I'm not sure exactly what's going through their heads.

I just hope it isn't ways to hurt us.

"Arr!" my pirate says, startling me as he climbs off my body. Before I can so much as move, though, he grabs me under the arms and lifts me like a child. As he places me on my feet, I will my knees to lock so I don't crumple back into a heap on the floor.

"Tie them up," the hook-handed pirate says. He's just been watching the whole time, not bothering to join in. Maybe he's at a disadvantage with that hook. Frankly, I'm glad he didn't try to stop either one of us; the tip of that prosthetic looks pretty sharp.

"Why?" Lincoln asks, which causes all the pirates to turn to him. "You can get answers from us just as well if we're *not* tied up."

"Aye," the hatted pirate says. "But ye'll be runnin' away afore ye can give us our answers. So ye'll be tied up like the swine ye be."

"Seriously?" I whisper to Lincoln. He shoots me a warning look and turns back to the pirate in the hat.

"If you tell us what you're looking for—"

"Treasure!" my pirate screams. "Arr!" He grabs me by the front of my sweater with one meaty hand. "Where's me treasure?"

"I don't know!" I squeak. My eyes feel so wide. Lincoln's don't look much better. He reaches up and gingerly pokes at his head. His fingers come back covered in something dark, and he shoots the hatted pirate a glare.

"This is a shitty way to conduct business. If you're just going to yell at us and abuse us, you're not going to get what you want."

I know the words are a mistake as soon as they're out of his mouth. He probably realizes it, too, but only after the pirate has already lashed out with his sword. The scream sticks in my throat. *What happened? Is he bleeding? Did the blade—*

"Ow." He looks over at me, his expression strange. I can't see anything wrong . . . until a few seconds later when the dark stain starts to seep through the front of his t-shirt.

"Oh, my god. Lincoln . . ."

"Stay back," he says, his voice fierce as he shoots me a warning look. "Don't."

I realize I'm about an instant away from kicking ol' arr-face right in the nuts. He's so focused on his partner skewering Lincoln that he doesn't even see how pissed off I am. He's standing there with this eager, psychotic smirk.

"Riley."

I turn back to Lincoln. He gives his head a quick shake.

"Tie them up," the hook-handed pirate says again. He shoots me a squinty frown, almost like he's trying to see me better. I don't know how these guys can see much at all. My phone is gone—*where the hell did it go?*—so the only light is from the lantern that's still sputtering away on the side of the fountain.

The two pirates still in possession of both hands drag me and Lincoln closer, then slam us back to back. It's a good thing he's taller than me, or our heads would've collided for sure.

"Sit ye down, scurvy curs."

I don't even know who's talking. My heart's beating so hard that my vision is jumping all over the place, and I can't seem to focus on anything. *Relax*, I tell myself. *It's just a Reverie. These morons can't actually hurt you.* I know that's not actually true, though. While they might not be able to cause any lasting damage, they can make us feel pain. At my back, I feel Lincoln start to sink to the ground. He's not fighting it, so I figure I better not try, either.

When we're sitting, back to back, on the hard floor, the hatted pirate disappears into the nearby store. He returns a moment later with a coil of rope. It looks like something you'd use to climb a wall or a rock face. Something synthetic. But the pirate doesn't comment on that. He hands one end to his loud shipmate and starts wrapping the rope around our chests, binding us together.

"Not so tight," Lincoln says, his voice sounding pained.

"It be tight or ye'll escape."

"Where are we going to go? There are three of you and two of us. You've got swords. None of you are injured."

"Arr!"

"Shut up," I mutter under my breath. Maybe the pirate doesn't hear me. Or maybe he's just ignoring me.

"If you want us to—" Lincoln breaks off with a grunt as the rope tightens painfully. "If you want us to talk, we have to be able to breathe."

The hatted pirate looks over at the one with the hook, who shakes his head.

"Your ability to breathe is sufficient."

"How come *you* don't talk like an idiot?" I ask. I guess all the adrenaline coursing through my system is making me bold. Or stupid.

"There be nothin' wrong with talkin' like a matey," the hatted pirate says before his more erudite companion can say anything at all.

"You sound stupid."

"Riley," Lincoln says, his voice weary. "Stop."

I bite my lips together and lean back into his body. The pirates finish tying us up, using some bulky knot that might or might not be done correctly. In any case, it doesn't look like something we'll be able to wiggle out of. My arms are pinned at my sides, and I can barely move at all.

Instead of interrogating us as I expect, though, the pirates step away to have a little huddle. I turn my head as far as I can so I can keep my voice low.

"Are you all right?"

"Yeah. I'm great." He takes a deep breath that I can feel through the rope. "Never better."

"Please don't die, okay?"

He lets out an amused grunt. "You want to stay in this Reverie?"

"No. But I don't want to be strapped to a dead body, either."

"The Reverie would end the moment I died. But I don't think that's going to happen any time soon."

"You just got stabbed."

"Barely. He poked me with the end of his sword. I don't think it went in very far. Enough to bleed, but . . ."

"So you're *not* going to die?" My voice comes out sounding disappointed. He chuckles weakly.

"I'll chalk your waffling up to the stress of the situation."

"There's no waffling. I want this stupid Reverie to end. I just don't want you to have to die to make that happen."

"I'm touched."

I feel the familiar annoyance creeping back in. It's almost a relief. But it's also a distraction. I shake my head and lower my voice a little more. "How do we get out of this?"

"Hell if I know."

"It's your Reverie."

"So?"

"So, if you're going to include vicious pirates, you should have a way to defeat them."

"Maybe we're not supposed to defeat them."

I snort. "What are we supposed to do? Befriend them?"

"I don't know, Riley." He sounds so tired. I'm not sure if it's because he's been stabbed—well, more like mildly pierced, if he's to be believed—or if he's just tired of having Reveries with someone who's not into it at all.

"I . . ." I begin. The words seem to stick in my throat. I swallow hard. "I'm sorry."

"For what?"

"It's one thing ruining my own Reveries. But this is yours. So . . . I'm sorry."

"How are you ruining it?"

"The same way I ruined all the others."

He sighs. "You didn't ruin anything. Those Reveries were amazing. Especially for a beginner. A little intense, but . . ."

"A little?"

"Just a little." He shifts. A moment later, I feel one of his hands on my own. I grasp it gratefully, trying to get a good grip on his fingers at that awkward angle. "I'm the one who's sorry," he says, his voice so soft that I almost can't hear him. "I never should've forced you into those situations. And I'd get you out of this one right now . . . if I could."

I shake my head, understanding what he means. "Why don't we just try to finish? I'll do my best."

"You don't have to do that for me."

Yes, I do. It's the least I can do. I look over at the pirates. They're not paying attention to us at all; they're so engrossed in their conversation.

Actually, it looks like there's a bit of an argument going on. There's a lot of hand—and hook—waving, and plenty of ridiculous pirate-speak. I'm not sure if the guy who keeps saying "Arr!" is entirely with it.

The floor suddenly feels cold. I jerk a little as I realize that what I'm feeling is wetness. *Holy crap. Did I just pee my pants?* My heart races as I take a few sniffs, trying to figure out what happened. But it's not pee I smell. It's something familiar. Something I haven't smelled in months. Not since I went to the beach.

"Um . . . Riley?"

"What?"

"Why are my pants wet?"

"Shit," I whisper. I look over toward the lantern, watching where the golden glow is being cast on the floor. The ripples of water flash in the faint light.

"I swear, I didn't piss myself."

"It's seawater," I say. "The doors in the food court must've given out."

"Great . . ." He draws out the word.

"It's not that deep."

"Not yet. Remember how high up the doors the water came? If it gets that high in here . . ."

I pull up my legs and brace the soles of my boots on the floor. "We need to stand up."

"And then what? You think we can run like this?"

"I'm not suggesting it. But unless you want to stay sitting and eventually drown . . ."

He lets out a groan. "Ritch is going to hear about this."

"Where is he, anyway? If he's your Cicerone, shouldn't he be here?"

"Not necessarily. Rainraven obviously isn't a major character in this scenario." He presses his back against mine. "You ready? If we lean against each other, we should be able to get up."

"Okay. Yeah." I fumble around for his other hand until I'm holding both. "Ready?"

"Go," he says. I try to brace my boots and push back hard, but before we can get more than a few inches off the ground, my feet slip out from under me on the watery floor, and we both go down with . . . well, not a splash. It's more like a wet plop.

"Ow."

"Sorry," he says.

"I can't get a grip with my boots."

"Neither can I. Maybe—"

"Avast!" the loud pirate shrieks, waving his sword in our direction. I pull back in alarm as I see him rushing over.

"What?" I shout, my panic making me unable to modulate my volume at all.

"Ye be tryin' to escape!"

"No, we're not."

The hatted pirate strides closer, drawing his own sword. I squeeze Lincoln's hands as the pirate positions himself beside us and points the tip of his sword at Lincoln's head. I choke back a squeak of fear.

"Please," I say. "Let us go."

"We be wantin' our treasure," he says.

"We don't have it!"

"Ye know where it be."

"No! Why would we know where your treasure is?"

"Ye be in the company of that scurvy cur."

"What? Who?" I ask, frowning up at him in the gloom. *Does he mean Lincoln?* But the pirate just waves his hand back the way we came.

"Farley. That mangey sea-dog."

"What does he have to do with any of this?" I ask, twisting to try to see Lincoln, but giving up before I can wrench my neck too hard. "How does Farley know these guys? They're not even from the same era!"

The pirate wiggles the point of his sword closer to our faces, and I flinch. "Farley be stealin' our treasure ev'ry other week."

"Arr," the unhinged pirate agrees. "Until we be takin' out his eyes."

My own grow so wide that I'm afraid they're going to pop right out. "Lincoln . . . Lincoln . . . Please don't—"

"It's fine. Relax. They're not going to—" He grunts as the sword flashes out toward his face. I let loose a scream that echoes around the cavernous space, and start to struggle against the rope.

"Fuck you!" I scream, nearly toppling us sideways in my attempts to free myself from our bonds. "You lousy assholes! I'm *never* telling you where your treasure is now. Never!"

"Riley," Lincoln says.

"*Never!*"

"Riley!" He digs his fingers into my hands. "I'm fine. He missed."

My body goes limp. "What?"

"He missed."

"Arr!" the crazy one shouts, then dissolves into laughter. He sounds like a deranged hyena. "That be why Morgan don't be doing the disembowellin'. His aim be worse than a nought-eyed water flea's."

I look up at Morgan. The light from the lantern is reflecting off the water now, casting wavy reflections of gold all over the space. His expression is hard to pin down. He might be embarrassed. He might be angry. He might be trying to puzzle out what his friend meant by "a nought-eyed water flea." But he's just standing there, like a statue out of a nightmare, still holding his sword pointed toward us.

"Arr?"

Morgan and the hook-handed pirate ignore their companion's sudden—and oddly inquisitive—outburst. The crazy pirate shuffles sideways, passing us and moving into the shadows behind me.

"Arr!"

"What be wrong with ye, Holler?" Morgan asks. But the man doesn't answer. I hear wet footsteps as he makes a quick retreat. Morgan and the other pirate glance at each other, then turn to look at me and Lincoln. "What be wrong with him?"

"How should we know?" Lincoln says. "But maybe you should follow him."

They glance at each other again. They look like they might be considering it. I frown and twist my neck to whisper to Lincoln.

"What is this? A plot hole?"

"What?"

"Why is he running?"

"How should I know?"

I turn back to face the pirates, not wanting to take my gaze off of them for too long. "It's your Rev—" My voice catches as I see the flash behind the hook-handed pirate's shoulder. A flash of movement. And a flash of . . . metal. "Oh, shit."

"What?" Lincoln says, detecting the alarm in my voice. "What's wrong?"

I start kicking at the slippery floor in an effort to get to my feet. "Stand up!" I shriek. "Now!"

"Why? What's going—"

"Mirror," I say. As if the word breaks some sort of spell, both the remaining pirates slowly turn. When they see her standing there, two stores down, they let out a collective gulp. It's almost like something you'd hear in a cartoon. The next thing I know, they're sprinting past us, splashing water everywhere.

"What's she doing here?" Lincoln asks, then doesn't wait for an answer. "Wait!" he shouts, aiming his desperate plea at the rapidly retreating pirates. "You have to untie us!"

I continue to struggle to stand, even as I watch the horrible vision materialize out of the darkness in front of me. Just like before, her face is nothing but a blank mirror with subtle contours, reflecting the room and the meagre light from the pirates' forgotten lantern. She looks a little different this time. I guess she looks a little different every time. *Air, fire, earth, and water,* I remind myself. And this version of Mirror fits perfectly into the pattern. Her arms are covered in fine, silvery scales that catch the light. Her dress seems to be made of seafoam, studded with tiny starfish and seahorses. None of them are moving, though, and I suspect they're dead. Her hair appears to be made of water itself, twisting and reforming in the air. Droplets separate for an instant, only to be reabsorbed into the watery coif. As she moves closer, I look down at her feet . . . or, where her feet should be. But it's almost like her dress is trying to become one with the water on the floor. I can't see her feet, in any case.

"This doesn't make any sense," Lincoln says, almost to himself.

"Why not?" I snap, keeping a wary eye on the supernatural woman moving ever closer. I have no idea what kind of torture she has in store for us this time, but I'm pretty sure it's not going to be pleasant. In fact, I suspect it's going to be something out of Lincoln's worst nightmare, given her appearance. "You created her."

"Yeah, for *your* Reverie. Why is she in one of mine?"

"We don't have time to figure that out," I say, trying again to push against the floor. But the salt water is making the surface slick. My boots might be great on ice and snow, but they suck when it comes to liquid water. "Come on! Work with me, here."

"I'm trying." He grunts, and I hear a splash. "The floor's too slippery."

"No shit!"

"Keep trying. Maybe if we—" He breaks off in surprise as the rope binding us suddenly goes slack. I don't know how or why, and I don't really care. I let go of his hands so I can pull the rope off over our heads. He jumps to his feet and grabs me by the hand. I don't ask any questions. I just hold tight as we start to run, our feet splashing. The water's well over our ankles now, and it's hard to get any sort of speed going.

I let out a yelp as he stops, wrenching my arm. I look back at him and see the expression of horror on his face. It isn't until I see him lifting into the air that I realize he didn't stop on purpose. I glance over at Mirror, only to see her standing with one arm stretched high into the air, her hand curled almost like she's holding someone by the back of the neck.

"Let go," Lincoln says, his eyes wide. I hold on tighter, then use my other hand to reinforce the grip. My feet leave the floor, and I hear them dripping as we rise into the air. "Let go!" he screams, his eyes wild. It so startles me that I lose my grasp. I'm not that high yet, so I manage to stay standing as I splash back into the water.

All I can do is watch as he moves upward, away from me. Mirror seems to have some sort of plan, because she's not moving him straight up. She seems to be pulling him backward at the same time. I let my gaze fall, spotting the fountain. And I suck in a gasp.

All the times I've been to this mall, I've never paid much attention to the fountain. I might have when I was younger, since I loved to throw pennies into fountains to make wishes. But I've never thrown pennies into *this* fountain. It's too new, built when the mall was renovated a few years ago. So I've never really noticed the sculpture in the middle, the one with the stylized metal waves that jut up like silver knives into the open space above.

"Why?" I ask. My voice comes out in a whimper. I pull my gaze away from Lincoln, who's being held in the air by some invisible force—probably the same invisible force that pinned him to his own bedroom wall when we first encountered Mirror—and turn my attention to the terrifying water spirit. She doesn't seem to notice me at all. Her focus is entirely on Lincoln, who's now hovering about twenty feet above the fountain . . . and about ten feet above the deadly points of that sculpture. "Hey!" I shout, my voice shaking only a little. "Water bitch! What the hell do you want from us?"

She doesn't turn. But she does let her hand fall.

Lincoln screams as he plummets toward the sculpture.

6

IN WHICH
I MAKE
A CONFESSION

I scream, too. The sound catches in my throat, though, as I watch Lincoln fall. It looks like he passes right through the sculpture . . . although, that may be some sort of optical illusion brought on by the meagre lantern light and all the tilting golden reflections. When he hits the bottom of the fountain, a terrible cracking noise ricochets through the space. I really hope it's an auditory anomaly . . . but I know it's not.

I reach the edge of the fountain and find him crumpled in a heap on the bottom. Despite the fact that the water on the floor is past my ankles, the bottom of the fountain is dry. And he's just lying there, panting, among a smattering of glinting coins.

"Riley," he gasps. "Watch out."

I whip around, searching in the gloom for the threat. But I don't see anyone. The space Mirror occupied just moments ago is empty. Turning back to Lincoln, I shake my head.

"She's gone."

"Of course she is." He presses his forehead against the bottom of the fountain and sucks in a few breaths. "You need to go."

"Excuse me? I'm not leaving you here by yourself." I step over the knee-high lip of the fountain. Only when I move closer do I see the problem. I close my eyes, but not fast enough. The retch that follows echoes through the space.

"What's wrong?" he asks. There's a pause. "Oh."

I shake my head and open my eyes. And I very purposely keep my gaze away from his left leg, even though I can still see it—and its completely unnatural curvature—out of the corner of my eye. "We need to get back to the others."

"How am I supposed to get there?"

"Lean on me," I say, bending down to offer him my hand. But he just looks up at me in disbelief. In the dim light, I can see where Morgan caught him with the sword. The deep cut is bleeding. Half an inch higher, and he probably would've lost his eye.

"I can't," he says.

"Well, you can't stay here!" My voice comes out in a shout. "This level's flooding, and if you don't want your worst nightmare to come true, we need to get to higher ground."

He pushes himself up with his fists. A strangled roar emanates from between clenched teeth. "Damn it! I can't, Riley. It hurts too much. Without crutches or something, I—"

"So I'll find crutches. Or something else that . . ." I trail off as I look over in the direction of the outdoor outfitter.

"What?"

I scramble out of the fountain, grabbing the lantern as I go. I hold the light high as I plunge into the lapping darkness of the store. Displays of tents and campfire setups crouch in the gloom, the smaller items floating in the rising water. I bypass the racks of outerwear, hurry past the wall of hiking boots, and ignore the freeze-dried food display. I'm about to let out a wail of frustration, but then I finally spot what I'm looking for, loosely looped around the rigid hands of a mannequin. I set down the lantern on a nearby shelf so I can extricate what I need.

"Riley!" Lincoln calls. My heart surges. Has Mirror returned? I grab the lantern and my prize and hurry back to the fountain. Lincoln's right where I left him, trying not to look at the new angle in his lower leg. I set the lantern down on the edge of the fountain and climb back inside.

"Here," I say, handing him the long, skinny object.

He takes it slowly, a bemused expression on his face. "What am I supposed to do with one ski pole?"

"It's not a ski pole. It's a hiking pole. And you're going to use it—and me—as crutches."

"I don't think—"

"I don't care what you think," I snap. "Once you brought Mirror into it, you lost the—"

"Whoa," he says, staring up at me with wide eyes. "You're blaming *me* for this?"

"She's your character. This is your Reverie." I step closer and crouch down beside him, trying to get into a good position. "Why are you torturing yourself?"

He presses his lips together and doesn't say anything. I tug on his arm. "Come on. We have to get out of here. It won't be long before the water starts spilling *into* the fountain. And then . . ."

"I can swim."

"You really want to swim in dark water with that broken leg flopping around? Sure. That sounds like a great plan."

"And hopping all the way to Phantasmazine is a better one?"

"You want to go to Phantasmazine?"

He shakes his head wearily. "I'm just saying." He quickly swipes his fingers over his eyes, and I realize he's crying.

"Why are you doing this?" I ask, my voice gentle. He turns to me in surprise.

"Doing what?"

"Hurting yourself. This is your Reverie, right?"

"Yeah." He sighs. "Yeah, it is." Grasping the pole with one hand, he reaches around my shoulders with his other arm. "I apologize in advance if I end up screaming in your ear."

"Is there a pharmacy in the mall?"

He snorts. "I don't think a couple of aspirin are going to help."

"Maybe there's something stronger."

"You want to kill me with an overdose?"

My lip trembles. I let my butt fall onto the hard bottom of the fountain and turn my head away. He leans closer, resting his head against mine.

"I'm sorry," he whispers. "It's just the pain talking."

"You think I want you to be in pain?"

He's silent for a moment. When he finally takes a breath to speak, I can hear it shake. "I think *I* want me to be in pain."

I frown and pull away a little so I can turn to him. "Huh?"

"Maybe I *am* hurting myself on purpose."

"No kidding. But why?"

He shakes his head slowly and looks down at the coins glinting in the dim light. "I'm punishing myself. At least, that's what Ritch thinks."

"Punishing yourself for what?" I ask, my annoyance growing along with my confusion.

"This." His voice is small.

"The Reverie?" My confusion deepens. "All the Reveries? Lincoln, you always fared worse than I did. Except the first time, but that was—"

"That was my fault, too," he says miserably.

"I got sick and hit my head. Not your fault."

"But it was." He stares at me, his gaze intense. His eyes look a little shinier than usual. "I'm the reason you were sick. I pushed too hard. You weren't ready. Ritch told me to take things slowly, but then I went ahead and threw you into another scenario. I told myself I was going to explain everything, but then that Reverie with the dragon was so intense. And you freaked out about the graphic novel, so I never got a chance." He shakes his head as he closes his eyes. A tear detaches and rolls down his cheek, catching the glow from the lantern. "And then I went and did it *again*. I pushed you into it, even though you didn't want to be there. I could've listened to you when you told me. We could've just gone back to the beginning and ended it."

"So why didn't you?" I ask, keeping my voice as gentle as I can. He looks like he's on the verge of dissolving into full-on sobbing, and I don't know if I'm ready to see that. Not from him. Not from the self-assured Cicerone who confidently navigates the batshittery of the Reverie world.

He keeps his eyes closed as he takes a deep, shaky breath. "I didn't want to lose you."

I don't say anything. What can I say? I'm not even sure what he means. Lose me as a charge? A Reverie companion? A friend?

Something else?

He pulls his arm away from me so he can swipe the tears from his cheeks. "By the time I realized how badly I'd messed this all up, you were so pissed off with me. All I ever wanted was to give you what Ritch gave me. I loved the Reveries . . . and I thought you would, too. But now I've screwed up so bad that you don't even want to write anymore, and I—"

"I'm still writing," I say, stopping him before he can say anything else. If he doesn't cool it, I'm going to end up crying, too.

He frowns at me. "You're still writing?"

"Not a lot, but . . . there's something I've been playing with for the last couple of months."

Another blink sends more tears cascading down his cheeks. "Historical fiction?"

I shake my head. "Not exactly." I bite my lip as I try to think. Do I tell him? Do I deny it? Twist the truth? I don't even know anymore. Glancing over at the lantern, I sigh. "I'm trying something new."

"Something new . . ."

"See, there's this girl who lives with her aunt in a beautiful little town in a river valley. When she's eleven, her town is attacked by airships as part of the ongoing war. Only a few people survive, and she vows to get revenge. Years later, when she's seventeen, she's learned to be this badass. She joined one of the regiments of dragon riders in the south, and she's pretty good with a rifle, too. But when she's shot down during a raid in the north, she's taken prisoner by a handsome young captain. She can't decide whether she wants to kiss him or kill him, even though his people slaughtered hers. I guess you could say she's conflicted. But they end up having to work together when a new threat comes at them from the west, forcing unlikely alliances and taking the war in a whole new direction." I suck in a deep breath, then let it out in a quick sigh.

Lincoln just stares at me for a moment. "Is that all?" he says at last.

"What?"

A sad little smile creeps onto his lips. "I knew it."

"You didn't know anything," I say, a twang of annoyance creeping into my voice. It doesn't help that his smile is growing. "Okay, fine. Shut up."

"It's hard to . . . *not* do it, eh?"

"Not do what?"

"Write. Think about writing. It's just what we do."

"I guess."

"For what it's worth, I think that sounds like an awesome story."

"It's a work in progress. I've still got a lot of loose ends."

He nods and swipes his fingers over his cheeks again. "So . . . what was the threat from the west?"

"Promise you won't laugh?"

He nods and uses his index finger to make a quick "X" over his heart.

"Zombies."

He laughs.

"Shut up."

"I'm sorry. But that's . . ."

"Stupid?"

"No. Perfect. It's perfect." He reaches out again, slipping his arm around my shoulders. "If you can have a bilateral air force comprised of dragons and steampunk airships, why can't they be fighting a common zombie enemy?"

"When you say it like that, it sounds stupid."

"Some of the best stories sound kind of stupid when you condense them down into a single sentence. If you're writing it, I'm sure it'll be anything but stupid." His fingers tighten on my shoulder. "We should get going."

I blink, a bit disoriented by the sudden change in subject. Beside me, a ripple of water splashes over the lip of the fountain. My heart surges in alarm.

It takes what feels like an eternity to get him onto his feet. But with the support of the hiking pole on one side and me on the other, he manages to stand up. He's shaking, though, and I know it's only going to get worse. Leaving him for a moment, I step away to grab the lantern, just as another small wave tumbles over the lip of the fountain. A second later, and the flame probably would've been extinguished. I turn back to him, lifting the light a little higher. He looks pale and queasy, and I can't blame him at all. The way his leg is just sort of hanging there does not look right. I step forward to rejoin him, but he shakes his head as he angles his body toward the edge of the fountain.

"I should probably do this part by myself," he says.

"Do what?"

"Get out of here. I have to get my leg over that lip, and it'll probably be easier on my own."

I frown. "You sure?"

He nods and hops closer to the edge. The movement seems to jar his leg, and he sucks in a sharp breath. "Damn. No sudden moves."

"Be careful," I say, stepping closer so I can give him as much light as possible. He leans on the pole as he carefully lowers himself down onto the edge of the fountain, then swivels sideways and gets his good leg out. Before starting the rest of the manoeuvre, he hands me the pole.

"Here goes nothing." He takes a deep breath, blows it out, and carefully grasps his lower leg in both hands. As he lifts it up and over the lip of the fountain, he grits his teeth so hard that I can hear the awful sound of them grinding together.

"You're allowed to scream," I say, but he probably doesn't hear the last word. I don't even hear it over the sound of agony that pours out of him.

He lets go of his leg, letting it fall into the water. It looks like an unnecessary jostle, and I don't know why he's done it . . . until I see his head wobbling. I quickly set down the lantern in the (mostly) dry fountain, drop the pole, and hurry to grab his shoulders as he starts to tilt. "Lincoln. Lincoln!" Grasping his face in both hands, I twist his head to face me. "Hey. Don't do that. Please, don't do that. I need you to—" He sucks in a gasp as his eyes go wide.

"Treasure," he mumbles.

"What?"

"What?" He blinks, trying to focus on my face. "What happened?"

"You passed out a little."

"A little?"

"Please don't do that when we start walking."

"No promises." He pulls out of my grasp and looks down at his leg. "Jesus Christ. Why the hell does this have to hurt so much?"

"Because your tibia and fibula are snapped in half?"

"It's a Reverie. The least my brain could do is dial down the pain. It doesn't *have* to hurt this much."

I straighten up with a frown. "So . . . dial it down."

"I would if I could." He shakes his head slowly. "I've always been all in with these things. Why stop now?"

"Because we might not make it out of here if you don't."

He looks up at me. "Riley, I want you to promise me something."

I narrow my eyes. "What?"

"Promise."

"Not until I know what I'm agreeing to."

He sighs and looks away, toward the lantern. "Might want to pick that up."

I look over at the lantern. Water is lapping around the base. In fact, there's enough water in the bottom of the fountain now that the strap on the hiking pole is starting to float. I grab the lantern and pull it up out of the water before passing over the hiking pole.

"I want you to promise me that, if I *can't* make it upstairs . . . you will."

I shake my head. "I'm not leaving you here to drown."

His gaze is intense in the golden light as he stares up at me. "If this is our second chance . . . I mean, if this Reverie is mine, and you're my Cicerone, then the connection is back on. Or . . . *a* connection is back on. And I—" He breaks off, his lip trembling. "What is *wrong* with me?" he whispers.

"What do you mean?"

"I'm doing it again. Forcing you to keep a connection that you don't want." He shakes his head and looks away. "I'm sorry. Never mind."

Gripping the lantern's handle tightly in one hand, I step over the edge of the fountain into the nearly knee-deep water. Curiously, it feels warm. More like a swimming pool than a rogue ocean tide. I get into position on his right and offer him my free hand.

"I'm not letting you die in here, okay? Forget the connection for now. I'm doing this because I don't want you swimming with the fishes."

He snorts. Weakly. But I'm relieved to see the twinkle of amusement in his eyes.

"And if I have to keep putting up with your annoying presence to save you, then that's the price I'm willing to pay."

"I'm touched."

"You should be."

He regards my hand for a moment before grasping it. Using me and the pole, he manages to haul himself to his feet. When he's standing, he sort of throws his arm around my shoulders and leans against me, head bowed. He's breathing hard.

He might not be able to do this. What then? I'm not leaving him down here. I'm not. We're doing this. We're getting out of here. We're going to finish this Reverie and figure out what's going on.

"Slowly," I say as I slip my arm around his waist. His whole body is shaking.

"Not too slowly. The water's rising fast."

I don't even want to think about that. Instead, I focus. I try to conjure up a mental map of the mall. The escalator is too far. At least, the one we used before is too far. There's another that I know of, but it's even farther. I feel my body start to sag. And then I remember.

"Come on," I say, tightening my grip on his body and turning in the opposite direction. Away from the rest of the mall. Toward the glass elevator on the far side of the fountain.

The water pulls on my lower legs with each step, and I can't even imagine what it's like for him. Well, I *can* . . . but I'd prefer not to. I'm probably going to have bruises on my shoulder when this is all over. And I'm never going to forget the sound of his stifled little sniffle-sobs in my ear. It's almost worse than the sound of his wheezy whimpers after being roasted by the dragon because, this time, death is nowhere even close. He just has to put up with the pain and hope we can figure out how to finish this Reverie.

If it involves running, though, we're screwed.

It takes what seems like forever before we finally reach the elevator. When we come to a stop in front of the closed doors, I start to panic. *What if it's shorted out from all the water? It might not even work. And then we'll have to go back the way we came, and you've just added another hundred feet or so to this torture march—*

"You going to press the button?" he asks. His voice is strained, but now that we're not moving, he seems to be able to breathe a little better. Using the hand gripping the lantern handle, I extend my index finger and angle it toward the button, my heart pounding. The lantern bangs against the wall, then leans as I press my finger against the brushed metal circle. As the edge lights up in red, I suck in a breath and hold it, listening.

"It's not working," I say, my voice coming out in a devastated whisper. I almost burst into tears right then and there.

"Give it a minute," he says, turning his gaze upward. I follow it and spot the triangles above our heads. The one pointing down is lit up, the bluish glow seeming to hang like mist above us.

Still, I don't dare to get my hopes up until I hear a strange gushing noise. The doors slide open in front of us, and water rushes into the little box, pulling at our legs. Lincoln lets out a cry and falls against me, almost as if crushing my body is going to help his pain. His head, pressed against my own, seems to be vibrating.

"Breathe," I remind him, because he seems to have forgotten. He sucks in a few breaths in quick succession. "Not so fast."

"Make up your mind."

"You're going to hyperventilate and pass out."

"I wish I would."

"How would I get you back to Phantasmazine?"

"Drag me. It would probably be easier than this." He reaches out with the pole and whacks it against the edge of one of the doors as they try to close. "Let's go. I have to get out of this water."

I don't argue. I just move forward, into the elevator, and try to get us into a convenient position. The light from the lantern reflects against the glass walls, making it next to impossible to see outside. Not that there's much to see, other than a fountain that's slowly filling up with a supernatural storm surge. I press the button for the second floor and hold my breath.

I worry that the weight of the water will pose a problem, but the elevator's obviously pretty strong because it moves smoothly upward, hardly making any sound. The water drains between the doors as we rise, but not quickly enough. When the doors open, the first thing that exits the elevator is a gush of seawater. It spills out over the floor, glistening in the lantern light. I regard it warily as we step forward, onto the slick surface.

"Be careful," I warn him.

"You, too. If you fall, we're both going down."

He's right. There's no way we're not going to slip at some point. I let go of his waist and turn to him with a frown. "Can you stay standing?"

"As long as I don't move. Why?"

I don't answer. I just hurry away, heading for the nearest store, which sells—by some miracle—household linens.

7

IN WHICH
WE FOLLOW
THE TOWEL BRICK ROAD

I head straight for the bathroom section of the store and sweep as many towels as I can carry into my free arm. I dump them just outside the door, then go back for more. It takes at least five trips (I kind of lose count) before the shelves are empty. Returning to the knee-high pile, I grab a couple from the top before stepping carefully over to Lincoln.

"Here," I say, handing him the lantern. "Hold this."

He does, looking bemused. I shake out one of the towels—a grey one—and spread it on the floor in front of him. It soaks up the water immediately, going dark. I place the next one beyond it, the seams just touching.

"Riley, you'll never soak up all the water."

"That's not what I'm trying to do," I say, returning to the pile and grabbing another few towels. I lay out the next one, angling it slightly to create a bit of a curve toward the railing. By the time I get the path of towels to the railing itself, they're not going dark quite as quickly. I hurry back, using the makeshift path, and grab another armful of towels. Lincoln just watches in silence, holding the lantern. I can tell his arm is shaking by the way the light is bouncing around, but I don't say anything about it.

It takes a few trips back and forth, and by the time I run out of towels, I'm around the corner, couched in the darkness of the mall. I can't see the water glistening on the floor on either side of me, but I don't think it's that wet here. Sure enough, when I bend down to press my fingers against the last towel, I feel nothing but dry terry cloth. I hurry back to Lincoln, careful not to trip on any folds or edges. When I can see the lantern again, my feet start making squelching noises on the towels.

"I really don't know if I can do this," he says, handing me the lantern. I get into position beside him once more, wrapping my arm around his waist.

"Yes, you can. We'll go slow." I take a step forward, onto the first towel. He leans heavily on the pole and on me as he makes a tentative hop. A grunt escapes him. "Once we get over to the railing," I say, "you can use that. It'll be more stable than the pole."

"Great." His teeth are clenched again. I keep my gait slow—like, snail's-pace slow—and concentrate on making our journey as smooth as possible. He holds his left leg up awkwardly, trying to keep his toes from dragging on the floor.

"It's better without the water, isn't it?"

"Marginally." He blows out a breath. "Seriously, Riley. I don't think I can—"

"Shut up. We're doing this. If it takes all day, we're doing this. If it takes a week—"

"If it takes a week, I'm throwing myself over the railing and ending this Reverie." We step onto the towel nearest the railing, and he holds the pole toward me. I try to grasp it in the same hand as the lantern. It's awkward, but I manage. He reaches out and grabs the railing. I notice the difference right away. There's less pressure on my shoulders, and he's able to move a little faster.

We move around the circular walkway that overlooks the fountain, our feet squishing on the sodden towels. He doesn't say anything—he's probably too distracted by the pain—but my mind is awhirl. When I catch myself frowning, I shake my head.

"What can a Cicerone do?" I ask.

He grunts as he makes another hop. "What?"

"If I'm the Cicerone here . . . what can I do?"

"Not much. We usually set things up before the Reverie."

"What things?"

"Any specific characters we want to throw in. The genre. The setting."

"Like the library?"

"The library was already there. Just like my neighbourhood and the park were already there."

"But you tweaked the settings," I say slowly, trying to remember.

"Yeah. The auroral storm. The heavy smoke. The switch from day to night."

My frown deepens. *This* Reverie switched from day to night. Did I do that?"

"I don't know. Did you?"

I shake my head. "I didn't know I was creating a Reverie at all." I think back to our encounter in the food court before all of this started. My sudden nausea. My run to the bathroom. "Is that possible?"

"What?" he asks absently. He takes a larger hop to get over the overlapped edges of the towels, letting out a grunt as he lands.

"Creating a Reverie without knowing you're doing it."

"I don't know. Maybe."

"Have you ever done it?"

"No. When I was working with you, the Reveries were always on purpose."

"How does that work, anyway?" I ask, casting a sideways glance at him. "Do you just . . . barge into my thoughts?"

"I didn't . . ." He sighs. "It's about getting on the same mental wavelength. Something about brainwaves. Ritch explains it better."

"So you don't even know how you do it?"

"I just do it," he says. "We writers are always on the edge of that sort of mental state. It doesn't take much to push us all the way in."

"What sort of mental state would that be?"

"Daydream, basically."

"Oh."

"So if you're going there, then I just match my state with yours and . . ."

I shake my head slowly. "Why isn't everyone always zoned out, then? If it's that easy, how come people aren't just doing it with every random person on the street?"

"Because they're not in a Cicerone relationship. I don't know exactly how it works, Riley. All I know is that you have to have a connection to make the connection." He stops moving. I don't realize why until I look down and see the towels veer away from the railing, off into the darkness of the mall. "Can we rest for a sec? My good leg feels like it's going to give out."

His whole body feels like it's going to give out. The trembling is getting pretty violent. I tighten my hand on his waist, hoping it feels a little more supportive. He gives my shoulder a squeeze.

"You're doing a good job," he says.

"Of what? Pulling you into a Reverie where you get stabbed, you nearly get your eye poked out, and you have your leg bones snapped in half?"

"One, that so-called stab wound would be lucky to get a single stitch. Two, my eye is fine, thanks to Morgan's terrible aim. And three, I'm the one who came up with Mirror. I can't blame you for my own creation attacking me."

"Still."

He grunts in amusement. "If you really want to blame yourself, go ahead. But *I* am not holding you responsible for any of this. You have no training as a Cicerone. It's ridiculous to expect you to know what to do without it."

"You know what to do."

"Do you think I spent those five years with Ritch just farting around with my own Reveries? He was training me, too."

I don't say anything. My arm is getting kind of tired, and the lantern has fallen almost to my side. I lift it again, feeling my muscles shake.

"Let's go," he says as he reaches for the pole. I somehow release it (my fingers are stiff from holding it in such an awkward grasp), and he jams it against the floor. We continue down our road of towels, moving deeper into the second floor of the mall.

The soaked towels stretch farther than I remember, but, luckily, the last one is still dry as we step onto it. And when our feet clomp onto the bare floor at the end of the path, they do so steadily. Lincoln pauses to give my shoulders a quick squeeze. It feels something like a hug. I turn to him with a smile . . . but it dies a moment later as I see his face. He looks awful. His hairline is soaked with sweat. The cut under his eye has stopped bleeding, but the skin around it is dark and swollen. His lips are pinched to the point of invisibility.

"Are you okay?"

"Define 'okay.'"

"'Not about to die.'"

He shakes his head slowly. "I'm not that lucky."

"Lincoln . . ."

"Sorry."

"We're . . . almost there."

"Don't lie."

"Fine. We're not even halfway there. Happy?"

He shifts his weight toward me and hops forward. "At least . . ."

"At least what?"

"Never mind."

"Tell me."

He sighs. "Don't get weird about it."

"Why? What were you going to say?"

"Just that . . . I'm glad you're here with me. This time."

This time. Not like the time I left you with your lower half crushed under a boulder. Or when I left you blistered and oozing on the street in front of your house. "Are you . . . I mean, is that your choice?"

"What?"

"Me being here. This is your Reverie, so—"

"You still have free will, Riley. Even in my Reverie." He grunts as the next hop jostles us both. "So thank you for staying with my sorry, broken ass."

"I think your ass is the only thing that isn't damaged right now."

He chuckles weakly. "I don't know. I came down on it pretty hard when we were trying to get out of that rope."

An awful thought occurs to me, and I raise the lantern a little higher as I peer into the darkness. "They're still in here," I whisper.

"Who? The pirates?"

"Yeah. And we're sitting ducks."

"If they show up again, maybe we'll get lucky and Mirror will make another appearance. They seemed to be pretty scared of her."

"How do they even know her?"

"I doubt they do. They can probably just sense . . ."

"That she's an evil bitch?"

"No. They can sense she's powerful. Haven't you felt it?"

"Yeah," I whisper. I've felt it. My whole body has felt it. Whenever she's near, it's like . . . I don't know. Almost like electricity is filling up the space. Any spark could start an explosion. It feels precarious and dangerous and terrifying, all at once. "Why the hell would you create someone like that?"

"I wanted a good villain."

"Well, you got one. But I really wish you'd stop putting her in the Reveries."

He grunts. "I didn't put her in this one."

"Are you saying I did?"

"I don't know. Maybe. Not consciously," he says as I glance at him in disbelief. "But she's showed up in your last two Reveries. So you might've been expecting her this time."

"I guess . . ."

"I'm not blaming you, by the way."

"Good. Because she's *your* stupid villain."

"Noted."

"I don't ever want to see her again."

"Okay."

"She gives me the ultimate creeps."

"Then I guess I did my job as a writer."

"I'll be sure to make note of that in my review."

He grunts. I can't quite tell if it's from amusement or pain. "There's going to be a review?"

"Oh, yeah. I'm already writing it in my head as we speak. 'A mélange of misery and plot holes from start to finish. The main characters are too stupid to live, and the mall setting is both pedestrian and materialistic. The villain is terrifying, but she's a little over the top. One out of five stars. Do not recommend.'"

"You," he says, his voice distorted by a chuckle, "sure know how to boost a writer's self-esteem."

"I try."

We fall silent as we make our way slowly through the mall, heading back toward Phantasmazine and the rest of the Reverie's characters. Well, hopefully not the pirates. Our passage is almost silent, except for the sound of Lincoln's shoe as he hops, and his little grunts as he lands. Above us, the mall's skylights are beating out a strange rhythm. It's rain, no doubt, but it's kind of regular, too. Almost like a rhythmic dripping noise. But it sounds sharper than that. Like knuckles rapping on the glass.

Or the glass cracking.

Whenever we can, we veer close to the railings so Lincoln can use them for support. After what feels like an eternity, I happen to glance over one of the railings and see the still escalator below. At least . . . I see part of it. The water has risen a lot, and only the top few steps are actually exposed. I can see the seawater lapping and sloshing as it moves, like water in a swimming pool slapping against the sides.

Lincoln blows out a breath. "Thank goodness we didn't try for the escalator."

I just shudder as I think about it. We'd be under water by now. Possibly dead. He said he can swim, but if he passed out from the pain . . .

"Look," he says. I frown into the darkness. I can sort of see something up ahead: a tiny point of light, skimming along at around waist height. I turn to Lincoln.

"What the hell is that? A will-o'-the-wisp?"

He squints. "I don't think so. A firefly?"

"In the mall?"

"I don't know." He sighs. "I'm tired of guessing."

But we don't have to guess for too long. As we get a little closer, I see the light fly back the way it came, passing by the top of the escalator. And I can hear the sound accompanying it: little footsteps.

"Mommy!" a childish voice calls, just as the point of light comes to a bouncing stop.

"It's Harper," I say, watching as the light zips off to the right, away from Phantasmazine. Perplexed, I try to follow it with my gaze, but lose sight of it in the gloom.

"Does she usually glow?"

"No." I frown, peering into the darkness. I can hear more now. Voices. Coming from off to the right. I don't want to move too fast, but Lincoln seems to be quickening his hops. I adjust my speed to compensate. As we approach the escalator, I see movement emerge out of the shadows.

"Riley?" someone calls. It's a female voice. Young. I squint, trying to see better.

"Yeah," I say. "It's me. And Lincoln."

Two figures hurry forward, and then we can see them in the lantern light. One is Emmeline. The other is Jessica, followed by Harper. As they get close, I can see that the bobbing light we saw before is some sort of glowing tiara perched on the little girl's head.

"Nice crown," Lincoln says.

"Sorry." Jessica rushes to his other side, grabs the pole and hands it to Emmeline, and pulls his arm across her shoulders. We're both shorter than him, but once we give him some support, we're able to move a lot faster. "She saw it behind the counter and wanted it. We needed some more light, anyway."

"I'm a princess," Harper says, spinning in a tilting circle on the toe of one boot. She nearly tips over, but manages to catch herself.

"Actually, that's an elf queen's crown." Lincoln watches her as Emmeline grabs her hand and pulls her out of our way. "It went missing many years ago. Treasure hunters have been searching for it ever since."

I turn to him as my breath catches in my throat. "Is that the pirate treasure?"

He snorts. "Unlikely," he says, leaning close to my ear so he can whisper. "It's made of plastic."

"Are you sure?" I ask, peering at the crown.

"Yeah. Twenty-nine ninety-five, plus tax."

"So was the sword. And that looked pretty damn real."

He sighs. "You want to take it from her?"

"No. But if those pirates show up . . ."

"We'll deal with it then."

They lead us over to the circular arrangement of benches in the middle of the space, where three other figures are sitting. I recognize Farley right away; he's easy to spot with his long cane clutched in his fingers. I shudder as my gaze catches on his eyes. They must be glass. No wonder they don't look quite right. Now that I look at him, I see that he's not exactly dressed like someone from the twenty-first century. His dark coat is simple, with buttons instead of anything as modern as a zipper.

The other two figures seem unfamiliar at first, but then I realize I *have* seen them before. It's the man and woman the pirates had cornered at the outdoor outfitter. They're both dressed in modern clothes. The woman's ears are full of piercings, and she's got a massive, bleeding gash across one cheek. The guy is cradling one hand in his lap; it's wrapped up in what looks like his jacket. As we get closer, I smell the unmistakeable tang of fresh blood.

"You okay?" Lincoln asks as we approach. The guy just shakes his head.

"His hand's hanging by a thread," the woman says. Her voice sounds dull. She's just staring straight ahead, probably in shock.

"Keep pressure on it," Jessica says. She leads us over to an empty bench—one that's facing the railing—and positions Lincoln in front of it. "And you," she says, addressing the guy sagging between us, "sit down. Carefully."

"No. I think I'll sit down recklessly."

Jessica frowns. I shake my head.

"He's in a lot of pain."

"I can see that," she says, staring at his leg. "You need to elevate that."

"No, I need surgery. But that's not going to happen. It doesn't matter, anyway."

She gives him a dark look. "Who's the nurse here?"

"You, I'm guessing."

"That's right. So you're going to listen to me. Now . . . sit. Carefully."

We help lower him down onto the bench. He keeps his leg pulled up, though, as if he's afraid to let his foot touch the ground. I don't blame him.

"Where's Rainraven?" he asks, peering dully around the space. There's a weird glow in here. It's almost like there's a full moon and it's sending silvered light down through the skylights. But we can still hear the incessant rain. The wrongness—the illogicality of it all—makes my skin crawl.

"She went for a walk," Emmeline says. Lincoln turns to her in disbelief. "A *walk?*"

"That's what she said."

"In the dark."

Emmeline shrugs. "She said she'd tell us if she found a better place."

"I want to go see Santa," Harper says quietly.

"Santa's not here right now," Jessica says. "Remember?"

Emmeline shudders. "Thank goodness."

"Why?" Lincoln asks.

"Because his castle is underwater."

"I thought it was a workshop," I say. Lincoln shakes his head.

"There's a little workshop, but it's attached to this massive ice castle. It's almost two storeys high." He turns and peers into the darkness. "We'd be able to see it from here if the lights were on."

"Be glad you can't," Emmeline says. "It's got a bad case of crabs."

I snort. "Excuse me?"

"I'm serious. Like . . . crabs the size of large dogs. They're crawling all over the castle. Well, the part that's sticking out of the water, anyway."

"How did crabs even get into the mall?" I ask.

But she just shrugs again. I sit down beside Lincoln, setting the lantern on the bench next to me. As soon as my butt hits the hard surface, I realize how weary I am. And teary. I didn't realize how much I was looking forward to getting some answers.

"Hey," Lincoln says, and the next thing I know, he's slipping his hand into mine. I turn to him as my eyes fill with tears. "It's fine. We'll figure it out."

"How? Rainraven is the only one who might know what's going on. And she's not here."

He shakes his head slowly. "Getting answers out of her was a long shot, anyway. She's not going to tell us the really important stuff, like why we're stumbling around in a dark mall in the first place when the connection should be broken."

"We just got locked in after hours," Jessica says. She's staring down at Lincoln's leg, which is just sort of dangling there. "You can't hold it like that forever."

"What do you suggest?" he asks. "Besides putting it up. That's going to hurt, and I don't want to freak your kid out when I scream."

Harper, who's been standing off to the side, humming something to herself, takes a step toward her mom. Jessica shakes her head.

"We'll do it slowly. But if you don't get that elevated, you could lose—"

"Nobody's losing anything," he says. He turns to me, squeezing my hand. "Let's figure this out. What are we dealing with here?"

My eyes widen. "You want to just . . . talk about it? In front of them?"

"They'll ignore anything that's not part of the main narrative."

"Really?" Glancing at each of the people surrounding us, I shake my head. "Why?"

"No idea. But that's just the way it works. Unless it's some meta story *about* Reveries, they won't pay much attention when we talk about it."

"Weird."

"I know. So, what do we know so far?"

I try to focus my thoughts before I begin. "It's the middle of the night. We're trapped in a mall. It's raining so hard that a pirate ship ran aground in the flooded parking lot, and now the lower level is full of water."

"Good. What about the characters?"

I look up at Jessica. She's looking at us, but she seems to be . . . well, on a different wavelength. She's probably still thinking about Lincoln's broken leg, not listening to the weird conversation that implies she's nothing but a figment of someone's imagination. "There's us. And Rainraven. Ritch, I mean."

"Right."

"Jessica, Harper, Emmeline, Farley . . ." Trailing off, I twist around so I can see the couple on the next bench. "Those two. I don't know their names."

"Buford," the guy says, just managing to get the name out through gritted teeth. He looks like he's in about as much pain as Lincoln. Maybe more.

"Buford?" Lincoln repeats, his amusement evident in his voice.

"It's your Reverie," I mutter. "I came up with a guy named Hube in my last one, though, so I'm not going to judge."

He grunts.

"That's Misty," Buford says, tilting his head toward his companion. She looks pretty out of it.

"Okay," I say. "Buford and Misty. Plus Morgan, Holler, and . . . the guy with the hook."

"The name is Carrington," a voice says. My tense body jerks in surprise, and Lincoln's hand tightens on mine as we turn to look at each other.

"Oh . . . shoot," he whispers.

8

IN WHICH
I CONFOUND SOME PIRATES
AND GO ON A TREASURE HUNT

Lincoln turns his gaze in the direction of the voice. When I do the same, I see the three shadows emerge out of the darkness and step into the eerie skylight glow. Morgan and Holler, flanking their hook-handed companion, draw their swords.

"Oy, Farley!" Morgan shouts. "What did we be tellin' ye 'bout meetin' again?"

Farley stands up quickly, his glassy eyes wide. He raises his cane in front of him like a sword.

Holler lets loose a sound like a hyena. "This time, we be takin' yer tongue for yer scurrilous lies!"

"Your sister will still be a whore whether you touch my tongue or not."

I didn't think it was possible for Holler to look even more deranged than he already does. His eye practically rolls as he raises his sword and lets out an undulating roar.

Harper screams.

"No!" I say, turning to Lincoln in desperation. "Stop. You have to stop this! These people are innocent. And Harper's just a little kid."

That little kid is making quite a ruckus, too. She's practically climbing Jessica, like she wants her mom to pick her up and whisk her out of here. Jessica's just staring at Holler as he steps forward. Maybe she doesn't realize the danger. Or maybe she's just overloaded by the weirdness of the situation. She's a modern woman, after all. Being accosted by a trio of sword-wielding pirates in a shopping mall is not a normal thing to expect on a Saturday afternoon. Or night. Whatever.

But before things can get too intense, Carrington grabs Holler by the coattails. He yanks him back, causing the deranged pirate's arms to pin-wheel comically.

"Shut the scallywag up," Morgan says, jabbing his sword into the air in front of him, like he's miming skewering an enemy. "Or we'll give 'er somethin' to scream 'bout."

"Back off," Lincoln says. He pushes himself up to a standing position, even though I'm tugging on his arm to try to keep him in place. "Let go, Riley."

"Be caref—"

"Arr!" Holler shouts, his voice echoing up toward the skylights. Harper lets out another ear-piercing scream. And she abandons trying to get Jessica to pick her up. Instead, she turns and races into the darkness, away from the pirates. Toward Santa's Workshop. I don't know if it's a conscious choice, or if it's a simple flight response. Jessica immediately follows, shouting her daughter's name.

"Shut up, will you?" Lincoln says, addressing the pirates. "You're scaring the poor kid." He wavers a little on one leg. I stand up and offer him my arm. He leans on me heavily as he fixes his gaze on the advancing trio.

"You be wantin' another piercin'?" Morgan asks, his one eye glinting dangerously. He smiles, revealing a darkened grin. In this light, it's hard to tell whether he's missing a bunch of teeth or if they're just rotten. "I be skilled at the Prince Albert."

"Arr!" Holler says, following the exclamation with a snicker. He seems to have forgotten all about Farley, who's still standing there brandishing his cane at the foes he can't see.

"With your aim," Lincoln says to Morgan, "I'd probably end up with a nipple piercing."

The pirate's expression darkens. Dangerously. I know I have to do something. I suck in a breath and step in front of Lincoln. *Are you insane? That's a very real sword, you know.*

"I know where the treasure is!" I blurt. Morgan frowns. But Carrington nods, drawing my attention back his way.

"I know you do." His voice is soft. Too soft. It doesn't go with the funk of menace that's emanating from the three of them. "And you were just about to tell us, weren't you?"

I nod as I feel Lincoln's hands settle on my shoulders. For some reason, their warm weight fills me with strength, almost like they're charging a battery. "Yeah," I say. "I will. But first, you need to tell me exactly which treasure you're looking for. Because this place is . . . a treasure trove."

His eyebrows rise in a familiar way that makes me think of the boy standing at my back. "A treasure trove, is it? And whose treasure is hidden within these walls?"

"Um . . . all sorts of people's," I say. But that answer doesn't seem to satisfy him. He assumes an annoyed pose, resting his lone hand on his hip.

"Be more specific," Lincoln whispers in my ear. For a moment, I panic. But then the answers start to come. They don't make a lot of sense . . . but I'm hoping these three won't notice that.

"Do you think you're the first pirates to stash your booty here? No. There are all sorts of things cached away in these, um, caverns. Smartphones. Flatscreen TVs. Step-counters. Uh—"

"What be a step-counter?" Morgan asks, his voice suspicious.

Good one, Riley. Now you've stepped in it. Behind me, I hear a soft chuckle. But now is not the time to get annoyed. "It's a magical device," I say. "You wear it strapped to your wrist, and it can count the number of steps you take in a day."

"Arr!" Holler shrieks. "That be witchcraft!"

Carrington's frowning. "And what's the purpose of this device?"

"You might want to know how many steps you've taken."

"Why would you want to know that?"

I chew on my lip. Lincoln's fingers gently squeeze my shoulders.

"You're off track," he whispers. "Get back on."

"Never mind the step-counters," I say. "I'm just pointing out that there's *lots* of treasure in here. There might even be some gold."

"Arr," Holler says, his overly wide eye lighting up with greed. "Now *that* be a treasure."

"But is it *your* treasure?" I ask. His face takes on a perplexed expression. "I'm only going to help you find your treasure. If you want anything else, you'll have to find it yourself. And fight the rightful owners for it."

The three pirates exchange a look. Then they turn back to me.

"That's fair," Carrington says. He takes a step forward. As he gets closer, I can see that his eyes are a watery sort of grey. His face is covered in wrinkles, especially around the eyes, but I have a feeling he's not as old as he appears. He's probably just been out in the sun a lot, squinting and getting sun damage. "So where is it?"

"First, *what* is it?"

"Oh, I think you already know."

A surge of frustration hits me, and I almost swear. *What is wrong with these characters? I thought Lincoln was better at Reveries than this.*

But maybe I'm giving him too much credit. These pirates might not even know what they're looking for, other than some vague notion of treasure. And I think I know exactly where I can get some of that. Stepping sideways, I turn and give Lincoln a stern look. "Sit. Stay here."

His eyebrows rise. "Who do you think I am? William?"

"Air, fire, earth, water," I say. He just blinks. But then he seems to understand. He sinks back onto the bench, wincing as he hits the hard surface. I turn to the others. "Does anyone have a piece of paper and a pen?"

Emmeline shakes her head. I turn to Buford and Misty, but they're just sitting there in terror. Besides, neither of them look like they're carrying anything useful. I turn to Lincoln in desperation.

"Check a store," he says.

"How?"

He shrugs. With a growl of frustration, I turn back to the pirates. Beyond them, I can see the corner of the nearest store. There's probably a pen at the checkout. And receipt paper. I just need to get to them.

"I'm going to do some magic," I say, my voice hesitant. "But I need to get something from that cavern first." I point. All three of them turn to look, then turn back to me. "You can come with me if you're afraid I'm going to run away."

"Ye won't be runnin' away," Morgan says. He steps closer, raising his sword. "Ye run, and we'll be doin' the same thing we did to Farley to yer friend 'ere."

I look at Lincoln and swallow hard. He gives me an encouraging nod, but I shake my head.

"Go on," he whispers.

"You think I'm going to leave them here with you after he's said something like that?"

"What? Were you planning on running away?"

"No. But I don't trust them not to do something stupid just for shits and giggles."

"Arr," Holler says, looking confused. "What be shits and giggles?"

I frown at him. "Let's hope nobody finds out." With a last glance at Lincoln—who gives me a quick, pained smile—I turn and edge around the pirates, who step back to let me pass. *Now* they're going to be gentlemen?

I try not to think about what I'm going to come back to as I walk briskly to the store. I don't dare run for fear I might make them think I'm trying to escape. My boots seem so loud, but they're not quite loud enough to drown out the pounding of my heart in my ears.

I realize as soon as I reach the gaping doorway that I should've brought the lantern. It's nearly pitch black inside, and I can't see much other than shadows. Pausing for a moment, I consider going back for the lantern. But if those pirates see me coming back empty-handed, they might think I'm trying to trick them. And I don't think it would take much to push them over the edge. Especially Holler.

So I just move slowly, feeling with my hands and feet as I shuffle into the darkness. I *think* this is a clothing store, and I vaguely remember seeing the sales counter in the middle of the space. That's where I head, moving at such a slow pace that I start to panic. If I'm gone too long . . .

Don't think about it. Besides, this is his Reverie. He wouldn't actually let those pirates cut out his eyes . . . would he?

I don't know what to think anymore. After all, he did end up with a minor stab wound, a bash to the side of the head, a pretty serious cut on his face, and a severely broken leg. Maybe he *is* punishing himself.

Maybe I've been making him feel like he has to.

Yeah, I was angry about the Reveries. I still am. But not as much as I was. And, if I really think about it, the whole idea is kind of cool. If he'd done this *properly*, I might've been into it. Actually, I would've been excited about it. My own private playground to try out story ideas? Sign me up. A cute guy as my guide and muse? Hell, yeah!

But he screwed up. I don't know if I should blame him entirely, though. I mean, he's still pretty new at this, too. Ritch definitely should've been monitoring the situation more closely. He's old. He should be a lot more wise.

I trip on something (it might be the stand of a clothing rack) and sprawl forward. Luckily, my hands slam into something solid, preventing me from ending up on the floor. I get my feet more securely under me and start running my hands over the smooth surface. *The counter. Finally.* My fingers trail over the empty space before my left hand hits something hard and cold with a spiral cord. The scanner? Probably. But that means the cash register is close. I edge sideways, fumbling in the darkness. But before I can find anything large, my fingers find something much smaller. I grasp it in both hands, feeling its contours desperately.

"Yes," I whisper as I feel the delicate leaf of paper. It's the POS card reader . . . and there's a tiny scrap of paper sticking out of it. I grab it and pull, but it won't give up much. Not that I need much. So I tear off the piece, making sure I get as much as I can. There's probably something printed on it, but if I can find a pen, I can take care of that with a quick scribble.

I have to actually go around to the other side so I can access the shelves underneath. I find a few things that feel like pens, but I don't know if they all work. So I just grab a few. I don't want to have to make a return trip if I happen to grab one that's out of ink. Then I hurry back toward the dim glow of the mall.

As I get closer to the skylights, I can see my prize a little better. There's actually nothing on the receipt paper, which is a relief. I quicken my pace as I hurry back to the benches. The pirates are standing where I left them, much to my relief, and I can see the others beyond that. Jessica is back, sitting next to Lincoln with Harper curled up on her lap. The light in the kid's tiara is still glowing steadily, making a little pool of light on her mom's chest.

"Ye be findin' yer magic supplies?" Morgan asks. I nod and hold up the paper and pens. The pirates move apart to let me pass, and I step over toward the escalator. I can hear the water sloshing against the steps, and when I get close enough, I see that the level has risen even more since I last looked. Little waves are lapping at the third step. *If we don't get out of here soon, the second floor is going to flood.* I shake the thought from my head and crouch down beside the escalator. The floor is wet due to the intermittent splashes coming from below, so I press the paper against the glass under the railing and click out the nib of one of the pens.

I've never actually done this before. I don't even know if it will work. All the other times we created things from pages, we used printed words . . . not handwritten ones. *And this page thing was* your *idea, too,* I remind myself. *How do you know it's even going to work in one of Lincoln's Reveries?* The truth is, I don't know. But it's worth a try. So I press the pen to the paper and write:

A wooden chest full of gold and jewels.

"Where be yer magic?" Morgan calls. I ignore him as I stand up and crumple the paper in my fist. When I look over at the three of them, though, I see the dangerous look in Carrington's eyes.

"Writing isn't magic," he says. "If you're trying to trick—"

"I haven't done the magic yet," I say, my voice shaking. I walk closer to the escalator and step onto the very top step. The next one is shallow, and I carefully slide onto it while I grasp the rubbery railing in my free hand. The water is lapping just below my toes on the next step, and I know I need to do this carefully. If the paper floats away, the treasure won't be reachable. If I don't get the paper in just the right place, the heavy chest could go rolling down the escalator when it pops into existence.

"Arr!" Holler shouts. "Hurry!"

"You can't rush magic!" I shout back at him. "Cool your jets."

He lets out a puzzled grunt, but he doesn't say anything else. I crouch down, clutching the crumpled paper in my fist, and lean forward as I keep a tight grip on the handrail. I pinch the paper between my thumb and forefinger and move it into place on the step below me, trying to keep it wedged between the step and the riser. I feel the paper start to soften and uncurl from its ball. But I don't let go.

What if this doesn't work? I don't have any other ideas. They want treasure, and if they don't get it—

I squeak as the space in front of me suddenly explodes into form. I don't even have time to pull my hand back, which results in what feels like a punch to the knuckles from a very solid, very hard wooden chest. I stand up quickly, staring at the thing in disbelief, and stumble as my heel catches on the step behind me. Luckily, I'm still holding the handrail.

"There's your treasure," I say, stepping off the escalator and pointing. Morgan and Holler rush closer, and I skitter back, casting my gaze over toward the benches. Lincoln's just sitting there with this weird smile on his face, looking like a proud parent. A very tired, very pained parent. He looks absolutely awful. But that smile is making me feel like I could do just about anything.

"Arr!" Holler shouts, drawing my attention back to him and his companion, who have sheathed their swords so they can use all their hands to haul the chest off the steps. "It be heavy wit' treasure!"

I look over at Carrington. He's staring at me, his eyes narrowed ever so slightly. I edge toward the bench, but he gives me a little shake of his head, almost a warning.

"Open it," he says, turning and striding over to the chest. Morgan's fussing with the lock now. I didn't even think about a key, but it turns out he doesn't need one. He just draws his sword and smashes the handle down on the rusty padlock. It breaks away, scattering dark flakes of oxidized metal on the wet floor.

Everyone's kind of interested now. Lincoln's watching intently. Emmeline has her phone out to record what's happening. Buford and Misty are staring at the pirates with glazed expressions. Jessica's leaning forward, and even Harper is watching out of the corner of her eye. The only person who doesn't seem to care what's in the chest is Farley, but that's understandable; this whole treasure thing is probably a bit of a sore spot for him.

As Morgan sheaths his sword, Holler hefts the lid. The skylight glow catches on the gold coins and sparkling jewels within. Now that I think about it, I'm not sure how two men even lifted something like that off the steps. With such a cargo, the chest must weigh a ton.

"We be rich," Morgan breathes, reaching in to snag what looks like a fist-sized ruby from the top of the pile.

"Arr," Holler growls. "Take yer filthy paws off me treasure."

"Yer treasure?"

"Arr!"

"Enough." Carrington's voice is quiet but commanding. He steps forward and slams the lid shut with his hand. Holler narrowly misses getting his fingers smashed. "This isn't what we're looking for."

My heart sinks. "But . . . you wanted treasure. This is treasure."

"It's not our treasure."

"Arr!" Holler shrieks. "It be mine!" He pries at the lid, but Carrington slams his boot on top and holds it closed.

"It's not our treasure," he repeats, staring at me. "You tricked us."

"N-no," I say, looking over at Lincoln in desperation. Then I wish I hadn't, because I probably just gave the pirates some very awful ideas. I turn back at the sound of Morgan pulling his sword from its sheath. "No! I gave you what you asked for. If you're not going to tell me exactly what you're looking—" My voice catches in my throat as Morgan whips his sword toward it, and I wince when I feel the cool metal brush my skin. Lincoln sucks in a breath.

"Riley—"

"I'm fine," I say, glaring at Morgan, even though I want to look anywhere but at the man who's probably about to accidentally slit my throat. "Be careful with that thing."

"Ye be lyin'."

"I didn't lie. I thought that was the treasure you were looking for." I shift my gaze to Carrington, who's still got his boot on the chest. Probably because Holler's still doggedly trying to get into it. The crazy pirate's got his sword out now and is trying to wedge the blade into the gap between chest and lid like a crowbar. "How am I supposed to know what you . . ."

Oh, my god, Riley. You idiot.

Carrington must see the realization in my eyes. He nods. "Morgan. Let her go."

"But she be—"

"She knows where it is."

I watch the sword waver and finally fall. Only then do I let out a sigh of relief. I rush to the bench and grab the lantern. Then, without a word, I walk quickly back into the mall, lighting a golden path ahead of me.

"Hurry back," Carrington says, his voice low and dangerous. I glance over my shoulder, only to see him watching me. I turn and hurry down the concourse as quickly as I dare. The stores pass in a parade of eerie darkness and tilting shadows until, finally, I spot the familiar silhouette of the Phantasmazine sign. I turn and go inside, heading straight for the wooden stand I remember from before. The sword is still there, gleaming in the lantern light. It looks far too fancy for a grubby pirate like Carrington . . . but I know this is what he's after. He's the only one of the three without a weapon. Holding my breath, I grab the handle and lift the sword from the stand. It's heavier than I expect. This thing is definitely real. I smile a little as I carefully lower the sword to my side and hurry back into the mall.

It's over. It's over. It's over. The gleeful refrain lights up my mind as I run back down the concourse. There's no reason not to go as fast as I can. The pirates can see that I'm coming, not going. And I've got what they're looking for. As soon as I give Carrington his sword, the Reverie will end. At least, I think it will. I've never actually ended one by finishing a story. Although, this isn't even *my* Reverie. So maybe Lincoln needs to be the one to hand over the sword . . .

My boots' rhythm slows as I get closer to the benches. My heart picks up its pace, even though I'm not sure what's wrong. But something is. The mall feels colder all of a sudden. And yet, it seems to be getting brighter, too. I almost don't even need the lantern. I lower it to my side and speed up again.

When I get close enough, I see the chest sitting abandoned. The pirates have edged away. Actually, nearly everyone has. They're huddling on the far edge of the space, not quite in the shadows. Jessica's holding Harper, and the kid won't even look in my direction. I come to a stop, feeling breathless, and glance at the benches. Lincoln's where I left him, still holding his leg in that awkward position. He's shaking violently, though, and I know he won't be able to hold his leg up for much longer. Beside him sits Rainraven.

A rush of hot anger courses through me, and I storm forward. "Where have you been?" I shout. But I don't have time to wait for an answer. I wouldn't have heard it, anyway, over the terrifying roar that echoes through the space. It sounds like the death moan of an ancient god, or something equally dramatic, and I'm afraid the sound might actually kill me. My hands go slack, and both the sword and the lantern fall to the floor. The latter smashes and goes out, but it doesn't matter. The supernatural glow in here is plenty to see by.

"What the hell was *that?*" I shriek, my panic keeping my volume dialled all the way up. Lincoln stares at me with wide eyes.

"It's coming from the water."

"But what *is* it?"

Rainraven tilts her head. "Could be a kraken."

I gape at Lincoln in disbelief. "You're going to throw a kraken into this?"

"You think I'm doing this on purpose?"

"We don't know what you're doing! And this one"—I point a shaking finger at Rainraven—"is no help. Are *all* Ciceroni so inept?"

He shakes his head, looking like he might cry. I follow his gaze out past the escalator, where the water is churning and frothing as if some sort of monster is about to rise from the depths.

"Oh, god," I breathe. I turn back to him and step toward the bench. "We have to get out of here."

"Where am I supposed to go? How am I supposed to get there? In case you haven't noticed, I'm—"

"So stop it! Stop hurting yourself. Stop creating pirates and krakens and who knows what else, and just end this." I turn and look for the sword. "If you give the sword to Carrington—"

"Riley."

"What?"

"Look out."

"What?" I repeat, and turn my gaze back to him, just as he winces and throws his hands over his head.

Time seems to fall out of sync. The first thing I feel is the hard rain of glass pelting down upon us. The sound comes a moment later.

9

IN WHICH
I REFLECT ON MY LIFE CHOICES
AND MAKE A STARTLING DECISION

Harper's screaming. I think I am, too. I throw myself toward Lincoln, trying to shield him with my body, even though it's already too late. He falls back against the bench, and his leg jostles against the ground. The sound that comes out of him makes me think his soul's being ripped right out of his body.

"I'm sorry," I pant. "Lincoln, I'm sorry. End this. End it!"

"I . . . can't."

"Yes, you can! It's your Reverie. All you have to do is hand over the sword, and the story will be over."

He shakes his head. The rest of him has gone limp as he sprawls there in the pounding rain that's now falling freely from above through the broken skylight. He doesn't seem to want to move. I sit back a little and check him over. Crumbs of glass sparkle in his hair. I brush at them gingerly, afraid I'll get cut.

"It was the sword in Phantasmazine," I say. "That's what Carrington wants. Once he has it—"

"It's not Carrington you need to be worried about, love," Rainraven says, drawing my attention to her. She looks fine, if a little wet, even though she just had skylight glass rain down all over her, too. I glare.

"Then what *do* I need to worry about?" I snap. "We just want to get out of here, and you're no help."

"You don't need my help," she says. "You'll figure it out."

"Not without both of us getting PTSD!"

She shakes her head slowly. "If you don't like this story, tell a new one."

"But it's not my story!" I wail, looking at Lincoln, who's got his head tilted forward and his eyes closed. "And he doesn't know what to do. If you weren't doing this weird method-acting thing . . ."

She smiles enigmatically. "We're all actors, love. We all play our roles. Some of us just play a few more than others."

"I don't get it."

"I know." She pats my arm, then points into the dark mall, back toward Phantasmazine. I peer into the gloom . . . and nearly throw up when I see the flash of silver.

"No." I stand up and take a step back. Rainraven shakes her head. "No," I wheeze. "Not now."

"If not now, when?"

"What the hell are you talking about?" I shout. But I can't tear my gaze away from the woman moving slowly, inexorably, out of the shadows toward us. Now I understand why the rest of them—including the pirates—are all huddled up on the far side of the space. That energy is back, that terrifying, ancient energy that I felt right before she launched half a hillside at me and Lincoln in the last Reverie. She moves as if floating, the foam of the hem of her dress sliding like froth against the wet floor. Her reflective face is turned toward us, but she's got one arm raised like a conductor, her delicate fingers pointing into the air. I turn to Lincoln in terror. "We have to go."

"I can't." He doesn't even open his eyes.

"You have to." I look over at Mirror, who's still moving toward us. Her head is tilted slightly lower now. She has her prey in her sights.

And it's not me.

"Lincoln, get up!" I hiss. I throw myself onto the bench next to him and try to pull his arm around my shoulders. But he leans away. "Stop it!"

"It's over," he whispers. "Just let her do whatever it is she needs to do."

"She's going to kill you."

"I know. Maybe that's what has to happen."

I shake my head. "You don't have to do this. I have the sword. You don't have to die for this to—" My voice catches in my throat as I see the movement out of the corner of my eye. I whip my head toward the water beyond the escalator, just as something massive emerges, dripping. In the time it takes for me to realize what it is, the bundle of tentacles is already coming down. I brace myself and shrink back against the bench.

They slam right through the railing with a clatter of metal and a crunch of glass. The accompanying splash hits me right in the face, and I'm sputtering as I wipe the water from my stinging eyes, so I barely see what happens next. One moment, Lincoln's sitting beside me. The next, he's on the floor. His head slams backward, sounding like a hollow coconut. But he doesn't stop. He slides, scarily fast, toward the gap in the railing. I don't even think. I just throw myself after him.

He screams and twists, just as my stomach hits the floor and my hand closes around his wrist. But then I'm moving, too, closer to the water. I try to get up on my knees, but the floor is slick. I grab his wrist with my other hand instead, and turn my head to scream at the others.

"Help me! Please!"

"Riley. Don't let go."

I look up to see Lincoln's face, pale and panicked. I tighten my grip on his arm, but it's not helping. We're both getting pulled toward the edge. I can see the thick tentacles wrapped around each of his legs, slithering back into the black water. "Somebody help us!" I scream.

Footsteps splash beside me, and someone grabs his other hand, the one that's been clawing uselessly at the floor. I dare just a glance. It's Jessica. She keeps her legs in front of her as she holds on to him, sliding along on her butt . . . until her feet brace against the lip under where the railing used to be. Lincoln's lower half is out over the water, still being pulled by the awful tentacles. I scramble to mirror Jessica's posture and manage to get my boots braced in the same way.

"Somebody get the sword!" I shout over my shoulder. "Kill the monster!" As soon as the words are out of my mouth, I realize how futile they sound. That sword, as deadly looking as it is, isn't going to do much against a behemoth like this. I dig my fingers into Lincoln's arm. The pull increases, and he lowers his head as he screams. A moment later, Jessica and I both jerk backward as something releases with an awful tearing sound. But then the tentacles resume pulling, and we're almost yanked into the water. One of Jessica's feet slips off the edge. She manages to plant it again, but I know neither of us can last much longer.

I turn my head and spot Mirror. She's standing much closer than I thought. Her blank face stares down at Lincoln as he's pulled like taffy between us and the monster.

"What do you want?" I scream. "What do you fucking *want?*"

For a moment, she doesn't move. And then, her hands rise into the air, almost as if she's lifting something with them. I turn back to Lincoln, only to see another set of tentacles rising out of the water behind him. *How many does this thing have?* With a speed that reminds me of a whip, they snap out audibly . . . and wrap themselves around his face.

"No!" I scream. I can't even see his features anymore. Just thick, slippery muscle as it pulls back against him. He can't possibly breathe like this. His hand starts writhing, clawing at the air.

"It's going to break his neck!" Jessica shouts. "We have to let go."

"It'll kill him!"

"It's going to kill him anyway." And then, to my horror, she releases her grip on his hand. The full force of the tug of war pulls against my shoulders so hard that I scream. My fingernails tear into his flesh. But I can't hold on. I can't . . .

My scream echoes through the mall as the smothering tentacles pull him out of my grasp and into the inky darkness. I scramble to the edge and grip it with bloody fingers as I search the still-churning depths. "Lincoln!"

It's over. It's over. It's over. Just a few more seconds. Then it'll be over. Then you can apologize for letting him be consumed by his worst fears. I'm breathing hard, watching the water try to settle. A terrible, moaning roar emanates from the water, and all the hairs on my body stand on end. I start to cry, even though there's no point. I better do it now . . . and not in the bathroom where I'm going to exit the Reverie in a moment. I dash away the tears with the backs of my hands, feeling the sting of seawater in my eyes.

Nothing's happening. Oh, god. Is he suffering down there? Why won't he die? How can he possibly still be alive when—

I suck in a breath and turn around to face Rainraven. She's just sitting there, as if a kraken didn't snatch the boy from the bench right beside her. Standing on shaky legs, I move closer. A small smile pierces her features.

"You think this is amusing?" I ask.

"No, love."

"He's dead."

"I suspect he is."

I jerk, as if she's just slapped me. "But . . . I'm still here."

"You are."

"I shouldn't be."

She raises her eyebrows. "Why not?"

"Because this is his Reverie."

"Is it?"

"Well, it can't be mine."

"Why not?"

"The connection was broken. He died in my last Reverie."

"Did he?"

I stare at her, aghast. "What are you talking about? He was buried in a landslide."

"Oh, I know. He told me all about it." She picks at a bit of sodden lint on the edge of her cloak. "I'm sure he *thinks* he died. But there are such things as air pockets and unconsciousness."

"Oh, my god," I whisper. I turn around to face the water once more. There's no trace of Lincoln there now. There's just Jessica, picking herself up out of the broken glass and swiping ineffectually at her sodden jeans. My mind stutters, then crashes into disappointed despair. "Was this my Reverie? Was he my Cicerone?"

"He'll be your Cicerone until the connection is broken," Rainraven says. I whirl around to face her.

"Then it's broken for sure this time!" My voice comes out in a wail, and I start to cry again. My hands curl into fists as they press against my temples. "This isn't fair! Now that I know . . . Now that I understand . . ."

"What is it that you want, love?" The old woman's voice is gentle. I should be angry with her. I really should. But the only person I can muster up any anger toward right now is myself. My whole body sags.

"I want him back," I say. "I want the Reveries. I want to learn how to be a Cicerone myself. I want . . . I want to be a writer."

"I know you do."

"But it's too late!" I wail. "He's already dead. And now—"

"Riley, love, it's never too late. Think about where you are."

I sniff hard. "A mall?"

She laughs softly. "A Reverie."

"So?"

"So, who makes the rules in a Reverie?"

I chew on my lip for a moment. "I do?"

"You do. So if you want him back . . ."

"But he's dead," I say, my voice small.

"What is death in a place like this?" She shakes her head slowly. "Truly. What is death in any place?"

I just stare at her. "I don't understand."

"Yes, you do." She smiles and leans back on the bench. "Of course you do."

I'm almost ready to snap at her. Who knew Lincoln's Cicerone could annoy me as much as the boy himself? I turn and look back at the water, which is settling into an inky sheet. Then I turn and look at Mirror. She's still here. Still just standing there. Or floating there. I can practically hear the soft fizzing sound of her seafoam skirt as the water laps gently at its hem.

"She's powerful," Rainraven says quietly. I tear my gaze away from the supernatural bitch and frown at the old woman.

"Too powerful."

She tilts her head. "Is there such a thing?"

"She's more powerful than me."

An infuriating little smile is all I get.

"Riley," a small voice says. I turn and see Harper standing a few feet away at the edge of the darkness. Her tiara is still glowing, illuminating her damp hair. But she looks different than she did before. There's a look in her eyes that makes me want to take a step back. "Mirror," she says.

"It's . . . okay," I say. "She doesn't want to hurt you."

The little girl smiles. "What do you want?" The question echoes weirdly in the space, and I hear it again, almost word for word. The sound is deeper. Louder. It takes a moment for me to realize that it's no echo I'm hearing. I peer into the shadows, to the people standing behind the child. They stand as still as statues, the same question on their lips.

Shit. Is this Reverie broken?

"What do *you* want?" I ask. "What do you want from me?"

"We want what you want," Harper says, and the way the rest of them switch up their refrain to match her words makes me shudder. I shake my head and back away from them. But I have nowhere to go. I look at Rainraven in desperation. She's just watching the nine others as the words slip off their tongues. She's not freaked out by any of this. She knows what's going on. She's just not willing to tell me—

My eyes go wide. I snap my attention back to the group, and they fall silent.

"The Council," I whisper. Harper's face lights up, and she begins to bounce on her toes. But she doesn't say anything. "This was never Lincoln's Reverie, was it?" I ask, turning to Rainraven.

She merely raises her eyebrows.

I frown and chew my lip. "He didn't die in the landslide. The connection wasn't broken. But . . ."

"But what?"

"He would've known he was acting as my Cicerone, wouldn't he?"

"Would he?"

My boot stomps in the water before I can stop it. "Will you just give me some goddamn answers?"

She smiles. "You already have the answers, love. Just like you've always known what you wanted."

"I didn't!"

"Yes, you did." She shakes her head. "You and Lincoln are so much alike. It's a good match."

I cough indignantly. "We are *not* alike."

"You're not both confused teenagers who try so hard to deny what they really want that they end up causing themselves no end of problems?"

"Lincoln's not confused," I snap.

"No?"

"No. He always wanted to be a Cicerone."

"That's true."

"Then how is he confused?"

"He likes you," Harper says. I whirl around to face her.

"That's . . . none of your business."

She giggles. "Lincoln likes Riley! Lincoln likes Riley!"

"Stop it!"

Her face suddenly becomes serious. "Don't you like him?"

"That's not the point." I turn back to Rainraven. "Whether we like each other or not . . . What does it matter?"

"Oh, it matters, love." She waves her hand over toward Mirror, almost like she's introducing an esteemed guest. I frown.

"I don't get it."

"Lincoln created her."

"Yeah, and she's done nothing but attack him since. He's obviously some sort of masochist."

She laughs softly. "Riley, what is Mirror?"

I look over at the preternatural being, who angles that mirrored mask in my direction. I quickly lower my gaze. "A villain."

"No. Not a villain. Merely an antagonist."

"Same difference."

"No, love. It's not the same. Mirror isn't evil. She's simply a reflection."

"Of what?"

"Of you," Harper says matter-of-factly. I turn to her in disbelief.

"What did you say?"

The little girl just smiles. I shake my head and turn back to Rainraven.

"Is that really what he thinks of me? That I'm some crazy bitch out to hurt him?"

"You were angry with him."

"That's an understatement."

"Riley, Mirror is a reflection of the way he sees you."

"Yeah, I get that."

"No, you don't. Look at her. Take a good look. And tell me what you see."

I don't want to, my mind whimpers. But I do it anyway. I stare at her face, feeling the magnetic pull, and I find myself stepping closer. The skylight glow provides enough illumination for me to see my own face reflected back at me. It feels like I'm making eye contact, even though the only eyes I can see are my own.

"What do you see?" Rainraven asks.

I could describe any number of things about her. But at the moment, there's only one word that fills my mind. I loosen my dry tongue and take a deep breath, watching my own lips move in the reflection. "Power," I whisper.

"Yes, love," Rainraven says. "Power. Intimidating power."

"But I'm not powerful."

"He thinks you are."

I frown, still staring into the depths of Mirror's shiny face. "What was it that he wanted?" I ask quietly. Rainraven doesn't answer for so long that I don't think she's going to. But then I hear her take a deep breath.

"You need to ask him yourself. It's time the two of you started being completely honest with one another."

With a massive effort, I manage to pull my gaze away from Mirror's face and turn around. "What does it matter now?" I say miserably. "He's dead. Even if this was a second chance . . . we blew it."

"So unblow it."

"That's not a thing."

"Why not?"

I grunt. "He's *dead*."

"So?" She raises her eyebrows and shoots a darting glance at Mirror.

"She takes life. She doesn't give it."

The old woman shakes her head. "Riley . . ."

I feel like I'm missing something. And I'm disappointing everyone while I'm doing so. I look over at Harper and the others, hoping for a hint. But they remain silent. I close my eyes as I feel my lips start to twitch with the effort of trying not to cry.

What am I supposed to do? I guess I could find the sword and hand it to Carrington. Would that do it? But if Lincoln is dead when I end this, that's it. No more second chances.

I want this. I want him. I want . . .

Air, fire, earth, and water. Mirror controls them all. If she's a reflection of me, then . . . do I just tell her to do something? Or—

My eyes snap open. I turn to Mirror, seeing the smile on Rainraven's face out of the corner of my eye.

"Anything can happen in a Reverie," I say quietly.

"Yes, love."

I take a deep breath and reach out. Mirror doesn't move. It's almost as if she knows exactly what I'm doing, and welcomes it. My fingers close around the edges of her mask, dipping into her watery hair; when I give a little tug, it comes off in my hands. Making sure to keep it at the same level so I don't have to see what is (or what isn't) underneath, I bring it slowly toward my own face. My whole body trembles. I might be about to make things a whole lot worse.

The mask warps and inverts itself like a sheet of liquid mercury, settling over my features with a tingle of electricity. Strangely, I can see through the mask, even though it has no eyeholes. I can breathe somehow, too. But I can't move my mouth at all. The mask feels like it's sealed my lips together, and, for a moment, I panic. *You're in control,* I remind myself. *You have the power now.*

My head feels wet, and I see tendrils of water splashing out around my field of vision. I lift my arms, only to see that the clothes I was wearing have disappeared. Shimmering scales appear on my arms, moving from my hands all the way up to my shoulders. I look down toward my feet and see only a froth of foam where the bottom of my dress meets the floor. Actually, I can't even feel my feet. Do I have any?

The space in front of me that Mirror occupied just a moment ago is empty. I turn around slowly, my skirt hissing as I move. Rainraven looks up at me from the bench, a satisfied little smile on her face. The nine others watch me from the shadows. Even the pirates—who seemed so afraid of Mirror before—are just regarding me calmly.

I turn to the water as an urge overtakes me. Without really knowing what I'm doing, or how I'm going to do it, I raise my arms. A wave heaves just beyond the broken railing, spilling water over the floor. *Is it really that easy? Is this really all I have to do?* I let my arms fall, allowing the water to settle back into itself. And then I try again, this time with a particular image in my mind. I imagine the water like a gentle hand, scooping Lincoln's body from the briny depths and buoying him up to the surface. I can feel something, almost like a force pulling at my arms. I lower my head and try to make the mental picture a little clearer. The water heaves again . . . and something breaks the surface.

The body rolls and tumbles onto the floor, surrounded by a rush of liquid that looks like a rather disgusting soup full of pebbles, shells, and lengths of ropey seaweed. The hem of my dress dissolves, only to re-form a moment later, frothier than before. I glide over to him and sink down so I can roll him onto his back. The mask prevents me from moving my face at all, so I can't even burst into tears at the sight. *It's too late*, I think, staring at the saddest thing I've ever seen. It's not just that his lips have lost all their colour; or that the broken part of his leg has been ripped clean off, leaving the leg of his jeans hanging empty; or that his forearm still bears the jagged nail marks from my desperate attempt to save him from the kraken. Cashel Lincoln should *never* look like this. Not even in a Reverie.

And the worst part of it all is that he thinks this is what he deserves.

I take his face in my scaly hands. There's no resistance; all his muscles are slack. *I'm sorry, Lincoln. You were right all along. I did want this. Well . . . not this. But I do want the Reveries. I want you to be my Cicerone. And I want you to be my friend.*

He's so still. It's not right. It's not fair. I turn and look over at Rainraven. She just shrugs. A flare of annoyance surges in my core.

He's dead. It's over. I can't just bring him back to life . . . can I?

I turn back to Lincoln as hope buoys in my chest.

Why not? I controlled the water and pulled him out. The human body is made mostly of water. So why can't I fix this?

I place one hand on his chest, then shake my head slowly, sending my watery strands of hair swaying. He's not bleeding now, but as soon as his heart starts beating again, he's going to bleed out through that severed leg. I look around and spy the seaweed. It appears strong enough, so I grab the longest piece I can reach and proceed to tie it around his thigh, hoping I can get it tight enough to cut off the circulation. There's no point in bringing him back only to have him die from blood loss.

When the makeshift tourniquet is as tight as I can make it, I lay my fingers on his chest once more, over the little tear in his t-shirt made by Morgan's sword. The fabric is almost clean (probably from being soaked in the water). But his body is so still and cold under my touch. I bow my head as I try to imagine what I want to happen next.

Blood . . . flowing.

Heart . . . beating.

Lungs . . . filling with air.

I keep the image in my mind as I will Mirror's power—my power—through my fingertips and into his chest.

Blood . . . flowing.

Heart . . . beating.

Lungs . . . filling with air.

Blood . . . flowing.

Heart . . . beating.

Lungs . . . filling with air.

Blood . . . flowing.

Heart . . . beating.

Lungs . . . filling with—

He sucks in a strange breath that sounds blocked and wet. A moment later, water fountains from his mouth, and I realize that maybe I should've done something about clearing his lungs before trying to fill them with air. His chest shakes as he tries to suck in another breath. Under the trembling, I can feel the thump of his heart. It's faint at first, but it grows stronger as my fingers linger there.

"Riley," he rasps.

I want to tell him I'm here. Before he opens his eyes and sees me like this. Before he opens his eyes and sees his very own nightmare bending over him. But the mask is still sealed over my face, and I can't move my mouth.

"Riley," he says again. He's struggling to breathe. Something's wrong. He's not moving the rest of his body. Jessica's shout right before the kraken took him echoes in my mind: *It's going to break his neck!*

I pull my fingers from his chest and move both hands to his cheeks. I'm careful to keep my thumb away from the cut below his eye, which has started bleeding again. Leaning closer, I will him to somehow hear my silent words.

I'm here. I'm right here, Lincoln. I understand now. And I want to tell you . . .

His eyelids flutter, then go still. Gently, I brush my thumb over the swollen skin just below the cut that nearly took his eye.

Lincoln. I want . . .

He opens his eyes slowly. At first, they don't seem to want to focus. I can see the moment when they do, and when he understands what he's seeing. I remain still, afraid to make things any worse with sudden movements. Waking up, unable to move, trapped in the literal grip of your worst nightmare has got to be one of the scariest things imaginable. So his reaction nearly has me letting go in surprise.

He actually smiles.

It's worse than I thought. He must've hit his head. Or the lack of oxygen damaged his brain. He doesn't really understand what he's seeing. I lean closer. He stares up into my face, his eyes making little movements as he searches for . . . something. He's probably just seeing his own reflection, but it seems like he's looking for something else. At last, his eyes slip closed again, and his shoulders hitch as he tries to take a deep breath. I shake my head, causing my hair to splash. *No! Lincoln, stay with me. We're not done yet. We have to—*

He opens his mouth. I tense as I wait for his words.

"Are we doing this?" he whispers.

For a moment, I don't know what he means. But then those simple words fizz into my consciousness like tiny bubbles, nudging me back toward reality. Understanding has me teetering on the border between both worlds. I nod, but it's no good. He can't see my answer. He needs to hear it. I pull my hands away from his face, and his head rolls to one side. My fingers dig into the edge of the mask as I grasp it to pull it away. The world burns white for a moment as a brilliant flash rips the air around me. I suck in a gasp, finding myself staring into my own reflection. But it's not in Mirror's mask this time.

I pull my hands away from the edge of the sink and look around, wide-eyed. Jessica and Harper are beside me . . . though their names probably aren't Jessica and Harper at all. I glance at the girl on my other side. She's still applying her lip gloss.

It takes all I have in me not to swear. I turn back to the mirror. I'm looking a little pale (and damp), but the nausea is gone. In fact, I feel fine. Just like I did after the last Reverie. When all the physical pain and discomfort were gone, and all that was left was . . .

My hands are still wet as I rush for the door and pull it open. This is *not* the time to stop for paper towels. I bolt down the hallway—the brightly lit, echoing with noise, greasy food-scented hallway—and rush into the food court. It's just as packed as when I went into the bathroom hours— No. It was only a few seconds ago. I shake my head and sprint toward the escalator, dodging shoppers and baby strollers and just generally trying not to trip and fall on my face. I get stuck in a clog of people on the escalator itself and have to wait through the interminable ride smushed between an old lady in a coat that smells of wet wool and a young guy who can't seem to keep his farts to himself. When I finally make it to the top, I blast away from the pocket of funk and run straight into the open space, where I come to a boot-squeaking stop. I look around for a moment, disoriented by the normalness of the setting. People move around me, completely unaware of what happened here in that other reality. The railing and the glass underneath it are both unbroken, and are decorated by illuminated garlands. The skylight over my head is intact; I can see the clear blue sky beyond the glass. My ears are vibrating from the level of noise in here, a mixture of adults talking, children squealing, the escalator humming, and an evil amount of Christmas music coming from somewhere. And yet, I can't help smiling.

I run down the concourse, glancing up periodically until I spot the gaudy Phantasmazine sign. It's lit up now, just like all the others, hanging over the store's entrance like a welcoming omen. I slow my pace as I get closer, but I don't stop.

I can't stop.

Phantasmazine isn't very busy at all, so stepping inside is almost like slipping out of a chaotic school of fish and into the calm ocean beyond. Another sort of music assaults my ears, this time some sort of medieval-sounding stuff that sounds like it should be in a video game. Stepping past the racks of graphic novels and shelves full of paint-them-yourself figurines, I head toward the counter at the back.

It's empty.

My heart nearly falls into my shoes. But before I can start questioning my sanity again, I see a familiar figure step out from around the corner behind the counter, his arms full of a stack of colourful boxes.

"Can I help you?" someone asks. The unfamiliar voice is female, and young, and coming from my right. I don't answer. I just walk forward, keeping my gaze locked with that of the guy behind the counter. He sets the boxes down as he watches me approach, giving no hint of recognition. I drink in the sight of him: uninjured, fully alive, and as annoyingly cute as ever. He raises his eyebrows in that familiar expression, and I'm not sure whether to burst out laughing or burst into tears.

"Can *I* help you?" he asks. I nod as I step up to the counter and stuff my hands in my jacket pockets.

"Yeah. You can."

"Awesome," he says, moving the boxes to one side so he can brace his hands against the edge of the counter. "What can I help you with?"

I hesitate. After everything we just went through, this all seems so anticlimactic. Standing here in this weirdly banal store, surrounded by all these props for the imagination that can't even come close to conveying the mind-blowing experience of a Reverie, is almost making my brain itch.

"Was there something specific you were—"

"Answers," I say before he can take this helpful-salesperson façade too far.

"Answers?"

"Yeah. What just happened?"

"You've forgotten already?"

I narrow my eyes at him. He just smiles.

"You finished the Reverie, Sadie. Properly this time."

"I didn't give the sword to Carrington."

"It wasn't about the sword."

I frown. "So what was it? A test?"

"Something like that."

My fists strain in my pockets as I press them down against the fabric. "You thought I needed to be tested?"

"It wasn't me." He shakes his head and looks down at his thumb rubbing the edge of the counter.

"But you're my Cicerone."

"Yeah, and I messed up. That Reverie was sort of . . . damage control."

I snort. "That was damage *control?*"

He pushes away from the counter and rounds it, coming to stand in front of me. I look up into his face, feeling my cheeks get warm. *Why does he have to be so cute?*

Damn it, Sadie. Focus.

"Can you answer a question for me?" I ask, remembering my conversation with Rainraven.

"Sure."

"What is it that you want?"

His eyebrows rise. "You don't know?"

"I can guess."

His lips twist in amusement. "Ah. So you're going to make me say it."

"Yep."

"I want the same thing I've wanted since I was thirteen years old."

"Perv."

He laughs. "Sadie, all I've ever wanted was to work with you. As your Cicerone. As your friend." His face takes on this gentle expression that's a strange mixture of affection and pride. "I could tell, even when I was just watching your dreams, that you were something special. You have amazing stories to tell the world. And I almost messed that up for you." He shoves his hands in his jeans pockets, suddenly awkward. "That's why the Council stepped in."

I blink. "They . . . stepped in?"

"Yeah. All those people—the pirates, the blind guy, the kid—they were—"

"I know who they were," I say. "I figured it out. Why didn't you tell me?"

He shakes his head. "I didn't actually know. Not until Rainraven told me. I should've clued in. There were nine of them."

"*Rainraven* told you?"

"She did. While you were off getting the sword from Phantasmazine."

"But I thought she wouldn't break character."

He smiles wryly. "She wouldn't have, if it had just been my Reverie."

I blink. "*Just* yours? You mean . . . it was ours?"

"As far as I can tell." He shakes his head. "Guess there's a first time for everything."

"That's why Rainraven was there," I say quietly, putting the pieces together. "And that's why it didn't end when you died. I was still alive."

"Exactly. You were the anchor. You kept everything going long enough to figure things out. And long enough to save my sorry ass."

I look away as my cheeks warm. "At least you knew what was going on," I mumble.

"I think Rainraven took pity on me. 'No point in unnecessary trauma,' she said."

"And then you got torn apart by a kraken and sucked into the depths."

He shrugs.

"You could've told me it was a test."

"Would you still have tried to save me?"

I nod, focusing my attention on his name tag. His shirt has flipped back on itself again, and all I can see is a bit of the pin where it's pierced through the fabric.

"Aw. I knew you cared."

"Shut up."

He chuckles. "I really am sorry, Sadie. For everything. You went through some weird shit in the last year, and a lot of that happened because of me."

"I forgive you."

His eyebrows rise again, this time in skepticism. "Really?"

"Yeah." I shrug. "What's the point of being angry now? Besides, I think you've been punished enough. We both have."

He frowns down at me. "Are you okay?"

"After seeing you get whacked in the head, stabbed in the chest, poked in the eye—"

"*Nearly* poked in the eye."

"Fine. Nearly poked in the eye, dropped into a fountain, dismembered by a kraken—"

"Dude," a voice says. "What the hell is she talking about?"

I frown at the girl who's kind of snuck up on us. She's probably the same one who asked me if I needed help, judging by the plastic name tag that reads DARRYN. I turn back to Cash, wondering how he's going to explain this. But instead of addressing the girl, he just sends me a smirk.

"She can hear us," he says in a dramatic stage whisper. "It's not like in the—"

"Shut up!" I squeak. He stifles a laugh and turns to Darryn.

"You've never played *Kraken in the Mall*?"

"No," Darryn says. "Jesus. What kind of game is that?"

"What does it sound like?"

"Tabletop? Video?"

"No . . . more like narrative RPG crossed with LARPing."

Darryn shrugs. "We don't carry the sourcebooks, do we?"

"God, no." Cash chuckles. "You want to get those onto the shelf? I told Ritch we'd have that display set up by the end of the day."

"Ritch?" I whisper as Darryn reaches past us to grab the boxes from the counter. As soon as she's stepped away, I shake my head. "Care to explain?"

"Do I need to? Ciceroni need day jobs, too."

"And his is running a nerd store?"

"There's nothing wrong with being a nerd." He smiles and gives his head a little tilt. Somehow, it makes him even cuter. "So . . . can I ask *you* something?"

"Ye-es?" I say, the word coming out like a slow-motion question. He leans closer so he can whisper in my ear. I hold my breath.

"Are we doing this?"

I pull back in surprise and look up. He's waiting for my answer—the same answer he's probably been waiting for since he was lying there, broken, on the wet floor of the mall—with his eyebrows raised in that expression that's become so comfortingly familiar that I can't help smiling in return. But my smile dies a moment later as I remember something.

"If I want the Reveries . . . don't I have to agree to be someone else's Cicerone? I don't think I'm ready for that."

"No?"

I snort. "Seriously? Do you think I am?"

"You'd better be."

Frowning, I shake my head as I continue to stare at him. "What do you mean?"

"You've already been assigned. Want to meet your first charge?"

I gasp. "Who?"

He chuckles as he pulls his hands from his pockets, flips the edge of his shirt, and points to his name tag. I gape at him in disbelief.

"That's not . . . That doesn't happen. Does it? Isn't Ritch your Cicerone? I thought you only got one!"

"Apparently," he says, leaning closer so he can keep his voice down, "the Council likes to err on the side of caution. Ritch is getting old, and they'd prefer not to leave me unattended in my own Reveries without a guide. I might get into trouble or something."

"Does the Council know something about Ritch that you don't?"

"I don't think so. It's just a precaution. And you wouldn't actually take over until after he's gone. In the meantime . . ."

"A Cicerone is going to train their next Cicerone. Right."

He grunts in amusement. "I never said it wasn't going to be weird."

"Yeah, but . . . do you even trust me enough for this?"

"Ritch will probably be around for years yet. He'll help me out. I'll help *you* out. You'll be ready."

"How will this even work?" I ask. "What if one of us dies in a Reverie?"

"I asked Ritch the same question."

"And?"

"Depends on whose Reverie it is. The connection would break for one of the relationships. We'd both have to die while acting as a Cicerone for all of the connections to break, though." He gives me a gentle smile. "I'm not worried. Even if that did happen, we'd still be connected. Maybe not with the Reveries, but we'd still have . . ."

"The mall?"

He laughs. "Yeah. We'll always have the mall." With a little shrug, he raises his eyebrows. "You never did give me an answer."

"What was the question again?"

"Are we doing this?"

To my own surprise, I don't even hesitate. "Yes," I say, pulling my hands out of my pockets and reaching up to throw my arms around his neck. There's a moment when I remember the last time I did this, after the steampunk Reverie, when he pretended not to know me, and I tense with a sudden anxiety. But then I feel his arms go around me, and everything just . . . Everything's . . . The world is as it . . . *Damn it, Sadie. You're supposed to be a writer.*

With my eyes closed, every other sense seems heightened. I smell the lingering, mouthwatering scents of the food court on his shirt. I feel the warmth of his body against mine as I linger in his embrace. I hear the rustle of his hands on my jacket as he adjusts them, gently holding me against him. Something starts to open inside me, something that feels like happiness and hope and possibilities. All the things I've been pushing back against for the last year. And why? Because I was afraid? *Of what?* I wonder as I pull back and open my eyes. I'm still so close that I can barely focus. Close enough that I suddenly feel bold. I lean forward a little. His eyebrows rise in answer.

So I kiss him.

If you had told me that day in the library that I would be standing here now, caught in a sweet kiss with this admirably annoying boy, I would have laughed in disbelief. But here I am. And here he is.

My Cicerone.

My muse.

My Lincoln.

He's the first to pull away, reluctantly, but I can still see the smile on his lips. "Are we doing *this?*"

"Can we?" I say, struck by an awful thought that maybe I've just made some sort of mistake. I lean back, frowning. "Is it allowed?"

"It's not *not* allowed."

"What if we break up?"

He laughs. "You're breaking up with me already? Wow, Sadie."

"No. I mean—"

"I know what you mean," he says softly, tucking my hair behind one ear. "And we can figure something out *if* that happens." He shakes his head slowly, smiling the whole time. I return the expression and go in for another kiss. "Careful," he mumbles between our lips. "You'll make the nerds jealous."

I pull back, just as he jerks his chin over at Darryn. She's watching us with this sort of wistful expression. A moment later, she shakes her head and goes back to arranging the display.

"So," Cash says, drawing my attention back to him. "Ready for another Reverie?"

I suck in a gasp, only to see the playful expression dancing on his features. Before I can stop myself, I've already whacked him on the arm.

"Ow!"

"Don't. You. Dare."

"Okay, okay." He holds up his hands in surrender. I take the opportunity to go in for another hug, this time around his waist. He lets out a contented sigh.

"I'm not ready yet," I say. "But when I am, I'll let you know."

"Fair enough." His arms tighten around me in a gentle squeeze. "We are going to have *so* much fun."

I'm not sure whether to laugh or get very, very worried.

Knowing him, I should probably do both.

ABOUT THE AUTHOR

Nissa Harlow wanted to be a writer from the time she was a small child, but it took a while before she finally did anything about it. In the meantime, she worked as a volunteer day-camp counsellor, a movie extra, and a digital-photo editor. She even once worked on a conveyor belt in a chocolate factory (which was as stressful—and delicious—as it sounds). These days, she lives in British Columbia, Canada and writes the types of stories she wants to read.

—

nissaharlow.com

ALSO BY NISSA HARLOW

NOVELS

Two Between Worlds
The Last Minute
No Such Thing

—

SHORT FICTION

Not Safe for Kids

—

SERIES

ELEMENTS OF MIND
Brainstorm
Dreamflare
Mindquake
Headrush